SEASIDE SKELETONS

ADAM LONGDEN

Adam Longden © Copyright 2019

Published by Goldcrest Books International Ltd
www.goldcrestbooks.com
publish@goldcrestbooks.com

ISBN: 978-1-911505-55-6
eISBN: 978-1-911505-56-3

This book is dedicated to all those who wanted a sequel...

PREVIOUSLY...

The long, hot summer of 1989. The paths of a teenage boy and girl cross purely by chance. But Jack is no ordinary boy: hidden from the world till the age of sixteen, he's a dirty secret, his father's cross to bear.

Music-mad Daisy sees it as her duty to introduce Jack to the real world – and a lot more besides along the way. It's a task easier said than done given Jack's numerous phobias and fears.

But as the summer goes on and the temperature rises so does the body count, as together they discover the truth of Jack's real identity.

Now Jack is in trouble. And on the run...

PART ONE

CHAPTER 1

Daisy

The light from the pub window was long gone. The lampposts were long gone. It was pitch black on the back lane to Wysall. A wanton veil of cloud didn't help. At first Daisy had run. And then she had trotted. And then she had walked, howling Jack's name into the darkness; a night-time marathon without end.

Unable to ignore the pain in her belly any longer, she ground to a halt, hands on knees, sucking in air. Wind and sobs caught in her throat; she didn't know whether she needed to burp or be sick. Her stomach was churning and there was too much saliva in her mouth. She spat on the road and groaned and cried some more. He'd gone. He'd gone, and there was nothing she could do about it. She might never see him again. 'Why, Jack? Why?' she cried.

She considered her options. Continuing to give chase, even if she could, would be futile; she'd never catch up with him. What about the van? Get home, get in the van and drive out this way? Keep going until she found him, even if it took all night? But which roads? What route? Knowing Jack he wouldn't be using roads; no way, especially considering the state he'd been in. He'd be going cross country, sticking mainly to the fields. But wouldn't that slow him down? Give her more of a chance to catch up? She had a brief and horrible vision of hurtling down a country lane in the dark, just as he was crossing it. What were the chances of that happening, though? At the sight of headlights he'd be off like a shot...

Face it, Daisy, he's gone. But she didn't want to face it, refused to. Wiping her mouth with the back of her hand, she stood up. But too quickly – that pain in her stomach again. She gasped. Hopefully it was just a stitch. She'd got to be more careful. Bitterly, and hobbling at first, she began the trek back home; in her desperation she must have run nearly half a mile.

As she walked she tried to make sense of what had happened, of what Jack had told her; the possible scenarios and solutions. She'd got to tell her mum. Maybe she could help to find him. But she knew what would happen – she'd want to tell the police. But perhaps this was right: if anyone could find him it was them. But wouldn't it be like dobbing him in for the sake of her own selfishness?

As all this was going through her head, something away in the distance caught Daisy's eye: a faint flicker of orange; a shimmering jack o' lantern in the night sky. Flames up on the hillside. The house. So it was true. This really brought it home to her. God only knew what else was up there. *Oh, Jack, what have you done? Why didn't you just go to the police? How does it look now?* How *could* she tell her mum? She'd immediately think the worst: that Jack was guilty, that he'd done this to cover his tracks, then fled. She didn't know his story, what his father was capable of. No, she couldn't tell her, not yet. *Sit tight and wait. See how it pans out.* Maybe try to find Jack the next day, when it was light; perhaps he'd even change his mind and come back.

Daisy soldiered on in the dark, bearing the heavy burden of a secret. She put her hand to her stomach. Two heavy burdens...

*****

The next morning when Carol Jones came down for breakfast she was surprised to see her daughter already in the lounge, glued to the telly. Daisy was still in the clothes she'd been wearing the previous night; she looked washed out, with bags under her eyes. 'What time did you get in last night? You look like...'

'Sshh!' Daisy hissed. 'I'm trying to listen.'

'Oh, sorry, madam,' said Carol. She turned to the telly to see what was so important. Unsurprisingly, the fire had made the local news. 'Hey, that's that place on the hill, isn't it? On the way to Bunny Wood.'

'Mum!'

Carol continued to whisper. 'I think there's some reclusive guy who lives there. Does furniture repairs or something.'

Daisy tried to digest the surprising fact that her mum knew of the house and of Jack's father, whilst she continued to listen to the newscaster. *'Early reports suggest that the body of a middle-aged man, yet to be identified, may have been found at the scene...'*

Carol gasped. 'There you go! I told you. Oh my gosh! How awful.'

'It is unclear at this stage whether the fire was started deliberately or accidentally. We will keep you informed throughout the morning as events unfold. In other news...'

'That poor man,' said Carol.

Poor man! Daisy wanted to yell, but she couldn't. 'So, how do you know the place?' she said instead.

'I don't. Only what I've told you. I don't think anyone does – it's that well-hidden. What's the sudden interest?'

'Nothing,' said Daisy quickly. 'It's just right on our doorstep, that's all.'

Carol studied her daughter. 'Have you eaten? Do you want some toast or something?'

'No, thank you.'

'No you haven't eaten, or no you don't want toast?'

'Mum, I'm fine.' Daisy could feel her mum looking at her. 'Honestly, I'm not hungry.' Carol walked off, shaking her head.

Daisy flicked over to Central, hoping for more information. The main news was on. No mention of the fire yet, thank God. She yawned, then flicked back to the BBC. Truth was, she *hadn't* slept. She'd debated all night whether to take the van out to try and find Jack. She felt that she should be doing something – anything. The longer she left it, the less chance she would have.

Daisy got up: she had to go after him. If she didn't she might regret it for the rest of her life. Leaving the telly on, she ran upstairs. In the kitchen Carol followed the sound of her daughter's footsteps. What had got into that girl?

Whilst Daisy got undressed, she put on her own telly. Still no further news. She showered in record time, pausing only to stare at her belly, then prod and squeeze it to see if it was changing. Could something really be growing in there? It didn't feel very different, a little firmer perhaps, the skin a little tighter; at least the pain had eased.

Afterwards, still glued to the telly, she located some clean jeans, wriggling into some black drainpipes but struggling to do them up. This was a worry. Donning the baggiest T-shirt she could find, one that covered her bum, she turned the telly off and left her room.

After grabbing the van keys from the table in the hall, and taking one last peek at the telly in the lounge – it pained her to be leaving it – Daisy went to let herself out. Her mum was still in the kitchen. 'Where are you going?' she called. 'You haven't had any breakfast.' Daisy briefly considered lying, saying she was going to see Jack. But wouldn't that make matters worse? Wasn't she lying to her mum enough already given the things she *wasn't* telling her?

'Back in a bit!' she said, avoiding the question altogether.

'Daisy!' The door closed behind her.

The morning was unseasonably cool. Daisy instinctively checked the VW's fuel gauge. Shit, the tank was low. This was a pain: she'd have to drive to Bunny first, then double back. Once you were on those back roads out Wysall way, there wasn't a petrol station for miles. Lucky she had some money with her; best get it out of the way. She went to put some music on for the journey. For once she wouldn't have minded listening to the radio for the news, but the aerial had snapped so she couldn't.

Turning left at the crossroads, it occurred to her she was going to have to drive past Jack's house. The thought of this made her shudder. If what Jack had told her was true, there would be, she could barely bring herself to say it, *bodies* up there. Human bodies ... his father's, poor Anne's, his mother's. It made her think of her dad at the mortuary. A sudden wave of nausea hit her and she had to lean out of the window. *Not now, please don't be sick now*, she begged herself.

The feeling passed, but Daisy's trepidation grew as she climbed the hill. She'd been in that house herself, seen that man, been trapped in a cellar with him – a murderer. And now he was lying there dead, unless he'd already been moved. Maybe he'd been burnt to death. And what about the other bodies? *Stop thinking about it!*

To her shock, a gaggle of vehicles was parked at the bottom of the lane, one of them a police car; she hadn't been expecting this. The police car was blocking the entrance to the lane along with some of that tape you saw on telly: 'POLICE LINE DO NOT CROSS'. A man and a woman in suits, probably reporters, were talking to a policeman. She tried to see past them, along the lane to the driveway. There were more vehicles further up, another police car and a van. Daisy had slowed right down, but when she became aware of the policeman watching her, staring right at her, she speeded up again, not wanting to be associated with the place.

After pumping a fiver's worth of petrol into the van with shaky hands, she went to pay for it, handing over a tenner. 'Have you heard what's going on up the road? The fire and that?' the man behind the counter said.

'No,' Daisy lied. Why did she lie?

'Terrible business. Everyone's talking about it. It's on the news and everything. A man died; they reckon it could have been deliberate.' He clung on to her change, whilst Daisy waited impatiently. 'Funny, I'd never noticed the place myself.' He noticed Daisy staring at the five pound note in his hand. 'Sorry, love. Listen to me waffling on.' He handed it over, and as Daisy left he watched her with a puzzled expression. Hadn't she just driven past the place? It was crawling with police.

Daisy drove off, back the way she'd come, her brain whirring. '*Everyone's talking about it*,' the man had said. Wait till they found the other bodies; the whole country would be talking about it. And what then for poor Jack? OK, he was long gone, but he couldn't get far, not really, not without a passport. Could he? She felt as if her head was going to explode as she waited for it all to unfold. It was like seeing a movie premiere before everyone else, knowing how it ended but not being able to talk to anyone about it. And for Jack's sake she hoped to God that he'd told her the truth about what had happened. Then she scolded herself for doubting him. Thing was, she couldn't remember much of what he'd said: it was all a blur. He'd been in a state, muttering something about his father falling off the roof ... something about a tank...

Driving down the hill, Daisy slowed down again, unable to help herself. She tried to look through the poplars, but they were at their most impenetrable this time of year. Had the house disappeared entirely? Been reduced to rubble? It was strange, but despite the dreadful experience she'd had at the bungalow and the way it had made her feel, the thought of it being gone made her feel even more emotional. Right now it was the only physical thing connected to Jack that was left – part of him, bound to him. And perhaps even this might have gone, just like their future together. As if he'd never existed.

Heading along Wysall Lane, Daisy had no clear plans. Where was she going, and how far? She tried to think like Jack. He'd avoid main roads, villages and people at all costs. He'd been terrified and determined. How far could you walk in one night? Five, ten, fifteen miles? Surely no further than that. But what if he'd run? And what if he'd regretted it? Realised it was foolish and turned back? It drove her mad not knowing.

Thinking it would be useful to know how far she'd travelled, Daisy made a mental note of the van's mileage. Then she turned the music up, but the song reminded her of Jack. She swapped tapes. It was no better. She turned the stereo off.

Daisy drove down country lane after country lane, through village after village: they all began to look the same. Only once did she cross a major road, trying to keep going in as straight a line as possible. This was hard when the winding lanes were dictating her route, and before long she wasn't sure what direction she was going in. All the while she looked from side to side, scanning the fields and hoping to see Jack. She kept on telling herself to slow down; even if she didn't see him, maybe he'd see the van. Part of her knew how futile all this was; he might not have gone this way at all.

After about half an hour she hit another main road; in one direction it ran through a village called Waltham-on-the-Wolds. She pulled to a halt to check how far she'd come – roughly eighteen miles. There was no way he'd have made it this far. She checked the fuel gauge; it wasn't looking too clever again. Now the oil light had come on. Shit. Why hadn't she checked it before setting off? If she broke down out here she was buggered. She hadn't even got her dad to rescue her anymore. This final thought did for her and she put her head on the steering wheel and wept. This was ridiculous; she was never going to find Jack like this. What was she doing out here in the middle of nowhere, miles from home? *You're trying your best, Daisy, that's what,* she told herself.

An aggressive honk from a car behind startled her, snapping her out of her misery. She looked in the rear-view mirror; an impatient man in a flash car was gesturing at her. 'Oh, piss off!' Daisy said, flicking him a V-sign in her mirror. She looked both ways, then crossed the main road, looking for somewhere to turn round. Typically the driver behind was going the same way, he was right up her arse. She indicated and pulled in. He accelerated past her, shaking his head; she gave him the V-sign again for good measure.

Daisy turned round and headed for home. Feeling as though she was letting Jack down, she took a slightly different route, trying to cover as much ground as possible. She just wanted to talk to him, to tell him she was sorry, to warn him that the police were up at the house. She wanted to hug him and hold him, to smell his deodorant and tell him everything was going to be all right. She wanted to tell him about the baby. She wanted him to tell her that everything was going to be all right. Putting on 'I Know It's Over' by The Smiths, she cried most of the way back home.

*****

As Daisy walked in, she heard her mum's voice from the lounge. 'Daisy, is that you?' Who else was it going to be? Daisy thought miserably. Her elder sister Lily was at work and her dad was dead.

'Er, yes…'

'You're not going to believe this. They've found more bodies up at that house!' Daisy's heart stopped as she put her keys down on the hall table. 'Quick! Come and look!' There was a hint of excitement in her voice, and it disgusted Daisy. She ignored her mum and headed straight upstairs. *'Daisy!'*

Once in her room, fingers trembling, Daisy put the telly on. '... *fire experts combing the scene for evidence stumbled upon the gruesome discovery in what appeared to be some sort of incinerator tank. Let's go live to our East Midlands correspondent, Dan Wrigley, who's at the scene. Dan, news is filtering through about two more bodies being found in the vicinity of the house. That makes three in total, doesn't it? What can you tell us?'*

A man with a microphone was standing in front of the police tape at the bottom of the lane. The fact that this was happening right now, this very moment, just up the road from her, struck Daisy as totally bizarre.

'*That's right, Hazel. Fire officers discovered the remains in what appeared to be some sort of purpose-built tank a short distance from the house. And when I say remains, these are skeletal remains, unlike the first body that was discovered. Early reports suggest that these bodies were deliberately burnt; the house fire didn't reach that far. There was also evidence on the ground surrounding the tank that it had been drained recently.*'

'*Drained of what, though, Dan?*' the newscaster cut in. '*Are you saying this could have been some sort of acid tank?*'

'*Maybe so. It's too early to speculate. But it's clear that what we're looking at here is no longer a straightforward arson enquiry. In fact, the case has rapidly escalated from an accidental fire investigation, through possible arson, to a potential triple murder enquiry. The original body of the man found at the scene, the presumed owner of the house, was only partially burned. He died from a physical trauma other than fire. But a petrol can was found near the body, although this could have been placed there afterwards. The forensic experts have now got a job on their hands to establish the identities of these three people, how and when they died, and if anything else might lie hidden on the property. On a side note, it's hard not to point out that this neck of the woods is no stranger to a murder enquiry. Less than six years ago, only a mile or so away, there was the tragic case of what was known locally as the "Keyworth Murder" — the first ever to be featured on* Crimewatch, *if you remember — a case which is unsolved so far, with the killer still at large. Coincidence, maybe? The police are in no way connecting the two crimes at the moment, I hasten to add, but it certainly makes for an interesting side plot. Back to you, Hazel.'*

'Dan, thank you for now. We'll speak to you again later in the day, no doubt, as events unfold in this intriguing case. That was Dan Wrigley reporting from a house on the Nottinghamshire–Leicestershire border that has been destroyed by fire, and where so far three bodies have been discovered.'

Daisy turned the telly off. She was sweating and her breath was shallow. She feared for Jack so much that it made her feel sick. He was the most private person she had ever known, yet he was possibly about to be implicated in a national, if not international, news story. It would be in all the papers – on the front pages. And what about her involvement? Would she be implicated somehow? In effect she was withholding information. She ought to tell someone – her mum at least. Surely all this could be explained away. Jack was innocent. But if they told the police – which her mum would insist on – there'd be a manhunt for Jack, he'd be the most wanted person in Britain. And she couldn't bear that. Despite what the law said, he'd be considered guilty until proven innocent. Didn't he deserve a chance to get away, to flee for good? Surely that was for the best.

And then there was all that crap about the Keyworth Murder, which had happened years ago – not long before they'd moved to the area. A poor girl had been raped and murdered, an incident that had made Daisy's parents, and most other local parents, fear for their daughters' safety. Perhaps it would prove to be a welcome diversion. Oh what to do, what to do…

Daisy lay back on her bed. The stress and the indecision were draining. She wanted to sleep to block it all out, to make it go away. But she didn't want to miss the lunchtime news. Setting her bedside alarm for five to one, she closed her eyes. Sleep quickly took her.

The alarm clock startled her awake, disorientated. She turned the telly on, turning the volume up. Impatiently, she waited for the news to start, and when the theme music began she felt her heartbeat speeding up. The opening five minutes were dominated by the story. But other than that the man might have died from a broken neck, there were no major developments to report since mid-morning. This would tie in with Jack's version of events, thought Daisy; his father had fallen off the roof.

Shortly after the news had moved on to another item there was a knock on Daisy's door. 'Can I come in?' It was her mum. How long had she been there? Daisy shot across to turn off the telly, then wished she hadn't; it jolted her stomach and she winced. She sat back on the bed just as her mum opened the door.

Daisy's face was pale and clammy. 'Why don't you open a window? Let some fresh air in. It's stuffy in here,' Carol said.

'It's always stuffy in here.'

Carol turned back to her. 'Are you sure you're OK? You look dreadful. Are you on your period or something?'

God, I wish, thought Daisy. 'No, just tired, that's all.'

'I've made you some lunch, a sandwich. Lily's home. I want you to come and join us.'

Daisy groaned. 'I'm not hungry.' She was, but knew she wouldn't be able to eat a thing. And what was Lily doing back home?

'I don't care,' said Carol. 'To my knowledge you haven't eaten since yesterday teatime – and then you only picked at it. No wonder you feel faint. I want you downstairs in a few minutes. Lily's got to go back to work soon.'

'What's she doing home?' said Daisy. Lily hardly ever came home for lunch.

'Oh, she wanted to watch the news; everyone's talking about it in town apparently. Have you heard the latest?'

Daisy was appalled: they were no better than rubberneckers at a car accident, the whole lot of them. 'No, I haven't,' she said dismissively.

Carol gave her daughter a long look. 'I'll see you downstairs.'

*****

As Daisy approached the kitchen door she could hear her mum talking. She slowed down to listen. '… obsessed with all this business up the road; she hasn't eaten a thing…'

'I wouldn't read too much into it. I think everybody's a bit obsessed with it,' said Lily. 'She's probably just fallen out with Loverboy again, that's all.'

'Will everyone stop calling him 'Loverboy',' Daisy snapped, as she entered the kitchen. Lily looked guilty. 'He's got a name, you know. It's Jack.'

'Yes, so you've told us. So when am I going to meet this Jack, then?' said Carol. 'I think it's more than high time, don't you?'

'I don't know,' said Daisy irritably, sitting down at the table.

'Told you, she's fallen out with him,' said Lily.

'Lily, will you shut up?' said Daisy.

'All right, you two, knock it off. We came to eat lunch, not argue,' said Carol. Daisy glared at Lily. Lily smirked and went back to her salad. Since the dust had settled after the funeral, it was true that normal hostile service was gradually resuming.

Daisy picked up her sandwich. Tuna and cucumber; she really didn't fancy it. Plonking it back down, she got up to get a glass of water. Carol watched her, exasperated. Daisy tried to eat, if only to stop her mum staring at her. It worked. She listened to the two of them prattling on about the news. They didn't talk about anything else. 'What about the Keyworth Murder? You don't think they're really connected, do you?' said Lily.

'Who knows?' said Carol. 'It really brings it back to you. That time. He was never caught, you know…'

'Oh, please,' said Daisy, hating that she was being dragged into the conversation. 'How are the two connected? This is a man who fell off a roof and broke his neck – he probably set fire to his house, then jumped off it because he'd murdered his family.' She took another bite of her sandwich.

'Who said he fell off the roof?' said Carol.

'Yes, I didn't hear that,' said Lily.

Daisy stopped chewing momentarily. *Shit*, she thought. 'What channel were you watching?'

'BBC, of course. We always watch the BBC for news,' said Carol.

'Oh, right. Well, this was ITV.'

'I thought you said you weren't watching it.' Daisy's mum looked at her with raised eyebrows.

'I wasn't really; it was just on in the background.'

'That's a development then, falling off the roof. Guess that rules him out being murdered – unless he was pushed, of course or, like you say, suicide,' said Lily.

'Yes, well, I think that's what they said anyway,' said Daisy, covering her tracks. 'Like I said, I wasn't really listening.'

'Anyway, back to the point – and the Keyworth Murder,' said Lily. 'I didn't mean the man, I meant those other bodies. Weren't they, like, skeletons or something? *They* could be connected.'

'*Please!*' said Daisy. 'Can we just stop talking about it? You want me to eat? How am I supposed to eat when you two are talking about dead bodies?' She got up from the table. One of those bodies was Anne – a human being. She'd known her, sort of, and it sickened her to have all these details discussed and dissected so flippantly over lunch, as if they were discussing the weather.

Daisy was right, Carol thought, feeling ashamed. They shouldn't be discussing morbid things like this so readily, especially so soon after… She suddenly wanted to cry. This happened a lot: anything could set her off.

*****

The next few days continued much the same. News kept filtering through about the house. Daisy had to put up with her mum and sister, like everyone else in the area, discussing it constantly. But they always went quiet when Daisy walked into the room, as if she was a baby who needed to be protected. Daisy, meanwhile, tried (unsuccessfully) to keep up the pretence of not being interested at all. The story had made the local and national papers, and in a so-called 'intriguing twist' it appeared that the two skeletons in the tank originated from different time periods – years, if not decades, apart. Everything Jack had said was true. It was a relief to hear it out loud. Now all she needed to hear was that Jack's father had died from falling off the roof; that was the big one, the one that would exonerate him once and for all. Maybe then she could think about telling her mum. Then they could see about trying to find Jack.

Daisy drove past the house again a few times. There was what her mum labelled a 'media scrum' camped at the bottom of the lane, even late into the night – and a twenty-four-hour police presence. No one but the forensics team and the police were allowed near the place whilst the investigation was going on, except for access to the farmhouse further up the lane. As one day dragged into the next, Daisy spent her time staring out of the window and crying a lot. She missed her dad and she missed Jack terribly. She was worried sick about him and wondered where he was, if she'd ever see him again and if he'd made it to the coast.

CHAPTER 2
The Bucket of Blood

It was dark when Jack reached the village. He'd been following a river for a few miles: it had gradually been getting wider, and he'd been hoping it would lead him to the sea. His goal had been to make it to the coast before nightfall; he was so close now he could almost taste it. But he was dog tired, every part of him hurt. His feet were blistered and raw, his hip joints burned and his stomach was a knot in an empty cavern. Judging by his map, it looked as though he was going to fall five to ten miles short. There'd be another day of travelling tomorrow.

For four nights and days he'd been at it. At night he'd slept rough, in outbuildings, barns and woods. During the day he'd walked and he'd cried, and he'd walked and he'd cried, his tears calling Daisy's name. He'd listened to her tape on his personal stereo, torturing himself by rewinding some of the songs over and over again. Eventually the batteries had run out.

He now knew what it was to be cold – bone cold – and he knew what it was to be lonely, when even the moon turns a callous, sickle-shaped shoulder to you and hunger is your only companion. He'd seen the earth at times of the day that only the animals and maybe some farmers saw. The early mornings when a blanket of fog hangs suspended in a perfect line over the rivers and fields, before the grey dawn turns pink as the first rays of sun, like probing fingers, creep over the horizon. Dusk when owls swoop, a blur of white on silent wings, and the bats flit and chirp in silhouette. Then in the dead of night, when God's lights litter the sky, Jack felt he was the only person in the world.

The river ran through the centre of the village, otherwise he would have avoided it as he had all the others. It seemed to be fate that led him towards an inn, its sign lit up; never had a pub looked more welcoming. It was crouched at the top of a grassy bank, overlooking the river, leaning slightly as if poised to jump in. There were mooring posts for boats and a path that led up to it. Two small boats were tied up, bobbing in the moonlit water and butting against the bank.

So far, Jack had been strict with himself. But he was nearly there now and a long way from home. He'd done it. He deserved a treat. Some hot food, warmth, a pint of cider and maybe a bed for the night. Maybe even a bath. One last stop and then tomorrow the world, his future, America. The yellow lamps, like miniature galleons, in the windows beckoned him. His feet were already on their way, his head incapable of making decisions or of putting up a fight.

The inn was made of stone, with a pointed central gable and a curved archway to the side that led to a car park. There were benches either side of the front door and hanging baskets of fragrant flowers. The swinging sign said 'The Bucket of Blood', its backdrop a weather-faded picture of a gruesome severed hand and a dripping bucket. *Strange name for a pub*, Jack thought; *ominous too*.

He walked past the windows to check it out. Men were hunched at the bar, a woman behind it, leaning on the pumps. Fear kicked in and he carried on walking. Out of the light he weighed up the risks. He hadn't spoken to anyone for days, not properly. There had been nothing but solitude. His old phobias reared up: the fear of people, the scrutiny. What if the authorities were already searching for him? What if there was a 'Wanted' poster of him, stuck up there in the bar like in the cowboy films?

Just then, the door banged open, startling Jack. A man with a roll up in his mouth, pulling a small, woolly, white dog stepped out. He too was startled by Jack's presence. 'Evenun',' he said. Jack nodded back. 'Come on, Scotty,' the man said, dragging the dog away. As Jack watched, they walked down the grassy slope.

The man unhitched one of the waiting boats whilst the dog hopped in, making it rock slightly. Reaching into the boat, the man put on some sort of helmet. Then he clambered in a little precariously and sat down. He saluted Jack before turning on a light on the helmet. Jack had to shield his eyes. The man began to row away, the oars licking the water. The dog stood with his front two legs on the side of the boat, watching Jack. The helmet light cast a triangular yellow beam on the water. There was something cartoonish about it – like the torchlight pictured in one of Jack's Raymond Briggs books.

If only it were that easy, thought Jack. If only *he* had a boat, he could row straight to the sea: it would save him walking the rest of the way. Perhaps there was someone else in the pub, a fisherman maybe, who would give him a ride. That man had certainly seemed friendly enough. He took a deep breath and opened the door.

Much-missed warmth hit him, together with that unique pub smell of cigarette smoke and ale. The change in temperature was considerable after he'd been out in the open for so long. There were candles on tables in a dimly lit bar. As Jack's eyes adjusted to the light, the black spot reared up in his vision, a curse since boyhood.

'What's 'e forgotten now?' a man sitting at the bar said, turning round. He stopped, a look of surprise on his face when he saw a stranger – especially one so young and dishevelled.

The landlady looked up from pouring a pint of lager, her hand on the plastic tap. Everyone else looked up. Jack's skin crawled. He gripped the strap of his rucksack tighter, ready to flee. ''Ow do, buh,' the same man said. The silence that followed was broken by the sudden dripping of liquid.

'Oh shit!' the landlady said, flipping the lager tap back up.

'Come on in, ol' boy. Don't be shy. We won't bite,' the man said.

'Leave 'im alone, Davey,' the landlady said, disappearing under the counter. Jack stayed where he was, his senses on high alert. A few men went back to their pints. Not Davey, who regarded him with interest. Jack averted his gaze.

The landlady popped back up, her face flushed from bending down, her chest too — she was wearing a low-cut blouse. She was buxom, middle-aged, with a kind face, fully made up, and masses of dark, curly hair. She took in Jack's rucksack, his grimy face. 'Can I 'elp you, love? Are yer lost or somefun'?' *Probably one of those Duke of Edinburgh kids*, she thought.

Jack cleared his throat, preparing to converse for the first time in days. He felt like a stray cat that had entered an unfamiliar home, hoping for a saucer of milk and somewhere warm to curl up, unnoticed. 'I ... I was wondering if I could perhaps get something to eat ... and a drink maybe?' His voice was quiet, shaky.

'Kitchen's closed I'm afraid, buh,' Davey answered.

'Do you mind, Davey? I run this pub, not you!'

'Well, when was the last time I got owt to eat after nine o'clock?'

'That's because you sit there on yer bloody arse all night till you know damn well I've turned everyfun' off, don't yer? Besides, you only live down the road; this poor lad's starving, look at 'im.' Jack shifted uncomfortably. 'I can probably rustle yer somefun' up. What were yer af'er?' She looked across at Davey, daring him to speak.

'Anything. I don't want to be any trouble – a chip cob or something?' He could just picture it, taste it, smell it – how the salt and vinegar would make his tabs laugh, as his sister used to say.

'Chip cob? Where are *you* from?' Davey said.

'Not from round 'ere, that's for sure!' the man next to him said. There was some amusement in the bar at this.

'It's a butty, ain't it?' Davey said.

'What, yer mean like a roll?'

'Ah, buh.'

Jack wished he hadn't said it; he'd only drawn more attention to himself.

'I can't do you any chips, I'm afraid, love, cob or uvverwise. The fryer's turned off.' The landlady paused for a moment. 'I suppose I could turn it back on again.' Davey looked at her with raised eyebrows, his pint halfway to his mouth. 'On second foughts, no I can't. I'd never 'ear the bloody end of it. Soup and a sandwich will 'ave to do – somefun' quick – I'm on me own, see.'

Jack nodded gratefully. 'Thank you.'

'No problem. Davey, will yer watch the bar for me a minute, please?'

'Aye. Won't be the first time.'

'Can I get you a drink while yer waitun', darl'?'

'Could I have a pint of cider, please?' said Jack

'I take it yer eighteen then?' the landlady said with a half-smile.

'Yes,' said Jack, reddening. He scratched at his stubble – the longest it had ever been – for emphasis.

'God love yer for a liar,' she said, and proceeded to pour him a pint. 'Right, that'll be one ten, please, love.' She put the pint on the bar. Jack panicked. Shit! His money was in his tin. He couldn't get that out in here! 'Oh, actually, pay me afterwards. I'll get that soup on.' The landlady waved her

27

hand, then walked off towards a door with a glass window in it behind the bar.

Relieved, Jack said in the loudest voice he could muster, 'Erm, where are the toilets, please?'

''Ere, I'll show yer,' Davey said. 'I need a piss, mesen.'

'You're meant to be watchun' the bar!' the landlady said turning round, her hand on the door.

'Oh, Big Dog'll watch it for yer, won't yer, Big Dog?'

'Ah, buh,' the large man at the bar next to him said.

'Good ol' boy,' Davey said, patting a meaty shoulder. The landlady sighed and looked to the heavens. 'Come on, this way, buh.'

Jack had no choice but to follow the stranger. It was a nightmare. He didn't need a pee for a start, he just wanted to get some money out of his tin. And if he did need one he wouldn't be having it standing next to this oaf. Why had this man latched on to him? It was the last thing he needed.

They headed out of the bar, up a step, through a door and into a corridor. The Gents was immediately on their right. The toilet was small; two urinals side by side – one with a pool of urine on the floor underneath it – and a cubicle. The whole room reeked of ammonia, so strong it made Jack's eyes water. He dived into the cubicle with his rucksack. Davey looked over his shoulder and chuckled as the door slammed.

To Jack's disgust, Davey broke wind loudly, saying, 'Better out than in,' then proceeded to urinate. Jack could hear it clearly; he could hear everything. This was a problem. He took his rucksack off his back and unbuckled his jeans, trying to make as much noise as possible, but also stalling for time. 'Where yer from then, buh?' Jack decided not to answer, pretending he hadn't heard. He heard the man zipping up his flies. 'Suit yersen, no odds to me.' Davey belched, then left without washing his hands.

Jack breathed a sigh of relief and pulled out his tin. To see all his life savings on show in a strange, faraway place like this made him feel vulnerable. He removed thirty pounds and quickly replaced the lid, burying the tin again at the bottom of his rucksack.

He left the cubicle to wash his hands. One of the urinals was now backed up with dark yellow piss. Jack looked into the cracked mirror above the toilet and saw his reflection for the first time in days. He was taken aback, barely recognising the boy who stared back at him. His face was grimy, red and wind-chaffed, and his short hair, recently cut and sticking out in tufts, surprised him. Wetting his hands again, he washed his face and ran his fingers through his hair, then took a deep breath before leaving the toilet.

A group of four men were now standing at the bar. They all had similar complexions – ruddy, weather-beaten. All of them looked up, scrutinising Jack. 'Been making some room, 'ave we?' Davey said. He let out a contagious bellow that rippled along the bar. Jack wanted to die. The whine of the kitchen door opening saved him. The landlady came out carrying two plates of steaming food.

'Come on, Marge, you've got a coo 'ere,' someone said.

'Sorry, fellas, be with you in a minute,' Marge said. She was wearing a pinny and looked flustered.

'Ey up. What's this? Food at this time of night? Is there a new world order or somefun'?' another man said. All the men's heads turned in unison, watching Marge as she came out from behind the bar.

'It's for this rum ol' boy 'ere,' said Davey, turning on his bar stool to wink at Jack.

'Yes, out o' towners get special treatment, apparently,' added Big Dog, without turning round. He was rolling a cigarette.

'Oh, give over, you lot. Honestly,' said Marge. 'Mind out me way, please, comin' through.' The men stood aside, reluctantly. She looked at Jack, rolled her eyes and tutted. ''Ere you go, love, come an' sit over 'ere. Don't mind them lot; they're only 'avin' a wind-up.' Jack quickly shimmied through the gap she had made in the small crowd, clutching his pint. There was the odour of fresh air on the men's clothes, and a faint whiff of fish.

The landlady placed the two plates on a dark wooden table. She moved a lit candle to one end of it. 'Sit yourself down here. I'll go and get you a spoon an' napkin.'

'Thank you,' said Jack. He put down his pint, took his rucksack off and plonked himself down on a cushioned settle. It was such a relief to take the weight off his feet that he thought he might never get up again.

In front of him were a bowl of brownish soup and a plate of cheese on toast. They looked and smelt wonderful. His stomach cramped in anticipation. 'There you go, darl,' said the landlady, returning. 'French onion in case you were wonderin'. Made it mesen. Enjoy it. Looks like yer need it.'

'Thank you,' said Jack again. He couldn't wait to get started.

'Right, you 'orrible lot. Oo's first?' said Marge, fighting her way back to the bar.

Jack picked up his spoon and started slurping soup. It scalded his tongue and lips and he winced, taking a large glug of cider to ease the burn. He set about his toast instead, devouring a quarter of it in one go, for once, not worrying about being watched. He grabbed another quarter, dipping it into the soup this time, waving it around to help cool the liquid. Little droplets of grease formed on the surface from the cheese.

As he went quickly onto his third quarter of toast, a voice disturbed him. 'Christ, 'e's 'ungry!'

'It's makin' *me* 'ungry,' Davey said.

'Ah, buh,' someone agreed.

Jack slowly looked up. All eyes at the bar were on him. His face burned and he wished he'd sat facing the other way.

'Stop gawpin', you lot, and leave the lad to his supper,' said Marge. The men reluctantly turned back. 'Right, Tom. What can I do yer for? The usual?'

'Aye, pint o' best, please, Marge ... and one for yersen.'

'You know me, Tom. Don't mind if I do, ta very much.'

'Ah, what've yer gone and covered 'em up for, Marge?' said Davey.

'Ey?' said the landlady. Davey gestured to the pinny. 'Dirty beggar,' she tutted, untying the apron anyway and putting it under the counter.

'That's better,' said Davey, nudging Big Dog.

Conversation started again, and the men left Jack to finish his supper. He listened to them as they smoked and talked. There was a distinct twang to their voices. To hear another dialect was a revelation. The only markedly different accent Jack had heard was that of his old boss, Peasgood: Scottish, yet easier to understand than these people.

When the landlady noticed he had finished, she made her way over. Jack was trying to pluck up the courage to ask for a room for the night. They seemed an amiable enough bunch. 'All done 'ere, love?'

'Yes, thank you.'

'Do yer want another pint bringing over? Yer must 'ave been thirsty.' She cleared the table in one quick swoop.

'Did you 'ear that, Tommo? Waitress service now as well!' said Davey. Marge shot him a look.

'Actually ... I was wondering if you might have a room I can stay in for the night,' Jack said, blushing, unable to look the landlady in the eye.

There were sniggers from the bar.

'Ooh aye, buh. Marge us always got a warm bed for an ol' boy like yersen. Ain't yer, Marge?' said Davey. There was more laughter and nudging amongst the men.

Marge spun round, reddening. 'Swear to God, Davey Fowler, one more word out of you tonight and yer barred!' She looked daggers at him. 'What must this poor lad fink of us 'ere? Bunch o' bloody 'eathens. I'm tryin' to run a business!'

'Well yer don't want to bar me then, Marge. I keep this place afloat!' Cue more laughter.

Marge turned back to Jack, exasperated. Sadly, there was more than an element of truth in Davey's statement: it had been a quiet night again. The unexpected revenue of a room would come in handy. 'Aye, I could do you a room, I suppose. I'll 'ave to get it ready fust, though.' A flicker crossed her face. 'You'll 'ave to pay up front as well. Don't want yer doin' a moonlight flit on me.'

Jack had no idea what a moonlight flit was, but was mightily relieved to have somewhere to stay for the night. 'That's fine. Thank you. How much will it be?' He hoped he wouldn't have to pay another visit to the toilet. It pained him to be spending his cash already.

'Will yer be wantin' breakfast?'

Jack considered for a moment. The thought of a cooked breakfast was tempting; it would set him up for the day. That soup and cheese on toast had barely scratched the surface. But he didn't want to hang around any longer than he had to – or draw more attention to himself. Better to get up and clear off. Disappear. 'No, thank you. Just the room is fine.'

'Yer sure? I do a mean full English.'

'No, just the room, thanks.'

'Call it twenty quid then. Saves me gettin' up early, I suppose.' Jack reached into his pocket, relieved at the amount. Marge faltered. 'Will yer be wantin' that other drink?' she asked.

'Er, perhaps just one more,' Jack said, holding out some notes. The cider had gone to his head.

'Yer not the first person who's said that in 'ere and regretted it, is 'e, Big Dog?' said Davey, nudging his mate again. He seemed determined to be part of the conversation.

'That's true,' sighed Marge, turning away. 'Pay me after. Me 'ands er full. I'll set yer a tab up.' It was another expression that was lost on Jack. What had ears got to do with it?

Davey was right. After another pint Jack was still in the bar. He'd intended to go straight to bed, to plan tomorrow and to pine for Daisy. But he'd figured he'd only get lonesome and depressed. Besides, the landlady hadn't got his room ready yet. She'd just finished serving another round of drinks. 'Right, I'm just nippin' upstairs to get that room ready. Davey, will yer do the 'onours for me again if anyone comes in?' Davey nodded. 'Ta, love.' *Strange relationship*, mused Jack as he watched her go. *One minute she's threatening to bar him, the next she's trusting him to run the pub for her.*

Jack was invited to come and sit at the bar. His shyness bubbled to the surface, and he declined politely. 'Ah, come on, buh. I've just bought yer a pint. The least yer can do is come an' drink it wi' me. Pass us that stool, Tommo,' Davey said. Jack remained seated. 'Don't upset me, ol' boy,' Davey said, patting the stool. Jack wasn't sure if this was a veiled threat or not. He didn't know the man well enough. Either way, he was in a room full of strangers, all of whom were watching him. He quickly weighed up his options. Figuring it seemed safer to move, Jack got up. 'Adda boy,' said Davey, grinning. 'Shift over, Big Dog, yer big lump. Make some room for … what's yer name, anyway, buh?'

'Er, J-ohn,' Jack corrected at the last minute, unwilling to give out his name.

'Yer don't sound too sure,' Davey laughed. 'Pleased to meet yer, John.' He held out a large, rough hand with nicotine-stained fingers. Jack had no option but to shake it. Davey squeezed Jack's hand hard, looking him in the eye. It seemed to go on forever, as if he was trying to assert control. Relieved when it was over, Jack sat down, squashed between Davey and Big Dog; he could smell them. Big Dog smelt of sweat, and the proximity of them both made Jack squirm on his stool. 'Fag?' said Davey, rolling one for himself.

'Er, no, thank you,' said Jack.

'Where yer from then, John?' the man called Tommo asked. *Here we go*, Jack thought…

He spent the next five minutes lying about where he'd come from and how he'd come to be in the area. One word answers, mainly. Finally, the landlady came back, thank God, smelling strongly of perfume. 'Right, all done,' she said.

It seemed a good opportunity to leave, and Jack made to get up. 'Erm, if I could pay you now, that would be great,' he said.

'Oh, don't leave us yet, John,' said Davey, putting a hand on his shoulder. 'It's Big Dog's round next. He wants to buy you a pint, don't yer, Big Dog?' Big Dog tutted and reached into his pocket. He didn't say a lot.

'No, really. I ought to be …'

'Sit down, relax. There's plenty o' time yet.' Davey applied a bit of pressure and Jack sat back down.

'Just one more then,' Jack said.

By the time he'd finished his next pint and another round was proposed, Jack was almost past caring about where it was all leading, or that he was being called John. He'd got his drinking head on, drowning his sorrows, and the men seemed to be enjoying having someone new to tell their stories to. Jack was just relieved the attention had been diverted from him. The landlady kept on standing near him, he noticed, wiping around the pumps with a bar towel, her ample bosom swinging from side to side, exuding that cloying perfume. She was knocking the drinks back too, matching the men round for round.

Soon everyone was laughing. A party atmosphere had sprung up. 'Turn the music up, Marge!' Davey said. He tapped his hands on the bar in time to it.

'Shots!' someone else cried.

'Yes, line 'em up, Marge!'

'Who's payin'?' said Marge.

'John'll get 'em, won't yer, John?' said Davey. Jack looked put out. He wasn't really sure what was going on, and had no idea what shots were.

34

'Ey, tha's not fair,' said Marge. 'Tell yer what. These are on me. I'll get some of me top shelf stuff down.' There were some groans at this. 'Ey, it's free, innit?' She reached up and grabbed a dusty and sticky bottle; the label had grapes on it.

A row of tiny glasses was produced and lined up on the bar. Marge filled them with the clear liquid. Whilst the men were spending as they were, she needed to make the most of it. This would encourage them. A glass was pushed towards Jack.

'Right, down in one!' said Davey. *What the hell*, thought Jack. They all drank. The alcohol was unexpectedly sweet, aniseedy and strong. It burned. Some men grimaced and shook their heads. Jack took a gulp of cider to get rid of the taste. 'Leave it on the bar, Marge,' said Tommo, tossing a five pound note on the counter. Marge picked up the note, smiling to herself. 'Right, oo's round is it?' someone said.

'One more shot first!' said Davey.

More shots were poured. And sunk. Jack's guard dropped further; for once it felt good to be amongst people. Perhaps this was a snapshot of his future – travelling and making friends along the way. He felt the urge to speak, to ask questions, his tongue loosened by the liquor – dangerously so. 'Does anyone here own a boat?' he slurred to Davey, having to shout over the music.

''Old up, John 'ere's speaking, everyone! Turn the music down a bit, Marge, John's speaking!' said Davey.

Immediately Jack wished he hadn't said anything. Everyone leant in to listen as he repeated the question.

'Aye, most of us 'ere 'ave a boat er some sort. Why you ask, buh?' answered Davey.

'How far is it to the coast from here?' Jack said in return.

'Not far. Fifteen minutes or so,' said Tommo.

'Where's the nearest port?'

'Yer askin' a lot er questions without givin' many answers, John! What kind er port? A fishin' port?' said Davey.

'Yer want King's Lynn for that, buh,' said Big Dog.

'No, a travelling port, for ferries,' said Jack.

'Well, there's nowhere round 'ere for that,' said Tommo.

'Yer plannin' on going somewhere, love?' said Marge.

'America,' said Jack, without thinking. The drink had got to him.

Davey spat out his ale, froth and all. Everyone laughed, except Marge.

'America!' said Davey. 'Listen to Chris Columbus, 'ere.' There was more laughter. Jack reddened.

'Leave 'im alone, Davey,' said Marge, wiping up the mess.

Davey regarded Jack, giving the impression he thought he was one sardine short of a tin. 'You're on the wrong side of the country for that, ol' boy. America is west, this is east. You're in the Fens now. Even Big Dog 'ere knows that.'

'Southam'un's probably yer best bet,' said Tommo, 'and that's down south… If you're bein' serious, that is.'

Jack was confused. He foolishly took another glug of cider. 'Well, does anyone have a boat that can take me there then? I can pay!'

'Where, America?' said Tommo. Everyone burst out laughing again.

'Aye, I've just got the *Discovery* moored down at the docks!' someone else cried. Most of the men were in hysterics now. Jack was starting to feel angry, braver in his inebriation. It seemed as if he'd gone from being an equal to a source of entertainment, a figure of fun. This showed on his face.

'Sorry, John,' said Davey, wiping his eyes. 'We're not taking the mickey, honestly… Marge, get this ol' boy another drink.'

'No, I don't want another drink. I've had enough.' Jack put his head in his arms. He wanted his bed, but didn't have the energy to get up. He could just go to sleep, right there on the bar. He closed his eyes, but his head spun.

Davey put a hand on his arm. 'Listen, there mus' be a dozen ports 'tween 'ere and Southam'un. It would take forever by boat, a fair bit o' gasoline, too. Someone could take yer to King's Lynn, m'be, for a price, but that's all.' Jack was listening – just. His plan was shot to pieces. He felt deflated. He'd walked all this way for nothing. Daisy's voice came back to haunt him: '*I don't think you've thought this through, Jack.*'

'You're probably be'er gettin' the train to Southam'un, buh,' someone said. There were murmurs of agreement at this. Jack brightened, forcing his head up to listen. Why wouldn't it stop spinning? 'You'd 'ave to get one frum Spaldun', that's the nearest station now – used to be one 'ere in the village. Still take yer a good few hours, though. An' then you'd need to get there.'

'I can take yer to the station in the mornun',' said Marge. 'Providun' it's 'fore openun' time.'

'Really?' slurred Jack. 'That would be amazing.' His plan was finally starting to take shape. But his head lolled again, against his will.

'Aye, we're not a bad lot out 'ere,' said Davey. 'No ma'er what they say.'

'Come on, love, let's get yer upstairs – while yer still can,' said Marge, pulling a fobbed key down from a hook. There were some sniggers and nudges at this. 'What er you lot sniggerin' at? 'E's 'ad enough, look, bless 'im. I don't wan' 'im being sick on me bar!' At the word 'sick' Jack's stomach joined in the spinning game, whirling round and round. He'd never felt like this from alcohol. Ever. Must have been that vile, sweet liqueur. He tried not to think about it.

'My rucksack!' he cried, suddenly alarmed. 'Where is it?'

'Pass 'im 'is rucksack, someone. It's down by that table,' said Marge. Some of the men were trying to shake his hand, patting him on the back and wishing him good luck. He was shepherded out of the bar, still muttering about paying for his room. 'Oh, give it me in the mornun', love. I don't think there's any danger of you goin' anywhere tonight.'

'Who wan'sa bet a quid she don't come back?' said Davey as the two of them left, and the men laughed.

'Pay no attention to them, love. They're animals,' said Marge out in the corridor. Jack hadn't even heard. He was trying to concentrate on lifting his feet up some creaky stairs. The stairs seemed to be going round in a circle, the last thing he needed. Finally they ended, and he vaguely registered another narrow corridor with black beams in the walls. The floor, which also creaked, seemed to be off kilter, sloping to the side – or was it just him? ''Ere we are.' The landlady stopped outside a door and Jack nearly bumped into her. As she unlocked it, she said, 'I've put you in a double … there's no other guests tonight.'

Marge walked in and turned on a bedside lamp. Jack followed her. He was met with a smallish beamed room, which smelt a little fusty. The bed took up most of it. There was tea-making paraphernalia on a mirrored dressing table and a TV that wouldn't stay still, attached to the wall by a metal bracket. 'Your toilet's through here,' she said, brushing past him, against him, too close. Jack still had enough of his wits about him to feel awkward up here in this small room, alone with her. Without being surrounded by cigarette smoke, her perfume smelt stronger than ever, sickly sweet like that liqueur.

She pushed open a door to reveal a small side room, painted cream, a toilet and a small basin. 'The bathroom's down the hall, opposite, if you need a shower, I'm 'fraid. Not all of the rooms are en suite.' Jack was horrified at the prospect of showering – not bathing – across the landing, but didn't say anything; he wouldn't be doing it tonight anyway. At least there was a toilet. And the bed looked like heaven. 'So, that's it then, I guess…' Marge gave him a lingering look, as if she expected him to say something. He didn't. 'Do you want me to wake you with a cup o' tea or an alarm in the mornun'?'

'No, that's fine,' said Jack, looking at the kettle.

'Well, if you're in no 'urry, 'ave a bit of a lie-in – looks like yer need it. I'll give yer that lift to the station – providun' it's 'fore eleven. I'll 'ave to be back for then.'

Jack nodded, too tired to think about it, his head still spinning.

'Well, night, love,' Marge said.

'Night,' Jack mumbled.

The landlady left. Jack listened to her creak away down the corridor. Fighting the urge to collapse on the bed, he lurched over to lock the door. Feeling slightly less vulnerable, he rummaged in his rucksack for his toothbrush and toothpaste. After sloppily brushing his teeth, swaying in front of the mirror, he got undressed and crawled into bed. It felt strange to be in an unfamiliar bed in a faraway place. He felt lonely, like a little boy. He stared up at the cracks in the ceiling, the cobwebs round the light fitting. They wouldn't stop moving. It made him feel sick so he turned off the light. Closing his eyes, he became aware of voices and laughter resonating through the floor from the bar. *Great*, he thought…

Jack was woken by the sound of a door slamming. His eyes shot open in the dark. Where the hell was he? Then he remembered. That lonely feeling returned, along with the nausea. He became aware of voices outside, below his window, impossibly loud. What was going on? And what the hell time was it? The sound of a motor started up. Again, too loud.

Wide awake, but still groggy, Jack shuffled over to the window. In the moonlight he could see a boat with three men in it moving away down the river. Another man, standing with his back to Jack, was urinating in the river. Two other men, unmistakably Davey and Big Dog, were struggling to start their boat. A light strapped to his head, Davey was tugging at the motor, but it wouldn't catch. Big Dog wasn't helping. He was sitting in the boat, rocking it from side to side and laughing. 'Pack it in yer great big fuckun' lump!' cried Davey. 'You'll 'ave us arse over tit!'

'Give it some choke,' said Big Dog. Davey fiddled with the motor, then tried again, unsuccessfully. 'Do you wan' me to start rowun' or what?'

'The state you're in?' Davey continued to swear and tug at the motor. After a few more goes it coughed into life. Big Dog cheered. 'Thank fuck for that!' said Davey, adjusting the choke. They set off, Davey steering the boat away from the bank and down the river. As Jack watched them go, it occurred to him that he would never see them again.

He crawled back into bed, but struggled to sleep. What time was it? Why hadn't he agreed to the landlady giving him an alarm call in the morning? As he lay there in the dark, he heard a door open and close within the building, distant footsteps on the creaky stairs. Must be the landlady going to bed. But the footsteps got louder, closer, squeaking down the hall. Surely she didn't live in this part of the building? This was the residents' bit. What was she doing? The footsteps slowed and stopped outside his room. Jack's skin crawled, and he pulled the bedcovers up to his chin. To his horror, the door handle turned. What the hell? Thank God he'd locked the door. Then a voice. 'Are you awake, love?' The landlady sounded drunk. Jack didn't dare breathe or move an inch. She tried the door handle one more time, sighed loudly, then went away.

Jack let out a huge sigh of relief. He felt like scarpering. What *was* this place? If there'd been a boat out there right now he'd have taken it. Followed the river to the sea. But how would he find his way out of the building in the dark? All the doors would be locked. And what if she heard him? He felt trapped. *What if she'd gone to get another key?* His key was in the door this side, thank God. But *she* didn't know that. The thought was enough to keep him up for most of the night. Eventually he drifted off. Torrid dreams plagued him – boats, keys, the landlady...

CHAPTER 3

Planes, Trains and Automobiles

When Jack woke in the morning his head was pounding. He opened his eyes and saw a stained, cracked ceiling. It all came back to him. Not just last night, not just the landlady, but everything... Daisy ... his predicament ... what lay ahead of him. He cried again then, the weight of it crushing him. He felt so alone, anxious and terrified. The alcohol in his system didn't help. He'd got to pull himself together.

Forcing himself out of bed, Jack went to fill the kettle. The rough carpet hurt his blistered feet and he winced. Whilst he waited for the kettle to boil, he scanned the room. Seeing the TV on the wall made him think of the news; the time. Pressing a few buttons, he eventually got a scratchy picture to come up, but no sound. Adjusting the aerial didn't help much; the picture zig-zagged from side to side. Trying a different channel, he got a breakfast TV show, and could just make out the clock in the corner of the screen: 8:45. *8:45!* He'd planned on leaving a lot earlier than that. Thinking he'd better get a move on, he turned the telly off.

First things first, he'd got to have a shower. It had been days, and it might be days again before he got another opportunity. But what about her? The landlady? What had she wanted last night? Again, he considered slipping out, leaving. But then he remembered he hadn't paid her. Shit! Why hadn't she accepted the money the previous night? And then there was that lift to the station. He looked down at his feet. The thought of walking there was horrendous.

Before leaving the room Jack got fully dressed, boots and all. His clothes reeked of cigarette smoke. He spotted a towel, draped over a chair: at least that was something. Leaving his tea to brew and clutching the towel, he unlocked the door. Cautiously, he ventured out into the corridor. It was deserted and quiet. Which way had she said the bathroom was? He couldn't remember, and tried to the right.

The first door he came to had a metal plaque that said 'BATHROOM' on it. So far, so good. The room smelt a little damp – like the bathroom at home. His head swam at the thought of home; he saw flames and wobbled slightly, as if he'd been punched. He had to lean on the basin for support. *Must block it out.*

Pulling back a stained shower curtain in the corner of the room, Jack was met with an equally grotty cubicle with spots of mildew between the tiles. He sighed: he hated showers – didn't trust them – and if there wasn't a lock on the bathroom door, he wasn't having one. Simple as that.

Fortunately there was. Locking the door, he quickly got undressed, wanting to get it over and done with in as short a time as possible. The shower went from scalding hot to icy cold blasts that either burned or took his breath away. There was barely enough power to rinse the shampoo out of his hair. Glad it was over, shivering and still wet, he got dressed again. His stinking clothes stuck to him as he made his way back to his room.

After gulping his tea down and quickly brushing his teeth, Jack checked he had all his belongings, including the notes in his pocket. Finally, he stuffed a load of milk cartons and teabags into his rucksack, thinking they might come in useful at some point. Who knew what lay ahead?

He made his way down the corridor. Reaching the stairs, he noticed a door the other side of the landing. Another metal plaque on it said 'PRIVATE'. Must be where the landlady lived. What if she wasn't awake yet? How could he go in there if it was private? Whilst debating what to do, he was alerted to a faint droning sound from downstairs. It sounded like a vacuum cleaner. Perhaps she was already up. Or what if it was a cleaner? He wasn't in the mood to meet another stranger. But he didn't have a choice: he needed to pay and he needed that lift.

As Jack gingerly opened the door to the bar, the sound of vacuuming got louder. But the landlady was nowhere to be seen. A tell-tale electric lead was plugged into the wall and led into another room. He headed towards a low, stone archway that he hadn't noticed the previous night.

A separate, more formal, dining area came into view. There were glasses on tables, some of them dusty, he noted, with burgundy napkins arranged in them. Amongst the tables was the landlady, vacuuming. Jack stopped, taken aback. The woman seemed to have aged overnight by at least ten years. She was wearing a dressing gown and slippers. Her hair, streaked with grey in the morning light, was tied back, and with no makeup her face was heavily lined.

Looking up, she noticed Jack, loitering. 'God, you frit me to death!' she said, putting her hand to her chest. She switched the vacuum cleaner off. 'Mornun', love. Did you sleep OK? I was gonna bring yer a cup o' tea up in a minute. You've caught me without me war paint on – not a pretty sight, eh?' Jack smiled awkwardly. 'Can I get yer some toast or somefun'? Cereal?'

'I'll just pay if that's OK. Thank you.'

'Good job you reminded me, love! I'd clean forgot!'

Jack pulled out his money and handed twenty-five pounds over, hoping it would be enough. Her hand was rough and dry as she took the notes from him. He had flashbacks to last night, the bedroom door handle turning. '*Are you awake, love?*' It made him feel squeamish: he couldn't believe this old crone was that same woman. 'Ah, just give us twenty, love. That should cover it. I 'ad a good night. A late one. Your turnun' up seemed to put 'em in good spirits.' She held out a fiver.

'But what about the drinks – and the food?' It was worth a fiver not to have to touch that hand again.

Marge considered for a moment, her eyes narrowing. 'Do yer' still want that lift?'

After settling his debt Jack was contemplating walking, just to get out of there. But now she had asked… 'Well, if it's no trouble.'

'No, I said I would. Call it twenty-five then. Yer a polite an' 'onest young man; there ain't many of *them* about these days, I can tell yer. I'll just go an' put some slap on an' get me keys.'

When the landlady returned she looked a little more like Marge again. 'Right, are yer ready then, love?' she said. Her car was a sun-faded red Mini Metro, which was sitting in the corner of a small car park. As in the room the previous night, it felt a little uncomfortable for Jack to be alone in the car with her; and the cloying smell of her perfume was inescapable. He clutched his rucksack for protection. 'Right, be good to me, darl,' she said, turning the key. The car whinnied for a bit, but didn't start. 'I don't use it much, 'cept for goin' to the cash and carry,' she explained, pulling out the choke before trying again. *Please start*, thought Jack. *Please.* The motor put up another brief fight, then revved to life, answering his prayers. Marge looked relieved. 'Good ol' girl,' she said, patting the steering wheel.

They set off, following the river briefly before veering off through more of the flat countryside. It was disheartening to Jack to realise they were travelling further inland rather than towards the coast. There were a few awkward silences, but mainly the landlady kept up an incessant patter; she liked to talk. 'So, America then, eh? What an adventure. God, I wish I could just up sticks and clear off out of this dump. Oh, to be young again! If only I could turn back time, I'd sure do things differently...' She paused then, and Jack stole a glance at her. She looked sad, old – too many late nights, too many gin and tonics. 'Anyway, too late for that now... So, are you on a gap year or somefun' then?' There was that expression again; Daisy's voice... Why did this keep happening? It hurt. Hearing her voice hurt. *Block it out.* 'Eh, love?' Marge was looking at him.

'Yes, something like that,' said Jack quietly.

'Well, yer very brave, I must say, travelling on yer own, young lad like you. And to America of all places! Yer didn't think of booking a ticket in advance then? Or goin' on a plane?' There was a pause.

'Erm, no... I wasn't sure where I wanted to go, you see.'

'Oh, bit of a snap decision, worrit? Wer gonna say, I thought yer were travellun' a bit light.'

'Sorry?'

'Yer rucksack – you ain't got much wi' yer.' Jack didn't say anything. She was asking too many questions. He could feel her watching him again, waiting for an answer. 'What are yer runnun' from, eh?' she said, surprising him. He thought it best to ignore her, but she carried on. 'Family? A sweet'eart, maybe?' Tears welled up in Jack's eyes and he fiddled with the strap of his rucksack. 'A sweet'eart, me thinks... Well, good luck to yer, love. Good luck to yer.' She patted his leg. Jack flinched and continued to stare out of the window.

There was silence for the remainder of the journey. Thankfully, it didn't take too long to reach the station, a large brick building bordering a main road. Jack gulped at the sight of it. The landlady pulled up outside, where cars and taxis were dropping off other people. He'd been wanting the car journey to be over so he could be on his own, but now he'd arrived the reality hit – that once he stepped out of this car he truly was on his own. He'd somehow stumbled across a mother figure in Marge – as odd as she was – and last night he'd had the company of friends. He'd enjoyed it. The building out there represented the real world – a cold place of flat lines and hard edges, people in a hurry, scurrying back and forth. Not like the earthy tones of his home – greens, browns and golds in comforting soft curves.

'Are you sure yer gonna be OK, love?' Marge said, noticing his hesitation. Jack took a deep breath, trying to compose himself.

'Yes. And thank you for everything.'

'Yer welcome.' She leant across and kissed his cheek, surprising him again. Her lips, like her hands, were dry and rough. 'Good luck,' she said.

Jack stepped out of the car and shouldered his rucksack. Marge pulled away from the kerb, and as she U-turned she pipped her horn twice in goodbye. Jack raised a hand in return. *Come on then*, he said to himself.

Once inside the station, Jack made his way to the ticket office. He stood in a small queue, getting increasingly nervous. Through the double doors at the back he could see the platform, a pedestrian bridge and people waiting. When it was his turn he said, 'Could I have a ticket to Southampton please?' The lady looked at him over the top of her glasses.

'Southampton?' she said.

Jack's stomach sank at her tone and he panicked. 'Er, yes… There are trains to Southampton, aren't there?'

'There are, but it involves a few changes. Let me see…' She ran her finger over some charts taped to her desk.

'Changes?' said Jack.

'Yes, changes. If you'll just bear with me a second… Yes, three of them by the looks of it. You would've been better going from Peterborough really.'

'Peterborough?'

'Yes. That's where your first change is.' Jack's head swam. Did she mean getting off and getting on a different train? What if he got on the wrong one? 'Then you've got King's Cross.' She looked up from the chart to see if he was taking it in, and noticed his pale, alarmed countenance. 'That's London... You have been on a train before, haven't you?' She was beginning to wonder. Jack didn't answer. At the mention of London he felt like fainting. *London!* He imagined the sprawling city. He just wanted to go to Southampton. Why did he have to go to London first? 'Do you still want the ticket?' Jack tried to bring himself back round. The lady was looking directly at him, her kind eyes magnified by her glasses.

'Er, yes. I think so.'

'You're sure? Because once I've printed it, that's it.'

'Yes. Yes, please,' he mumbled. What choice did he have? He'd got it into his head that the only way to America was from Southampton: he'd taken some drunken fisherman's word in a bar as gospel. And by hook or by crook he'd got to get there. Beyond that he had no plan at all; stowing away somehow seemed his only option.

'One way or return?'

'Er, one way.'

'Right. That will be...' She did some adding up on a calculator. 'Eighteen pounds fifty, please.'

Eighteen pounds fifty! thought Jack. *More money. Shit, money!* He'd done it again. His money was in his rucksack.

'Erm, is there a toilet around here, please?'

'A toilet?' the lady asked.

'My money, it's at the bottom of my rucksack...'

A flash of impatience crossed the woman's face. But the boy looked so flustered, bless him. She was just about to point with her pen, when a man behind Jack coughed. Jack turned around. A queue had formed again. He turned back to the lady, his face red.

'It's over there, behind you. I'll serve these people first. Your train's not for a while yet, so don't worry.' Jack thanked her and scurried off to the toilet.

Once there, he pulled out more money than he needed. He couldn't keep doing this, and his pile of notes seemed to be diminishing a little too quickly for his liking. But this was the bulk of his outlay, he told himself – the travelling.

When he returned to the booth, the lady printed off the train ticket and gave Jack his change. He stared at the ticket as if it was the most precious thing in the world. She wrote down some clear instructions for him, including his changes and what platforms he needed. 'Your train's not till ten past eleven, so you've got a bit of a wait I'm afraid, love,' she said. He thanked her and shuffled off, looking a little overwhelmed. The lady watched him go, shaking her head. 'Through the double doors and over the bridge to the other side. Platform three!' she called.

*****

Whilst Jack was waiting nervously for his train, back at the Bucket of Blood Marge was putting some fresh ashtrays on the bar tables. She sighed at the routine of it; another day, same old crap. Jack's brief stop-off at the pub had stirred something in her. The boy was moving on, passing through – his whole life ahead of him. She was stuck. It made her feel envious. The sound of a car, trundling through the archway of the pub to the car park, added to her woes. She knew that sound well; a customer. She looked at the clock and groaned. Ten minutes to opening time. Well, they could wait. Sod 'em.

She continued to go through the motions of getting the bar set up, turning the glass washer on, replacing the drip trays. She was just screwing the sparklers back on the real ale pumps when there was a knock at the back door. *Cheeky sods*, she thought, ignoring it. She needed customers, but not at ten to eleven. A few seconds later there was another knock, more persistent. It made her blood boil. She considered going to give them a piece of her mind, but then she'd have to let them in. Then they would have won. She chose to carry on ignoring it.

Marge listened for the sound of the car going away, but it didn't. Perhaps they'd gone to sit in it and wait. Good. Just then, two figures walked past one of the windows at the front of the pub, making her look up. She didn't see them clearly, but when they passed a second window she saw that one of them was a policeman. Marge's hackles went up. She'd always been nervous around the police, ever since she was a little girl. The sight of them made her feel as if she'd done something wrong.

She racked her brains, wondering what they could want. Meanwhile they had disappeared from view, presumably looking at the opening times by the door. *I know*, she thought, *I bet one of those local busybodies has complained about the bloody noise again.* Davey and co. starting their boats up and swearing and carrying on at two o'clock in the morning. She'd told them before about it – especially the boats – *'row out o' the village, then yer can start yer bloody motors up! You'll get me licence takun' off me, then where'll yer be!'* But they got drunk and forgot.

The two men reappeared at one of the windows, giving her a fright. The uniformed one cupped his hands over his eyes and peered in. Seeing Marge, he tapped on the glass and signalled to the front door. She sighed: better let them in and face the music. She picked up some post from the porch floor, drew back the bolts on the front door, and opened it. Bright sunlight flooded in, hurting her eyes. 'Mornun', officers. Bit early for a pint, innit?'

Her joke fell on deaf ears. 'Morning, madam. I'm Detective Chief Inspector Haslam, and this is my colleague, Sergeant Nichols,' the plainclothes man said. He flashed an ID card. 'May we come in?' As soon as he spoke, Marge knew he wasn't local, which ruled out a possible noise complaint. This was a relief. What could they possibly want?

'Sure. It's 'bout openun' time anyway.' She stepped aside to let them in.

Once in the bar, the officer in uniform took off his helmet. The landlady in Marge kicked in. 'Can I get you gents anythun'? Coffee, tea? Something stronger?'

'No. We're fine, thank you. In fact, we probably won't keep you long. We were in the area, you see, and just called in on the off chance. We've been doing the rounds of the village – petrol station, shops and so on. The thing is, well…' The man reached into his jacket pocket again and produced a bit of paper. He held it out. 'You haven't seen a young man fitting this description, have you? Passing through, maybe?'

There, in front of Marge's very eyes, was a sketch of a boy resembling Jack – or John as she knew him. Not quite a Photofit drawing, more rudimentary than that, but detailed enough – the high cheekbones, the tufty hair. Next to it were some handwritten statistics – approximate height, build, eye, hair colour and so on. The officers immediately clocked the recognition on the landlady's face; the look of shock, too. They looked at each other as if they'd struck gold. 'I take it you have come across the boy then?' the detective said. Marge didn't know what to say. She felt as if she was betraying him somehow.

'What's 'e done?' she asked.

'Can you answer the question please, madam?' The detective looked and sounded a hell of a lot more serious all of a sudden. There was urgency to his voice. Marge didn't see that she had a choice.

'Yes, 'e stayed 'ere las' night. 'Ad some food an' that.' The policemen looked at each other again.

'Where is he now? What time did he leave?' Haslam asked.

'I took 'im to the station this mornun'…'

'Which station? What time?'

'Spaldun' 'bout 'alf past nine, I s'pose.'

'Shit,' said Haslam. 'Sorry. Excuse my French. Pete, give the station a call. Tell them to get onto Spalding station right away, the local police station here too, deploy officers if necessary. I bet we've bloody missed him.'

'Yes, boss.' The man left, speaking into his radio.

'Tell me, you don't happen to know where he was heading, do you? It's important. Did he say anything? Anything at all?'

'Well, 'e said 'e was headun' to America.'

The detective looked at her as if she was joking. Clearly she wasn't. 'America? On a train?'

'No, by boat. 'E was goun' to Southam'un fust.'

'Southampton?' He produced a pen and notebook and began to scribble in it. 'And did you know the boy? Or did he give a name?'

'I didn't know 'im from Adam. He jus' showed up.'

'Yer sure? He's not a relation or anything?'

'Positive! Said his name were John – or that's what the regulars were calling him anyway.'

'John.' The detective scribbled again. 'And did any of these regulars know him?'

'No. Like I said, 'e jus' showed up.'

'Any surname?'

'Not that I can remember.'

'And you are?' Marge gave her name and details. 'Thank you. You've been a great help.' He slipped his notebook back in his pocket and hastened to leave.

'Detective, wait!' said Marge. 'What's 'e done? I need to know. 'E seemed such a good boy.'

Haslam paused for a brief moment, choosing his words carefully. 'We don't know that he's done anything just yet. Sorry, I can't say any more than that for now. But thanks again. We'll be in touch.'

*****

Jack hadn't been able to relax on the journey from Spalding to Peterborough. It had taken roughly twenty-five minutes. Unable to take pleasure in his first train ride lest he missed his stop, he'd stared out of the window instead, perched on the edge of his seat, his foot tapping. The black spot on his eye had accompanied him the whole way, a permanent addition to the landscape. Obsessively, he'd consulted the instructions the ticket lady had given him that he still clutched in his hand, the paper crumpled and slightly damp from sweat.

From the second he stepped off the train and onto the platform at Peterborough station something felt wrong. The station felt different to Spalding. Less friendly. Bigger, noisier, busier, more daunting. There were more lines, more trains; how was he supposed to find the right one? What if he missed it? There was no one kindly to ask, no bespectacled lady at a ticket booth. Everyone seemed to be in an even bigger rush, and there were smatterings of different coloured people, he noted. A loud ding-dong over a loudspeaker startled him, and a lady's voice announcing departure information echoed across the station. Spotting two policemen, one standing either side of the exit, added to Jack's unease. Did they normally have policemen at railway stations? There weren't any at Spalding.

He consulted his piece of paper for the umpteenth time. Platform two. 12:05. Peterborough to King's Cross, London. The name King's Cross rang a bell somehow; hadn't there been a fire there a year or so back? Jack scanned the station. He spotted platform two on the other side. This was some relief, but he was going to have to cross a bridge again. He was also going to have to walk past those policemen.

Keeping his head down he set off, the black spot a floating punctuation mark on his bit of paper. Out of the corner of his eye he saw one of the policemen talking into a radio pinned to his chest. *Don't look at them. Act normal.* It was strange, but as he neared them he almost expected them to reach out and grab him. He was prepared for it, ready to bolt.

What he wasn't expecting was to be grabbed from behind. Two arms looped through his, one in a brown suit – at the end of it a white flash of hairy hand with a wedding ring on it – and one in dark blue. There was a voice in his left ear: 'We need you to come with us, young man.' The two policemen guarding the doorway turned and walked ahead of him, shielding him, crowding out the light.

Jack was propelled towards the exit with force; he tried to struggle but it was no use. The same voice: 'Don't struggle, son; it'll only make things worse.' He struggled some more anyway; the authorities had finally got hold of him, his worst nightmare come true. His arms were twisted further behind his back, hurting him. He vaguely heard the loudspeaker ding-dong again on the platform. Then he felt his legs buckle, and the sensation of being dragged. Then the light disappeared entirely. His piece of paper fluttered to the floor behind him, unnoticed.

The next thing Jack knew he was being bundled into a waiting police car. His capture had taken a matter of seconds and, despite the busy station, had barely been witnessed. As he came round again, the man in the brown suit was saying, 'Is he with us? Is he back with us?'

'Yes, he's with us,' the uniformed officer said.

'Right. I am arresting you on suspicion of murder and arson at Bunny Hill, Nottinghamshire…' At the words Jack began to struggle again. The officers grappled with him. 'OK, cuff him, Pete, he's leaving us no choice.'

'Gladly.'

Jack's rucksack was yanked from him and his arms were twisted behind him again. Handcuffs were slapped on him, wrenching his shoulders into an unnatural position and biting into his wrists. He wanted to yell in pain, but refused to utter a sound. Then he was pushed into a sitting position and the plainclothes officer continued his spiel. 'You do not have to say anything. But, it may harm your defence if you do not mention when questioned anything which...' Jack stopped listening. The words became a distant drone. How had they found him? *How?* 'Do you understand?' he heard the man say. Jack gritted his teeth, staring straight ahead. His hands and the cuffs were digging into the small of his back. 'I said, do you understand? Suit yourself. Let's go, Pete.' As the car sped away, tears trickled down Jack's cheeks.

*****

The journey passed in silence, save for the odd bit of communication on the police radio. There were only two policemen in the car, the suited one in the back and the uniformed one called Pete driving. Jack felt dazed and shocked. Where the hell were they taking him? What were they going to do with him? After around fifty minutes he began to recognise place names on road signs again. Not even an hour, he reflected bitterly; it had taken him four days on foot. After another twenty minutes or so they came to a halt outside West Bridgford police station, on the outskirts of Nottingham.

Jack was rushed inside, flanked by the two men.

CHAPTER 4
Questions and Revelations

That evening Carol was in the lounge; the evening news was just starting. Five minutes before Daisy had been sitting there with her, then she'd sloped off upstairs. This had become a habit, Carol noted, as if the news was a personal thing that Daisy had to experience alone. It was most odd.

Moira Stewart was presenting the news; Carol liked her. '*Tonight's headlines...*' she said. '*Teenage boy arrested in connection with East Midlands so-called "Fire House Murders"...*'

'Oh my gosh!' said Carol, getting up. She called up the stairs: 'Daisy! Did you hear that? Are you watching the news? They've caught someone – a boy! Daisy!' There was no reply.

Carol returned to the lounge. '*Good evening. I'm Moira Stewart. In tonight's main news, a teenage boy has been arrested in connection with the so-called "Fire House Murders" on the Nottinghamshire–Leicestershire border. The boy was apprehended earlier today at Peterborough railway station in Cambridgeshire. The so-far unnamed youth is currently being held at West Bridgford police station, Nottingham. An hour ago, the superintendent for the division made this statement.*'

The news cut to a police superintendent, presumably outside the police station: '*I can confirm that earlier today, at approximately 11. 30 a.m., police officers apprehended a teenage boy at Peterborough station in relation to the recent ongoing arson and murder enquiry on Bunny Hill...*'

'*Has the boy been charged with anything?*' a reporter cut in.

The superintendent gave him a disparaging look before continuing. '*Nottinghamshire constabulary would like to state, for the record, that at this stage the boy has not been charged. He is currently being held for questioning. And that is all we have to say for now. Thank you.*'

'*How old is the boy?*' someone else said.

'*No more questions, thank you.*'

The programme cut back to the studio. '*Let's go live now to Dan Wrigley, our East Midlands correspondent, who's been following this case and is at West Bridgford police station. Dan, good evening. The police aren't giving much away about this young man, are they? What more can you tell us?*'

'*Good evening, Moira. No, they're not giving much away. But if you've been following this case from the start then I suppose, where the police are concerned, you could say that coy has been the watchword all along. As you may know, over the last few days the police have alluded to a possible piece, or pieces, of evidence being found at the crime scene, hinting that another person or persons might be involved. What this evidence is has been kept under wraps in order, we presume, to avoid jeopardising the ongoing investigation. They did, however, make an appeal to the public for anyone who has any information with regard to the house or the family, or indeed about anyone acting suspiciously in the local area. We are, again, presuming that today's breakthrough was made as a result of this appeal.*'

'*But what about the boy? What can you tell us about him? Peterborough's some fifty miles from Bunny Hill, is it not? I take it his identity is remaining undisclosed for legal reasons?*'

'*Well, yes and no. Very little is filtering through. What I can tell you is that the boy has been questioned from around midday. And what we have gleaned so far here on the ground is that he is either refusing or unable to speak. He was, as you said, apprehended some fifty miles or so away, apparently pretty dazed and confused. No one knows his name, age or anything about his background. There are even some rumours, all supposition, that the boy might have some minor mental problems...*'

There was a cry from Daisy's bedroom, '*JACK!*' followed by her bedroom door opening; then Daisy thundered down the stairs.

Carol shot to her feet. 'What on earth's going on?'

'It's Jack! The boy on the news. I know it is!' Daisy scrabbled for her keys.

'Now you slow down just one goddamn minute, young lady. What do you mean *Jack?* This murderer they've caught?'

'He's not a murderer! And I haven't got time to explain. I need to go to him. He needs me!'

'You're doing no such thing – not until you explain to me what's going on.' Carol stepped in front of Daisy, blocking the door.

'Mum!'

'Don't "Mum" me. So this is what it's all about, is it? Moping about, not eating, this obsession with the news? He's run away, hasn't he? Your Jack, he's run away!' Carol's face drained of colour. 'Oh my God! Are you telling me my daughter's been dating a murderer?'

'He's not a bloody murderer, Mum! He's innocent. Trust me. He wouldn't hurt a fly. If you'll just let me go, I'll explain everything later.'

'No! You're not going anywhere. This has gone on long enough. All this secrecy…'

'Mum, get out of my way!'

'NO!'

Daisy stormed off in the other direction.

'Where are you going?'

'Out the back door!'

'No you're not!' Carol grabbed her daughter's arm, and wrested free the car keys. Daisy extricated herself and spun round. She felt another wrench in her stomach, but was too incensed to care.

'Mum, give me those keys back, or I swear to God I'll bloody kill myself.'

Carol let out a gasp, then slapped Daisy hard. There was a brief silence as both of them struggled to comprehend what had happened. Daisy put her hand up to her face in shock, where a red mark had appeared. She hadn't been hit since she was a child. Carol went to her daughter, distraught.

'Oh my God, baby, I'm so sorry. I didn't mean to do that. Daisy, I'm so sorry.' She tried to stroke Daisy's hair. The keys were still in her hand, so without saying a word Daisy grabbed them, setting off for the back door again. Carol sank to her knees in despair. 'Daisy! Don't go!' she cried. 'I'm begging you!'

Just then a key rattled in the front door, surprising them both. The door opened and an alarmed Lily appeared: she'd heard the shouting from outside. Her mum was on her knees in tears, Daisy at the kitchen door. 'What the hell's going on?' said Lily, directing the question at Daisy. Neither Daisy nor Carol said a word, both of them feeling guilty in their own way, both of them breathing hard. Lily looked from Daisy to her mum, then back to Daisy again. 'Is someone going to tell me what's going on here or what? Daisy, why's Mum crying?'

'Oh, that's right! Automatically assume it's my fault.'

'Well?'

'Go on, tell her, Daisy. Tell her why your silly old mum is crying,' said Carol.

'What's the point? She wouldn't understand. Just like you don't understand. Why don't you tell her you hit me instead?'

Lily was taken aback. 'That would explain the red mark,' she said, trying to remain cool. Her mother looked even more shamefaced. 'Well, you must have done something to deserve it, Daisy. Mum's not in the habit of going around clobbering us, is she?'

'She wants to go and see this boy!' shrieked Carol. 'This criminal they've caught!'

'He's not a criminal!'

'You don't know that. Boys will say anything. Why have they arrested him then?'

'Didn't you listen to the news? He's just being questioned, that's all! Helping them with their enquiries or whatever.'

'Whoa! Wait a minute. Rewind,' said Lily. 'Are you telling me that boy on the news is Lover ... I mean, Jack?'

'Daisy seems to think so, and she would know. He's run away, hasn't he? Clearly guilty of something. And *she* thinks she's going to go tearing off to see him.'

'See?' said Daisy. 'This is exactly why I didn't tell you. You're so uptight these days I knew you'd automatically assume he was guilty before you'd heard all the facts ... and I don't *think* I'm tearing off to see him, I *am*. And there's nothing either of you can do to stop me!' She made as if to leave again, and Carol let out a wail of despair.

'Daisy! Stop!' cried Lily. 'Look what you're doing to Mum. Have you no heart? Hasn't she been through enough already?'

Daisy flipped. Flames of anger lit up her eyes as she spun round. 'Yes, she's been through enough already: we've all fucking been through enough already! But it's nothing compared to what Jack's going through right now. Yes, we've lost our dad. Yes, Mum's lost a husband. But Jack's lost his whole family! He's got no one. No one at all. He's all alone out there and probably scared out of his wits – it makes me sick to think about it. He's not used to people, and he's terrified of the police.' Saying this out loud broke her, but she carried on, sobbing the words. 'He's claustrophobic, and they've probably put him in a cell. I need to go to him, right now. You've got to understand, Mum. I'm sorry, but I'll see you later.'

'Daisy, wait!' cried Carol. 'Let me drive you. If you've got to go, and what you're saying is true ... at least let me drive.'

'No, Mum. You drive too slowly. It'll take forever.'

'Neither of you is driving!' said Lily. 'Look at the state of you both. I'll drive.' Daisy rolled her eyes.

'She's right,' said Carol. 'Let Lily drive. Then at least we can talk. You've got some serious explaining to do. And if you haven't convinced me by the time we reach West Bridgford, then you're not going into that police station.'

Daisy considered for a moment. 'OK, but we're going in the van.'

'I'm not driving that old thing. I'll take the Montego,' said Lily. Daisy was about to protest, then remembered there wasn't enough petrol in her van anyway.

So it was decided. They piled into the Montego estate, as if they were going on an impromptu family outing, Daisy reluctantly so. Lily had started using their parents' car since their dad had passed away – it was a connection to him. But Daisy had avoided it for the same reason; it reminded her of him too much. She took a deep breath before opening the door and slipping tentatively onto the back seat. Just as she had expected, it was a capsule of her dad frozen in time – the smell of stale tobacco smoke, the liquorice air freshener, his tin of boiled sweets, the cassette tapes with his writing on them neatly slotted between the two front seats; she tried not to look at them.

Settling herself on the back seat next to Daisy, Carol pulled a tissue out of her handbag and dabbed at her eyes. 'Right, start talking,' she said, pausing to blow her nose. 'You've got about half an hour to convince me why I should let my daughter see a boy whom I've never met, and is currently being held in a police station in relation to an arson and murder enquiry. I mean, a man's died – only this week – maybe killed. They still don't know what happened. What would you do if you were a parent?'

Daisy, who had been staring out of the window biting her nails, gulped and touched her stomach. *God, if only she knew*, she thought. Out of the corner of her eye she saw Lily watching in the rear-view mirror, waiting for her to speak. It annoyed Daisy. Just the fact that Lily was there annoyed her; she couldn't help thinking her sister was tagging along out of sheer nosiness, morbid fascination. And where did she start anyway? How could she tell Jack's story in the space of half an hour? How he'd never been to school. How he and his sister had been beaten. The awful truth of where he'd come from. How that man her mum seemed so concerned about was a rapist and a murderer. And then how it had all ended – what she knew of it anyway, how he'd disposed of the two girls to cover his tracks.

'Well?'

Daisy sighed and began.

*****

'Right. Let's try again, shall we?' the man in the brown suit said. He cleared his throat and switched on a small tape recorder sitting on the desk in front of him. 'I'm Detective Chief Inspector Haslam. The time is', he glanced at the watch on his hairy wrist, '6.35 pm. on Saturday the 29th of July. I'm here with my colleague, Detective Sergeant Brewster, and the as-yet-unnamed interviewee. Are you still refusing to clarify your name, son?'

Jack, slouching in a chair the other side of the desk, arms folded, stared blankly ahead. A heavy hand appeared from behind and squeezed his shoulder. It hurt and Jack flinched, but he still didn't speak. Haslam shook his head, sighed, then continued. 'The as-yet-unnamed interviewee who has been arrested in regard to the recent arson and murder case on Bunny Hill. This is interview number two. I will remind you once again, the unnamed interviewee, that it is in your interest to co-operate. By establishing your name, age and address, we can then assign you an appropriate adult to assist you in answering any questions you are struggling to understand...' His voice faded away again as Jack retreated into his protective shell. He stared down at his fingers, still stained black from having his prints taken earlier.

'Right. Let's start with the money this time, shall we?' Haslam continued. 'I ask you for the second time today, where did a young lad such as yourself get in excess of a thousand pounds in cash?' Jack was prodded from behind, and the room swam back into focus. The detective was dangling in front of him a clear plastic bag containing Jack's thick wad of notes. On the desk in front of Jack – similarly bagged – were the contents of his rucksack: clothes, underwear, tin, photos, toiletries, a map he'd bought from a petrol station, compass and his *Lamont the Lonely Monster* book, a childhood relic that had garnered a few raised eyebrows. It made Jack feel violated to see his things spread out like this; they were his private, personal things.

'What about these?' the man behind, Brewster, said in a gruff voice. He leant over the table to pick up Jack's compass and map. His large head appeared. 'Been travelling a long way, have we?' Jack didn't like this man; his breath smelt of coffee and cigarette ash, there was an air of violence about him. 'Where were you trying to get to?'

'What do you know about the Bunny Hill area?' Haslam cut in. 'What do you know about the fire there?' There was a flicker from Jack at this, but no more.

'Listen, you piece of shit,' said Brewster, coming round to face Jack and leaning on the desk, his face up close. 'You'd better start talking. We've got a trail that leads back there, so there's no use denying it. A bottle of milk and orange juice stolen from the doorstep of a farmhouse in Long Clawson – along with this jumper, I believe?' He picked a thick, navy, woollen sweater from the table, then threw it back down. 'A boy acting oddly, and found washing himself in a petrol station toilet in Waltham-on-the-Wolds. Best of all, though – and this one tickled me – frightening some poor old dear to death dipping your bits in a stream in Burton Coggles when she was taking her dog for a walk. There's a law against that kind of thing, you know? Got an exhibitionist streak in you or something, have you?'

All of this was true. The stream incident had been one of the most traumatic experiences of Jack's life. As for the orange juice and milk, when he'd come across the farmhouse he'd been wet, cold and gasping for some refreshment and sustenance. Feeling guilty, he'd left a five pound note tucked under a doormat – for the jumper as well. Unbeknown to Jack, an unscrupulous paperboy had turned up a little after him and extracted it.

'And let's not forget your little stay at the Bucket of Blood,' said Haslam. 'The landlady has been filling us in on that. Said you were planning on fleeing to America, of all places. Why was that? Why the sudden hurry?'

'Said you helped yourself to most of the tea and milk sachets in your room as well,' added Brewster, leaning in even closer.

'Yes, thank you, Detective Brewster,' said Haslam. Brewster backed away.

Haslam leant back in his chair. 'So, I'll ask you again. What do you know about the fire on Bunny Hill?'

The question hung in the air. The only sounds to be heard were the whirr of the tape recorder and the tap of Jack's foot under the table. Brewster turned away in disgust and ran his fingers through his hair. Haslam sighed again. 'Right, I guess you're leaving us no choice then.' He paused for a moment. 'Detective Brewster, can you put the gloves on, please?'

Brewster chuckled. 'Now, do you really think that's necessary, Detective Haslam?'

'Well, the boy's refusing to co-operate, isn't he?'

Jack started to pay attention at last. Whatever one of them needed gloves for, he didn't like the sound of it; his eyes flashed from one man to the other.

Brewster crossed the small room and reached into a drawer. He pulled two clear plastic disposable gloves out of a box, then made a show of blowing into one of them before, expanding it and stretching it over a large hand. He noticed Jack watching him and smiled. 'Ah, now we've got his attention,' he said. Jack looked away.

After performing the same routine with the other glove, Brewster leant on the desk in front of Jack again, staring him straight in the face, his gloved hands on the desk. Jack couldn't look at him. 'Detective Haslam, could you pass me the required items please?' Jack felt like wetting himself. If they were trying to scare him, it was working. Out of the corner of his eye, he watched Haslam slowly reaching into his suit pocket. What had he got in there? Some sort of torture device?

The detective rummaged around for a bit, watching Jack fidgeting and prolonging the tension. What he eventually pulled out of his pocket took Jack by surprise, a clear plastic envelope with a card or something in it. Jack breathed a sigh of relief. 'Detective Brewster, could you clear a space on the table please?' Haslam said.

'Certainly.' Brewster moved Jack's belongings to the edges of the table, leaving a space in the middle.

Haslam stood up. He passed the wallet to Brewster. 'If you'll do the honours, please,' he said. 'You've got the gloves on.'

Brewster reached into the envelope. Jack could now see that there were two photographs inside. As the man removed them, and laid them side by side on the table, Jack could not believe his eyes. They were two of his own photographs, both of his sister, Anne, when she was little. How was that possible? How had they got hold of them? He reached out to grab them. Brewster slammed one of his hands down on Jack's wrists. 'Leave them there, son.'

For the first time Jack allowed his eyes to meet Brewster's, indignation burning in them. Despite the threat this man posed, he was starting to piss Jack off, and at some point he was going to snap. He tried to remove his hand, but it took a few seconds for Brewster to relinquish it, just to emphasise who was boss. As Jack sat back in his chair his gaze returned to the two photographs. 'Who is *she?*' said Haslam, indicating with his finger. Jack barely registered the question; his mind was churning over the events of that fateful night. He tried to recall when he'd last had the photographs. He'd sorted them out and put them in his rucksack. Surely if any had been left in the house they'd have been burnt to a cinder. Then he remembered the stand-off with his father; showing him the photographs whilst at the foot of the ladder. Hadn't he dropped a couple of them in his haste? But surely he'd have seen them lying about; he'd walked past the body half a dozen times?

Detective Haslam answered the questions for him. He leant in and said in a new, more serious, voice, 'These two photographs were found at the crime scene on Bunny Hill. They were found, trapped, under a man's semi-charred corpse. Funny how you've got a wallet full of similar photographs in your rucksack, isn't it? So don't tell me you don't know who that girl is!' He banged a fist on the table.

'And more to the point, fingerprints matching yours are all over them – proving once and for all that you were at Bunny Hill, so you'd better start talking. *Now!*' barked Brewster.

'There was a fresh set of prints on these photographs as well. Whose were those? Did you have an accomplice?' said Haslam. *Oh my God*, thought Jack, panic-stricken. Those would be Daisy's. What had he done, getting her involved in this?

Brewster picked up the other photographs and began flicking through them. Jack hated this with all his heart, and had to restrain himself from trying to grab them again. 'Who's this other girl, then? There's two of them. Are they sisters?' Jack turned away. 'And here they are again at Christmas.' It was obvious which one he was holding up now.

'Are these *your* sisters?' said Haslam.

'And what's your connection to the dead man?' said Brewster. 'Is he your father? Did you kill him for killing your sisters?'

All these questions were making Jack's head spin, and this last one sent him over the edge. He felt trapped, backed into a corner. Groaning, he leant forward and began banging his head on the desk, butting it over and over. Brewster grabbed hold of Jack's hair and lifted him up. 'Start ... talking!' he said, pushing Jack backwards into his seat.

'Listen, son,' said Haslam, adopting his softer voice again. 'Just tell us your name, eh? That would be a start.'

The detectives both waited, expecting a breakthrough.

But none came.

Haslam tried again, beginning to run out of patience. 'Nobody's saying you're guilty of anything yet, you're just helping us with our enquiries, that's all.'

Silence.

'You're in deep shit is what you are!' shouted Brewster.

'All right,' said Haslam, sensing the situation was getting out of hand. 'I'm concluding this second interview at 6.45 pm. Detective Brewster, put the cuffs back on him and take him back to his cell.' He clicked the tape recorder off.

'Get up,' said Brewster, wrestling Jack to his feet.

'We can do this for as long as it takes, you know, son,' said Haslam. 'Over and over again. And all the while, as my colleague here pointed out, you're only getting yourself deeper and deeper in the shit. Take him away.'

CHAPTER 5
Red

Daisy was feeling nauseous, a combination of sitting in the back seat of the car, so-called morning sickness and the fact that the police station had just come into view. Outside there was a crowd of media and TV crews. She groaned in despair. What must Jack be going through?

'Oh dear Lord!' said Carol, echoing Daisy's thoughts. After the journey, their nerves were shredded.

Daisy had told Jack's story with such passion, such strength of feeling, that it was hard not to be moved by it. Carol had spent most of the journey in abject horror. Lily, meanwhile, had earwigged throughout and struggled to keep her eyes on the road. At first Carol had been sceptical, and even considered her daughter might be making the whole thing up. But it was all too far-fetched; how *could* you make that stuff up? Even more worrying was how Daisy knew this boy was telling the truth about what had happened that night. After all, she only had his word for it.

Carol had said as much, and Lily had murmured agreement. Daisy had gone on the attack. 'How could you say such a thing? This is why I haven't told you. I knew you wouldn't believe me – or Jack!' But Carol's doubts had sown a seed of doubt in Daisy's mind: if she acknowledged it, this might take root and grow, strangling and overwhelming like a vine. Daisy resented her mum for this.

Lily turned into the car park and pulled up as far away from the police station as possible. She applied the handbrake, then they all stared out of the window. 'Are you sure you want to do this?' said Carol.

Daisy gulped. She thought of her dad, his sense of justice, the importance of fighting your corner. 'I've got to, Mum. For Jack's sake. He needs me.'

Carol sighed. What was the hold this boy had over her daughter? 'OK, but I'm going in with you.'

'Me, too,' said Lily.

They all stepped out of the car. Lily locked up, and they began walking towards the police station, Carol in front. A few people noticed them and stopped what they were doing. Others began to turn round to see what was so interesting. Daisy, head down, auburn hair in full flame covering her face, elicited a few stares. One man with a camera even reeled off a couple of shots. Daisy pulled her hood over her head. 'Excuse me,' said Carol, trying to make her way through the throng.

A police officer stepped in front of the door, legs apart, as they approached. 'Sorry, madam. Nobody's permitted to enter the police station without prior arrangement.'

'We're here about the boy,' said Carol. 'My daughter knows the boy.'

'He's got a name, Mum,' said Daisy.

Sergeant Nichols's face changed; he suddenly looked flustered. 'Oh, right. Er, that's different then. Wait here a minute please.' He disappeared inside.

Murmurs went up, rippling through the crowd from back to front, '*She knows the boy!*' '*Who knows the boy?*' '*The girl with the hair, she knows the boy!*'

'Excuse me, miss,' a plucky reporter with a microphone said. 'How do you know him?' Daisy ignored him.

'It's her boyfriend,' Lily cut in.

Carol hissed, 'Lily!'

'And you are, miss?'

'Lily Jones. I'm her elder sister.' She stepped in front of Daisy to speak into the microphone.

'And do *you* know the boy?'

At this point a camera was pointed in Lily's direction. She paused to stand up straighter, and to flick her hair. 'Oh, yes, I've met him a few times.'

Just then Sergeant Nichols returned with a colleague. 'Right, if you'll come this way, miss. Ian, if you'll guard the door for me, please.'

'Certainly.' Another officer held open the door to let Daisy through.

'I'm coming too,' said Carol. 'I'm her mother. She's only a minor.' Daisy reddened. 'Lily, come on!'

Lily, pouting like Marilyn Monroe as the cameras clicked, was dragged inside. 'Hold on!' said Sergeant Nichols. 'And you are?'

'I'm her *sister*,' said Lily dismissively, stomping past before he could stop her. The sergeant sighed and followed them in.

'Right, you 'orrible lot, disperse please – you're blocking the entrance to a police station,' said the officer outside as the door closed.

'OK, slow down, you three. You need to sign in at the desk first,' Sergeant Nichols said. The three of them stopped to write their names and the date in a book, watched with interest by two staff behind the desk, a man and a woman. Daisy's hands were shaking, and she needed the loo. 'Right, follow me.'

They reached a corner and turned left onto another long corridor with lots of doors off it. At the end of it was another corridor stretching in both directions. It was a maze. Halfway down the corridor, they became aware of noises up ahead, a commotion round another corner – voices and the squeak of shoes. Daisy pulled down her hood to hear better. Just then, a plainclothes officer appeared at the end of the corridor. Behind him, handcuffed and being shoved in the back by another larger man, was Jack.

To see something so wild and untamed, yet so innocent as her Jack, shackled and prodded like a piece of cattle, did something inside to Daisy that she'd never experienced before. *JACK!*' she screamed.

Jack turned, startled, and so did the two men. '*DAISY!*' he cried. His immediate instinct was to run to her, and this he tried to do, forgetting he was handcuffed. Brewster grabbed the cuffs, yanking Jack's arms back, and he yelled in agony. The veins on his forehead stood out as he struggled. The other man joined in, restraining him. Carol was shocked at the sight of this emaciated, feral thing; he looked how she pictured the young Heathcliff, a black-haired, gypsy ragamuffin.

'Get off him, you bastards!' shouted Daisy, setting off down the corridor. 'Let him go! He's done nothing wrong.'

'Daisy!' cried Carol, mortified at her daughter's reaction.

But Daisy didn't get far before she was caught by Sergeant Nichols from behind.

'Woah! Easy there, red!' he said, grabbing hold of her.

Daisy bucked, fought and struggled, yelling the place down. 'Let me go! Take the cuffs off him, you're hurting him, you bastards!' Jack struggled, too, trying to force himself down the corridor on his knees, desperate to make physical contact with Daisy.

'Can I have some assistance here?' shouted Sergeant Nichols, realising he'd got a wild one on his hands. He had hold of Daisy round her stomach, but she was digging her nails into his hands and lifting her knees in the air to kick him.

Suddenly she cried out in pain, and her mum screamed, 'You're hurting her! Let her go!'

Jack was still crying Daisy's name as a female police officer came running down the corridor from the front desk. She took one of Daisy's arms, and Sergeant Nichols relaxed his grip, taking the other one. 'Right! Are you going to calm down, young lady? Or are we going to have to put some cuffs on you as well?'

Daisy made a last half-hearted attempt to free herself, but the fight had gone out of her. Her head hung down and she was grimacing in pain.

'Right. Get to your feet, *Jack*,' said Haslam.

'So you *have* got a name,' said Brewster. The two men dragged Jack to his feet.

'Are we all going to calm down here? Are we finished?' said Haslam, looking from Daisy to Jack. There was silence, except for heavy breathing all round and Carol's sobs. 'Good. Right. As for you, young lady, one more word out of you, or one more attempt at violence, and you're going to be in serious trouble yourself. Your boyfriend here's already in deep shit. Murder, arson, theft... We can now add assaulting a police officer to his rap sheet, along with you if we feel like it; not to mention your connection to his crimes...'

Carol gasped. 'Daisy, apologise right now.'

Daisy felt faint. There was a strange sensation of liquid running down the inside of her jeans, as if she had wet herself.

'Daisy?' said Carol.

Daisy looked up at Jack, her face shiny and pale. 'Oh, Jack,' she said, before looking down again.

Jack followed her gaze, not understanding. Her jeans had gone dark between her legs. Then, in between her trainers, there splattered a growing pool of scarlet on the tile floor. 'Daisy?' he cried. 'What's happening?'

Daisy passed out. '*Daisy!*' Carol and Lily screamed together.

'Jesus Christ!' shouted Haslam. 'Somebody get this girl to the hospital!'

'NO!' shouted Jack. 'Daisy! What's happening?' He tried to get away again, but was restrained. He screamed and screamed as Daisy was led away, stamping and shouting her name. It took three of them to drag him away.

*****

Daisy was taken to the Queen's Medical Centre in Nottingham. She had lost the baby. Carol, despite being in a state of shock, didn't leave her side. She was angry with Daisy, angry beyond belief, but unable to show it. How could she be so irresponsible? So stupid? And how could she keep it a secret from her? Angry didn't even come close to how she felt about the boy. 'You did know, Daisy, didn't you? You did know?' she said. Daisy nodded, ashamed; then confirmed she'd done a pregnancy test the afternoon of the fire. It was almost too much for Carol to bear; as Daisy slept, she wept. What she wouldn't give to have her husband by her side, his consoling arm around her; she didn't know how to deal with this stuff alone.

On Daisy's second day in hospital they received a surprise visitor, one of the detectives from the police station – Dave Haslam. He was carrying a small bunch of flowers. Carol was none too pleased at his arrival. It was obvious what he was there for – information. And Carol didn't want her daughter being harassed after all she'd been through; the fact that she was secretly pleased about the outcome, now that Daisy was on the mend, seemed irrelevant.

Her displeasure showed on her face. 'I'm here on a peace-making mission,' said Haslam. 'Here, these are for you – everyone at the station wishes you well.' He held out the flowers to Daisy. *Probably worried about getting sued more like*, thought Carol. Daisy took them from him, giving a trace of a weak smile. Haslam was a little surprised at her appearance. He barely equated this pale, vulnerable-looking thing with the feisty animal of a girl who had kicked up such a storm in the police station. The only thing that hadn't changed was that hair, lit up on one side, as if on fire, from the sun that penetrated the window blinds. His daughter would have been about the same age as her, he reflected – his wife, too, had had a miscarriage. They were going to call her Rebecca. Unfortunately this had left her unable to bear children, the one thing missing from their long, stable marriage. He hoped the same thing wouldn't happen to this poor girl; he felt a connection with her somehow.

'How's Jack?' Daisy asked; it was the only thing on her mind. She let the flowers rest on her stomach.

Carol tutted.

'He's…' The detective paused, not knowing how to word it. He didn't want to alarm the girl. He'd got to tread carefully – he needed her, and didn't need any more hysterics. 'He's doing OK, better than he was anyway… He dislocated his shoulder in all that commotion. We had to sedate him and get the doc to pop it back in again. That boy's stronger than he looks.'

Daisy breathed in sharply and closed her eyes, as if in pain. She could just picture him, strangers' hands on him, holding him down, a hovering needle. It killed her. He'd never been to a doctor's. Look how he'd reacted to having his hair cut.

'And his wrists were cut up a bit,' Haslam continued.

Daisy's eyes shot open. She clutched the bed covers. 'What? He didn't try to…'

'No! Don't worry. Just the handcuffs. He's calmed down now… The thing is…' He paused to glance at Daisy. She had sat back and her eyes were closed again; tears were spilling down her freckled cheeks. 'The thing is, he's not eating or drinking. And we're worried that – at this rate – he's going to end up in hospital himself.' That was it, Daisy started sobbing.

'That's enough, detective, I think you'd better go,' said Carol. 'I'm not having you upsetting my daughter like this. How dare you after what she's been through? It was your lot that did this

73

to her! And you can take your flowers with you as well.' She picked them up and tossed them in Haslam's direction.

Haslam, however, had dealt with much tougher cookies than a girl's irate mother. He had to put sentiment aside, put his work hat on. 'I apologise for causing distress, Mrs Jones, but whether you like it or not your daughter is connected to this case and *will* be questioned. We also feel that if we're going to get a single word out of the boy other than "Daisy" – or even get him to eat or drink anything for that matter – it's imperative that she helps us.'

'Certainly not! She's not having a single thing more to do with that … that animal…'

'Mum! Don't call him that!'

'Well he is – that feral thing getting my daughter pregnant … and despite what you've said, Daisy, the boy's still under suspicion for murder.'

'That brings me on to my next point, Mrs Jones. I understand your concerns, but some new information – forensic information and so forth – has been passed on to us today that could shed a very different light on the enquiry, and indeed the boy.'

'His name's Jack!' cried Daisy. 'Will everyone stop calling him anything but Jack?'

'Go on,' said Carol, her interest piqued.

'At present I'm not at liberty to divulge it.' Carol huffed disdainfully. 'I need to ask Daisy a few questions first.'

Carol sat with her arms folded, staring stubbornly ahead. 'So … may I?' Haslam said, gesturing to the bed.

'Mum, it's going to help Jack. They need to know the truth.'

'And he needs to start eating and drinking,' added Haslam.

'He could die, Mum!' cried Daisy.

'Five minutes,' Carol conceded. 'Then you can leave us in peace.'

'Thank you,' said Haslam, picking up the flowers, not knowing what to do with them.

'Here, give them to me,' said Carol. She got up, and took them over to a table. 'Daisy, do you want a drink of water?'

'No, I'm fine, thanks.'

The detective lowered himself onto the edge of the bed, pleased the hospital had put Daisy in a private room as requested. He removed a pad and pen from his suit pocket. 'There are so many questions we need the answers to that I don't know where to begin.' He glanced quickly at Carol, who was pretending to be busy with a jug and water. 'But first and foremost, what I need to know is your version of events of that night, and – providing we have time – the lead up to it. I mean, when you came into the police station you said Jack was innocent – innocent of what? Clearly you knew something of what went on or at least the build-up to it?' His pen hovered above his pad.

Daisy looked across at her mum. Carol looked back, concerned. It was the sight of the pen and paper, it all looked so formal. 'It's OK,' prompted the detective. 'You're not going to get in any trouble. We're getting a pretty good picture of what happened now – we just need to hear your version of it before we speak to Jack.'

Daisy cleared her throat and wiped a wet cheek. She could have done with that water after all. 'Well, I only know what Jack told me. And that wasn't a great deal. He was upset.'

'When was this?'

'That Monday night, the night of the fire.'

'Before or after the fire was started?'

'After,' said Daisy, as if that was obvious. The detective started scribbling.

'What time – approximately?'

'I'm not sure…' Daisy paused. She was going to say 'We'd arranged to meet at the phone box', but that sounded bad – as if they'd planned the thing. 'It must have been around nine, I guess.'

'And where was this? Up at the house?'

'God, no!' said Daisy quickly. 'We were at the phone box, near the crossroads.'

'The crossroads?'

'The crossroads to Wysall, near the Red Lion pub.'

'I see,' said Haslam, continuing to scribble. 'And what exactly did Jack say?'

'He said that his father had fallen off the roof; that he'd broken his neck.'

Haslam's upper lip began to twitch a little – after days of frustration and guesswork, he was finally getting somewhere. 'And did he say when this happened exactly?'

'I can't remember, I really can't … not exactly – possibly late afternoon, but I can't be sure.'

'Why didn't he tell you about it sooner? Wasn't that a little odd?'

'He wanted to wait … till it was dark. So he could set fire to the house.'

'So it *was* him that set fire to the house?'

'At what point do we need a solicitor here, detective?' cut in Carol.

Haslam waved his hand a little dismissively for Carol's liking, and nodded at Daisy to carry on. Daisy immediately wondered if she'd said the wrong thing; her voice became more urgent. 'Yes, but you've got to understand, he was desperate! We'd – he'd – only discovered that day what his father had done – where Jack had come from. His father had murdered them both, both his sisters. He's the criminal here, not Jack.'

'Wait, wait! Slow down!' Haslam was getting much more than he'd hoped for; his pen couldn't keep up. 'What do you mean, what his father had done and where Jack came from?' Daisy looked across at her mum again.

Carol went from looking cross to awkward; this was a distasteful topic, not the kind of thing you wanted to hear your daughter talking about. 'This boy, Jack, was apparently born as a result of that man forcing himself on his eldest daughter – Jack's elder half-sister,' said Carol.

'Oh my,' said the detective, his pen stopping momentarily. 'Poor lad. That would explain the older remains in the tank. And what about the others? Can you confirm whose they were?'

'His other sister,' said Daisy, 'Anne.' She bit her lip; it always got to her when she thought about Anne.

Haslam shook his head. The police had already managed to identify Anne themselves. But it was still a shock: how could two young women disappear off the face of the earth and no one bat an eyelid? 'And did she live at the house, with Jack?'

'Yes. She was like a mother to him.'

'Did she know what Jack knew?'

'About what their father had done? Who knows? She didn't let on.'

'And did Jack say what happened to *her?*' Haslam had stopped writing again, and was staring intently at Daisy.

'She went missing – around the end of June. We thought she'd run away; she'd met someone, you see.'

'Met someone? So someone else *did* know her?' He began to scribble again. 'Wait, we're getting side-tracked. We'll have to come back to this, it could be important. How did Jack's sister end up in the tank? What did he say about this?' The detective leant in, his face and throat flushed.

Daisy tried to rack her brains. 'Again, not a lot. He was in an awful rush, wanting to get away. He said something like his father had killed them both, they were in a tank. He'd only discovered them that afternoon – that's why he decided he'd have to set fire to the house, I expect. Perhaps his father had told him they were in there to taunt him. He used to beat Jack: he was a sick bastard. He kept him prisoner. Don't you see that? Don't you see that Jack is innocent?' Daisy was sitting up, straining with emotion. A shooting pain ripped through her belly and she gasped.

'Right, that's enough!' said Carol. 'And I mean it this time. You've asked your questions, more than enough. My daughter's in pain and I want you to leave.'

'Yes. I'm sorry. That's the last thing I want. Daisy, you relax and get some rest.' He patted her leg through the bed, then got up. 'You've been more than helpful.'

'When can I see Jack?' she said, still grimacing.

'That's between you and your mother. Besides, we still need to hear his version of events.'

'But that could be days! What if he still won't talk? What if he still won't eat or drink? He'll starve! You said you needed my help.'

Haslam looked at Carol. 'What?' she sighed, running out of patience.

'I've got an idea. If it's all right with you, Mrs Jones, I'd like Daisy to write Jack a note – I presume he *can* read?'

'Yes, he's not stupid,' said Daisy.

'Good. Well, write him a note, tell him to eat and drink, and that he's got to start talking. If he does all that then – again, providing it's all right with you, Mrs Jones – we'll bring him here to visit you. If it comes from you, Daisy, then he'll believe it.'

Daisy looked at her mum with her best puppy-dog eyes. 'Why do I feel my daughter's being used as a bartering tool?' said Carol, shaking her head.

'That's a yes,' said Daisy, overjoyed at the thought of a visit from Jack. 'Give me some paper.'

'There's one more thing,' Haslam said, whilst Daisy scribbled away. 'Later this evening, I'm afraid we're going to have to move you to another hospital.'

'Why?' said Carol.

'The press have got wind of where Daisy is – there's a gaggle of them outside the hospital. Bloody parasites – excuse my French. Daisy's appearance at the station yesterday, and her leaving a few minutes later in an ambulance, caused quite a furore, especially once they'd discovered her connection to the case.'

Carol groaned and Daisy stopped writing, suddenly pensive. 'Where?' asked Carol. 'Which hospital?'

'Melton – we've got a nice little room waiting for her. It's quieter there, smaller.'

As the detective left, tucking the note into his jacket pocket, Daisy suddenly called after him. 'Detective!'

'Dave, call me Dave.'

'Does he know? Does Jack know? About the, you know…' She put her hands to her stomach.

Haslam shook his head. 'No, he doesn't. We thought you'd want to tell him yourself.'

CHAPTER 6
The Note

When Haslam peered through the viewing hole in the cell door, Jack was still in the same position, doing the same thing – curled in a ball, knees up to his chest, rocking, his mouth occasionally moving. There were padded straps on his wrists. The detective sighed: to think this sorry mess might have been a father, he was no more than a baby himself.

Since they'd received the results of the autopsy, confirming that the man on the hill had died from a broken neck, most likely as the result of a high fall, everything had changed for Haslam. A length of cracked guttering at the house, a mighty lump on the deceased's head and an extended ladder all backed up the theory. Jack had quickly gone from being the bane of Haslam's life, someone who was making him look like a fool, to a victim. Meeting Daisy and finding out something about Jack's life had further enhanced his cause; he was just a poor, messed-up kid who had done nothing more than set fire to his house – understandably, given the circumstances – and there was no one pressing charges. It made Haslam wince inside to think how they'd hard-balled him, roughed him up, when he'd first come in – especially Brewster, he always got carried away. 'Open her up for us, Ian,' Haslam said. The waiting officer, keys already in hand, unlocked the door.

Haslam walked in with a tray; on it was food and water. 'Hi, Jack, how're you doing today? How's the shoulder?' Jack didn't look up, didn't even register that the man had entered the cell. The detective crouched down and placed the tray on the floor. Still not a flicker of response. Haslam didn't expect anything more. He reached into his pocket. 'I've got something for you,' he said, and pulled out a folded bit of paper. He put the note next to the tray, praying this was going to work. 'A note from your lady friend.'

There was a slight disruption to the rhythm of Jack's rocking, a faltering, before he resumed again. 'Says she wants to see you. I went to see her today at the hospital. She's doing fine. She misses you.' Again, there was a slight pause in the rocking. The detective waited. Slowly but surely he could see life returning to Jack's eyes – focus rather than a glassy stare, awareness of his surroundings. He could almost hear the boy's brain ticking, the cogs and gears of his mind grinding as he tried to digest the information.

Jack began to glance down in rhythm with his rocking. On the piece of paper he could see Daisy's bubble-shaped writing, and a large, underlined 'Jack'. It was driving him mad and he began to twitch. 'I'll leave you to it, fella. Open the note,' Haslam said, and put his hand on Jack's shoulder. Jack flinched, as if a hot iron had been placed against his skin. Nothing had changed: he still despised this man. The detective stood up and headed for the door. Experience had taught him that when you pushed certain people it worked the other way; they had to do things in their own time.

Jack registered the cell door being locked, but didn't look across. Outside, Haslam made a show of loudly sliding closed the viewing hatch. Then he did his little trick of quietly sliding it back again a couple of millimetres – enough to see into the cell, but not enough for an inmate to notice. The second Jack thought the hatch was closed he looked over at the door to make sure. Then he grabbed the piece of paper from the floor and scrabbled it open. Haslam smiled to himself. Jack held the note close to his face, his eyes darting backwards and forwards. All of a sudden his face crumpled and his body was racked with sobs. He read the note again, still crying, then curiously he held it up to his nose, as if trying to discern a scent.

The smile disappeared from Haslam's face: Jack's reaction had got to him in a way he hadn't expected. *Jesus, you're getting soft in your old age*, he said to himself. Jack suddenly looked across at the door again, his face red and streaked with tears. Haslam instinctively ducked, even though he knew he couldn't be seen. When he looked back again, Jack was guzzling the cup of water, the liquid dribbling down his chin and throat. The cup quickly drained, he set about the food, ravenously, caveman-like. He choked and coughed on it, grimaced and clutched at his chest, all the while glancing across at the door whilst trying to reread the note at the same time. The girl's mum was right; there *was* something feral about him. *Thadda boy, Jack*, Haslam said to himself, and walked away, whistling quietly.

The detective gave it an hour, then returned to the cell. He was carrying another cup of water. This time Jack looked up at the sound of the door opening. He looked a damn sight better already; he had stopped the incessant rocking and there was some colour back in his cheeks. But he still refused to look at Haslam. There was a nervous energy about him, as if he was ready to spring away at any moment. Or hopefully he was just eager to get on with it, thought Haslam. 'Ah, good lad,' he said, acknowledging the tray. 'You must have been starving. Here, have some more water.' He offered the cup. Jack glanced at it, but didn't make a move. The detective shook the cup slightly, as if trying to entice an animal.

Eventually Jack gave in and reached for the cup, careful to make sure their hands didn't touch. He grunted what sounded like 'Thanks' – the first word he had spoken directly to the police. Haslam breathed a 'hallelujah' to himself – it was a breakthrough, and all thanks to the power of love. He gave himself a mental pat on the back. After Jack had drained the cup in one go, Haslam said, 'Right, are we ready to have a little chat now?' Jack toyed with the empty cup, inspecting it, but didn't answer. 'I take it you read the note? That you understood it? Daisy's a lovely girl, Jack. You're a lucky boy.'

'When can I see her?' Jack said, the words only just distinguishable, as if he'd forgotten how to speak. But still, it pleased the detective. Little steps.

'After you've answered some questions. And answered them properly and truthfully. No one-word answers, otherwise the offer's off the table. We need to know what went on up there on that hill, Jack – the truth, your version of events, before you can speak to Daisy. I know some of it must have been traumatic for you, but we've been very patient with you so far. The time for silence is over; we're on your side. If you co-operate with us fully, then I'll drive you over to the hospital myself this very day.'

Jack continued to stare into the bottom of his cup. 'So, are we ready then?' Haslam said. The question hung in the air for an eternity. Jack appeared deep in thought. Then he nodded. 'Good lad. Come on.' The detective was about to put his hand on Jack's shoulder again, but as Jack recoiled he withdrew it, learning all the time. Instead he picked up the food tray, plucked the cup from Jack's hand and headed for the door. After a moment, and keeping his distance, Jack got up and followed him.

*****

There was a knock on the door of Daisy's room at Melton Hospital. Her stomach whirled and she quickly sat up in bed, rearranging her hair. She wished she'd got a bit of makeup on, but she didn't have any with her. She looked towards the door expectantly. 'Come in,' Carol said.

The door opened and a head appeared. Daisy's face lit up, then dropped. It was Haslam. 'Sorry to disappoint you, ladies,' he said. 'Mrs Jones,' he nodded. 'I've got a visitor who would like to see you, Daisy, lurking out here in the corridor – shall I bring him in?' Daisy beamed and nodded. Haslam smiled back; it gave him a warm feeling to be able to bring someone pleasure for once instead of bad news. 'Won't be a second.' He disappeared again. Carol and Daisy looked at each other, both a little nervous.

Out in the corridor Jack was standing with Sergeant Nichols from the station, jigging from one foot to the other. He'd been told in no uncertain terms that if he tried to run, or do anything stupid, they'd be back to square one. Getting him to the hospital had been no mean feat. Haslam had overlooked the small matter of the media scrum camped outside the police station that appeared to be growing by the day. They'd had to sneak Jack out the back in an unmarked car: for his own sake, it was imperative at this juncture that his identity remained secret – not that he appeared to have one. 'Come on, then, don't keep the young lady waiting,' Haslam said. He resisted the urge to ruffle the lad's newly washed and combed hair.

Jack followed Haslam into the small bright room. The first person he saw was Daisy's mum, and he appeared to shrink a little. She didn't exactly look welcoming. But then he turned and saw Daisy sitting in bed, her face glowing and tears smarting her eyes. It made him want to cry too. He had missed her; he had missed her so, so much. He wanted to go to her, to take her in his arms and smell her, but felt self-conscious, restricted by the gaze of two adults. So he stood there uncomfortably, not knowing how to proceed. There was an awkward silence until the detective cleared his throat. 'Erm, Mrs Jones, could I have a word with you in private please? There's something I'd like to discuss.'

'What, now? Can't it wait?'

'Please, Mum,' said Daisy.

Carol got the sense she was outnumbered – everyone was looking at her. But she was loath to leave these two alone unsupervised, especially after what had happened. Besides, she wanted to see what her daughter was so infatuated by. Then she remembered what Daisy had said about her being uptight. Perhaps she was right. When had she become such a prude? What were they going to do? Dive into bed together with her and two policeman outside? 'Very well,' she sighed, and got up.

Everyone looked relieved. Carol studied Jack as she passed him. He looked a damn sight better than he had done the other day – cleaner, and he'd shaved that bumfluff off. He shot her the briefest of glances before looking down again. Enough time for Carol to notice his eyes, a surprisingly striking blue.

The adults withdrew, but left the door ajar. Jack and Daisy looked at each other uncertainly, suddenly shy again. 'Come here, you,' Daisy said, patting the bed. Jack shuffled forward and sat down. 'No, come here properly,' she said, her voice wobbling, the emotions starting to flow now that they were alone. Jack leant forward and she took him in her arms. The physicality didn't seem real; that they could actually hug and hold and grip each other again at last.

Both of them were thinking the same thing. 'I thought I'd never…' Jack gasped, but Daisy stopped him.

'Shush. I know. Don't speak. Just hold me.'

They held each other for a while, shaking and crying, drinking each other in. Eventually Daisy patted Jack's back and pulled away, wanting to look at him. Jack could have stayed like that forever. 'Your hair's growing back,' she said, running her hands through it and searching his thin and haunted face. 'I must look a right state. My hair needs washing and I can't stop crying,' she laughed. Jack shook his head to disagree.

After a pause he said, 'I'm sorry, Daisy … about running away. I just didn't know what else to do, after I'd found…' A sob constricted his throat, convulsing his shoulders; his head bowed and he couldn't carry on. He'd had no one to talk to about discovering Anne; the bitterness he'd felt, the sense of loss, how he'd felt cheated and how he'd wanted to wreak revenge. It had all been bottled up inside him for the best part of a week.

'I know. You poor thing. I'm so sorry.' Daisy stroked his hair and brushed away his tears. 'I tried to find you that night, you know. I tried to come after you, but you were gone.'

'You did?' He looked up.

'Yes. I called your name, over and over, and ran after you, but my stomach…'

Jack looked down at her. 'What happened? What was it? I was so worried. They wouldn't let me see you, wouldn't even tell me how you were… That's how I did this,' he said, holding up his wrists.

Daisy took hold of them. 'That's what I need to tell you. That's what I've been trying to tell you for a week.' She suddenly looked grave. 'I had a miscarriage.'

Jack looked confused. 'A miscarriage? What's a miscarriage?'

'You're not going to believe this… We were going to have a baby. Me and you … but I lost it…'

Jack tried to understand what she was saying. 'A baby? But how?'

'How?' Daisy dropped his wrists and her shoulders slumped in exasperation. 'How do you think? You know…' She frowned and blushed at the same time, met his eyes, then looked away.

'Oh,' he said.

Daisy had expected more of a reaction, and she searched his face to see what he was feeling. But Jack didn't know; it didn't seem real. All he cared about was that he was with Daisy again. He moved to lie down with her, craving more physical contact. 'Ow, careful,' Daisy said, shifting across. 'I still feel a bit tender.'

'Sorry,' said Jack. He snuggled into her and put his hand on her stomach.

There didn't seem to be anything else to say, no need for anything else, so they lay there for a while. Then Jack said despondently, 'I never even got to see the sea.'

Daisy wasn't expecting this, and gave a sad smile. 'You will see it, baby, I promise. As soon as this has all blown over.'

There was another pause.

'I still can't believe you came after me that night. I didn't know.'

'Well, what would you have done if I *had* caught up with you? You were in such a state.'

'I don't know... Come back, I guess. I didn't want to go without you.'

Daisy sighed. 'Well ... I only wanted my Walkman back anyway.'

*****

That was how Carol and Haslam found them when they came back – snuggled into each other. Carol tutted. Haslam smiled. 'Right, you two lovebirds, reunion's over,' he said. Jack and Daisy were dozy, half asleep. They barely stirred, hoping the adults would by some miracle just go away. 'Come on. Jack's got to go back to the police station.'

Jack let out a moan, and something occurred to Daisy. She sat up. 'Hold on. Surely you can't detain Jack any longer. He hasn't been charged with anything.'

'We could if we wanted; we applied for it. But there's no need. Jack's going to be released, but he's still needed for further questioning. It's for me and Jack to go through back at the station.'

'But where's he going to go? You can't make him stay in a cell again.'

'No. Your mother and I have been discussing this...'

'What? Can he come back to ours? Please, Mum, *please*.'

'Er, I don't think so,' Carol said.

'It doesn't work like that,' said Haslam, and both Daisy and Jack's faces dropped. 'Jack needs to go into local authority care for the time being – especially whilst the questioning's still going on. His case is unique. He's a minor and has no parents, guardians or next of kin. There are designated places for cases like this locally, safe housing and that.'

Jack looked pale and shell-shocked. That he had no home to go to made him feel scared and vulnerable. And where were they going to take him? The thought of a new place terrified him. Still, it had got to be better than the maddening confines of that tiny police cell.

Just then, the door opened and Lily walked in with a waft of perfume. She was being chaperoned by one of the nurses who had been tending to her sister. The nurse looked serious. 'Right, it's getting far too crowded in here. I'm afraid two of you are going to have to leave – we only allow two visitors at a time here, it's the rules.'

'It's OK, nurse. Two of us are leaving now,' said Haslam.

'Are you OK, Lily?' said Carol, 'You look a bit flustered.'

'Er, I'm not sure… I think there's a reporter outside our house.'

CHAPTER 7
The Deal

The next few days were a whirlwind for Jack. He was transferred to what seemed to be a foster home. There were similar kids to him there, both older and younger, but he didn't have the time or inclination to mix with them. Most of all there were questions. Questions, questions, questions…

These all took place in a designated office at the safe house so Jack was kept away from the baying press. He had been allotted a liaison officer-cum-social worker, and she had accompanied him during the questioning. He was far from out of the woods. The fate of his father was more or less established, but they still wanted Jack to formally identify the body. The thought of this was horrific: he never wanted to see him again.

More importantly, the police wanted to know what knowledge Jack had of the apparent murder and disposal of his sister Anne; still a worrying area. It was clear that Jack couldn't have anything to do with the older remains, but they only had his and Daisy's word for it about when Anne disappeared and how she was found. Judging by the back of her skull, she had died as a result of a fatal trauma, administered by a heavy and blunt instrument. Of course, this was news to Jack and he broke down when he heard, which helped his cause.

There was also the small matter of Jack's background. Had he, as he and Daisy said, spent his whole life in apparent anonymity and isolation? And if so, where had he got that considerable wad of money from? Jack explained about his job at Peasgood's factory and Daisy backed him up. But when Haslam called to check this out, Peasgood, in a moment of panic, denied the whole thing, paranoid about being done for tax evasion or for utilising illegal workers, both crimes that were being cracked down on. Through his association with Jack and – more to the point, his father – there was also the threat of the pig scandal rearing its ugly head, a long-buried secret involving unfit and unlicensed livestock that could come back to haunt him.

This posed a problem for Haslam. Who did he believe? An upstanding, exemplary businessman or two teenagers who were clearly besotted with each other, yet whose stories so far had all checked out?

Haslam had grown to like Jack and Daisy, and took an almost personal interest in their story. It was unique, and he felt privileged to be the one who was dealing with it. He felt protective of them both – especially now the press had found out where Daisy lived. Despite Lily's best efforts it was her sister's picture that had appeared in the national papers (fortunately with her hair covering her face), accompanied by sensational and lurid headlines: *'Mystery redhead knows potential killer'*, *'What does teenage girl know about Firehouse Murders?'* and, worst of all, *'Is this the new Myra Hindley?'* It was shocking and awful. The best place for her was in hospital – her own little safe house – and that was where she would remain until things died down, although even the nurses had grown a little cold and uncertain around her.

To this end Haslam started to concoct a plan, a deal, to protect them both. It wasn't a new thing, it had been done before, but he would have to convince his superiors. He had initially mooted the idea to his long-suffering wife, Edna, who was used to him taking cases too personally; it was in his DNA. 'If those kids are let back out into the world round here, they're going to get eaten alive,' he said.

In an attempt to douse the flames of supposition and rumourmongering, Nottinghamshire Police made their first major statement since the murder enquiries had begun – and certainly since Jack had been taken into custody. The statement explained, amongst other things, that the deceased was considered responsible for the death of at least one of the bodies in the tank, his own daughter, Anne Hemsley. It had been impossible, thus far, to gain a positive identification or cause of death for the other body, owing to its state and the age of the remains. The presumption was that it was the man's eldest daughter, Charlotte Hemsley. The deceased himself appeared to have died accidentally from a broken neck as the result of a heavy fall, and the boy in custody had been released, pending further enquiries. The police also took the opportunity to re-appeal to anyone who knew any of the family members, Anne in particular, to step forward.

Of course the press wanted to know who the boy was. And of course they wanted to know his connection to the house – or if he was responsible for the fire. The police had deliberately avoided talking about this to see how everything panned out. But as no one was pressing charges, they could pretty much say what they liked. The statement did the trick. It turned the public tide from being negative about this mystery boy (and girl) to mere curiosity about their stories. At Haslam's request, and out of a sense of loyalty, Marge hadn't spoken to the press about Jack. Davey, however, had his 'five minutes of fame', telling reporters how he had met the boy 'John'. The most intense scrutiny switched to Jack's father, this reclusive monster who few people knew anything about, a man capable of murdering his own flesh and blood.

It was a Friday when Haslam met Jack in the office at the safe house. Jack was looking better, healthier, more like a normal teenage boy than that traumatised and feral mute they had captured that day. He no longer had the padding on his wrists and his face was less drawn. Haslam had a beige document wallet in his hand that looked important, and the air of someone who was pleased with himself – or so it appeared to Jack.

The detective sat down at the table and, after exchanging pleasantries both with Jack and the liaison officer, he opened the folder. 'Right, let's get down to business, shall we? In here are the outlines and conditions of a proposed deal we've set up. There are three copies. One for us, one for you and one for your representatives.' Haslam picked up two neatly stapled together documents and placed one in front of Jack; the other he handed to the liaison officer.

Jack stared down at the piece of paper in front of him. At the top of the first sheet it said, 'NEW IDENTITY PROPOSAL – CLIENT COPY'. He didn't read much further, it didn't interest him. All that he wanted was to see Daisy. He'd not been able to since the hospital, as visitors weren't allowed at the safe house, and he'd not even been able to talk to her on the phone. It had been days. Hell. He was morose.

The liaison officer, in contrast, was studying the document carefully. Haslam noted Jack's lack of interest. He was going to have to spell it out. 'Basically, this is a chance for you to start a new life – anonymously. Somewhere else, far away from here, where nobody knows you. Now, this isn't something new, we've done it before; it's similar to the witness protection scheme…'

'What about Daisy?' Jack cut in.

'I'll come to that in a minute.'

'What about Daisy?' Jack insisted.

Haslam sighed and looked up from the document. 'That's for Daisy and her mum to decide. Our main concern is you.

You're our responsibility; Daisy isn't. I know she's mixed up in all this, but…'

'Can she come with me or not? 'Cause if she can't I'm not doing it. I'm not going anywhere.' Panic was creeping into his voice.

'Now don't be hasty. Let's listen to what the detective has to say first,' said the liaison officer.

'No, you can't make me…'

'The thing is, we *can* make you. Your only other option would be to go into care, and then a foster home – and that could take months.'

'Aagh!' Jack suddenly leant forward.

Anticipating what he was going to do, Haslam put his hand in the way before Jack's head hit the desk. Making unexpected and unwanted contact with Haslam, Jack sat back again and closed his eyes.

'Listen, I'm not ruling it out altogether. Personally, I can see pros and cons for Daisy going with you – for both of you. But there's a danger it could compromise the whole thing and at the end of the day it's not my decision alone. Now if you'll just hear me out… You're going to be given a new identity, a new name, a National Insurance number, a chance to start again.'

'Where?'

'There are four different locations listed on page two, all in the UK of course.' Jack and the liaison officer both looked down. The names didn't mean a thing to Jack, but he'd heard of Manchester.

'Ooh, Norfolk's nice,' said the liaison officer.

'You can put all this behind you, go to college, get a job or an apprenticeship. There are some conditions and stipulations, of course, all of which are explained here. You're still technically under our control, for a start – don't forget you can still be charged with arson, theft and public indecency, they're all still hanging in the air. We *can* make them go away, but you'll have to co-operate. Most of them anyway. There's still the money and the Peasgood matter that need looking into further...'

'He's lying,' said Jack.

'So you say. We'll look into it. And as for your poor sister's demise, this is still under investigation – we've only got your word about what happened. Now, back to the rules... We can call you in for questioning or retract this offer any time we like. You're beholden to that. And also you're not allowed to leave the UK, or even try to leave the UK, for twelve months – not that you've got a passport. That's the term of our deal: twelve months. During this period you're not allowed to get into any sort of trouble, not so much as a scuffle. If you go into further education or an apprenticeship, your rent and utilities are taken care of, but not food. If you choose not to go to college, only the first quarter is subsidised; this incentivises your need to go out there and get a job. Now, with you being a minor, you'll initially have a designated carer living with you – three days on, three days off.' Jack looked up at this; he would be living with someone? An adult stranger? 'He'll get you set up, and it will be a male, and settled in; show you how to prepare your own meals and everything. He'll also be on hand on the off days. After that, his involvement will be on a sliding scale, depending on progress, until you're able to stand on your own two feet. He won't know your back story, won't ask for it, and you're not to tell it. At the end of the first full term, depending on good behaviour and if nothing else comes to light, you'll be set free from our restraints: you'll be free to go where you like, and be given the reward of a full UK passport.'

Most of this had gone over Jack's head – it all sounded like bad news – but his ears pricked up at the word passport. America!

'It sounds like a very fair deal, detective. Jack and I will go through it all together. Won't we, Jack?'

'I want to talk to Daisy.'

94

'I'll talk to Daisy first,' said the detective. 'And her mum. Explain the gist of it to them. Then we'll all meet up, somewhere neutral.'

*****

'Well, I think it sounds more than fair, just what the boy needs – a fresh start,' said Carol. They were all cooped up in the hospital room again, Daisy, her mum and Haslam. Daisy had her bags packed and was ready to go home. The sooner the better, as far as she was concerned: the room was stuffy and hot, and was starting to feel like a prison cell. The more the detective had explained about the deal proposed for Jack, the quieter she had become. Her mum, in contrast, had become more and more animated, the happiest Daisy had seen her for a while. 'But what about him being a minor?' Carol asked. 'I mean, wouldn't care be a better option, detective?'

'Call me Dave, please,' said Haslam. 'And yes, care *would* be the normal option, but Jack's case is far from normal. It doesn't provide the anonymity we require, for a start. And I'd worry for Jack ending up in the care system – the first thing they want to know is the kid's history and, well, Jack doesn't have one – not one that we'd care to divulge…' Haslam paused. A career in the police force had given him a good nose for behavioural traits and he too had noticed Carol's growing enthusiasm and Daisy's withdrawal. He turned to her. 'You've gone quiet. What do you think? It's the best thing for Jack, isn't it? A fresh start?'

'It doesn't matter what Daisy *thinks*, the deal is what it is,' said Carol. 'The boy…'

'Mum, if you call him "the boy" one more time, I swear to God…' They were both fractious, sick of each other's company and sick of the hospital.

'*Jack*, then, has got no choice. He hasn't got a home to go to for a start.'

'He could come to ours.'

95

'We've been through this, Daisy.'

'Why not? We've got a spare room.'

'No! And I'm not discussing it here anyway.'

'Dad would have let him.'

'Oh, don't you dare pull that one on me!' Carol's voice wobbled, and Daisy reddened, knowing she'd overstepped the mark.

'Ladies, please,' said Haslam. 'If I may save you the argument. Jack living at your house isn't really an option that's on the table. The idea is anonymity, protection. So far his identity has been kept hidden for that very reason – protection. If the press got hold of him they'd have a field day; they'd never leave him alone, hound him everywhere he went. *And* you, *and* your family – you don't want your lives to be ruined like that, do you? By the sound of it you've already been through enough.' He gave Carol a look; she was dabbing at her eyes with a tissue again. 'You'll still be able to see him, Daisy. He'll still be in the UK. We can't stop you doing that… But I'd wait till things die down a bit, if I were you – and if you *were* to go and see him, a word of advice: I'd probably do something with that lovely hair of yours first, or cover it up somehow…'

Daisy huffed and sat back with her arms folded, a stubborn look on her face. But then her brain started to tick over; the detective had given her an idea. 'Where is it he's going exactly?' she asked.

*****

Daisy was still deep in thought on the way home from the hospital; she'd chosen to sit in the back of the car. *Probably giving me the cold shoulder*, thought Carol. Who'd be a parent? She tried to think of something to break the ice. 'It'll be nice to get back home, won't it? To sleep in your own bed again? I'll run you a nice bath when we get back. Wash away the smells of hospital. You can take it easy… We could have something nice for dinner actually – I'll have to go to the shops, though;

I haven't got much in. Unless you fancied a takeaway for a change, a Chinese or something. You like Chinese, don't you?' Daisy didn't answer. Carol adjusted the rear-view mirror. 'Hmm?'

'I want to go and live with Jack,' Daisy said.

Carol's stomach sank. It took her a while to compose herself, especially as she felt like saying, 'Over my dead body!' But she knew her daughter well: the more she was told 'no', the harder she dug her heels in. Carol snorted. 'I hardly think that's practical. The police aren't going to subsidise you as well, you know! They wouldn't allow it, anyway – he's already got someone living with him for a start. And besides, it would, what do you call it, compromise the situation.'

'No it wouldn't. I could get my hair cut and dye it. No one's seen my face properly. I could be anonymous like Jack. We'd be miles away from here.'

'Honestly, Daisy, I swear you think you live in the movies half the time.'

'Well, what's wrong with that? Real life sucks. Bad things happen.'

Carol studied her daughter again; she was staring glumly out of the window. Daisy sounded so cynical these days. Her carefree girl was long gone. 'Well, like I say, it's not practical. How would you afford to live for a start?'

'I'd get a job.'

It was getting harder for Carol to suppress her anger. 'You're not throwing your life away and jacking in college over some boy!'

'A part-time job then – I could transfer my college course. Jack would be working anyway, there's no way he'll want to go to college.'

'And what if he can't get a job? He's not exactly employment material, is he? I'm not having my daughter holed up somewhere with a deadbeat who's got no future. I won't allow it, and that's final!' Carol yanked the indicator down to turn into their road, aware she'd just done the opposite of what she'd intended – she'd refused her daughter point blank.

Daisy was about to protest further, but she stopped, open mouthed. Outside their house there must have been getting on for half-a-dozen reporters and their vehicles. 'What the hell!' said Carol. 'This is getting ridiculous.'

'Keep going, Mum!' Daisy hissed. She lay down on the back seat.

Carol, panicking, accelerated, attracting more attention to the car than she would have done otherwise. She drove past their house and round the corner, then pulled up at the end of the cul-de-sac. Daisy sat up again, looking behind her. Both their hearts were beating fast. 'I'm sorry, Mum, but that decides it. I'm going with Jack.'

'It's that boy who's got us into this mess! Look at me, sitting here, round a corner, hiding from my own home. How did it get to this?'

'You can't keep blaming Jack for everything. It was my decision to have sex, you know? Mine! Not his. So if you want to blame someone, blame me!'

'Oh, I'm not talking about that, Daisy. That's another thing entirely. I'm talking about all the other stuff. The murders. That house. Those reporters!'

'Well, it's only going to get worse. They won't give up – the detective said that. That's why it's best if I just go away.'

'Forget it!' Carol snapped, but she knew she was losing the fight. Circumstances were conspiring against her. 'Right, that does it. We're going home. I'm not sitting here all day.' And she crunched the car into gear.

'Wait, Mum!' cried Daisy. 'I've got an idea.'

She ducked back down and instructed her mum to drive past the house again, and then to turn left, onto the main road through the village. 'Where on earth are we going? This is ridiculous!' Carol said, none too pleased at being ordered about. She just wanted to get home and have a cup of tea – or better still, a gin and tonic.

'Turn down Church Lane.' Carol tutted and did as instructed. 'Now pull up here,' Daisy said, springing back up.

'Why here?'

'It's Jack's … it's a cut through to the back of our garden. I'll climb over the fence. You pull up at the house, then let me in the patio door. It's genius.'

'I'm not doing this every day, you know. You can't keep hiding forever!'

'I might not have to,' said Daisy, kissing her mum unexpectedly on the cheek and getting out.

*****

'Mrs Jones, can we have a quick word?' said a reporter, as soon as Carol stepped out of the car. She'd nearly had to run them down to get on to the drive.

'Mrs Jones, how's your daughter? How's Daisy?' said another one. God, they even knew her name, thought Carol, ignoring them.

'Where is she, Mrs Jones? Is she still in hospital or with the boy?'

Carol put her hand on the door handle. 'Any chance of a few words, Mrs Jones? Anything at all?' said the first reporter again.

'No, there isn't!' Carol snapped. 'And you can keep off my drive or I'll report you for trespassing!'

Once inside the house, she peered through one of the glass panes of the front door. Some of the reporters were scribbling in their notepads, others were talking into Dictaphones; one man was scuffing his shoes on the ground, looking disappointedly towards the house.

Lily came downstairs at the sound of the front door closing. 'You're back. Where's Daisy?'

'Wait a minute.' Carol walked into the lounge. Lily, looking bemused, followed her. Her mum was closing the lounge curtains.

'Ah,' said Lily.

'Can you believe how many of them are out there?'

'They'll soon get bored.'

'I hope so… Right, I need to let Daisy in.' Carol made her sound like a cat.

'What took you so long?' said Daisy, already waiting on the patio.

'Sorry, it's those bloody reporters. I had to close the curtains. They even know your name!'

Daisy and Carol both turned to Lily.

'Don't look at me!'

*****

Over the next few days, with no sighting of the girl – and therefore no insights to be had into the mystery boy's life – the group of reporters thinned out a little. Carol continued to keep the front curtains closed, thereby keeping Daisy's whereabouts a secret. Daisy was hoping the reporters didn't disappear entirely, as they were a good bartering tool. In contrast to their waning enthusiasm, she had become increasingly determined that she was going to go with Jack: she couldn't stop thinking about it, her mind was made up. She was going to be eighteen the next month anyway. Providing the police didn't have a problem with her plan, she didn't really see that her mum could stop her.

She kept up her incessant barrage of good reasons: 'The house reminds me of Dad too much – his stuff is everywhere' (this was true). 'I need some time and space away from here to grieve properly. Jack helps me with that; he's not connected to this family. If I didn't go with him, I'd never be able to see him again. I'd be miserable. I've lost a baby too, Mum. Don't forget that – both Jack and I have. We need time to deal with that together.'

'How could I forget it?' an ever more resigned Carol replied. 'It'll haunt me to my grave… And what about me and your sister? Stuck here with no one but each other, rattling around in this big old house whilst you're God knows where. I need you *both* around me, *both* your support. Isn't it bad enough I've lost my husband?'

'Now you're laying a guilt trip on *me*,' Daisy said in return.

Carol knew she was right.

The five of them met at a secret location as planned – Haslam, Carol, Daisy, Jack and the liaison officer. Much to Carol's consternation, Jack and Daisy couldn't keep their hands or eyes off each other. Jack had the look of a condemned man about him, waiting to face the gallows. Unable to see or speak to each other, the last few days had been agony for him and for Daisy. Everyone was tense, on edge; there was so much riding on the meeting's outcome. Jack had no idea what Daisy had been planning, so he feared the worst. But Daisy had her spiel prepared. As for Carol, she wished Daisy had never met the boy; she felt he'd stolen her daughter from her. Her only hope seemed to be the detective.

'So, what's it to be, Jack? Have we had a good look at the papers?' said Haslam. Jack looked down glumly, disconsolate; he felt backed into a corner.

'Yes, we have, detective,' the liaison officer answered for him.

'Jack?' said Haslam.

There was silence in the room. A pulse in Jack's head throbbed as everyone waited for him to answer. He chased the black spot around his vision. Daisy squeezed his hand, which had quickly become moist, trying to prompt him to speak; she needed him to say it first. He looked across at her. Her eyes widened and she nodded slightly. He didn't know what it meant. Was she happy for him to go through with this? Was she rejecting him again? Or had the police and her mum brainwashed her?

He looked back down, unable to do it, unable to say the words that would commit him to a life somewhere without Daisy. She didn't see any other choice than to step in for him, and took a deep breath. 'Jack wants to go to Cromer, and I'm going to go with him.' Her mum groaned and rolled her eyes. Jack's face lit up.

'Now, hold on,' said Haslam. 'This hasn't been discussed. It would need running by the powers that be. Besides, it's Jack's decision, not yours.'

'For the record, I think it's a ludicrous idea, and she hasn't got my consent,' cut in Carol. Haslam gave her a sympathetic look.

'It's not ludicrous,' said Daisy. 'It's the only solution; think about it. Jack's only ever been looked after by his sister. He can't cook, can't wash, can't clean. He doesn't even know how to work a washing machine – do you, Jack?' Jack quickly shook his head. 'He's never been to school, never had a bank account – he's never even been shopping for food before! Who's gonna do all that for him?'

'Well, he'll have his designated carer for that, of course…'

Daisy cut Haslam off. 'What, a man? Some total stranger? What do men know about cooking and cleaning and all the little things? *I* can be his carer! He doesn't respond well to strangers – but I've done all this stuff with him before.'

'When?' scoffed Carol.

'This summer – when you were away. I introduced him to society!' Daisy was on a roll. 'I took him to his first pub, bought clothes for him, went to the chip shop with him, took him swimming and to the cinema. Got him his first proper haircut at a barber's. And trust me, that was just the beginning. Here, I've got it all planned out.' She produced a bit of paper from her jacket pocket, unfolded it and put it on the table with a flourish.

The three adults leaned forward. At the top of a neatly typed piece of paper was the heading 'Jack's Integration – A Step by Step Plan of Action'. Carol groaned again, then sat back; so that's what she'd been tapping away at on her typewriter in her room.

'Without me he'd just stay cooped up in his flat and go back into his shell,' Daisy continued, as Haslam studied the paper. 'He'd never dare go out there and get a job – would you, Jack?' Jack shook his head again, trying his best to look pathetic and useless. But it was getting harder and harder to suppress the grin that was trying to break out on his face. 'And just think of the money your department would save,' Daisy finished.

Haslam sighed. 'It looks like you've got it all planned out.'

'Yes, it's amazing the lengths she'll go to when she wants something,' snapped Carol. 'Shame she doesn't put that much effort into her college work.'

The detective sat back. He looked round the table. Jack, with that hangdog expression. Daisy, her face flushed with excitement and determination. Carol, thin-lipped, resigned. And the liaison officer, with a slight smile of admiration on her face for the girl and her performance.

Haslam thought long and hard, caught between a rock and a hard place. He looked at Carol again, then put his hands out, palms upwards, as if to say 'What can you do?' After a pause, he said, 'It's a risk, but I haven't got a problem with it personally…' Daisy and Jack let out squeals of glee and hugged each other. The liaison officer smiled broadly. It was hard not to be carried away by the young sweethearts and their story, they deserved a happy ending. 'But,' Haslam continued, 'I still need to speak to my superiors. And Daisy, Carol … please go home and see if you can come to some sort of an agreement, either way, whilst Jack and I thrash out the details. I'm not here to break up families.'

'I think you already have, detective,' said Carol, getting up. 'Come on, Daisy, we're going home.'

'But we've only just got here. I've only just seen Jack. I need to help him with all this stuff.'

'Suit yourself, you can find your own way home then.'

'I can give her a lift,' said the liaison officer. 'I don't mind.'

Carol gave Haslam one last accusatory look, then left.

Once it became obvious that Daisy wasn't going anywhere, Haslam sighed. 'So, Cromer is it, Jack?'

'Yes! Jack's never been to the seaside!' said Daisy.

'Let Jack speak.'

Jack nodded and grinned.

PART TWO

CHAPTER 8
Big Windows to Let In the Sun

It took about a week for the paperwork to be rushed through. Then, under the cover of darkness, Jack and Daisy were driven east to Cromer. It took around two and a half hours. They were both scared and excited in equal measure. For the first time in his life, Jack had a proper identity. He existed. In his pocket was a National Insurance card with his new name on it – new surname anyhow, he had been allowed to keep his first name. As far as Haslam was aware only a handful of people in the entire world knew it: Daisy's family, the liaison officer, and the police.

Jack's new surname was Gardner. He was glad to lose his father's surname; it felt like the severing of the last tie. After the final insult and trauma of having to identify his body, Jack wanted no more connection with the man whatsoever. He'd wanted his new surname to be Jones – same as Daisy's – then they could have been Mr and Mrs Jones. But Haslam had laughed and refused in a mockney accent. 'Jack Jones? Are you having a giraffe?' Despite the department's reservations, Daisy was allowed to keep her real name – she and her mum had insisted on this. It was her dad's name, and besides she'd have to enrol in college down the line and get a part-time job herself.

Daisy, like Jack, was also sporting something new. A different hairstyle. Taking Haslam's advice to an extreme, she'd had it cropped short and dyed a chocolate brown. Her inspiration had come from Edie Sedgwick, the tragic starlet who had died so young: Daisy had recently discovered her through a song, 'Edie (Ciao Baby)', by one of her favourite bands, The Cult. She'd left the haircut right up to the last minute, only having it done earlier that evening by one of Lily's work colleagues who had done a hairdressing course. It was a shock to everyone, especially Jack. He was mortified. Daisy noticed he wasn't as physical with her as she had been expecting – holding hands and snuggling into her on the back seat – on the eve of their great adventure. Under the flash of lamplight in the dark she kept catching him staring at her, then looking away; like an unsure toddler on visiting day with an estranged parent.

Lily was driving them in the Montego. Haslam and another officer were in a car in front. It seemed daft going in two cars, but Daisy had brought so much stuff with her there was no other choice. The rear of the estate car was chock-a-block with clothes, records, tapes, videos, posters, books, a hi-fi, a TV and video player – all the essentials. There were even some board games. Jack, in comparison, had nothing but his rucksack containing his meagre belongings – minus his savings (still confiscated, pending investigation) – and a cardboard box of second-hand clothes that Haslam and his wife had sorted out for him. Lily's other job was to be Carol's eyes: to report back whether the flat was suitable and in a desirable location.

Carol herself had refused to make the trip. She'd been in denial or at loggerheads with Daisy over the whole thing, right up until the last moment. She'd tried to come up with every reason possible to get Daisy to change her mind. 'You'll lose your job at the pub!'...'You'll lose your college place!'...'Don't expect a penny from me to support you! And you won't see any of your dad's money either – not until you see sense!'

The one thing Carol had demanded was that Daisy should get herself to the doctor's and go on the pill: 'If you don't do this one thing your mother's asking of you, I'll lie down in front of the car to stop you from going!' Daisy had gladly obliged; she couldn't go through a pregnancy again. Besides, she wouldn't be able to register at a new doctor's for some weeks yet, as Haslam had insisted she should lie low for a while.

Even this had failed to appease her mum, though. It wasn't until Daisy was about to leave that Carol had broken down, grabbing hold of her and pushing some notes into her hand. 'Make sure you call me as soon as you get there, to let me know you've arrived safely.'

'How?' Daisy had replied, beginning to cry herself and hugging her mum back. 'It'll be the middle of the night, and I doubt we'll have a phone!'

At around one-thirty in the morning they reached Cromer. It wasn't the auspicious arrival at the seaside Daisy had envisaged and hoped for. She had pictured them driving down the coast road on a sunny day, challenging each other to be the first to spot the sea – a game her dad had played with her and her sister. The town seemed a maze in the dark. Their flat was on a side street, with nowhere to park; it was a good job Daisy hadn't been allowed to bring the van, something else Haslam had insisted on.

In the end, the cars were parked on opposite sides of the street, neither of them particularly close to their destination. It quickly became apparent this was going to be a pain because of the amount of stuff Daisy had brought with her, and the fact it all had to be carried upstairs.

As they were unloading, none of them noticed a black car ghosting slowly past, then turning right at the end of the street.

*****

The first thing Daisy and Jack noticed was the temperature. OK, it was the middle of the night, and the flat had been vacant for some time, but it was warmer outside than in. The second thing they noticed was the immense size of the two front windows, framed by a pair of too-small, badly hung curtains. The flat was larger than they had expected – a huge open plan lounge, sparsely furnished, a ratty-looking brown sofa, and matching dining and coffee table. There was a kitchen area off this, and a bathroom off that. A corridor led to two other rooms, both of a similar size. The front one had a double bed and a wardrobe, and they soon discovered that, like the lounge, it faced a street with houses, flats and a shop directly opposite. Daisy was disappointed: in her romantic daydreams she'd imagined a sea view.

By the time everything had been hauled upstairs, they were all exhausted and the policemen were keen to get off, wanting to get home before morning broke. 'Right, everything's set up for you,' said Haslam. He looked tired, the naked overhead light exaggerating the sagging pouches under his eyes. 'The water, the electric, the phone line's connected – you'll have to get your own phone, though.' *Shit*, thought Daisy, she could have brought one from home if she'd known. 'Any problems with maintenance, don't call anyone local, call the top number here.' He handed Daisy a card. 'There are certain people we use. The number underneath is mine. The one underneath that one is yours, along with the area code. Your new address is there, too. We'll be in touch ourselves soon anyway. Get that phone sorted – a second-hand one'll do. And good luck to you both, especially you, Jack Gardner.' He shook Jack's hand and looked him straight in the eye.

Jack liked his new name – and having his hand shaken: it made him feel grown up. 'Thank you,' he muttered, 'for everything.'

'You're not out of the woods yet, young man – you're still ours. There's a lot of stuff needs ironing out. And remember, we can call you back in at any time. Don't forget what I said either – about lying low for a bit. Especially you, Daisy.' Haslam turned to her. 'People know you, know your name – not that they'd recognise you now, I'd expect. But don't go enrolling anywhere for a bit or signing up to anything. Give it a month or so…'

Lily was keen to get off too. Daisy thanked her for her help and they hugged awkwardly before she left; it was something neither of them was used to.

And then it was just Daisy and Jack, left alone in their new lounge, marooned in a sea of boxes. Daisy became aware of Jack staring at her again. 'Why do you keep looking at me like that?' she said.

'Like what?' Jack said, reddening.

'As if you don't know me!'

Jack shrugged. 'It's just…'

'I know, my hair… You said the same thing last time I dyed it.'

'Yes, but this is different.'

'You'll get over it. You're gonna have to. Come here.' She walked over to give him a hug. Jack relented a little. It felt weird, though – normally he'd bury his face in her hair, but now there was nothing there except skin and ear. Eventually he succumbed to the smell of her embrace. 'I had to get used to *your* new haircut,' she said.

'Can we go and see the sea?' Jack asked, pulling away and walking over to the large windows.

'What, now? It's still dark out,' Daisy said, following him. 'We don't even know the way. Besides, I'm absolutely knackered.' The stress and lack of sleep had worn her out.

Jack stared out of the window trying to get his bearings and adjust to his new environment. Daisy stood next to him and yawned. 'Let's wait till the morning, eh? When it's properly light. I want it to be special. We've got to make the bed yet anyway.' She pulled him away. Jack reluctantly left the window. 'We'll set the alarm for nine and go down first thing before it gets too busy. We might have the beach to ourselves!' She squeezed his arm.

After making the bed, they couldn't locate Daisy's alarm clock. Jack no longer had his sister's. So, after giving up and brushing their teeth, they collapsed into their new bed in their new home. The bed wasn't very comfortable and squeaked terribly, but they were too exhausted to care. 'I hope you don't mind it being the three of us,' Daisy said, playfully nuzzling her threadbare teddy bear's nose into Jack's cheek – there was no way she could have left Denim behind.

Jack laughed. 'As long as I get the most cuddles.'

*****

When they awoke it was already mid-morning. The sun was streaming in through the bedroom window and there was a lot of noise from outside. Noise that they weren't used to: traffic, people, and something else too.

'Jack,' said Daisy, shaking him awake. 'Listen.' Jack opened his eyes and came face to face with Daisy and her dark, shorn hair. His eyes widened in shock. 'Can you hear the seagulls?' Jack listened. How could you *not* hear them? Honking and screeching. 'I suppose you don't notice them after a while,' Daisy said.

She got up and walked over to the window. Jack sat up, excited at the prospect of seeing her in her underwear. Unfortunately she was still wearing all her clothes; they'd both been cold when they'd gone to bed. Daisy gasped. 'Oh my God, come and look – it's so busy!' Jack quickly got up and joined her at the window. Cars were queuing up on their street, all facing in the same direction, and there were hordes of people, holidaymakers in shorts and hats, families and children, strolling down the pavements.

Little did Jack and Daisy know, they'd arrived slap-bang in the middle of Carnival Week, the town's busiest time.

'Jesus,' said Jack.

'What time is it? It must be getting on for midday.' Daisy looked at her wrist, but she didn't have her watch on. 'Actually, what day is it? It's a Monday, isn't it?'

'Do you think it's always like this?' said Jack. If it was, he didn't think he was going to like living there.

'Well, I guess it's still the summer holidays. I bet it dies down come September… At least it's a nice day out there by the looks of it. Come on, let's get our skates on – I need a cup of tea, then we'll go down to the beach. You can finally see the sea!' She looked at Jack. 'What's wrong? I thought you'd be chomping at the bit!'

Jack was staring down at the street. 'It's just, just all those people.'

'Well, at least we'll be anonymous! Oh no, we've not got any milk. I'll pop to that shop down there. It looks like a newsagent's. That could come in handy.'

'You're meant to be lying low.' He looked uncertain.

'We've got to eat and drink!' Unlike Jack, Daisy couldn't wait to get out into a new environment. She was beginning to feel excited about everything: their new home, the seaside, the sunshine, their new lives. Her new hairstyle as well: it made her seem like a different person. She could feel her sadness ebbing away already. Before Jack could stop her, she planted a big kiss on his cheek and headed for the stairs. 'Put the kettle on. I'll be back in a minute!' she called.

'Have we even got a kettle?'

'Yes, there's a little travel one somewhere. See you in a minute.'

Daisy disappeared and Jack drew himself away from the window. After putting the kettle on, he went to stand at the front windows of the lounge. The sun was painting a rhombus-shaped rug on the floor. He stood in its warm glow. But with Daisy out of sight, in a strange place with all those people about, an irrational unease crept in. Eventually she appeared at the shop doorway, clutching a bottle of milk and a loaf of bread. It took him a second to recognise her; she almost looked like a boy with her new haircut and sunglasses. He watched her cross the street, and then she disappeared from view again. Then he heard a banging from downstairs that made him jump. It must be their front door.

He raced downstairs and opened it. 'I forgot the key,' said Daisy, stepping inside. 'We need to remember that or we'll be locked out. I can't believe how busy it is out there! Do you know there's some sort of office downstairs? There are people in there right now.'

'Really?'

'I spotted a phone box a few yards away as well, which is a bonus. I'm gonna give Mum a quick call actually, before I forget; she'll be whittling. You could have got some mugs and teabags out…'

'Sorry, I couldn't find them.' Truth was, Jack hadn't even looked; he'd been distracted by the window.

'They're in the boxes somewhere, same one as the kettle I think. Have a look, I'll be back in a minute.' She dumped the milk and the bread on the side, then ran back downstairs. 'I'll leave the door on the latch!' she called.

Jack didn't like being on his own. He trudged back into the lounge for some mugs. As he searched he wondered who had lived here before them. Ghosts in the system like them. Or regular, everyday people; a family even.

Five minutes later, to Jack's relief, Daisy returned. 'How was your mum?' he asked, as she slurped her tea.

'OK, I suppose… She still didn't sound too happy, but she was relieved I called. I gave her our number and address – Grandma wants it apparently. We really need to get a phone, though – I only had 50p in change and that soon ran out. God, I'm starving.' Daisy reached for the bread. Then she let out a groan. 'Shit, we don't have a toaster!'

'What do you need a toaster for? Use the grill on the oven,' said Jack. They'd never had a toaster at home, so this was normal for him.

'Good idea,' said Daisy, opening up the small electric oven. 'You see, you're already starting to think for yourself – and it's me that's meant to be showing you!'

The oven clearly hadn't been cleaned for a while: it smoked out the kitchen, smarting their eyes, until they located the switch for the extraction fan and opened the bathroom window. They found a fridge for the milk under a kitchen counter. Like the oven it was neglected; stained and sour smelling. 'Oh, gross!' said Daisy, turning it on. They had so much work to do: the whole place needed a proper deep clean. Even the counters were tacky.

Then there were all the boxes to unpack. They sat amongst them on the squashy brown sofa to eat their dry toast and peanut butter. The unpacking and cleaning could wait: they were young and they'd got all the time in the world. The sea and a beach were waiting out there for them.

CHAPTER 9
Standing on a Beach

Leaving the safe haven of their flat (and remembering to take their key with them), they stepped out onto the street. There were people everywhere. For Jack this was a little daunting to say the least, and his black spot joined them. But there was a sea breeze and the wafts of warm air were pleasantly different to the still cool of the flat. Daisy pulled him along and into the throng. Jack took a deep breath; it was like preparing to dive into the current of a fast-flowing river. Daisy was wearing her denim shorts, which were pinching somewhat, a vest and sunglasses. Jack was wearing jeans and a T-shirt. He didn't own a pair of shorts.

They followed the flow, which was mostly heading in the same direction; to the seafront they guessed. They passed a car park, pubs, lots of shops, and had to cross over a couple of roads. Standing at a pedestrian crossing, Daisy suddenly squeezed Jack's hand. 'Look!' Between the tall buildings of the narrow street ahead, in the distance, was their first glorious sight of the steel-blue sea. It shimmered and sparkled behind a heat haze, blending into the sky. Jack stood agog. A tear came to his eye, and for a moment the crowds and his worries melted away. Daisy couldn't imagine what it was like never to have seen the sea before.

The pedestrian crossing beeped, startling Jack, and Daisy pulled him across the road. They headed down the street. There were no cars here and the crowds were thicker than ever, with people milling around, clutching ice cream cones and trays of chips that smelt divine. Jack kept his eyes glued on the sea; at least it gave him something to focus on. The shops were all of a similar type now, mostly with colourful beach items out front, inflatables, buckets and spades, and postcards on stands. There were ice cream parlours and sweet shops, windows stacked high with sticks of rock. They saw a fish and chip shop where people were queuing out the door and down the street. Jack and Daisy looked at each other in amazement.

After they had passed one last pub on a corner, the street opened out onto the elevated seafront. The breeze increased, cooler now, and there it was in all its glory – the North Sea. Jack grinned as his hair ruffled in the wind. There were large boats in the distance, bobbing on the water, and an old-fashioned pier, crowded with people, that reached for the horizon. From where they were, despite being high up, they couldn't see the beach. Daisy pulled Jack forwards to the wall in front to see better. There it was, down below – and there went Jack's stomach, that sickening, spinning feeling. He took a step back. The beach stretched in both directions as far as the eye could see, divided into sections by wet, charcoal coloured stumps. Families littered the sands, some hardy souls braving the sea. It was a wonderful sight.

'Come on, let's go down,' said Daisy, heading for a steep concrete walkway that snaked back and forth. People were sitting on walls with trays of chips in their hands and cans of pop by their sides. Gulls squawked and wheeled overhead. When they reached the beach they found themselves underneath the pier, which was so huge it made them feel like ants. The metal struts that supported it were criss-crossed with an intricate design that was entwined with seaweed. Waves crashed against the rocks at their feet. Jack's imagination ran wild with images of smugglers, shipwrecks and pirates.

Daisy sat down to take her shoes off and told Jack to do the same. But he was hesitant. 'Come on! We've not come all this way for you not to even go in the sea!' Daisy cried. She had a point. Barefoot and clutching their shoes, they followed the gentle slope of the beach to the waves, the sand cool, wet and firm. Dozens of cream and grey seagulls watched their progress with beady eyes, perched in rows on groynes of ever decreasing height, as if they were preparing to start a race. The sea's icy grip took their breath away at first, and as the waves lapped the beach, then receded, Jack lost his balance and stumbled.

Steadying himself, he looked at the giant structure above. He noticed small feet, children's feet, hanging over the edge of the pier, and long lines of twine dangling into the sea. 'What are they doing?'

'Crabbing,' said Daisy. 'You can't come to Cromer without going crabbing. They're the best in the UK, or so they say.' Jack stared in wonder as a bucket was hoisted back up; it was like catching bullheads in the brook, but with a more sophisticated pulley system. He thought he'd like to try it.

Growing accustomed to the temperature of the water, they made their way along the shore as the waves foamed, unfurled and laughed around their ankles. There was something raw and unbridled, a sense of freedom and nature, about paddling barefoot. They stopped to hold hands and look back at the town. There were pastel-coloured houses – pink, blue, mint green and beige – and weather-beaten hotels that looked past their prime, some with turrets and domes. Colourful beach huts stretched away towards cliffs, and there was a hilltop shantytown of caravans in the distance. Above the town, Godzilla-like, and highest of all, was a square church tower with spires, apparently constructed from pebbles – Jack had never seen anything like it before.

'Come on, let's go on the pier,' said Daisy.

Up on the promenade it was different again. There was a helter-skelter, fairground rides, amusement arcades, music and bells ringing. Daisy felt as if she had stepped into *The Lost Boys*; that she had moved to a seaside carnival town. 'People Are Strange' by Echo and The Bunnymen started playing in her head. Her mum was right; she *did* think she lived in the movies. Negotiating the wooden boards of the pier, Jack got the faded seaside glamour feeling again that he'd felt when he saw the hotels. It felt as if he had stepped back in time. The word 'vaudeville' popped into his head, though he had no real idea what it meant. He half-expected to see soldiers in uniform, smoking roll-ups, arm in arm with young women in old-fashioned clothes.

They headed on to the pier, past the children crabbing, bare knees in shorts, overseen by their parents. Leaning on the railings to watch, Jack made the mistake of looking down again. There was that sickening feeling in his stomach again; the urge to jump off. How could the kids just sit there like that? They were so high up. Jack looked out across the beach instead. The sand was wet and shiny, caramel coloured potter's clay peppered with mottled black pebbles, like sultanas studded in dough.

Moving on, they made their way to the furthest point of the pier, where there were fewer people. They looked out to sea, Jack apparently mesmerised. Above them the sky was a blue and white atlas of wispy jumbled continents. Daisy turned to him as the sun screamed down, burning her dark hair to chestnut. 'So, what do you think? Is it everything you'd hoped for?'

'Apart from the crowds, yes. Everything and more!'

'Don't worry. When the holiday season's over, we'll practically have this place to ourselves, I bet.' Daisy removed her sunglasses and they kissed, their first proper kiss in an age – since before the fire. It had been too long. Jack ran his fingers through Daisy's newly cropped hair, trying to get used to it. She pressed herself to him. Passion surged in them both, swelled like the ocean. And for a moment it was just them and their mouths and the sea and the sky.

They made their way back through the crowds and up into the town. There was only one thing on their minds now (well, two actually) – chips. The queue had died down a little, but was still spilling out of the shop. After waiting for about ten minutes, stomachs rumbling, they finally got to the counter. They ordered a tray of chips each and a can of pop to share. Cider didn't even cross Jack's mind; through no choice of his own he had weaned himself off it. The last time he'd had any alcohol was at the inn – and look how it had made him feel. Daisy had to pay, which annoyed Jack, and he scowled as he doused his chips with salt and vinegar. He'd got over a thousand pounds to his name – money that he'd earned – and he didn't have access to it. It was Peasgood's fault, the bastard, lying though his teeth. Why would he do that? Spite? It made Jack determined to get another job, to pay his way. He felt as if he was ready.

They wandered back down to the seafront with their chips and ate them sitting on a wall, looking out to sea. They were the best Jack had ever tasted. He was famished and picked out every last crispy scrap with his fork. He could have managed another portion. Daisy saw him looking at hers. 'Oh no you don't!' she said, speeding up to polish them off. After dumping their wrappers and the empty can in a bin, they headed back to the flat; there was work to do.

Taking a different route back, they passed more amusement arcades. It was hard not to notice them as they were so brash and loud, but that was the idea, they drew you in. Jack stopped to look at one of them. People – adults and children alike – were standing at colourful machines with bells and lights, full of shiny coins that intermittently poured out of them. It was like a money factory! Perhaps he could earn his fortune in there. 'What are these places?' he asked.

'Arcades,' said Daisy. 'They're lethal.'

'Why? Look at all that money.'

'Trust me, you put more in than you get out.'

'What do you have to do?'

'You feed money into the slots and hope it knocks more money over the edge of the shelves and out the bottom.'

'Sounds like fun. Surely there must be a way to win.'

'Everybody thinks that at first – well, kids and idiots anyway – I know I did. Me and Lily used to be addicted to them, always dragging Mum and Dad down here. But as Dad used to say, "The house always wins".'

Jack didn't look convinced. Daisy sensed he'd still like to have a go, and that she was being a cynical adult. It was easy to forget that he saw things like this – new things – through a child's eyes; she shouldn't take this away from him. 'We will have a go, we've got plenty of time. Just not today. Come on.' And she pulled him away.

A few doors down they passed a restaurant with chairs and tables outside – all taken; the place was busy. Waitresses and waiters in uniform were bustling between tables, serving meals and pouring wine. Wonderful smells of seafood filled the air. As they passed the entrance, a handwritten notice next to the open door caught Daisy's eye: 'Kitchen assistant required. Full or part time. Training provided to right candidate. Apply within or call the number below'. She grabbed Jack's arm. 'Look! Kitchen assistant required.'

'So?'

'So? You need a job, don't you?'

'Yes, but not here. What do *I* know about cooking? Look at this place!'

'Well, it says training provided.'

'I don't think so. It looks too busy.' Jack tried to walk away, but Daisy pulled him back.

'*I* would,' she said, looking up into his eyes. 'For us. But I can't – not yet. Remember what Haslam said.'

She was right. He was being a chicken. He remembered that feeling of Daisy paying for the chips. Here was an opportunity, and he was too scared to ask. 'OK,' he said bravely. 'I'll give them a ring later. Have you got a pen?'

'You can go in right now – it says "apply within".'

'I know, but they look a bit busy.'

'I'll come in with you if you want. Besides, what's the point in paying for a phone call when you can just walk in and ask?'

But he wasn't ready. 'I'll call in tomorrow.'

Daisy sighed. 'You promise? It would make such a difference.'

'Yes, I promise.'

They left the restaurant behind.

Climbing the stairs to the flat, they both felt worn out; it must have been the sea air and all the walking. On opening the door they were faced with the boxes. It was overwhelming. 'Come on,' said Daisy, 'We've got to get this over and done with. But first, I need some music – I can't tackle something like this without music.' First she had to set the hi-fi up, then she rummaged for what seemed like an age, picking up and discarding tapes. She seemed unable to decide.

'Just put anything on, then we can get on with it,' said Jack. 'I've got my tape if you want that.'

'No, it's got to be something significant. It'll be the first song we play in our new home. I want it to remind me of this moment for ever.'

Jack shook his head; she was so particular about her music. In the end she went with 'Mersey Paradise' by the Stone Roses, one of her all-time favourite songs from the band. Not that they were anywhere near the Mersey, but this was *her* little piece of paradise. The song opened with a line about splashing against the rocks, which seemed apt, and it was sunny and jangly just how she felt... Until something catastrophic occurred to her. She went into a blind panic. 'Oh my God, Jack. Oh, fucking shit! Where's my diary, where's my diary!' She began frantically rifling through boxes, chucking books out of them.

'What? What's wrong?'

'*The concert. The fucking concert!*' He still didn't understand. What concert? 'The Stone Roses gig! I've got a horrible, horrible feeling we've missed it! What date is it?'

'I don't know.' Jack had never paid any attention to what the date was.

Daisy finally found her diary – the diary she hadn't written in for weeks, and shook it violently. The two precious tickets, still tucked in the back, fluttered to the floor. She grabbed one and turned it over. The date read 'Saturday 12th August'.

Her heart pounded. She dropped the diary and the tickets, still in a panic, as Jack looked on helplessly. Then she grabbed her TV and dragged it over to the aerial socket. 'Help me, Jack. Help me!'

'What do you want me to do?'

'Find the remote control!' He did, and chucked it over.

Daisy immediately put Ceefax on. In the corner of the screen was the date – Monday, 14th August. They'd missed the concert by two days. Daisy dropped the remote and sank to her knees, letting out a moan. She put her head in her hands and began to sob uncontrollably. Jack was distraught: he could remember how much the concert had meant to her. Her dad had bought her the tickets not long before he'd died. It seemed so long ago now that she'd asked him to go with her. 'How could we be so stupid?' she cried.

'Hey, it's not your fault. It's not surprising it slipped your mind.'

'But that concert will never, *ever*, come round again. It's gone forever. It would have been my first one – and my dad bought me the tickets especially!' This set her off again, and she was inconsolable. Jack didn't know what to do. In the end, he told her to go and have a lie down while he started the unpacking. Head bowed, and still in tears, Daisy went off to their bedroom.

Once she had gone, Jack let out a sigh. Why did this have to happen? On their first day, too. Everything had been going so well, but now the day felt tarnished, bruised. He really felt for Daisy, and blamed himself: if it hadn't been for him they would never have had to move here. Then she would have remembered.

Jack began to half-heartedly pluck video tapes out of a box; he didn't know where Daisy wanted them to go, and it wasn't as if they had shelves to put them on. In the end he stacked them by the telly. Once he'd done this, he moved on to the cassettes and the books, trying his best to be useful. In half an hour or so, he emptied three large boxes. What should he do next? He wanted to see Daisy, to find out how she was; it wasn't the same without her. Then he noticed a box of clothes; those would have to go in the wardrobe. It was a good excuse to check up on her.

Daisy was lying on her side when he walked in. Although it was only late afternoon, she had the curtains closed. At least she'd stopped crying. 'I came to see how you were doing,' Jack said sheepishly. Daisy gave him a put-on smile to show that she appreciated the thought. Jack put down the box and lowered himself onto the bed. He took her hand, not really knowing what to say. 'I unpacked quite a few boxes, but I didn't know what to do with the clothes.'

Daisy didn't answer for a while. Then she said, 'Sorry for losing the plot. I've ruined the day, haven't I?'

'No, not at all.'

'I just feel so ... foolish – and guilty. How can you forget something so important?'

'You shouldn't feel guilty. If anything, it's my fault.'

'It's not,' she sniffed. 'Things happen. I wanted to come here.'

'You don't regret it, do you?'

Daisy looked up; he looked so sorrowful. 'Coming here? Don't be silly. Course I don't. I just wish I'd remembered the concert that's all... I suppose I haven't been writing in my diary lately, or even looking at the *NME*. It was like when Dad died; suddenly it didn't seem so important.' She propped herself up on one elbow; it felt better to talk. 'It's funny, isn't it? The really big things, the life-changing ones, and you don't document them – it's the trivial things like records coming out that you mention.'

Jack shrugged – he'd never kept a diary; God only knows what he'd have written about. 'Won't they do another concert?' he said, trying to help. 'I mean, I don't know how these things work...'

'I guess they will at some point, but it won't be the same...' She trailed off.

No, it probably wouldn't be the same.

*****

'Let's try again, shall we?' said Daisy, half an hour later, slipping a Kate Bush compilation into the hi-fi; she felt like listening to something meaningful.

Under Daisy's instruction they split up, one of them cleaning and the other unpacking. Daisy started on the cleaning, figuring Jack would be useless at it. Fortunately her mum had packed some stuff for her – sponge scourers, Jif, J-cloths – the only input she'd had.

Jack carried on unpacking. Daisy really had thought of everything – plates, cutlery, condiments, shampoo, loo roll...

He tried to remain focused, but kept getting distracted as Daisy squatted down and bent over in her shorts; he was starting to get used to her hair now.

Little things kept occurring to Daisy. They didn't have a washing machine or a vacuum cleaner, for example; it really was like starting from scratch. Where would they do their washing? And the carpets needed a serious vacuum, maybe even a shampoo. It made Daisy's skin crawl to think of all the dirt and mites that might be in them – it was the same with that old sofa. It was all going to take time. And money. This was what worried her most.

By the time they'd finished, even having put up Daisy's posters in the lounge and bedroom, they were filthy, tired and hungry. But the place was starting to look more like home – or lived in at least. 'Right, I'm going to have a bath. I feel absolutely gross,' said Daisy. 'And we need to think about what we're gonna have for tea. Have a look to see if the shop's still open.'

'Yes, looks like it.'

'What can we get that's not too expensive? We've got to make our money last. They don't have a massive selection there anyway.'

'Beans on toast?' suggested Jack.

Daisy pulled a face. 'Suppose so. Bit boring, though. But beggars can't be choosers... I think I saw tinned stuff. Do you want to grab some money out of my purse whilst I run a bath. I hope there's some hot water left.'

Daisy disappeared, whilst Jack located her purse. He extracted a pound coin, then made straight for the bathroom. Daisy was bent over the bath, moaning about the water not being very hot. Jack reddened and felt guilty all of a sudden, as if he was intruding. He cleared his throat. 'I've got the money.'

'Well, what are you bringing it in here for?' Daisy stood up, her face flushed. She still didn't seem in the best of moods. 'Go and get some beans.'

'Me? Why?' said Jack.

"Cause I'm going to have a bath, that's why – and besides, you need to start doing this stuff. I'm the one that's meant to be lying low, remember, not you.' Jack stood there. 'Go on.' She pushed him out of the bathroom. 'And don't forget to put the door on the latch,' she said as she closed the door. 'I'm not getting out of the bath to let you in!'

Jack pictured this as he padded through the kitchen. It was a provocative image. 'Actually, take the key!' Daisy called. 'Anyone could wander in off the street.' Jack grabbed the key off the side and reluctantly headed downstairs. He stalled for time, fiddling about with the door catch to see how it worked. He couldn't recall ever going into a shop without Daisy – and certainly not buying something himself. *Come on, Jack*, he said to himself, *you're Jack Gardner now. He can do this sort of stuff*. And with that he took the plunge and opened the door.

The shop was bigger than he'd expected, more than just a newsagent's. Jack was hoping to slip in unnoticed, but the lady behind the counter, a woman in her fifties who bizarrely resembled the Queen, said, 'You'll have to be quick, we're closing in a few minutes.' Jack blushed and hurried out of sight. He circled the shop until he found the tinned section, took a can of beans, then cautiously looked towards the till. The woman was peering at him over the top of her glasses. He had no choice. Best to get it over and done with. He kept his head down as he approached and put the tin on the counter.

'Moved in over the road, have we?' the woman said, tapping away at her till. Jack's heart stopped for a second. How the hell could she possibly know that?

The drawer of the till shot open, startling him. He could feel the woman looking at him. 'Erm...'

'I met your girlfriend this morning,' she said. *What the hell?* thought Jack. What had Daisy been saying? The woman thought she'd embarrassed the boy or he was a bit simple – so

127

she gave up. 'That's thirty-five pence please.' Jack handed over the money and got his change, not once looking her in the eye. He thanked her and left. She watched him go.

Jack let himself into the flat and shut the door behind him. He stood with his back against it, breathing heavily. So much for being anonymous.

Back upstairs, he knocked on the bathroom door. 'Daisy?'

'It's OK, you can come in.' *God, no*, thought Jack, nearly dropping the tin. He didn't think he'd be able to handle seeing Daisy reclining in a bath; they hadn't been intimate for weeks, and certainly weren't used to having this freedom around each other. And what about when it was his turn? Or what about when he needed to go to the toilet – properly? What if she barged in? He would die of embarrassment. He hoped there was a lock on the door.

'Erm, it's OK… Daisy, what did you say to the woman at the shop?'

'What woman?'

'The woman behind the counter with glasses.'

'What, the one who looks like the Queen?'

'Er, yes.'

'God, is she still on? She was on this morning.'

'Yeah, what did you say to her?'

'Nothing, nothing at all, other than "hello", "thank you" and "goodbye". Why?'

'She knew where we lived and that you were my girlfriend.'

Jack heard a big splash. 'You're joking! Nosey cow. She must have been watching us. You didn't say anything, did you?'

'No.'

'Well, good. We need to be careful. Did you get the beans?'

'Yes.'

'Are you OK making dinner, while I finish off?'

'Yes, no problem.'

'Can you put the kettle on as well. I wouldn't mind a cup of tea with it.'

Cup of tea, thought Jack – *at this time of the day?* For the first time in weeks he had a proper pang for alcohol; it must have been sparked off by that nosey woman.

Whilst he was finishing off dinner, Daisy emerged from the bathroom wrapped in a towel, her cropped hair scraped back. She looked scrubbed and pink, but a perfect picture. 'I've left the water in for you – it's not very warm, I'm afraid.' She half-smiled apologetically. Jack watched the shape of her in her towel as she walked over to the windows in the lounge. The shop was closed now. There was a window above it with a net curtain across it. Possibly someone's flat; maybe the shop's owner's, maybe that woman's. Daisy drew their own curtains as best she could, but they were pretty useless. 'We need to get some nets,' she said, then waltzed off down the corridor. Jack watched her go.

After dinner and a quick bath for Jack (with the door locked), they were both ready for bed. It was still early, but they were tired from their exertions. And Daisy was clearly still down about the concert. They sat up in bed for a while, compiling a list in her notebook of things they needed; a vacuum cleaner, a washing machine, an iron, a phone, some net curtains... How were they going to afford it all? On top of the money her mum had given her and a little cash of her own, Daisy also had a Halifax Building Society account that her dad had set up for her years ago. It had around five hundred pounds in it and wasn't to be touched till she was eighteen. Her parents had figured it would come in handy, to put towards a car, for example: the camper van wasn't going to run forever. Turning eighteen had always seemed so far in the future, but it was actually only a few weeks away. This money was her back-up plan if they got desperate. But it didn't seem right spending it in such a fashion. She wondered what her dad would have thought of her winding up in her current situation ... or what he would have thought of her forgetting the concert.

Daisy chose not to mention the building society money; it might delay Jack from looking for a job. She brought this up with him when they switched the light out. 'So, are you gonna be OK going in and enquiring about that job tomorrow? You know, at the restaurant?' Jack had already forgotten about it and his stomach sank. Besides, as soon as the light was out, he had been thinking about something else entirely. Despite Daisy's sombre mood this afternoon, after watching her cleaning and wandering around in that towel, and now her being snuggled into him, a feeling had been building inside him – he was getting … twitchy.

'Jack?' She nudged him. 'You're not asleep, are you?'

'No,' he said. Far from it.

'So, are you? I can go with you if you're worried. I don't mind.'

He sighed. 'No. I'll be fine. Honestly. You can't come in with me anyway. I'll look like an idiot – as if you're my mother or something.'

'I am like your mother in a way.' She snuggled into him further, pleased that he'd agreed. *Oh, don't do that*, he thought. If she moved her leg a few inches further up now, he'd be sprung – and embarrassed. 'Night,' she said.

'Night.'

Jack lay awake in the dark. Frustrated, and listening to the sounds of revellers on the street below. He'd been too tired to notice them on their first night.

CHAPTER 10

'Service Please!'

The start of the next day was pretty similar to the previous one. Jack and Daisy were awoken by the sound of gulls trying to outdo each other with their morning karaoke. Daisy's alarm clock hadn't surfaced yet, nor had her watch; she must have left them both behind.

'Are you OK?' said Jack, turning to her. 'You know, about…' He meant the concert.

'Not really. But I'll get over it … I guess. Best not to talk about it.'

'Sorry.'

They got up, then warmed themselves like a pair of lizards in the sun at the lounge windows. It was mid-morning already. They watched the crowds below for a while. Then Daisy decided she wanted scrambled eggs on toast, so she went down to the shop for some bits. She also bought a newspaper to see if there was any further mention of the fire or the murders. There wasn't: the story was slowly slipping out of the limelight.

Returning to the kitchen, Daisy remarked that they'd got to find a supermarket; the shop over the road was way too expensive. Then she groaned as she remembered they didn't have a microwave: she'd always scrambled her eggs that way back home, it was so quick and easy.

'Just do it in a pan,' said Jack. 'That's how Anne used to do them.' Then he had a sudden flash, like an electric shock to his brain: an image of his sister cooking at home that was so clear it felt as if he could reach out and touch it. The heart-wrenching pain in his chest that followed took him by surprise; he'd been so preoccupied of late that he hadn't been dwelling on the past. He leant on a counter to steady himself.

Daisy wasn't aware of any of this, she was too busy rooting around in cupboards to see if there were any pans. There was one tall cooking pot, but nothing that was any good for a couple of scrambled eggs. She slammed a cupboard door and screamed in frustration. 'I'm sick of bloody peanut butter and beans on toast. I want some proper food!' Jack was surprised at this outburst, especially so soon; it had only been a couple of days. He was used to a frugal existence and going without, but she was clearly accustomed to home comforts and a full fridge and larder.

It made him feel guilty, and sorry for her. 'We'll get a pan today. There's got to be somewhere open.'

'What, add it to the list, you mean? Where's the money gonna come from? Mum's money won't last forever and we need to eat! It'll have to be a second-hand shop.' Daisy grabbed the loaf of bread, then realised she'd have to put the oven grill on for toast. 'You know what? I can't even be bothered.' She slapped the pathetic little travel kettle on instead. Jack watched her, feeling useless. He took her hand.

'I'll go straight to the restaurant today. See if I can get that job.' Jack tried to sound braver than he felt. Daisy let herself be pulled towards him. Her stomach rumbled against his. 'We'll have to get some chips again,' he said, not minding the idea at all.

'We'll get scurvy at this rate. Or fat. Well, me anyway – you'll never get fat.'

'You won't get fat.'

'I will. I already am. Then you won't love me.'

'Don't be silly,' he said. 'And I'll always love you.' He kissed the top of her head.

'Sorry for being grumpy,' she said, looking up. 'It's just... frustrating, that's all.'

'I know.'

*****

They set out just before midday and joined the crowds again. It was still a bit of a shock, having them right on their doorstep. Daisy was wearing her sunglasses as she had before: they made her feel like a celebrity who was trying not to be recognised. Feeling a little indulgent, they headed straight to the chip shop – both deciding they could barely think straight, never mind enquire about a job, on an empty stomach. Besides, chips were a cheap meal. They ate them on the seafront, soaking up the unfamiliar carnival atmosphere.

Feeling better, and unable to put it off any longer, they headed back to the restaurant. It had been empty when they'd passed it earlier, but now a few tables were taken. Daisy squeezed Jack's hand. 'Are you sure you don't want me to go in with you?'

'No. Honestly. I've got to do it myself.' Jack had gone a little pale. A waiter standing at the door in an apron was watching them.

'Well, if you're sure... Best get it over with before it's any busier. Good luck.' Daisy pecked him on the cheek.

Jack shuffled towards the restaurant, hating to leave her. His head was swimming. Not only was he nervous about speaking, but he was also feeling the pressure: he couldn't screw this up, not with their finances being what they were.

As Jack reached the door, the waiter said, 'Table for two, sir?' He eyed the scruffy lad suspiciously.

'Er, no.' Jack was flummoxed. He hadn't expected to be accosted straight away. He tried to speak, to explain about the job, but was tongue-tied.

'The toilets are only for paying customers, I'm afraid,' said the waiter, trying to read between the lines.

Jack reddened, but Daisy had seen enough and stepped in; he'd be a nervous wreck by the time he got in there. 'He's enquiring about the job. The one advertised in the window.'

'Oh, right!' said the waiter, immediately changing his tone. 'My apologies. Step this way, young man.' He ushered Jack inside.

The interior of the restaurant was dark. When Jack's eyes adjusted, he found himself in a larger room than he had been expecting, with cane chairs and glass-topped tables. Broad-leaved plants in huge pots were dotted amongst them. A girl in uniform was setting out cutlery, alongside an array of glasses and napkins. There was a small reception desk with a lady behind it, and a bar where a smart-looking barman was polishing glasses. 'Welcome to the Crab's Claw,' the waiter said. The lady at reception looked up. 'We've got a young man here enquiring about the kitchen assistant position. Is Chef busy?'

The lady studied Jack, looking him up and down. He was starting to feel like cattle being weighed in at a market. 'I'm not sure. We've got a few twos and a four in. I'll give him a ring.' She punched a number into the phone. 'Hi, Chef, we've got a young gentleman here enquiring about the kitchen job... I don't know, I'll ask. Full or part time?'

Jack shrugged and forced himself to find his voice. 'Either,' he croaked.

'Either,' she repeated. 'OK. I'll send him through. Dan, could you take him through, please. Chef will see him now.' Jack gulped. 'Table for two, sir?' Behind Jack another couple of diners had wandered in.

The waiter hesitated. 'Er, Jeanette, could you escort this young man through to the kitchen please? He's here about the job. I need to get back out front.' It was strange how they seemed to be addressing him formally now, as if he was a customer.

The girl laying the tables sighed, then walked over. She gave Jack a smile. 'Follow me.' She was about his age: blonde, slim, her hair tied into a bun. He felt shy in her company.

There were round windows in the double doors in between the reception and bar, and Jack had his first glimpse of the kitchen. His stomach churned. Jeanette pushed one of the doors open and held it back for him. Straightaway he was hit by the sounds – the rush of the extraction fans, the clanging and banging of pans, the barking of orders. Then the smells – a rich and pungent mix of roasting meats, seafood, garlic, fresh herbs and frying chips. But most of all he was struck by the heat; the restaurant seemed air-conditioned in comparison.

There must have been three or four chefs in there, all in white jackets and navy striped aprons, and one lad, about Jack's age, maybe a little older, wearing a T-shirt, jeans and an apron, who was washing up in a corner. Everyone had a tea towel draped over one of their shoulders. Most of them looked up at Jack's arrival. The lad washing up grinned, as if he was pleased to see him, as if he knew him. 'There's a lad here about the kitchen job, Chef,' said Jeanette to a man behind a brightly lit counter.

'Yes, I know that,' the man replied sarcastically, looking up briefly from four plates of food. He was large, a little overweight, red-faced and glistening with sweat. The plates were huge and white with very small portions of food artistically arranged on them. Jack had never seen anything like it. After placing a dainty green herb on top of some tall, eye-catching stacks, the chef said, 'Right, these can go to outside four, please.' He consulted a small slip of paper that was hanging up, then barked over his shoulder, 'Side of asparagus. Where is it?' Then he stuck the ticket on a spike.

'Coming now, Chef,' said a voice from the bowels of the kitchen.

'What have we got?' Jeanette said, fishing two cloth napkins from out of her pinny pocket.

'Two red mullet, two pigeon.'

The girl picked up two plates, using the napkins. 'Outside four, yes?'

'Yes. Outside four.'

'All right,' she said, scurrying off.

'*Asparagus!*'

A harassed-looking young chef brought a black metal pan of asparagus to the counter.

Chef felt the vegetables with the back of his fingers, then began transferring them to an oval serving dish. 'Black pepper!'

'Shit, sorry, Chef,' the young lad said. He grabbed a peppermill from a nearby work station, then proceeded to twist it over the asparagus. 'All right, don't go fucking mad!' said Chef, pushing the lad away. He consulted another ticket hanging up and shouted over his shoulder. 'How are we doing on a parfait and a tartare?'

'Here, Chef.' Two more pretty plates of food were brought to the counter by another chef.

'Keep an eye on the fingerprints, yeah?' he said, rubbing the rim of one of the plates in a circular motion with a damp cloth.

'Chef.'

Jeanette returned, and groaned at the food queuing up. 'Can you ding for me, please? These want a drinks order. Oh, and check-on.' She pulled another ticket out of her pinny and slapped it on the counter. It had blue handwriting on it.

Chef picked it up. 'Check-on. Two fish and chips!' he said, sticking it up with the others.

'Chef!' the brigade answered in unison.

Jeanette waltzed away, somehow managing to balance the serving dish on her wrist as she carried the other two plates.

Chef banged a bell on the counter, the kind Jack had seen in *Fawlty Towers*, and shouted, 'Service please!'

Jack stood there, totally overwhelmed by it all. The man finally acknowledged him properly for the first time, still garnishing a plate. 'Right, here about the job, are you?' Jack nodded quickly. 'What's your name?'

'Jack,' he mumbled.

'Sorry? You'll have to speak up in here.'

'Jack,' he said louder. It felt as if he was shouting.

'Have you got any experience?'

'Er, not in a kitchen… In a factory, though, making sausage rolls and that.'

Chef snorted. 'Sausage rolls?' He looked at Jack properly for the first time. 'How old are you?'

'Sixteen.'

'Looking for part time, then?'

'Well, anything really… The more hours the better, I suppose.'

'You don't want to say that in 'ere,' Chef laughed. 'You're not at college then?' Jack shook his head.

'You're not intending on going? 'Cause it's not just a summer job – there's no good us training you up just for you to piss off when September arrives.'

'No.' Jack shook his head again.

'*Service, please!*' Chef barked again, banging the bell and making Jack jump. 'And it's evenings and weekends as well.'

'Yes, that's fine.' Jack was starting to think he might have a chance.

'Come in tomorrow evening for a trial. You'll have to start from the bottom. Learn the potwash first, like what Aitch is doin' over there. Peelin' spuds and that as well.' He tilted his head in the direction of the lad washing up. Jack nodded again. 'I won't be here tomorrow night, but Whizz'll look after you, he's my sous chef.' And then louder, over his shoulder, he said, 'Won't you, Whizz?'

'Aye,' said Whizz, a beanpole of a man, possibly in his twenties: unshaven, a bit manic-looking, his chef's jacket hanging off him as if from a coat hanger. Surprisingly, he tilted a cider bottle in Jack's direction, took a swig from it, then poured the rest of it into a saucepan.

'Jesus Christ, where the fuck are they? This tartare won't be tartare anymore, it'll be cooked!' Chef turned off the bright lights of the counter just as Jeanette returned for the other two plates of food; she looked a little flustered.

'Sorry, check-on again,' she said, another ticket in hand.

Chef snatched it off her and glared at her. 'Where've you been?'

'Taking a drinks order for outside four. They want a house salad now as well.'

'One house salad tout suite! Where's everyone else?'

'Hilary's taking orders and Dan's busy – we've had a six walk in – and Owen's serving.'

'Why haven't you got anyone else on? It's Carnival Week!'

'We have at one. Craig's in.' She scuttled off again with the plates. 'I'll be back for that salad!' Jack felt sorry for her.

'Fuck's sake, another table of four,' Chef said, studying the new check. 'Right. See you tomorrow, er, Jack, we're getting a shaftin' here. Check-on…'

'What time?'

'Eh?' Chef said distractedly.

'What time shall I come in?'

'Er, quarter to six, sharp. Check-on! Two moules to start…'

Jack beat a hasty exit, wondering what he'd let himself in for. As he reached the door he heard Chef banging the bell again and shouting, *'Fucking service, please!'* Jeanette was on her way back in. She raised her eyebrows at Jack in exasperation. He left, smiling.

He was still smiling when he got back outside. The bright afternoon sun made him wince and he could smell food on his clothes and hair. Most of the outside tables were taken now. 'I take it you got the job, then?' said Daisy.

'I've got a trial shift!' Jack beamed.

Daisy squealed and hugged him. 'See! I told you... I knew you could do it!'

'Whoa! Slow down. I haven't got the job yet.'

'You will, though, I know you will. Once they see how hard you work.'

'We'll see.'

They walked off, hand in hand. 'I feel like celebrating,' said Daisy. 'Do you fancy an ice cream?' She stopped outside an ice cream shop.

'Not really,' said Jack. What he really wanted was a drink. He felt like celebrating as well, but he was also only too aware of their lack of money. 'Besides, we've got to get a pan yet, haven't we? If we're going to spend money, it ought to be on stuff like that.'

'God, you're so sensible,' Daisy said, dragging herself away from the enticing array of ice creams on offer. 'But you're right, I suppose. Come on; let's see if we can find a second-hand shop.'

They did, well off the beaten track: it sold, amongst other things, refurbished electrical goods, cookware and camping gear. They found a pan that would do the job, and an alarm clock too; they even spotted an old-fashioned telephone and a vacuum cleaner. 'Does this phone work properly?' asked Daisy.

'Yes, it's a Bakelite, been refurbished – here, I'll show you.' The shopkeeper unplugged the phone on his desk and plugged the old-fashioned one in. He held it to his ear, then to Daisy's. It appeared to be working.

'How much is it?'

'Twelve pounds.'

'Twelve pounds for an old phone? I could probably get a new one from Argos for that!'

'Perhaps you could, young lady, but not in this town. There isn't one. You're not from round here, I take it?' Daisy didn't answer. 'Besides, it's an antique. From the war, that is.' Daisy wasn't convinced, but she liked it. It was straight out of a black and white movie.

'We'll just take the pan and the clock for now,' she said.

Exploring the town further, Daisy spotted a Halifax branch; they passed by without her drawing attention to it. They also found a second-hand clothes shop, a proper supermarket not far from the flat and a tempting little second-hand bookshop, but managed not to spend any more money. The one shop they didn't find, which struck Daisy as both odd and disappointing, was somewhere selling records; still, it would only be a temptation. They also came across a canoe hire place, next to a bowling green and set back from the seafront. This looked like fun.

Exhausted from walking so far, they made their way back to the flat with mixed feelings. The initial euphoria about the job trial had given way to frustration with the money situation. They'd seen so much today, so much they wanted to do and buy, but it was all intangible, all out of reach – for the moment at least. 'I guess it's scrambled eggs for dinner, then,' Daisy said, a little glumly.

'I guess so.'

'You can make it, though. You need all the cooking practice you can get now!'

'That's fine by me,' said Jack, giving the pan a few experimental tosses, as if he was flipping a pancake. 'Hey, we could have an omelette,' he suggested.

'But what would we put in it? We haven't even got any cheese – we could have got some from the supermarket; I'm not buying any from that shop!' They had reached the flat and Daisy let them inside. The cool air immediately hit them as she pushed the door open.

Something on the floor caught her eye. An envelope; a small white envelope with elegant handwriting on it that must have come in the second post. '*Grandma!*' she exclaimed, picking it up.

It was so strange seeing something physical from the outside world, from their other life, making its way into their new secret world; as if it had been deposited through a time portal. Daisy excitedly opened the envelope. She pulled out a little card with a painted daisy on the front. 'Ah, typical Grandma, bless her,' she said. Inside the card was a note in the same lovely old-fashioned writing, saying: '*A little something to tide you over till your birthday. Make sure you're eating properly. Good luck at university. How exciting! Love, Grandma. x.*' University? thought Daisy. There were two twenty pound notes. 'Bless her,' Daisy said again, and a tear came to her eye.

That was it: she burst into tears. Her grandma's kind words and much-needed gift had hit a raw nerve. It was a reminder that there were certain people you could count on, who had your back no matter what. People who loved you. Family. And this brought guilt, because she'd turned her back on them. And for the first time Daisy questioned whether she'd done the right thing. She'd been so hell bent on her actions, so wrapped up in them – her way of dealing with the grief and the miscarriage – that she hadn't really considered the people she was leaving behind.

Little did she know that Lily had found her mum crying in Daisy's empty room both nights so far; it would have killed her if she had. And little did she know that Carol hadn't had the heart to tell her mother that Daisy had pretty much absconded with a boy and was lying low; she'd said her daughter was starting at Norwich University in September. Carol knew she'd send Daisy some money. It was a way of looking after her, whilst hoping that she'd see sense and come home.

'Hey, what's wrong?' said Jack, wrapping his arms round her. 'This is a good thing, isn't it? The money.'

'I know. I'm sorry. It's just everything, I guess. It's all been so stressful. And I still don't think I've grieved properly, you know, about Dad.'

This Jack could understand. He felt exactly the same. Little things like the mention of Anne's name could set him off. He could go from a high to a low so quickly. And he felt as if he was bottling it all up, the fact that his sister was truly gone, forever, and that at some point it was going to come gushing out. 'It's OK. Don't be sorry. I know how you feel.' They held each other for a while until Jack realised he was still clutching the pan. 'So ... scrambled eggs, then?'

'No, I don't think so. I think we can do better than that now.'

*****

Daisy was adamant they were going to have something special for dinner, courtesy of Grandma, to celebrate the job trial. Jack, cautious as ever, wasn't so sure. 'Shouldn't we save the money just in case?'

'In case of what? What's the point in living if you can't celebrate when something good happens? Dad always said you should celebrate stuff. You've only got one life.'

'I know, but I haven't got the job yet. What if I don't get it?'

'You will.' Daisy wouldn't take no for an answer. 'Come on, let's make a list, then go to the supermarket!' Who was Jack to argue? It was her money after all, and it was good to see her so happy again.

Daisy decided on spaghetti bolognese. It was inexpensive and easy to make, but would feel like a proper meal. Their first proper meal in their new home. She said she would show Jack how to prepare the vegetables, it would come in handy for his new job. That pan left in the cupboard would be just right for the spaghetti.

Walking round the supermarket with a basket was a strange experience for Jack – for both of them really; it made them

142

feel like adults. Daisy suggested they should buy a bottle of white wine to go with their dinner, all very grown up. She chose a bottle of soave as it was cheap. They added a few essentials then, feeling pleased that they had still only spent a tenner, headed back home.

Daisy told Jack to put the wine in the fridge whilst she put some music on. She couldn't cook without music. Then they began. She showed him how to peel and finely chop the vegetables, and soon the enticing smell of frying garlic, onion, celery and carrot filled the kitchen, making them both hungry.

Whilst the sauce was simmering, Daisy set the table, humming along to the music. They didn't have any wine glasses, so they had to drink their wine out of mugs. But it didn't matter, it was still one of the best meals they'd ever had. They clinked their mugs together and said 'cheers'. The wine went straight to their heads, as it was the first drink they'd had in weeks. Jack had never tasted wine before, and couldn't believe how strong it was. He treated it like cider at first and guzzled it until Daisy told him to slow down. By the time they'd cleared up the kitchen the bottle was empty; they were both drunk, but wanted more alcohol.

The shop opposite was closed, so Daisy suggested they should get a couple of take-out bottles of cider from the pub down the road. Jack didn't know you could do this. He was too scared to go on his own, and would sooner have gone without, so Daisy went instead. She was too inebriated to worry about lying low, or about not spending money.

But when she returned she said, 'We can't make a habit of that. Nearly two pounds each, these cost! We could have got two big bottles from the supermarket for that!' They wondered whether to put a film on, but decided to stick with the music instead; the drink made them want to talk. There would be plenty of nights when they could watch films.

They were still talking as they climbed into bed. 'You know when we're walking round town,' said Daisy, slurring slightly.

'Do you feel, I don't know how to describe it … as if we're in a bubble and we're not like anybody else? It's just us and them. The crowds, I mean. I know it sounds daft, but it's like we're outlaws or something … like Bonnie and Clyde … living outside society, like Patti Smith sings in 'Rock n Roll Nigger'. I kind of like it. God I'm drunk,' she giggled.

'Me too,' said Jack.

'Come here.' Daisy pulled him closer. They kissed, and it felt natural and drunken and good. It had been too long. The drink was the catalyst, as usual. Their hands explored each other. After a few minutes of fumbling, despite Jack's brain saying 'yes, yes, yes!' another part of his body was saying 'no'. This had never happened before, and he didn't understand it. Daisy was aware of it as she pressed herself against him. 'What's wrong with *him* tonight?' she said, 'I don't know whether I should be offended. I hope it's not my hair!'

'No,' he said embarrassed.

'Are you sure? Why don't you pretend I'm someone else? You might like it.' The drink talking.

'That's a dreadful thing to say!'

'Well, what is it then?'

Now that Jack thought about it, he could probably put his finger on what was subconsciously putting him off. 'I think it's the other thing.'

'What other thing?'

'You know…' He didn't want to say it, but kept picturing the blood. 'What happened at the police station…'

'Oh, don't worry about that. I'm fine now, honestly. Back to normal.'

'But what if, you know, what if it happens again? A baby, I mean?'

'It won't,' she said. 'I'm on the pill.'

'What pill?'

'*The* pill. The pill that stops you getting pregnant.' She couldn't believe she was having to explain it.

'But how…'

'Stop asking questions and kiss me, Jack Gardner; you're ruining the mood. Just trust me.' She slipped her hand inside his boxer shorts. 'Do you want me to talk to you? Will that help?' she purred, coaxing him with her hand.

It did help.

And the bed made an awful racket.

CHAPTER 11

Feeding the Monkey

It was Carnival Day, the highlight of the week, and the sky around Cromer was filled with parachutists and old-fashioned aircraft. It made for quite a spectacle, only adding to the magic of their new lives.

Thanks to the unexpected bonus provided by Daisy's grandma, they returned to the second-hand shop for the phone; this they considered to be their biggest necessity. They bought a cheap throw for the sofa, too. The vacuum cleaner would have to wait – see if Jack got the job first. Then they headed to the supermarket, so Jack could eat before his trial shift.

Back at the flat, after unpacking their shopping, the first thing they did was to plug in the phone. It worked, which was a relief; and they took it in turns to hold the heavy black receiver to their ears. Hearing the dial tone was exciting, a connection to the outside world; it made the flat feel more like home. Daisy cut out a little circle to put in the middle of the dial, with their number written on it in biro. 'We'll need to get a phone book,' she said. 'I'll stick it on the list.'

Daisy made sausages, mash and onion gravy for tea; another cheap and tasty meal. But, much to her annoyance, Jack was so nervous he could barely eat a thing. All he wanted to do was crack open the big bottle of cider they'd bought – old habits, quickly re-forming. Daisy was adamant that he shouldn't. 'You can't turn up stinking of booze on your first shift,' she said. 'This is too important. You need your wits about you too – you can't go handling knives and hot things when you've been drinking!'

Jack briefly pictured the chef who'd been drinking cider – Whizz, was it? – which made a mockery of that comment. Daisy was probably right, though, he seemed to get drunk a lot quicker these days. 'I'm not going to be handling knives, I'm washing up,' he mumbled, getting up and scraping the majority of his dinner into the bin. Daisy tutted at the waste.

Remembering what the lad washing up had been wearing the previous day, Jack donned some jeans and an old T-shirt. Then he did his teeth and combed his hair, in silence. Watching him pace about as she washed the dinner pots, Daisy could sense his anxiety. When it was time to go he loitered by the stairs, pale-faced and doing his customary nervous jig. 'I'll just get my jacket and I'll walk with you,' Daisy said, drying her hands.

'No, it's OK. I'll go on my own.'

Daisy was taken aback. 'Why? You're not ashamed of me, are you?' she joked.

Jack wasn't in the mood for jokes; he felt as if he was going to be sick. 'It's just best I go on my own. I need to prepare myself.' This was true, but he also knew that turning up with Daisy would make him feel like a little kid – like when Anne escorted him to work on his first day. The thought of her made him feel sad again.

'Well, if you're sure.'

Jack nodded solemnly.

'Good luck, then. You'd better be going.' She gave him a big hug and kissed him on the cheek. 'I think you're being really brave, and I'm so proud of you. You're gonna do fine. I know it.' He wished she would stop; he was starting to well up. 'Just do as they tell you, and work as hard as you can.' She followed him downstairs and let him out. 'What time did they say you would finish?'

'They didn't.'

'Oh, well. I'll wait up for you anyway. Just bang on the door and I'll let you in — it's gonna be weird being in the flat on my own. We'll have that cider later to celebrate! Fingers crossed!' *No pressure then*, thought Jack miserably as he walked away. 'Love you!' Daisy called. He turned and mustered a half-smile.

The town felt strange without Daisy. Bigger, lonelier, cooler. There were fewer people about; they'd not been out at this time of day before. Jack would have rather been doing anything else, and suddenly realised how much he missed the fields and woods back home. Alone, he began to doubt himself, to panic. The black spot reared up, then the voice in his head. *What's the matter, Jack? Can't you remember the way?* 'Shut up!' he replied. *Relax. Just follow your nose and don't think about it.*

Somehow he managed to find the restaurant, remembering the pedestrian crossing on the way. The restaurant was closed, confirmed by a sign on the door. What the hell? Feeling foolish and nervous, Jack peered inside. It was dark, but there were lights on and he could see staff moving about, which was a relief. But no one had spotted him. The lady wasn't at the front desk. What should he do? Knock on the door? He was just trying to pluck up the courage when a friendly voice from behind startled him. 'I did that on my first shift too!'

Jack spun round. It was Jeanette, the girl from the other day. He breathed a sigh of relief to see a familiar face. She was flushed and dismounting from a bicycle. 'The staff entrance is round the back. You're not allowed in through there, Hilary would kill you. Come on, I'll show you the way.' She pushed her bike in the direction he'd just come from. Jack followed awkwardly. 'So, are you nervous then?' she asked, brushing her blonde hair out of her face as she turned to him. Jack shrugged. He felt tongue-tied again. 'You'll be all right. At least Chef's not on tonight. Whizz has his moments, he's a bit up and down and can get a bit stressed, but he's generally OK. And Hilary can be a bit of a bitch – she's the manageress – but other than that everyone else is really friendly. We're in here,' she said, turning down an alleyway.

She took another right, this time through a gate marked 'Private', and they arrived in a courtyard. There were a couple of rubbish skips on wheels – the type they had back at Peasgood's factory – a log shelter and a huge cage of flattened cardboard. Sitting outside the back door, which had a sign above it saying 'Private. Staff and deliveries only', was Whizz. He was at a pub table with a dirty umbrella, smoking a cigarette. Jack's heart raced at the sight of him. 'Here he is!' Whizz cried. 'You two know each other or something?' Jack didn't follow.

'No, we just arrived at the same time,' said Jeanette, padlocking her bike next to another one.

'Oh, thought that was quick, even for you!' said Whizz.

'Oh, piss off!' Jeanette said, shouldering her bag and disappearing inside. Jack was amazed to hear her speak like this to the chef, but he seemed to take it in good part.

Making sure she'd gone, Whizz said, 'I'd watch out for that one, er … what's your name again?'

'Jack.'

'Jack. She may look like butter wouldn't melt, but let me tell yer…' Without finishing, he took one last wheeze on his fag, then stubbed it out in an overflowing ashtray. 'Right, let's face the music, shall we?' Jack followed him inside. 'Here's the staff changing room. Ours anyway. The ladies are next door, so no drilling holes in the wall or anything.' He pushed open a door to the right to reveal a small room with a desk, a filing cabinet and lots of clothes hooks. It smelt unpleasant, of grease and fryers. There were normal clothes hanging up, and chefs' uniforms, some of them dirty, littered about. On the desk, Jack noticed, was a small stack of magazines – the top one with a naked woman on it – and he went bright red. 'Have you got anything to hang up?' said Whizz. Jack managed to shake his head. 'Not the best, is it? Could do with a tidy up actually. It's not until someone new comes in that you notice it. Might get Aitch to do it tonight if we're not too busy – seeing as there's two of you on. Here, take this apron. It'll do for tonight, but if you're gonna start 'ere full time, you'll get yer own set to take home to wash – it's the best way.'

Jack took the dirty apron. It was tacky to the touch and he inwardly grimaced. But he was pleased to hear that the smiley lad from the other day would be there. They left the room and walked past another door to their right. 'Lookin' good, Jeanie,' said Whizz as he passed. Jack briefly saw Jeanette putting some lipstick on before she slammed the door. They passed a glass-fronted office, then Whizz pushed his way through some hanging plastic strips, a fly screen between the staff quarters and the kitchen. Then they were in, and Jack's heart speeded up.

The kitchen looked to be immaculately shiny and spotless, especially compared with the rooms behind the scenes. The heat and the smell hit him again, the sounds and the brightness, the hustle and bustle. Steam belched from the central cooking range. A percussion of clanging pans and knives on chopping boards filled the air, competing with the rush of the extraction fans. People spoke in loud voices. Someone was singing. Aitch was mopping up something that had been spilt on the tiled floor. He looked up and grinned. Jack smiled sheepishly back. The place had the feel of a galley on a ship, of comrades and teamwork. 'Right, I'll show you around quickly, then I'll leave you with Aitch. He'll show you the potwash.'

Whizz guided Jack around the kitchen, introducing various chefs and telling him what different areas were called. The men nodded as Jack passed. Most of it went over his head, including some of the chef's names. There seemed to be about four chefs on, plus Aitch, and one chef in a separate section entirely, which was cooler, called 'pastry'. This was confusing. Was that all he did, make pastry? Another section was called 'sauce'. What sauce? 'And this is where you'll be tonight, with your inmate, Aitch here – in the slammer. Some don't make it out alive. Some escape fairly quickly. Aitch here is a lifer, but he likes it in 'ere, don't you?'

'Wouldn't 'ave it any other way, Chef,' grinned Aitch, standing to attention, still clutching his mop.

'Right, put that mop down and show Jack here the ropes. You can show him the veg store as well. Oh, and the monkey needs feeding.'

'Yes, Chef,' said Aitch. 'I'll explain later,' he mouthed to Jack.

When Whizz left, Jack felt a bit awkward being on his own with a stranger. 'Right, stick your apron on and I'll show you how the potwash machine works,' said Aitch.

It was all pretty straightforward. Jack had used a similar setup at the factory.

The bell on the food counter dinged, and someone shouted, '*Staff food!*' Jack looked over, and a couple of chefs were placing large trays of food on the counter. The food steamed and looked good under the lights. He wished he'd eaten more dinner at home now; the smell was making him hungry. 'Do you want something before it all goes?' asked Aitch. Jack shook his head. No matter how hungry he was, he wasn't going to be eating in front of a load of strangers, no way. 'I'm gonna grab some. I'm starving! It's cottage pie tonight.' And Aitch dashed off.

The double doors to the restaurant kept opening as staff from out front came in. The clock above them said ten to six. The waiting staff queued up on their side of the counter, whilst the chefs helped themselves from their side. 'What's the vegetarian option?' asked Jeanette, and the chefs groaned.

'Er, mashed potato?' one of them teased.

'Don't you like meat, Jeanie?' another one sniggered.

'Hilarious,' she said, picking up a spoon.

'I'm surprised you're on tonight, actually – thought you'd be on one of the floats with your Miss Cromer crown on,' said Whizz.

'Well, you know, you've got to give the other girls a chance...'

'You'll always be my Miss Cromer,' another chef said.

To Jack it seemed as if they were a big, squabbling family. And this struck him as a way of saving money as well, if he was able to pluck up the courage to eat with the others. Aitch kept on getting pushed to the back of the queue, which wasn't so nice. 'Get back, scumbag, you're last in the pecking order,' a chef said, holding him back. Jack didn't like this, and felt for him.

But soon Aitch came back proudly clutching a steaming bowl of food. He leant against the potwash machine to eat – too quickly – and he burnt his mouth. 'You sure you don't want some? There's some left,' he said between mouthfuls, noticing Jack watching. Jack shook his head again.

'Right, get this lot off the pass, you pair. It's service time!' someone shouted from the food counter.

'Come on, that's our job,' said Aitch. 'Here, you'll need one of these.' He grabbed a thick tea towel from on top of the potwash machine and draped it over Jack's shoulder. Together they headed over to what was clearly called 'the pass' to collect the dirty trays.

Just then a waiter, a tall youth with his hair in a ponytail, burst in with a check in his hand. 'Check-on, chef,' he said, passing it to Whizz.

'Fuck me, it's not even six yet.'

'I know. They're queuing up out there,' the lad said, disappearing again.

''Ere we fuckin' go then. Get the lube ready, boys, could be in for a shaftin'!' Whizz spooned the last of his dinner into his mouth and dumped his plate in Aitch's hand as he passed. 'Check-on!' he shouted. 'Two covers. Guess what it is?'

'Fish and chips!' a couple of the chefs called back.

'Corr-rect! That's Carnival Week for you, folks!' Whizz seemed to have developed another persona now that service had started and the head chef wasn't there. There seemed a different atmosphere to the previous day. More relaxed.

'Right, I'll have that bit,' said Aitch, back at the potwash area, spooning the last of the cottage pie into his bowl. 'Are you sure you don't want to try some?'

'Well, maybe just a bit,' said Jack. The cottage pie looked so good: fluffy mash, glazed and crispy with baked cheese. Aitch passed him a spoon.

'Always keep one of these in your back pocket,' he said, grinning.

Jack looked around to make sure no one was looking, then took a spoonful of pie. It was the best he'd ever tasted: rich, salty and savoury, cheesy and full of flavour. Aitch could see the pleasure on his face. 'And that's just the staff food,' he said. 'You wait to see what comes back from the customers – steak and everything. One of the perks of being in the slammer, my friend!'

The rest of the night went by in a bit of a blur. Endless 'check-ons'. Endless dinging of the bell and the shouting of 'Service, please!' by the chefs; then 'Mains away!' from the waiting staff. Endless plates, plastic tubs, pans and trays to scrape and scrub and clean and put through the machine; some of them were incredibly stubborn – what Aitch referred to as 'soakers'. The waiting staff seemed a lot friendlier with Aitch than the chefs, stopping to have a joke and a chat with him, boys and girls, most of them about the same age as Aitch and Jack. The lad with the ponytail said something strange to Aitch that Jack didn't understand, just, 'Got any?'

'Aye, you know me. Only personal tonight, though, I'm afraid.'

'Love Shack later then?'

'Yes. Tell the others.' What was this secret coded talk? Jack wondered.

The potwash section was also being constantly barked at to fetch food for the chefs, either from the veg store, the dry store or a huge refrigerator room that you could actually walk into. In between all of this they were expected to peel an entire sack of potatoes, which Aitch carried back on his shoulder from the veg store – a cool dark place, full of shelves bursting with coloured vegetables, mushrooms, peppers, tomatoes, carrots. It reminded Jack of *Fantastic Mr. Fox*. Aitch seemed to be perennially cheerful, saying how easy it was as there were two of them on; he didn't seem in much of a hurry with anything. The monkey, it turned out, was a large plastic bin. 'Feeding it' was filling it full of peeled potatoes.

Aitch showed Jack how to peel a potato efficiently and safely, using some ferociously sharp-looking metal peelers. 'If you're not careful and you don't concentrate, they can bite you,' he said. 'Right, I'm nipping outside for a smoke. Back in a minute.' And he waltzed off. 'Just nipping out for a fag, Chef!'

'If you've got time to smoke, you've got time to clean that changing room!'

'In a bit. Just got the monkey to feed first!'

In between potatoes, Jack found himself distracted by what was going on around him. Everything seemed to happen at a million miles an hour. One lad seemed to be getting a lot of stick, messing things up and getting shouted at constantly. Jack recognised him from the asparagus incident the other day. But peeling potatoes wasn't so bad. Once you got in a rhythm it was quite satisfying; he'd done a lot worse jobs.

Aitch returned, smelling of cigarettes, and said, 'Bloody hell, Jack, slow down, you're makin' me look bad. He'll have me cleanin' the changing room at this rate.' Jack did as he was told, and they peeled side by side. Then Jeanette appeared, dumping a pile of plates next to them. 'Having fun, boys?'

'Just emptying my sack, baby,' said Aitch. Jeanette rolled her eyes. 'Hey, you coming to the Shack later? I've got some squidgy.' Jack listened as he peeled. What was this shack? And what the hell was squidgy? So many questions…

'Depends what time I get finished.'

Just then a pain shot through Jack's thumb, and he cried out and dropped his peeler. He hadn't been concentrating, and had peeled the corner of his thumbnail off. The flap of skin he had opened began to pour with blood. He was mortified – a combination of embarrassment and the fact he might have messed everything up with his carelessness. It wouldn't stop bleeding.

Aitch laughed, totally unconcerned. 'Hey! Your first cut! It won't be your last, I tell you. At least you haven't burnt yourself yet.'

'It's not funny, Aitch,' said Jeanette. 'That looks quite bad. Here.' She fished a paper napkin out of her pinny pocket and casually took hold of Jack's hand. With her other hand she wrapped the napkin tightly around his thumb. Jack's first instinct was to yank his hand away; he'd never been touched by a girl other than Daisy and his sister. It felt strange. 'Now keep that on tightly or you'll drip everywhere. Follow me and I'll show you where the plasters are kept.'

'Special treatment, eh?' said Aitch. 'You didn't show me where the plasters were kept when I cut myself for the first time!'

'Maybe in your dreams.' Jack looked at Aitch. He grinned and gestured for Jack to follow her. 'Jack's cut his thumb, Chef,' said Jeanette. 'I'm just showing him where the plasters are.' Jack looked down, utterly ashamed.

'Fuck's sake. Don't be long!' said Whizz, looking up briefly from the pass, where he was dressing some plates.

Some of the chefs cheered. 'Ey! New boy's got his first cut. That didn't take long!'

'Make sure that's all you're showing him, Jeanie!' one of them called.

'Drop dead, Aidy!' she replied.

Jeanette led Jack out of the kitchen, back through the fly screen and out into the staff corridor. They went into a room with a small basin, a toilet and a cupboard on the wall. She removed a box of blue plasters and opened it. Pulling a couple out, she told Jack to remove the napkin and hold out his thumb. He blushed and said, 'It's OK, I can do it myself. Thank you.' He removed the napkin, but it stuck to the flap, opening it up and making it bleed even more. It stung like hell and he grimaced. His thumb looked pale and unnatural where the nail had come off.

'Go on, let's see you then, brave boy,' said Jeanette, passing him a plaster. 'Let's even see you get it open!' He couldn't, and reddened further.

'See?' she said, taking the plaster back.

Jack stood there uselessly as she proceeded to stick not one, but three plasters around his tender thumb. It seemed to take an age. 'Jeanette, are you in there?' someone called from the corridor. Jack looked alarmed.

'Yes, I'm bandaging the new lad's thumb. He's cut himself.'

'Well bloody hurry up, will you, we're getting shafted out here!' That word again: 'shafted'.

'All right, I'm coming! I'll have to leave you to it. Stick all this stuff back in the cupboard, and put the wrappers in the bin.'

'Thank you,' Jack muttered.

'You can call me Jeanie, by the way.' She glanced at him. 'Most people do.'

After tidying up, Jack rushed back to the kitchen, still fretting that he'd messed everything up. The pots were piling up. 'Stick a rubber glove on and crack on with the pots,' said Aitch. 'I'll finish this sack. You won't be able to peel with all those plasters on.' Jack did as instructed, annoyed with himself – and also wondering how you were meant to keep up with all this work on your own.

Eventually the checks stopped coming on; it was around nine-thirty. Then there was a final flurry of clearing down: cue another influx of dirty pans and plastic tubs. By ten most of the chefs had gone. The kitchen was a lot bigger and quieter without them. Whizz was still around, popping in and out of the walk-in fridge and the stores with a clipboard. Then even he disappeared. Who was Jack supposed to speak to? How did he know if he'd got the job?

The moment Whizz disappeared, Aitch reached up to a shelf and turned on a grubby-looking radio cassette player with foil attached to its broken aerial. He pressed play and turned the music up loud, bobbing his head to it. 'Right, as soon as the music's on you know the two Russians are on their way!' he shouted.

'The two Russians?'

'Yep. Clearup and Fuckoffsky,' he grinned.

The clearing down jobs seemed to be endless; spraying and wiping surfaces, draining the potwash machine, taking bins out, sweeping and mopping. And all the time there was only one thing playing on Jack's mind. 'Who do I speak to about the job?' he finally said; he needed to know.

'Oh, Whizz'll still be here – in the office doing the ordering. Probably best grab him before he goes or he'll forget, knowing him. Once he's finished service there's only one thing on his mind – same as all of us, that's why they call him Whizz! Here, take this bin out and that one over there: you'll have to go past the office anyway, the skips are out the back. Don't look so worried. They call it a trial shift, but everyone comes back at least once; well, most people anyway. I'm still here, aren't I?'

Jack smiled. Aitch made him feel at ease, and he appreciated his help.

As instructed, he carried two bulging black bin liners out to the skips. The office was still lit up, and Whizz was on the phone. There was a bottle of cider next to him. After dumping the bin liners in the stinking skips, Jack loitered by the window. Whizz noticed him and held up a nicotine-stained finger. Then he put the phone down and beckoned Jack in. 'How did you find it, mate? Bit manic, I guess?' Jack smiled and nodded. 'You don't say much, do you? We'll have to knock that out of you if you want to get on here. Still, early days I suppose. Anyway, I'm not quite sure what Chef's got in mind – between you, me and the walls I think he's looking for someone full time to train up and replace Aidy, who's about as useful as a ladle with holes in it. So best you come in and speak to him. We'll need your details anyway – contact number, address, National Insurance number – so pop them in tomorrow morning. Chef's back then, and he'll have a chat with you. You've done well, though, except for peeling your thumb! Don't worry. We've all done it.'

Jack breathed a huge sigh of relief, thanked Whizz and returned to the kitchen. Aitch was sweeping the floor, or was supposed to be – he was on his knees performing an over-the-top guitar solo with the brush. Jack laughed.

By the time they had finished it was getting on for eleven o'clock. Jack couldn't believe it, Daisy would be wondering where he'd got to. They returned to the changing room to hang their aprons up. 'Do you want to come back to mine for a smoke?' Aitch said. This took Jack by surprise, and he didn't know what to say. 'Some of the others are – I've got my own caravan in the garden called The Love Shack. Jeanie'll be coming, I bet, she loves a smoke; and Tom – that's the guy with the ponytail – and his bird.'

So that explains it, thought Jack. 'No, I can't, thank you. I've to get back.'

'Strict parents, eh? You at college? I haven't seen you around.' As Aitch was talking, he picked up the magazine with the naked woman on the cover and nonchalantly began to flick through it. There were similar magazines underneath. Jack couldn't believe it, and went bright red again.

'Er, I've really got to go,' he said, and rushed to the door.

'Oh. Suit yourself then,' he heard Aitch say.

Jack made his way back through the courtyard and gate, down the alleyway and onto the street. He looked both ways, trying to get his bearings. To the left he could see an infinite darkness between the buildings, and could hear the unmistakable roar of the sea. He became aware of the fact that his heart was racing. He felt exhilarated at what he'd achieved. The kitchen. The whole thing. He'd done it! And it hadn't been so bad – he'd worked in a new environment, a scary one, and actually enjoyed it. And he'd been asked back!

Breaking into a jog, he headed for home, dodging couples and lampposts and drunks. He couldn't wait to tell Daisy; she'd be so proud of him.

*****

After successfully navigating his way back in the dark, Jack knocked on the door. When Daisy appeared a few moments later, he realised how much he'd missed her and gave her a big hug. 'Woah! Someone looks happy. How did it go? Phew! You stink!' she said, pulling away.

'It was amazing!' Jack stepped inside and followed Daisy upstairs. 'It was so busy, and there were loads of chefs, and the pots were never-ending, and me and Aitch had to peel a sack of potatoes – I cut my thumb!'

Daisy turned round. 'Oh, dear, that's not a good start. Who's Aitch?'

'He's a lad I work with, about our age. He's really nice. And my thumb wouldn't stop bleeding and Jeanie had to wrap it up and put plasters on it.'

'Who's Jeanie?' They were back in the kitchen now.

'Oh, one of the waitresses – she's really nice too.'

'Is she now?' said Daisy, studying his excited countenance. He was clearly buzzing. It made her feel strange. 'Sounds like you enjoyed it.'

'Yes, it was amazing!' he said again. 'And the best thing is I've got to go back in tomorrow to see Chef about more shifts – maybe full time!' He grabbed hold of her again and gave her a kiss, unable to help himself and bursting with pride.

'That's brilliant news. Well done! See, I told you you could do it... Now go and have a bath.' She pushed him away. 'I ran one for you earlier, but it's probably gone cold by now. And I opened the cider. I got bored of waiting.'

She watched Jack pull his T-shirt off as he went. She got that strange feeling inside again, as if she were casting her mind into the future; an awareness that maybe it was no longer going to be just the two of them, that she might have to share her Jack.

They stayed up late, really late. Talking and drinking and listening to music. All the cider was finished. And when they hit bed, drunk, they made love again. This was never in doubt.

CHAPTER 12

A Cappuccino of Wild Mushrooms

When they drew back the bedcovers the next morning there was blood on the sheets. Jack looked at Daisy in alarm. She pulled up her T-shirt to inspect her pants. Jack looked away at first, but then looked too. There was no sign of blood. Then he became aware of a vague throbbing from his thumb. It was stained with dried brown blood: he had reopened his wound during the night. They breathed a sigh of relief. 'We need to get you a plaster for that,' said Daisy. 'And it looks like we need to make our first trip to the launderette. Come on, help me get these off.'

As they stripped the bed together, Daisy said, 'I spoke to Mum last night. And Grandma.'

'Really?'

'I was bored, so I thought I'd try our new phone out. Don't worry, I didn't stay on long.'

'What did they say?'

'It wasn't the best really. Mum anyway. It started off OK – they were both relieved we'd got a phone in case of emergencies... Mum said I sounded funny, sort of tinny – must be the old phone – and Grandma couldn't hear a lot at all; I had to keep shouting. I had to lie to her about going to uni as well, which I hated. I wish Mum hadn't told her that. They both asked if there was anything I wanted for my birthday.'

'When is that?' asked Jack, struggling with the poppers on the duvet cover.

'The twenty-first, Monday. Bit of a boring day to have your eighteenth birthday on, but there you go! I told Mum we needed a vacuum cleaner, and that's when she got all upset, saying, "What has it come to when your daughter's asking for a Hoover for her eighteenth birthday? What kind of a present is that? We should be having a big party for you here at home!" And then she started getting upset about Dad, and that it would be the first birthday without him. That upset me as well – so in the end we were both crying! Ready?' They peeled the duvet cover back together, and Daisy dumped it on the floor. 'Then she was begging me to come home for my birthday – said she'd pay for the train, for you as well if that's what it took. I said that we couldn't because you'd got a job…'

'You didn't!' said Jack, stopping mid-tug at a pillowcase.

'Well, you have – sort of.'

'Yes, but not properly yet.'

'Well, you will have. I believe in you… She didn't offer to come out here, though. I think she was too stubborn to ask. And I didn't ask her: I want to get the place done up better first, more homely. I didn't tell her about the concert either – I thought it would upset her even more 'cause of Dad, and she didn't mention it. She's either forgotten or can't remember the date of it.'

Jack thought for a minute. 'You can go back, you know, if you want to for your birthday. I wouldn't mind.' He would, but was trying to do the right thing.

'No. Thanks, anyway. It's too soon. What's the point in moving out here only to go back a week or so later? It would only remind me of Dad anyway. And besides, I want to spend my birthday here with you.'

Jack was relieved. He couldn't imagine being in their new home without Daisy. 'You never know, I might be working on your birthday,' he said.

'God, I hadn't thought of that. I hope not. What are we going to do? Something special?'

'I don't know,' Jack shrugged. 'It's your birthday. You choose. We've still got to be careful with money, though, I guess.'

'We don't have to spend money to have a good time. I'll have a think. Right, this lot is going to have to go in a bin liner.'

*****

Daisy and Jack headed into town. Jack was in proud possession of his National Insurance card, and not so proud possession of a full bin liner of washing, slung over his shoulder; he felt like a coalman. Daisy was carrying another bag of dirty laundry, mainly underwear. They went to the launderette first, where Daisy tried to work out how to use the machines. In the end she had to ask for help. Jack hung back whilst she dealt with it all. 'More money,' she sighed as they left.

Next they headed for the restaurant, so Jack could speak to the head chef before service started. He was nervous about meeting him again. Daisy left him outside and said she was going to go and buy some plasters; she would meet him back there.

The restaurant wasn't open yet, so Jack used the staff entrance at the rear. It was strange being back, passing the office and the changing rooms. He felt like an interloper as he hesitantly peeled back the plastic strips to the kitchen. The smell and heat hit him straightaway. Aitch was the first to spot him. He was tilting what looked like a giant silver cauldron on an axle and pouring its contents – golden liquid and bones and vegetables – through a large colander into an equally large pan on the floor. 'Jackeroo!' he called. The other chefs looked up and nodded a 'hello' or an 'all right'. It made Jack glow with pleasure to be acknowledged, to be noticed for once.

'How's the thumb?' said Chef, who was chopping at the pass.

So he'd heard. Jack gulped and walked up to him, a bag of nerves. 'Erm, OK, thanks. I've come to bring my National Insurance card in, and my... my address and that. Whizz asked me to.'

'Chef,' said Chef.

'Chef,' said Jack. He imagined this was what going to school was like, addressing a teacher as 'Sir'.

'Yes, Whizz left me a note.' Whilst he spoke Chef reduced a lemon to a dozen or so slices in the blink of an eye. Then he dinged the bell, something he seemed to love doing. 'Won't be a minute.' He placed the lemon slices in a glass dish.

Alison, a girl with purple streaks in her hair who Jack remembered from the previous night, came in from the restaurant. She smiled. 'Hi, Jack.' Jack smiled back sheepishly, glowing inside again. 'Thanks, Chef.' She walked off with the dish.

'Right, come into the office. I've got five minutes,' said Chef.

Jack followed him out of the kitchen. Aitch grinned through a cloud of fragrant steam as he passed, still struggling with the giant cauldron. They entered the office.

'Have you got all your details?' said Chef, sitting down at the desk.

Jack handed his National Insurance card over and a piece of paper with his phone number and address on it. It seemed a significant step. Chef plucked a pen from the front of his tunic, and wrote down the number. He handed the card back. 'I'll give these to Hilary,' he said. 'She deals with the wages. You should get paid cash in hand for what you've done this week – they're good like that – then anything after that, providing we take you on, will be weekly on a Friday through the books – all above board. You'll have to work a week in hand, though, same as anyone who starts, so you won't get paid again for a couple of weeks.'

Jack nodded his head, trying to keep up. 'Regarding shifts ... where are we today? Thursday. If you come in tomorrow night and Saturday night – they're two of the busiest shifts – you can work alongside Aitch again, but I'll get you to look at the garnish section as well, veg and that – give Silly Bollocks a bit of competition. We'll see how you get on. After that, if all goes well, we'll have another chat. See about giving you some regular shifts. How does that sound?'

'Amazing,' said Jack. 'Thank you.'

'Good. Right, I'll see you tomorrow night. Five-thirty at the weekends.'

Jack left with his head spinning, excited but apprehensive at the prospect of working alongside the head chef as well as trying to keep an eye on two different areas of the kitchen. It all seemed too quick. To his dismay Daisy wasn't outside the restaurant when he returned to the street. Why did he always fear the worst? After about five minutes of spiralling anxiety he spotted her amongst the crowds. Relieved, he walked over to meet her. She was clutching a paper bag. 'It took me ages to find a Boots,' she said, holding it up. 'Plasters. How did it go?'

'OK, I think. I've got to go in tomorrow night and Saturday night.'

'That's great! See, I told you.'

'Yes, but it still doesn't mean I've got the job. It depends on how I do.'

'You'll be fine.'

'I don't know... They want me to look at the garnish section or something as well.'

'What's the garnish section?'

'I've no idea – something to do with vegetables.'

'Wow! They must have been impressed. Well, I hope you don't have to work Monday – I think I've found what I want to do on my birthday!' Daisy took his arm and led him down the street.

'Where are we going? The laundry place is that way.'

'I know, but I want to show you something.'

They headed towards the seafront and turned right at the pub on the corner. Daisy led Jack over to a sign on a lamppost. It read:

EAST RUNTON FUNFAIR.

CROMER'S PREMIER FAMILY FUNFAIR.

**TRADITIONAL AND MODERN RIDES FOR
ALL AGES.**

FROM THE 4th. TO THE 26th AUGUST.

ON THE A148 1½ MILES FROM CROMER.

BUSES EVERY HALF HOUR.'

'A funfair?' said Jack.

'Yes, I love them! I go to Loughborough fair every year. It's amazing.'

'There's one by the seafront, isn't there?'

'That's not a proper fair, it's just a few rides for kids. This one will be huge, I bet, with all the best rides – like, I dunno ... the orbiter and the meteorite. Trust me, you wouldn't get kids on those. I bet you've never even been on the dodgems, have you?'

'No. I've heard of them, though,' said Jack, a little put out.

'There you go then! You'll love them. Oh, can we, please? We can catch the bus there...'

'It could be fun, I suppose, and like I said before it's *your* birthday...'

'Oh, it will be. I just hope you're not working, otherwise we'll have to go on the Sunday instead.'

'Fingers crossed then, I guess,' said Jack, not sounding too sure: some of the rides sounded terrifying.

*****

Friday and Saturday night were a blur, a frantic, exhilarating blur. Service was madness – for Jack anyway. If he thought his first shift was busy, the weekends were cranked up to an entirely new level. The kitchen was a man down for a start: Aidy, or 'Silly Bollocks', hadn't shown up on Friday; maybe he'd got wind of his impending possible axing, or maybe he'd just had enough. This meant Whizz had to manage two sections – sauce and garnish – which, fortunately, were next to each other. The chef from pastry had to muck in as well.

Chef stood at the pass as usual – sweating and shouting and dinging his bell, rejecting anything that wasn't up to scratch. None of the chefs seemed in a panic, though; it was more a case of organised chaos. Jack didn't get to see much: he was mainly fetching and carrying and helping to keep up with the pots. The closest he got to doing any cooking was delivering a pan of hot mushroom soup to the pass. Chef told him to wait whilst he decanted it into four tiny cups. He showed Jack how to put a swirl of froth on the top of it, which Jack somehow managed to replicate, despite his shaking hands. The soup was then finished with a twist of black pepper and a sprinkling of finely chopped chives – a 'cappuccino of wild mushrooms' apparently. He was dismissed, smiling; he'd passed his first real test.

At the end of Saturday night Jack flew home, proudly clutching his pay packet – exhausted but buzzing, the glow of the flat door a beacon in the night. Despite the late hour, Daisy was waiting up for him, starved of his company. After a bath and a bit of supper, as he clutched his cider Jack filled her in on service. Daisy listened, enthralled but also a little envious. It sounded exciting, and Jack clearly enjoyed it. He was earning money and making friends; this much was clear: 'Oh, Aitch did this' and 'Tom said that – it was hilarious!' – or worse, 'Jeanie did this' and 'Alison said that'. Who were these girls? She wasn't used to sharing Jack with anyone else, especially girls. Meanwhile she was stuck there in the flat – 'lying low'.

Eventually she steered him with some difficulty to a conversation about music — *her* world. Jack was her student, and she loved playing him songs and introducing him to bands. At around three in the morning they were still sitting under a blanket on the sofa, surrounded by tapes, records, bottles, plates and cans. Finally they retired to bed to make love.

Sunday morning was a treat: Jack wasn't back at work until Tuesday. He could lie in and relax, knowing he'd got two days off and, more importantly, knowing he'd got more work ahead of him. Daisy was still asleep, facing away from him. He stared at the back of her neck as she slept, something he loved to do. Along with her hair, her neck was one of the first things that had so beguiled him as he sat on the bus behind her. And now, cuddling into her back, he had a front row seat. Every morning.

CHAPTER 13
Happy Birthday

'Happy Birthday,' Jack said excitedly, entering the bedroom clutching a tray.

He'd been up since the crack of dawn. Never having celebrated anyone's birthday before, he felt as if it was his own first proper birthday party.

Daisy groaned and stirred. Jack stood there awkwardly, not knowing where to put the tray. On it were boiled eggs, orange juice, tea and toast – and of course Daisy's birthday card; just as Anne used to do it for their so-called father. The card he'd bought from the newsagent's across the street; everything else he'd been into town for.

As he wasn't paid until Saturday night, Jack had spent all Sunday in abject frustration, his pay packet burning a hole in his pocket. Early Monday morning, as soon as the shops opened he was out of the door like a shot, a scrawled list in his hand. He'd told Daisy the previous evening not to get up until he came back into the bedroom. This had suited her; all the late nights were taking their toll.

'What time is it?' she croaked, shielding her eyes.

'Birthday time!' Jack said, grinning, unable to stand still. 'Come on, wake up!'

Daisy dragged herself up, smiling now, more at Jack's enthusiasm than anything: anyone would have thought it was *his* eighteenth birthday. 'I bet I look a state,' she said, smoothing her hair across her forehead.

'As fresh as a Daisy! Here.' He placed the tray on her lap. 'Happy birthday.' Jack kissed her on the cheek. It felt so good to say it to someone and mean it.

'Wow, I could get used to this.'

'Open your card,' he said, sitting down on the bed.

'Hold on! Let me have a sip of juice first, I'm thirsty.'

Jack watched her, bouncing up and down.

'Stop it!' she laughed. 'You're making me spill it.' She picked up the card. 'Where did you get all this stuff from? It must have cost a fortune.'

'Not at all. From the shops in town – the tray was from a charity shop. Come on, hurry up and open your card!' There were presents waiting in the lounge.

'OK!' She ripped open the envelope, inspected the front of the card and smiled, then opened it. Inside was Jack's unfamiliar, spidery handwriting. She did her best to read it out loud. 'To Daisy… Happy Birthday… Love from Jack. Kiss. Kiss.' She stared at it for a while in silence, misty-eyed.

'What's wrong?' said Jack, mortified.

'Nothing. I just don't think you've ever written anything to me before, not properly – it's special, that's all.' She leant forward to hug him, feeling happy and sad.

'Sorry it's not very good.'

'It's perfect.'

'Back in a minute!' Jack dashed out of the room.

When he returned a few moments later, he was clutching two parcels wrapped in shiny purple paper with silver stars on it, and two more cards. Daisy looked up from dipping toast into her egg. 'You shouldn't have!'

'Why not? I'm earning money again.' He sat down on the bed again, slopping tea everywhere. 'Sorry!'

'Let me finish at least one egg!' she said, taking the presents from him. 'It seems a shame to waste them.'

Daisy carried on dipping soldiers as she tried to open a card with her other hand. 'No guessing who these are from – Mum and Grandma are the only two people who know our address, unless Mum's told anyone else.' She opened her mum's first. Inside was fifty pounds in notes. More significant, to Daisy anyhow, was the message: '*Love from Mum and Lily. We miss you.x*.'

Just 'Mum and Lily'; the first card like that. It took Daisy by surprise and she began to well up again. 'Jesus, what's wrong with me this morning? I'm an emotional wreck!' She dabbed at her eyes. 'Can you get me some tissue, please?'

'Sure.' He left the room again, a little confused at all this sadness on a birthday morning.

When he returned Daisy had put her breakfast tray to one side and was still staring at the card. 'Here,' he said, passing her some loo roll.

'Thanks.' She wiped her eyes, then took a deep breath. 'Sorry. I didn't mean to spoil everything.'

'Don't worry. It's fine.' Jack wanted to prompt her to open her grandma's card, so she could get on with his presents, but he knew he had to be patient.

Eventually she opened the card. Her eyebrows rose. She bit her lower lip and looked at Jack. Plucking out a cheque, she slowly turned it round to face him. He took a sharp intake of breath. 'A hundred pounds! Daisy, we're rich!'

'It's too much,' she said. Then she pulled out one of her grandma's trademark notes: '*Dear Daisy, Glad to hear you're settling in by the coast. I'm envious! Please use this money as you see fit. You're only eighteen once! Mum said you'll have to catch the bus to university. Car? Love, Grandma. x. P.S. let me know you received it safely.*'

A hundred and fifty pounds to add to the money that they had left. Daisy's mind whirled with the possibilities – there was so much they needed. She was lost in thought for a moment, and forgot Jack's presents until he nudged her with a tube-shaped parcel.

'Sorry... Now, I wonder what this is?'

'What? Do you know?'

'Well, I'm guessing a poster – unless you've wrapped up a tube of wrapping paper!'

She began to tug at some of the Sellotape strips he'd haphazardly stuck at vertical intervals. 'Where did you even get Sellotape from?' she said.

'Woolworths. I looked at it as an investment.'

After unpicking the last strip of tape, Daisy unrolled a black and white poster. Instantly she knew what it was, and her eyes lit up. She'd been wanting it for ages – a *Boys Don't Cry* poster by The Cure; iconic, and quite apt really, considering all the crying she'd been doing this morning. 'Wow. Thank you. How did you know I wanted this?'

'I didn't,' he beamed. 'I just knew you liked the band, and I knew you hadn't got it.'

'Where did you get it from? I've been looking for one for ages.'

'Woolworths again!'

'This picture always reminds me of you actually – the way he looks from behind.'

'Really?'

'Before you got your hair chopped, anyway.'

'Come on, open your other present,' Jack said impatiently. This giving presents thing was addictive.

'Now I'm not sure what this is, but I'm guessing a book,' she said, picking it up.

'Maybe,' said Jack, bouncing on the bed again.

Daisy opened the parcel. Inside was *The Return of the King* – the last instalment of the *Lord of the Rings* trilogy – a second-hand copy, but in really good nick. Now this Jack had known she'd wanted; she'd mentioned it when they were unpacking. She'd already read the whole book – her dad's copy – but only had the first two volumes herself. 'Oh, thank you. That's really thoughtful.' She leant forward and gave him a kiss. Jack beamed again, pleased with himself. 'Where did you get it, the second-hand place near the seafront?'

Jack nodded. 'Yes. It was amazing. I wished I had more time in there – I wanted to look for some of my books that I... you know...' It was his turn to look sad.

'Oh, we will. We've got all the time in the world – and money now. Wow! I'm such a lucky girl,' Daisy said, looking around her. And she meant it. For some reason, despite the lingering absence of her father, it felt like the best birthday ever: surrounded by cards, wrapping paper, presents and more money than she knew what to do with; the sound of the gulls outside and another sunny day painting its announcement across the room; and the fair to look forward to. 'Hey, I've thought of something we can do today – and you've got to say yes, you've got to!'

'What?' Jack was getting the impression he wasn't going to like the idea.

'Swim in the sea! I can't believe we haven't done it yet. And it looks like a nice day again.'

'Oh, I don't know about that.' It was all the people that put him off, all of them watching him – a public display. Swimming at Stanford Hall had been bad enough, but on a beach in a pair of shorts in full view of the whole world...

'Oh, we've got to! Pleeease.'

'But I haven't got any shorts, remember.'

'Oh, you're not trying that one again. We'll buy you some – some that fit properly this time.'

Jack groaned.

'It *is* my birthday... I'll make it worth your while...' She leant forward to kiss him.

Just then, the phone rang from the lounge – for the first time. Its lovely old-fashioned ring was so loud it startled them both. 'I bet that'll be Mum!' said Daisy, shooting out of bed. Jack watched her dash off, a vision of creamy limbs and jiggling flesh in prawn-pink pants. He groaned again.

Full of high spirits, Daisy picked up the phone. 'Hello,' she said breathlessly into the receiver. But the voice that answered wasn't the one she'd been expecting.

Back in the bedroom Jack half-listened as he surveyed the birthday mess strewn across the bed. It was hard to make out what Daisy was saying, but it didn't sound like a light-hearted birthday conversation. He hoped nothing had happened to her mum or grandma: they didn't need anything like that, especially not today. The conversation stopped and Daisy's head appeared round the door. 'Jack, it's for you.'

'For me?' Who'd be calling him? The restaurant?

'It's Haslam.' Jack had the same sinking feeling that Daisy had experienced when she'd heard the detective's voice, like a pin being stuck in a birthday balloon. He immediately felt as if he'd done something wrong. It wasn't that either of them disliked him – look what he'd done for them – but he was a reminder of a world and a past they wanted to forget.

'What does he want?'

'Just checking up, I guess. Or so he said, but I got the sense there was something more. It's you he wants to talk to anyway.' Jack looked pensive and got up. What if Haslam wanted to call him back for questioning? 'It's nothing serious, I'll bet,' Daisy said, sensing his unease. She hadn't seen that look on his face for ages: he was so relaxed now, a different person, and she resented the change in him.

'Why did he have to phone today?' Jack said as he passed her.

He picked up the receiver with trepidation. 'Hello.'

'Hello, Jack Gardner.' The infiltration into their world was exacerbated tenfold by the sound of his voice, and Jack's head swam. More flashbacks: the maddening confines of that cell block, the interrogation room, the tape recorder, not knowing if he was ever going to see Daisy again. 'How are you, young man? I thought I'd give you a quick call and see how you're settling in...' The familiar East Midlands voice, so different to the accent in Norfolk.

Unused to phones, Jack didn't answer, forgetting that he had to speak.

'It's been a week or so,' the detective added, and laughed awkwardly, too loudly.

'I'm fine, thank you,' Jack finally said.

'Good, good.' Haslam sounded relieved. 'How's the flat? Everything working all right? No problems?'

'No, it's fine. A bit cold, but fine.'

'Hmm. Those storage heaters don't give out much heat – not that you should need 'em yet anyway. It's summer. Need to keep your costs down... And how's that young lady of yours? You looking after her?'

'Er, yes. I suppose.' Haslam laughed awkwardly again. It was starting to seem like how Jack imagined a conversation with a well-meaning but slightly annoying distant uncle.

'No other problems then? You both keeping your heads down? Anything else you want to tell me?'

Jack was going to mention his job, but decided against it. It would only prolong the conversation. His mind was already drifting back to the image of Daisy's buttocks squashed into her pants underneath that T-shirt. She'd just come into the room, fully dressed now. Her hair had grown enough that she could tuck a little of it behind an ear to listen as she settled on the sofa. 'No, everything's fine.' He rolled his eyes at Daisy.

'Good, good. All's fine here too. Things are quietening down... The papers are full of that boat tragedy yesterday. Dreadful business...' There was a pause. 'You've seen the news?'

'Er, no.'

'It was in London. Fifty-odd people drowned...'

175

'Oh, right.' Jack looked at Daisy again. Why was Haslam telling him this stuff?

'Anyway … whilst I've got you, there are a couple of things I want to run by you.' *Ah, here we go*, thought Jack. 'Firstly, and I hope you don't mind talking about this – I don't want to reopen old wounds or anything – but at some point you're going to have to decide what you want us to do with the remains…'

'Remains?'

'Yes, your family. All three of them. When they finally get signed off, of course.'

Jesus. This was something Jack hadn't thought about. He didn't give a damn what happened to his father, and he didn't really want to think about the other two either. He'd said his goodbyes and had his funeral when he'd set fire to them.

'I mean, we have a facility we use … in certain cases … where we can get them cremated for you. No ceremony. No fuss. Nothing like that. We just hand the ashes over.'

'The ashes?' Daisy was listening intently now, starting to cotton on.

'Yes. There's a charge, though. Normally.'

'A charge?'

'Yes. It's not free, I'm afraid.'

'Well, I've got money. I've got over a thousand pounds – if only I could have it back.'

'That money is currently evidence – but it does bring me on to my next point. I've been to see your supposed former employer, Mr Peasgood. And I hate to say it, Jack, but he's sticking by his story: he's adamant he doesn't know you from Adam. Neither does anyone else there.'

'What, you went to the factory?' Jack couldn't believe it.

'Yes, and everything seems above board. I chatted with Mr Peasgood in his office, then he gave me a tour of the place. All very professional. I even spoke to a couple of workers on the floor…'

'They're lying! They're all lying. They never liked me, any of them. They never even spoke to me. It's my money and I want it back!'

'So you keep saying, but it puts me in a difficult position. Who do I believe? Are you *sure* there's nothing else you want to tell me? About the money, for instance? I mean, throw me a bone here…'

Daisy was trying to mouth something to Jack, but he couldn't make it out whilst he tried to listen to Haslam at the same time.

'What?' he said to her.

'I said, are you sure…' said Haslam.

'Sorry. Hold on,' said Jack. And then to Daisy, 'What?'

'Put your hand over the mouthpiece,' Daisy hissed. Jack did as she said. 'Say you can describe Peasgood. You can describe the whole factory. Tell him.'

Jack hadn't thought of this, and he took his hand off the mouthpiece to speak into it. 'I can prove it. I can describe Peasgood, I can describe the whole factory. I worked there for five months or so. Ask Daisy. She'll tell you!'

'I already have, remember. You know it's a crime to lie to the police, both of you. And what you're accusing this man of – an upstanding and reputable businessman – lying to the police himself, illegal workers, tax evasion… This is serious stuff, Jack… OK, go on then,' Haslam sighed. 'Describe him to me.'

Jack gave a detailed description of Peasgood: his red complexion, his white hair, beaky nose and gnarly hands, his Scottish accent. He even gave a brief description of the factory. The detective appeared to take it all in his stride. 'And how do I know he's not a distant relative of yours or your father's, a family friend you've fallen out with or got it in for?'

'Family friend? We didn't have any family friends! Why are you believing him and not me?'

'Because he's got too much to lose. You've got nothing to lose.'

'Only a thousand pounds!'

'Look, this is going nowhere.' Haslam sighed again. 'I don't want to have to bring you in again, Jack, I really don't. But at some point you're going to have to come up with a different story – or one of you is. Or somewhere down the line someone's going to find himself in serious trouble. Have a think about that, and also about what you want us to do with those remains. There's no rush for now; let's just say to be continued… I'll call again in a couple of weeks or so. I'm glad you've settled in OK, and Daisy. Keep on keeping your heads down, the both of you – for the time being at least. Goodbye, Jack.'

The detective hung up, more confused than ever about who was telling the truth.

*****

After much palaver (and a lengthy phone call from Daisy's mum, who also wanted to discuss the boat tragedy), Jack stood at the edge of the sea in his new navy swim shorts and a T-shirt that he refused to take off. Daisy, already in the water, splashed him as she tried to entice him to join her. But it was no use: she couldn't get him to venture any further than knee deep. *Jaws* had kind of ruined swimming in the sea for Jack: he didn't mind looking at it – or at Daisy in her black bikini – but he couldn't bring himself to submerge himself. Things kept brushing against his ankles, making him jump. Sharks? Jellyfish? No, just seaweed. So he stood, shivering, watching her swim and frolic about, at the same time keeping a beady eye out for dark shapes, or worse a sinister fin, to emerge from the foam and swell behind her.

Eventually he left her to it, retreating to their towels and bags. It was a welcome relief: he felt warm again, and the sun turned the wet sand sticking to his feet and ankles to fine grains. It was taking a while for him to shake off that phone call. His mind kept drifting back to it: the injustice of it all and the questions Haslam had asked. He didn't want to think about any of it. He just wanted his money back.

After ten minutes or so, Daisy rejoined him, shiny, dripping and giddy from the sea. Jack looked around to see if anyone else was looking at her, a little perturbed as usual at her being half-naked in public. Surely it made everyone else feel how he felt, looking at her? He quickly passed her a towel. 'God, that was amazing!' she said. 'So refreshing. You should have joined me!'

'Umm, I don't know... You can't see what's under the water.'

'There aren't any bloody sharks in Norfolk!' she said, towelling herself off. Jack looked glum. 'You OK?'

'Yes, just, sit down,' he said, patting the towel next to him.

They both looked out to sea for a while. Then Daisy said unexpectedly, 'You know what I'd really like to buy for my birthday?'

'No. What?'

'I've been thinking about it for a while, and being here today, but more because of seeing your writing in that card... You know what occurred to me?'

Jack shrugged, intrigued but with no idea what she was talking about.

'I've not got a single photograph of you, nor you of me – nor any of us together. I don't know why it's never really occurred to me before. There was just so much other stuff going on, I guess...' Daisy's voice trailed off, and they continued to look out to sea: at the boats, the pale bodies striped with sunburn, the colourful floats and dinghies. They'd both been through so much that summer. Stuff that neither of them could have envisaged, stuff that had consumed them. And yet here they were, still together.

'So, you want to buy a camera?' Jack said finally. He turned it over in his head, glad for something new to distract him. He'd never had his photo taken. Ever. What would he look like? Like he did in the mirror?

'Yes. It'd be fun, wouldn't it? And when will I ever have the money again? Cameras aren't cheap, not for a proper one. And it could come in handy if I go back to college. I wouldn't mind doing something like photography.'

'It's your money,' Jack said, putting his arm round Daisy. A large and inconsiderate cloud had covered up the sun and she was shivering slightly. 'You can do whatever you like.'

So it was decided. With Daisy still drying off, they found a camera shop. The store owner, a sincere elderly gentleman with shaky hands, talked Daisy into going for a good quality second-hand camera, rather than a new one: in his opinion, what with her being a novice she didn't need anything with all the modern 'bells and whistles', and spending anything more than a hundred pounds would be a waste of money. The camera cost eighty-five pounds – still a considerable sum. She put down a ten pound deposit, and Jack, not Daisy, gave the man his name and their phone number. Daisy explained they had to wait for a birthday cheque to clear before they could pay the rest.

They returned to the flat to get changed, dump their things and to collect Grandma's birthday cheque, so that they could pay it in at the bank. Back in town, Jack had his first go in the arcades, and unsurprisingly left empty-handed. And Daisy finally had the ice cream she'd been hankering after; it took her an age to decide what flavour to have. They also finally bought that second-hand vacuum cleaner, and lugged it back to the flat. Then they spent the rest of the afternoon in bed (daytime love-making was becoming a necessity). Afterwards, whilst polishing off a bottle of wine that was meant for the evening, Daisy came up with the hare-brained and drunken plan that the next summer they should tour the music festivals – Glastonbury and Reading and suchlike – with their own ice cream van. They'd make the ice cream themselves: weird and wonderful flavours, such as white chocolate with cranberry ripple, lemon and ginger, and liquorice. 'Everybody loves ice cream!' she said. 'We'd make a killing!'

Jack wasn't so sure. He could take or leave ice cream.

CHAPTER 14

Too Long at the Fair

They were meant to wait for darkness to fall before setting off to the fair, as according to Daisy funfairs only really came alive when it was dark. But running out of alcohol propelled them out the front door early and into a night full of treasure that was waiting to be plundered. Their destination was the pub on the corner near the seafront, where they planned on having a pint or two before catching the bus. Hand in hand they strolled, both of them in high spirits, the spectre of the morning's phone call long gone.

They got to the seafront just as the sun was setting. And what a sunset it was. They'd caught glimpses of it through the gaps in the buildings as they walked. Instead of going straight into the pub, they headed on to the promenade to take it all in. Off to the west, the sun was a shimmering, liquid-gold disc, a lozenge melting into the sea. Syrupy rivulets like veins of fire surrounded it, as if the sun's very mass was dissolving before their eyes, turning to flaming lava. And as it disappeared, taking the light with it, they turned to look at each other in wonder as they leaned on the promenade wall. 'I wish I had my camera already,' Daisy said wistfully.

'Yes,' said Jack. 'Come on, let's go and get that pint.'

The pint helped to quell his nerves, and they were both excited when the bus arrived to whisk them to their destination. It was strange to be staring out of the window at the dark of a new and unexplored landscape, seeing the coast come and go, the sea and the cliffs and the haunting trees, all silhouetted against the rusty sky. The moon was up, and its many-splintered reflection glistened like a flock of silver birds on the shifting expanse of water. Its size and beauty humbled them both, sobered them a little.

Cromer was soon left behind them, and a couple of stops came and went. Before long it was time to get off, with the cry 'Next stop fair!' from the bus driver. Quite a few people stood up. Jack gulped as his nerves returned. Daisy squeezed his hand, smiling, full of nervous anticipation herself.

The bus pulled to a halt and they disembarked. Immediately they heard the distant thump of music and saw the flashing glow of coloured lights in the sky: a man-made Aurora Borealis with a disco soundtrack.

Jack and Daisy followed the throng, adults and youngsters alike, children holding their parents' hands, everyone chattering. After a minute or so, they all veered off to the left, down a muddy track that led to a field. Up ahead, through an open gate, they saw the flashing lights properly for the first time. The music was louder and they heard screams. An amplified voice was stirring the punters up, egging them on.

The fair was much bigger than Jack had expected; it seemed to be a mini village of canvas-topped stalls, tents, rides and rides ... some of them huge. And as for the noise, it took some getting used to. Jack could feel the pulse and beat of the music in his chest and throat.

He stopped and stared for a while in wonder. There was one particular ride that rose high above most of the others. People were standing in a circular cage, being spun round at a sickening speed. They were all facing each other and screaming. The cage slowly tilted until they were almost spinning vertically, defying gravity and any modicum of good sense. It looked terrifying. The more it tilted, the louder they screamed. How anyone was still standing was anybody's guess. Daisy saw him looking. 'Do you want to go on it?'

'Huh! Not a chance!'

'Come on. Let's see what else there is.' She took his hand.

Each stall was omitting its own distinctive aroma. The tang of fried onions filled the air from burger and hot dog stalls. Bags of fudge and coloured sweets dangled from awnings, accompanied by the sweet and savoury smell of frying doughnuts. 'Oh! I've got to have some candy floss!' said Daisy. They waited as a man, clearly used to being watched, expertly spun a stick over a hole in a buzzing metal cylinder. Slowly but surely, thin threads of cotton candy, like electrodes, began to attach themselves to the stick. He poured in more pink gloop and the pale rose-coloured bush got bigger and bigger; he manipulated it against the sides of the cylinder to shape it. It was one of the most amazing things Jack had ever seen. Then it was done, and the man handed it over. Daisy paid, smiling. 'Here, try some!' she said. The floss was sticky, sickly sweet, and quickly melted to nothing in Jack's mouth. He wasn't a fan.

They moved on, Daisy absentmindedly picking at her candy floss like a child, whilst Jack's senses were bombarded. Along with the music, there were screams, bells and whistles, carnival music from the carousel, children's happy, flushed faces, the pneumatic drill sound and stink of generators and the startling crack of pellet guns from the shooting ranges. The stalls were endless – hook a duck, the coconut shy, all of them bursting with prizes: huge, fluffy, stuffed animals, balloons and inflatable dinosaurs, some of these attached to children's prams, their parents passing in a blur of perfume and cigarette smoke.

'So,' said Daisy, fighting to be heard, 'what are we going to go on first?' Her face was lit up by the coloured lights.

'I don't know. Some of the stalls look like fun.'

'Oh, we can do them later. I want to go on a ride!'

'Well, something on the ground then.' They'd just passed a big wheel, where all Jack could see were legs and shoes, dangling from rickety tin tubs, swaying precariously in the starry sky. Why would you want to do that? It was so unnatural; it made his stomach spin just looking at it.

'I know. We'll start with the dodgems! That'll break you in nicely,' said Daisy.

She insisted they went in different cars so they could bump into each other. Jack couldn't get the hang of it, and spent most of his time stuck or going the wrong way, much to Daisy's amusement but not that of the ride operators – they kept having to take over to steer him out of trouble as he was causing traffic jams. The more he did this, the more people deliberately bumped into him – causing his neck to violently snap forwards. And this was meant to be fun? He felt traumatised! And just when he was getting the hang of it, and had accomplished a couple of free circuits with the breeze blowing in his hair, it was over. They both stumbled away, Jack realising that he'd enjoyed it in the end – the exhilaration, the shower of sparks from the ceiling, the pounding music and the electronic buzzing sound. He could do it again.

'What next?' Daisy said, out of breath.

'How about the carousel? The horse thing?'

'That's for children! You can't go on that!'

'Well, it looks, you know, safe.'

'What about the sizzler?'

'What's the sizzler?'

'I'll show you.'

It took them a while to find it. And when they did, and Jack saw the speed and heard the screams, he said, 'No way!'

'Oh, come on: it's one of my favourites.' She pulled her puppy-dog face.

'Sorry, Daisy. Not this time. Look at it! Look at the people's faces! I'd throw up.'

'Spoilsport.'

'You go on. I'll watch.'

'No. I'd have to sit with some stranger!'

'Maybe later, then. I've got to build myself up first.'

'I know! What about the ghost train? That doesn't go very fast. It's more for children really as well. Come on!' And she dragged him through the crowds again.

They paid their money and sat in a little carriage on a track. Suddenly it lurched forwards, propelling them towards a ribboned curtain similar to the fly screen at work, and into the unknown. Everything went pitch black, and suddenly their carriage speeded up. Jack wasn't expecting it; his stomach went funny and he let out a shriek. Then they slowed down again. Things hit his face, skeletons popped out at him, something touched his shoulder, lights flashed on and off. There was ghoulish laughter, creaking doors, and buzzes and shrieks. In the brief moments when he could see properly he felt as if he was in one of those runaway mine carts in *Indiana Jones and the Temple of Doom*. Then they went round a corner: everything went dark and the carriage got faster again. Suddenly it hit a dip and Jack's stomach seemed to lurch into his mouth. He screamed in horror and Daisy howled with laughter; he could have killed her. And then just as suddenly the ride slowed, they hit another fly screen and they were back outside in the coloured light.

Daisy couldn't stop laughing. Jack's face was a picture, even his hair seemed to be standing on end, like in a cartoon. 'I hate you!' he said. 'You tricked me. I'll never trust you again!'

'Oh, come on. It wasn't that bad!' she cried, as they clambered out and down the steps. 'Don't you love me anymore?'

'No, I hate you!' But he realised he was smiling himself, and as with the dodgems there was part of him that had actually enjoyed it. He'd felt alive – on edge and terrified, but alive.

They were still laughing and getting their breath back when a voice surprised them. 'Hey! Jackeroo! Fancy seein' you here!' They both looked up. It was Tom, the waiter. He was with Alison, his girlfriend with the purple hair, and Jeanie. 'How's it going, man?' He gave Jack an unorthodox handshake, which Jack had no idea how to return.

'Fine, thanks,' he said, blushing, and not knowing what else to say. They all looked at each other for a second, awkwardly.

It was strange seeing them all out of work, especially in their normal clothes. Tom had his hair down and was wearing a long coat and black drainpipes. He was smoking a funny smelling rolled up cigarette. Alison was dressed in black too; she was wearing a Sisters of Mercy T-shirt, and it looked as if she'd dyed her hair a different shade, unless it was just the fairground lights.

Jeanie was dressed more fashionably in a jacket, a cropped vest that revealed her stomach, jeans and trainers. 'You didn't tell us you had a girlfriend, Jack,' she said, offering what appeared to Daisy to be a superficial smile. The girls looked each other up and down.

Jack blushed again. 'Erm, no. I mean, yes...this is Daisy.' *Shit!* he thought. He'd said her name. Too late now.

'Hi, Daisy!' they all said. Daisy said 'hello' back, but was feeling shy.

'I like your hair,' said Alison. 'I wish I was brave enough to have it that short.' Daisy smiled thanks.

'So, how long you been here?' said Tom. Jack and Daisy looked at each other. 'At the fair, I mean,' he added.

They both breathed inward sighs of relief. 'Not long, we've just got here,' said Jack.

'What've you been on? Anything good?' said Alison.

'Not really... Like I said, we've just got here.'

'You ought to try the orbiter – it's awesome!' said Jeanie.

'Yes, it's wicked, man,' said Tom, blowing out smoke.

Jack smiled and nodded. Then no one spoke again.

'Right, well, catch you later, Jack.' Tom gave Jack another one of those handshakes. 'When you in next?'

'Er, tomorrow, I think. Yes, Tuesday.'

'Ah, me too. I'll see you then, dude.' Tom put his arm round Alison.

'See you at work, Jack,' said Jeanie.

'Bye, Daisy!' Alison called over her shoulder, as they headed off. 'Nice to meet you!'

'Yes, you too.'

Jack looked at Daisy, shrugged and smiled. Despite giving away her name, he felt good, really good. For the first time in his life he had friends; people who recognised him, acknowledged him and made him feel wanted.

'So, who's the skinny blonde then?' said Daisy.

'Eh?' said Jack.

'*You ought to try the orbiter – it's awesome!*' Daisy mimicked in a silly voice.

'Oh, that's Jeanie.'

'The one who bandaged your thumb up, right?'

'Er … yes. Why?'

'No reason. Come on, Mr Naive.' Daisy began to walk off and Jack trotted after her. He really didn't understand girls sometimes. When he caught up with her, she said, 'You didn't tell your new friends you had a girlfriend?'

'Well, no. We're meant to be lying low, aren't we? Especially you.'

This was true, Daisy supposed. 'You didn't tell me two of them were goths either.'

'What's a goth?' said Jack, over the music.

'Someone who dresses in black and dyes their hair – wears black nail varnish and stuff. The music's cool, Sisters of Mercy and that.'

'Oh, right.'

'You know he was smoking marijuana as well, don't you?'

'Who, Tom?'

'Yes, the guy with the long hair who called you "Jackeroo".'

'What's marijuana?'

'Oh, never mind!' Daisy sighed.

They stopped briefly to devour a hotdog each, but afterwards, despite her best efforts, Daisy couldn't get Jack to go on any of the scarier rides. So they stuck to the stalls for a while – the hoopla, the coconut shy – frittering away their money. But they did manage to get a prize in the end; Daisy chose a fluffy stuffed tiger, as she missed Sookie, the family cat. Next they passed an intriguing looking wigwam with a sign above its entrance that read 'Rosalina's Palmists'. 'Hey! A fortune teller, let's get our palms read!' cried Daisy.

'No. It might be bad.' Jack pulled her away.

'Why would it be bad?'

Jack didn't answer. His attention had been piqued by some risqué and colourful artwork on the next attraction. It was a rodeo ride. Huge scantily clad cowgirls looked down at them, with glossy lips and bursting cleavages in halter-neck tops, their prominent nipples depicted in eye-popping detail. There was loud square-dance music playing, and people were making fools out of themselves, paying to take it in turns to be thrown off a mechanical bull. Daisy looked at Jack.

'Forget it!' he said.

They'd pretty much done the rounds by this time, and Daisy was feeling a little put out that she'd not been on any proper rides. All she had to show for the night (and her money) was a stuffed tiger and a ketchup stain on her jacket. But then, looking down the last row of attractions, something bright caught her eye – the waltzer. She'd always loved and loathed this in equal measure; the way it made her stomach feel made her giggle uncontrollably. 'I can't believe I forgot it. Come on!'

Jack moaned. 'That? I'm not going on it if it goes in the air.'

'It doesn't,' she laughed, pulling him along, 'so you've got no excuse.'

They stood and watched for a few minutes; the ride was in full swing. A skinny tattooed man with a roll up dangling from his mouth was negotiating the undulating boards between the carriages with ease, spinning random carriages at will; he was bathed in a red glow, as if on stage. There were children on the ride, Jack noted, all screaming and laughing – so it couldn't be that bad. And at least the carriages were fixed firmly to the ground. Strange Wurlitzer music was playing, similar to the carousel. A young couple chomping on toffee apples came to stand near them, waiting their turn. Eventually the ride began to slow down, but not to a standstill. People clambered off, a little unsteady on their feet, as if they were trying to disembark from a moving roundabout in a park. Some of them were a tad green around the gills, others were still laughing.

Jack and Daisy took their places with everyone else. The man locked them in with a metal bar that dug a little uncomfortably into Jack's lap, and took their money. A silver medallion swung from his open-shirted hairy chest as he leant forward to pay them their change. The ride began to slowly rotate again, and their carriage began to turn naturally on its pivot, bobbing gently up and down as if on waves. Her stuffed toy in her lap, Daisy smiled at Jack and he smiled back. It was all quite pleasant for a while. Then they had their first spin...

It wasn't even a big one. The man just gave their carriage a one-handed tug of encouragement before moving on. But straightaway the centrifugal force kicked in, making Jack's stomach go into spasm. He gripped the bar tighter. Daisy let out a whoop, clearly enjoying the feeling. Thankfully it didn't last long, and their carriage returned to normal. But then the man did it again, harder, and that sickening feeling, more intense this time, seemed to go on forever. Daisy let out another squeal, and couldn't stop laughing. Jack's smile turned to a grimace. What had he let himself in for? And why was the man picking on them – almost singling them out?

And then there he was again, legs straddled, leaning into them, blowing cigarette smoke in their faces, using both of his tattooed arms this time. To make matters worse, the whole ride seemed to be faster and the maddening music seemed to be louder. Instead of bobbing gently on a calm sea, it was like negotiating choppy waters on a pirate ship to hell. The hungry, restless boards were bouncing and creaking up and down. Jack could see through the cracks to the mechanism and grinding cogs; he could smell the grease, the lacquer of the painted slats. Everything else rushed by in a blur. He felt nauseous, bilious; he was going to throw up. He burped as the hotdog repeated on him. It was how he'd felt that night, drunk, at the inn. He turned yellow, grey, then white. He was going to pass out...

Daisy noticed his face and stopped laughing. But the man spun them again. Laughing sadistically. '*No, stop!*' she cried. It wasn't fun anymore. 'Jack!' But he was gone, passed out. Her palms were sweating. She was clammy. But still the carriage wouldn't stop spinning and the ride wouldn't end. There was nothing she could do but close her eyes and sit it out, clutching on to her tiger and to Jack's moist hand...

When it was finally over, Daisy shook Jack, desperately worried. 'Wake up!' He came to, his head lolling, no idea where he was. The ride was still moving slowly and he groaned.

'Aagh, I think I'm going to be sick.'

Daisy panicked and tried to lift up the bar, but it seemed to be stuck. The man came over and did it for them, still laughing. Daisy gave him a filthy look. She managed to help Jack up and they both stumbled off the ride. Again, the feeling of wanting to be sick gripped him. It came in waves. He hated being sick, and tried to fight it.

'Just keep walking,' he said, groggily.

They passed stalls in the dark, trying to make for the exit. Everything that had seemed exhilarating when they arrived at the fair now seemed hideous. The strobe lights, the infernal racket, the screams and laughter, the depressing beady-eyed goldfish in bags, the sickly sweet cloying smells from the doughnut stalls, the dirty cooking oil. Jack just made it past the last tent and into the dark, then succumbed. The contents of his stomach shot out onto the grass — mainly hotdog and onions. Daisy felt awful, and put her hand on his back. 'Happy birthday,' he mumbled.

CHAPTER 15
The Love Shack

As Jack settled into his new job, the working week fell into some sort of routine. Despite waking up late, they always found time for sex and a hurried breakfast before Jack's daytime shift. Daisy usually walked into town with him, kissed him goodbye, then trawled the second-hand shops for bargains, mainly clothes. It had turned a little too cool to sit on the beach, but she still wandered down there to try out her new camera, her new plaything. She was proud of Jack, but envious: she was getting bored.

Afternoons consisted mostly of Jack filling her in on his shift. Then it was time for dinner prepared by Daisy and for Jack to get back to work. Daisy already begrudged this: she missed him most in the evenings, when she got most bored – and cold. Jack returned after work with his hair and skin smelling of food. After his bath they finally relaxed. Cue another late night – music, alcohol and sex.

With the flat to herself, almost every day Daisy had taken to doing a Jane Fonda workout video of her mum's that she had brought with her. She was becoming a little conscious of her weight; those few extra pounds she had put on whilst pregnant seemed to have stuck. Being on the pill didn't help – it said so on the packet. Neither did the boredom eating. Unlike

Jack she seemed to be constantly hungry, forever picking. She wanted to look skinny like Edie (her current style guru) in *Ciao! Manhattan*.

Daisy had bought a Velvet Underground and Nico LP – the classic album with the Andy Warhol banana on the front – when she discovered a Saturday market in the Town Hall that sold records, tapes and books. The album, which featured the song 'Femme Fatale', written about Edie, blew her away. She was instantly hooked, and it provided a soundtrack to her days and nights as she dressed up and experimented with her new image, taking self-portraits with the self-timer feature on her camera. She could be who she wanted to be, and heavy, coal-black eye makeup, eye pencil on her cheek, dangly earrings and leopard print accessories were all tried out.

Jack was as bemused by it all as he was irked at her taking random photos of him, even when he wasn't doing anything: shots around the flat, in bed or just lounging around. But it was an exciting moment when they got the first film developed: a red letter day. Daisy had gone for a thirty-six exposure black and white film, which was slightly more expensive than colour, but worth it. More arty: she wanted to replicate her screen idols. And the images of them that came back were indeed striking, possessing a stark and fresh beauty that they couldn't possibly appreciate till they were much older. Daisy thought her face looked puffy and that she looked too young, too posey, as if she was trying too hard. A kid dressing up. But there was a particularly sweet one of them together (again taken with the self-timer), which was just what Daisy had been wanting. It would be going in a frame.

Seeing photos of himself for the very first time, Jack was in turn fascinated, embarrassed and horrified. All he could see in himself was his father in those old photos of him with Carla, the black and white adding to the effect. Daisy thought he looked amazing: Matt Dillon out of *Rumblefish*.

As for the kitchen, Jack was enjoying it more than he could ever have imagined. Work had always been drudgery to him, whether it had been at home or in the factory. He never dreamed you could get paid for doing something you actually enjoyed. There was a lot to learn; boy, was there a lot to learn! And some of it could be monotonous – picking crates of spinach, and peeling and chopping onions for example – *and* he had been thrown in at the deep end. But he approached the tasks with his trademark fastidiousness, determined to complete them quickly and to the best of his ability.

His shifts were filled with a constant bombardment of smells and colours – a never-ending assault on his senses. Picking sweet-scented basil leaves for something called pesto. The fragrant aroma that was released when peeling and chopping a parsnip. The chicken soup smell of simmering stocks topped with a lid of fresh herbs and vegetables – thyme, rosemary, onions, garlic, carrot and celery. The liquorice assortment nature of a tray of prepped, brightly coloured, Mediterranean vegetables – peppers, aubergines (which he'd never heard of), some unusual purple onions, courgettes and tomatoes; all for something called ratatouille. Who'd have thought food could be so stimulating?

But it was the camaraderie he loved as well – the banter, the running jokes – especially when Chef wasn't there. It seemed everything or everyone had a silly nickname or expression. Jack (now Jackeroo) had never heard so much foul language in his life, and it took some getting used to, but soon it became contagious. And then there were his new friends – Aitch, Tom, Alison and Jeanie – who'd accepted him so readily and didn't question him or his past, or about Daisy. They lived for the moment, the present.

Nuances from Jack's work life were creeping into his home life. He took more of an active role in the preparing and cooking of dinner, peering over Daisy's shoulder and wanting to get involved, to show off how finely he could chop an onion. He paced the kitchen with a tea towel draped over his shoulder, getting under her feet, moaning that their chopping knife wasn't sharp enough. Sometimes he tried things with a spoon and say that it needed a little more seasoning. At this point Daisy would tell him to clear off, or 'make his own bloody dinner'. He was even proud of the new striped burns he had on his forearms, just like the other chefs. When he was telling Daisy about his day, his speech was increasingly peppered with swear words and work expressions, such as, 'it was dead' or 'we got shafted' or, much worse, 'we got a raping' – without any real thought about their true meaning. 'That's a terrible thing to say!' Daisy would remark in return, but soon even she got used to it.

What she couldn't get used to were the boredom and loneliness. They were starting to get to her. For weeks now they'd been in Norfolk, with nobody bothering them and no mention of events back in the East Midlands. With no trial for the media or public to follow, no one to hate and no police van to throw rocks at, the story had quickly – nationally anyway – become old news. Daisy's frustrations came to a head one Friday night when, to her despair, Jack didn't return home from work at the normal time…

At first she presumed they'd had an extra busy service – a 'shafting' – with lots of late tables, but as the clock went past twelve she began to worry. It was totally out of character for Jack not to return home; he practically ran back some nights. What should she do? Go to the restaurant to look for him? Call the police? Too soon for that; besides, what sort of attention would that draw to them? She had no choice but to sit and fret, and wait in the cold flat under a blanket. She felt lonelier than ever, not having anyone to turn to and not knowing anyone in the town. It was too late to ring her mum: she'd only worry, and it would give her another excuse for Daisy to come home. In her letters to her mum, Daisy was always careful to portray a rosy picture of their new life – which was true; most of the time…

It was gone one o'clock when she finally heard the door open. She'd worked herself up into an absolute state, and for ten minutes or so she'd been staring at the phone in tears. She shot up from the sofa as Jack came bounding up the stairs. He was clutching a random black bin liner. When she saw the grin on his face she could have murdered him. 'Where have you been?' she cried.

'Sorry! Jesus, what's wrong? Have you been crying?'

'Yes, I've been crying. I've been worried sick!'

For some reason, Jack appeared to find this amusing. It was as if he was drunk. 'Oh, come here, baby. Did you miss me?' And he went to hug her.

But this only angered her further, and she pushed him away. 'Don't you baby me! Where have you been? And why … oh my God! Have you been smoking? You smell like an ashtray!'

Jack giggled again. What was wrong with him? 'Only a bit,' he said.

'Only a bit? Where, at work? Have you been there all this time?'

'No! If you calm down a minute, I'll explain!' He was still smiling and his eyes were a little glazed.

'Well? Go on then. Explain! And you're not coming near me until you do.' Daisy had her hand on her hip, just like her mum when she was angry.

'We went back to Aitch's. It was in totally the opposite direction, near the seafront. I wanted to let you know but didn't know how – and there wasn't time.'

'Why didn't you ring?'

'There wasn't a phone box anywhere. And I'd forgotten the number.' He looked apologetic for the first time.

'Who's "*we*" anyway?'

'Just me and some of the gang, Tom and that.'

'And that? What, girls? Was *she* there?'

'Who?'

'That bloody Jeanie!'

'Yes. Why?'

'You bastard!' she cried. And totally unexpectedly she started laying into Jack.

'Jesus, Daisy! What's got into you?' He grabbed her wrists to stop her from slapping him, but she carried on struggling and crying.

'I hate you! I'm stuck here, bored to tears and worried sick about you ... on the verge of calling the police. And you're carrying on with some slut from work.'

'Slut from work?'

'I wish I'd never come here. I want to go home!' Jack had never seen such genuine animosity towards him, and it killed him. She wrested her hands free and sank to the floor, her back against the kitchen cupboards.

Jack dropped to the floor alongside her, heartbroken and suddenly sober. 'Don't say that, Daisy, please don't say that! What's wrong? What's got into you? I'm nothing without you, and I'm certainly not carrying on with some girl. How could you think such a thing?'

'Because I'm stuck here and I'm lonely and I've got nothing better to do than think. Your mind plays tricks on you – I want a job, like you, or to go to college. If I don't, I'm gonna go out of my mind.'

'But I've got something to tell you about that. Look!' And Jack reached for the bin liner he'd been carrying. He ripped it open, and out spilled some pristine chef's jackets and striped blue aprons, wrapped in clear plastic. 'These are mine, Daisy! The restaurant owners bought them for me. I'm going to be a chef, a proper one. Can you believe it? Chef said I'm doing really well!'

Despite her misery, Daisy couldn't help but smile. He was clearly so proud. She wiped away a tear. 'Well done. That's amazing … for you anyway. But what about me?'

'That's the thing. There's a job going at the restaurant. Some guy walked out during service, a waiter; it was so busy! Hilary, the manager, was really angry. She wouldn't stop swearing. She said he's not coming back even if he begs, and she was asking if anyone knew someone looking for a job. I said I'd ask you. What do you think?'

Daisy dabbed at her eyes again with her shirt cuff. She let out a relieved laugh. Perhaps everything *was* going to be all right. It was just the lift she needed: for something to happen, to get back out into the real world again, to start living and earning money. 'She sounds terrifying,' she said. 'But I'd love to… Do you think it would be safe? You know, do you think it's too soon?'

'Perhaps … but we can't put it off forever. They've seen you now, anyway. It's a risk, but I hate seeing you like this. I thought we were happy! I know I am.'

'I *am* happy. It's just the boredom, that's all – when you're at work…'

'There's nothing going on with Jeanie, by the way. She's just a…'

'I know. I'm sorry.' She leaned in towards him. 'Just me being stupid. I was upset. I was genuinely worried about you. I didn't know what to do – I was going to call the police! And then when I saw that smile on your face…'

Jack chuckled, as if remembering something.

'What are you laughing at?'

'Nothing. It's just that stuff Aitch smokes. Well, they all do actually…'

'What, marijuana? Have you been smoking marijuana?!' She turned to him, incredulous.

199

'Well, *they* call it gear. And, yeah. Only a bit, though. It goes straight to your head. It felt like drinking a strong home brew. Have you ever had any?'

'No, can't say that I have. I can't believe you've been smoking marijuana! And without me.' Jack smiled sheepishly. 'That lot are a bad influence on you. It's a good job I'm coming to work there – to keep an eye on you! And that slut Jeanie.'

Jack shot her a look.

'Only joking,' she said.

And so they made up.

Even though it was late – very late – there was no question of going to bed: there was too much to talk about. Once they'd settled under the blanket in the lounge, Jack explained to Daisy how they'd ended up going back to Aitch's, and how they'd asked him to after pretty much every service. It was a bit of a routine with the work gang – a smoke after work. This time everyone was going; they were all buzzing after a busy service, and from being paid. Jack felt like celebrating getting his chef's uniforms. It had sealed the job, so to speak. And it was getting embarrassing to keep on saying no. Daisy nodded her head, understanding. Why shouldn't he socialise – even if she was stuck at home. She was pleased for him; things were working out. He'd come such a long way since they'd first met. Secretly, she wasn't sure about the marijuana thing, though – or the girls being there…

'Aitch has got this really cool caravan in his garden – it's his bedroom,' Jack said, excitedly. 'He calls it The Love Shack after a song or something.'

'Yes, The B-52's. I know it,' said Daisy.

'Yes, that's it. Anyway, that's where everyone goes to smoke. It's amazing, almost like a den. And he's got all these sculptures made out of melted candle wax – he's got candles everywhere.'

'Sounds a bit weird if you ask me,' said Daisy. 'And dangerous!'

'Ah, you'd love it! We were listening to The Cure and the Stone Roses – and … Sisters of Mercy, is it? That was Tom's choice. And we played a card game called Shithead. It was brilliant!'

She would probably have loved it as well; it sounded like fun. It had been ages since she'd mixed with anyone her own age apart from Jack – far too long. And she loved a game of cards. 'Well, you never know – maybe I'll get an invite to The Love Shack before long,' she said.

CHAPTER 16
Oh, You Pretty Things

And so Daisy went to work at The Crab's Claw, Cromer's premier restaurant. It was a nerve-racking moment when she had to hand over her personal details for wage purposes, thus giving away her full identity. But Hilary didn't bat an eyelid, not a flicker; perhaps people in East Anglia had no interest in what was going on in other parts of the country. Being Daisy, she fitted in easily – she was a likeable girl and a hard worker. The gang took to her straightaway, and Jack was thrilled to see her standing the other side of the pass.

The only person who wasn't too pleased was Jeanie. Her nose was put out of joint by this pretty new girl showing up, with her short hair and her air of mystery. Jeanie was used to being Queen Bee and having a monopoly on male attention; she enjoyed wandering into the kitchen and having a little flirt with the chefs, especially Jack, taking advantage of his good nature. But she tried her best not to show her displeasure, readily flashing Daisy a false smile and chatting away with her.

Daisy didn't buy it for a second: it was blatantly apparent this girl fancied Jack. She had a habit, Daisy noticed, of scratching the top of her thigh, just underneath the hem of her barely there black skirt when she was talking to him; she had that gap between her thighs that skinny girls have. But Daisy, too, was careful not to let her feelings show. For the sake of harmony, they both kept up an act: the way Daisy saw it was, in the words of the old saying, 'keep your friends close and your enemies closer'.

It wasn't long before she had her first invitation to The Love Shack, her first Friday in fact. But she politely declined. It was too soon: she didn't feel comfortable enough. Jack was a little put out as he would have liked to have gone himself, and didn't feel as if he could without Daisy. He'd been thinking how the 'gear' had made him feel; he'd kind of liked it. But they had their first social night out in Cromer the following Sunday. This was the only night the restaurant closed, so most of the staff treated it like a Friday or Saturday night. There was a band playing at the local pub, the Drunken Sailor, that they all used because they got served there. The band were local, too, with a bit of a cult following in North Norfolk. They were called Bone Dry Joe and the De-humidifiers – an indie outfit with a fun edge to them.

Daisy and Jack were half-cooked by the time they headed out, nervous and excited beyond belief. Daisy couldn't wait to see a live band for the first time. She'd wanted to take her camera with her, but was worried it might get damaged or stolen. Jack was buzzing because he was going to be spending the evening with his mates.

When they cautiously entered the pub, Daisy didn't go unnoticed even though it was rammed. Autumn had bared its teeth early on the coast, and the sea breeze had turned a little fresh to say the least, so Daisy saw their night out as an opportunity to don a second-hand fur coat she had purchased. Along with her cropped hair and striking makeup, she made for an eye-catching sight. Jack was brimming with pride to be out with her. A stranger asked if she was in the band, to which she blushed and shook her head.

They found the gang at a table, squashed into a corner. Tom was wearing his trademark black. Aitch was grinning, already stoned. Alison and Jeanie were there, too. All of them were smoking cigarettes; the air was thick with them.

'Jackeroo!' cried Aitch.

Jack grinned back. Tom got up.

'Oh my God! I love your coat!' cried Alison, complimentary as ever. Daisy blushed again. Jeanie looked her up and down and gave her that smile – more of a grimace. It reminded Daisy of standing on the cool north side of her house back home, where the sun didn't quite reach.

'Drinks!' said Tom. 'I'll come with you.'

'So will I,' said Aitch. 'It's my round. Same again, everyone?'

'Aye,' said Alison, holding up the remains of a pinkish concoction in a plastic pint glass. It seemed everyone was drinking out of plastic glasses.

The boys fought their way to the bar, whilst Daisy was left with the two girls. She had to squash up against Jeanie, who didn't appear too pleased. Daisy would rather have been sitting next to Alison. There was an awkward silence for a moment.

'It's so nice to see you out of work, Daisy – and I just love your style!' shouted Alison, leaning across Jeanie.

'Thanks. I like yours too! What's that you're drinking?' Daisy said, acknowledging Alison's glass. 'It looks interesting.'

'Snakebite and black – half cider, half lager and a dash of blackcurrant.'

'Aaah,' said Daisy. She'd heard of it. 'Sounds like a cocktail!'

'Do you drink cocktails then?'

'Sometimes, yes.'

'Oh my God. I swear you're so sophisticated – and glamorous. Isn't she, Jeanie?'

'Umm,' said Jeanie, draining the last of her glass.

The evening continued, the drinks kept flowing and the band finally appeared. They had to walk through everybody to get to the stage – just a cordoned off section of the pub. There was an aura about them, and a buzz of expectation rippled through the crowd. People cheered and patted them on their shoulders as they passed. Tom, Aitch and the girls got ready to move towards the stage with everyone else. Jack stood up, nervously. He looked at Daisy and she squeezed his hand.

It was hard to get close to the band, as there was a group of about a dozen hardcore followers monopolising the makeshift barrier at the front. But once the music started this didn't matter a bit. Wow! Daisy had dreamt about this moment her whole life – seeing and hearing a live band. She was gobsmacked at how loud it was: the thump of the bass pedal, the crisp snap of the snare drum, it was like being continually punched in the chest. Even the echoing reverberation of the guitars seemed to be tangible, as if you could reach out and touch the riffs. OK, it wasn't the Stone Roses, but the band was still polished – manic but tight – and the music was infectious, with catchy call and response vocals between the drummer and singer. Everyone was bobbing or pogoing up and down, especially at the front, the groupies hollering out the choruses. It made Daisy's skin pimple with ecstatic feeling, and it was impossible not to be caught up in it all. She'd never thought music could sound better than on a record or tape – until that night.

Everyone was jostling for position. At first this was alarming for Jack. The slightly violent atmosphere that had sprung up surprised him, and in any case he still wasn't used to crowds. The gang began to split up. The last he saw of Aitch was when he shouted, 'I'm heading for the mosh pit!' before fighting his way to the front. Jack did his best to keep hold of Daisy, but they were both shoved from all sides. Trying to clutch on to a pint glass became impossible. Eventually he gave up, drained his glass and tossed it to the side. Now he knew why plastic glasses were being used: they were constantly being chucked into the air, sometimes still full. It was madness.

By the end most people were drenched and sticky with sweat or alcohol, or both. Jack nearly got into two fights trying to protect Daisy. But he'd also been aroused on several occasions as Daisy was constantly backing into his crotch while he tried to keep hold of her. Despite the mayhem she'd become aware of this, and kept on looking over her shoulder and wiggling her bum into him. It was driving him insane! He just wanted to go back to the flat.

This had to wait, because as soon as it was kicking out time they headed to The Love Shack, all except Jeanie who said she was calling it a night. Daisy had her first experience of marijuana that night. What the hell ... everyone else was doing it. And she was drunk: she was up for almost anything when she'd been drinking. A joint was passed round, and before long Daisy and Jack both felt as if they were floating. Things that weren't even funny became hysterical. Soon everyone was crying from laughter and from the smoke. Music had never sounded so good, if that was possible after the night they'd had: it was enhanced, with a new clarity, with more depth to the lyrics. They took it in turns to choose songs, and every one sounded like the best song ever. People kept saying as much: 'Is it just me or this the best song ever?' and then, 'Will everyone stop saying that?' It was a running joke that was always the cue for another round of laughter. When it was Jack's turn he put 'The Caterpillar' on. And he and Daisy couldn't take their eyes off each other, both thinking that the other had never looked so attractive, so alluring.

After a very long game of Shithead, and another couple of joints, the laughter gave way to a dreamy sense of shared euphoria. Tucked away in the little cabin, they all found themselves staring into space. Alison had fallen asleep, her head on Tom's shoulder. Even the usually irascible Aitch, sporting a new black eye, had gone quiet. He was melting some candle wax with his lighter and watching it drip. Daisy, who had taken to looking at everything as a potential photograph, rued not having her camera with her. It would have been the perfect opportunity to take some reflective shots of everyone with their guard down. A moment captured in time, and a memento of the evening.

It was time to go home. Aitch let them out into the fresh air of a starry seaside night, which hit their heads. The gang, now the best of friends and elegantly wasted, hugged and shook hands before making their separate ways home. Jack and Daisy walked through the quiet town in a stunned silence. They didn't have to say anything to each other. They both knew how the other was feeling. What a night!

And when they got home, they had to make love. Their first time stoned together. The best time ever; it went on forever. Their Velvet Underground album was playing. The seven minutes of 'Heroin' in all its majesty sounded particularly apt. They soared like condors: Jack had never felt so uninhibited and he gave Daisy all his best moves. And some new ones, too…

CHAPTER 17
At It Like Rabbits

Daisy woke Jack up the next morning with a cup of tea. She was standing at his side of the bed with nothing on but her fur coat. It was open. His 'Venus in Furs'. He pulled her back into bed…

This act pretty much personified the period that was beginning. The Velvet Underground album on constant repeat; a rapid descent into marijuana dependence. Jack bought his own from Aitch, and he and Daisy smoked it at the flat in the perpetual cold. Their days and nights were spent at the restaurant; intermittently manic, but always stimulating and social. It had quietened down a little since most of the tourists had gone, but only slightly. They had been replaced by locals and foodies, who had come crawling back out of the woodwork.

But above all else, that autumn was about the sex. Fuelled by marijuana and alcohol and with no one to stop them, they had the arena to themselves. Jack was unlocking the secrets of the female species – some good, some not so good. Tights, and how funny they looked over Daisy's knickers, monthly blood, tampons, makeup, the fact that girls grew hair on their legs and under their arms – just like him. He hadn't realised they shaved it off; he'd always thought they were naturally smooth! But he was also finding stuff out about himself. He liked to watch Daisy doing the housework. Her cleaning the front windows or vacuuming the floor was enough to get him worked up. Daisy indulged him in this, sometimes in her underwear, freezing her arse off in the process: she'd quickly gone from being modest about her body to being practically an exhibitionist. Having given up on fighting her few extra pounds, she'd decided to embrace them instead. Jack didn't seem to mind: he couldn't keep his hands off her. At least her tits were bigger, she thought. Boys liked big tits – that's what she'd gleaned from her male friends at school anyway.

Daisy had her own little quirks as well. Sometimes she asked Jack to put on his chef's gear for her at home. He looked so handsome. She loved the way the white looked against his beach-tanned arms and face. Undoing his apron, she imagined that they were at work, and that they were doing it in the kitchen in front of everybody.

They might have set records that autumn for how many times a couple could make love in a week. The bed was on its last legs, the headboard gone. A red-faced guy from the office downstairs posted a letter of complaint through their door about the noise – too embarrassed to knock on the door. Daisy kept the letter as a memento and pasted it in her diary. They even sneaked down to the beach one night, drunk, to do it; one for Daisy to tick off her list. Sex had become a way for them to deal with the grief that they were undoubtedly still going through: it banished it to the corners, kept the lights on. Even on the day of her dad's funeral it had been some sort of weapon, a release.

One day Daisy and Jack were in the newsagent's. It was a Wednesday. Since they'd started smoking regularly, any sense of planning and organisation regarding food and drink had slipped. Money wasn't so tight for a start. They'd fallen into the habit of nipping across the road for most of their bits and pieces, almost on a whim or when they got the 'munchies'.

That morning, amongst other things, it was Daisy's music paper and Jack's cigarette papers.

As Daisy rifled through the newspapers, trying to find the *NME* – she seemed to be the only person in Cromer who bought it – out of the corner of her eye she could have sworn she saw Jack furtively glancing up at the top shelf. She pretended to carry on searching for a second, even though she'd found the paper, then stood up and shot a glance at where he was looking. It appeared to be at a prominently displayed adult magazine. The cover was taken up by a model who was bending over with her back arched – olive skin, and white knickers cutting across her bum. Daisy didn't know how it made her feel. Had she imagined it? Jack wasn't aware that he'd seen her looking, and she didn't say anything.

But it stayed with her: it made her feel curious, a little jealous, but also strangely aroused. And so next time they were there, buying the Saturday paper – her mum had always bought it for the TV guide, and so Daisy did the same – she thought she'd give Jack a little test to confirm her suspicions. 'I've just got to get a few bits of food. Can you grab the *Mail* for us?'

'Umm,' said Jack, still drowsy from a late night smoking and drinking.

Daisy gave him a few seconds, then moved to where she could watch him but was out of view. He scanned the row of papers, and quickly found the *Mail*. But before he went to grab it, to Daisy's astonishment there it was again – that furtive, but definite, glance up at the same magazine. It was still in position; obviously not many people bought them. Daisy felt funny. *The little so-and-so*, she thought, as he grabbed the paper before turning round again. Daisy didn't say anything, pretending to be studying tins, but she felt shaky as they paid.

Back at the flat, she made a decision to teach him a lesson. But it would have to wait...

By now, Daisy knew what staff were on at the shop, which days and times. The owner, Queenie as they now called her, always had Tuesdays off: Jack's first day back at work. This was perfect because a young lad worked in the mornings. He was about the same age as Daisy and a bit wet behind the ears, she thought, someone she didn't feel threatened by, and wasn't a nosey parker. She suspected he might fancy her a little, because he always went bright red around her, a bit like Jack used to.

Once Jack had gone to work, Daisy necked a large glass of cold white wine. It tasted gross so early in the morning and made her grimace, but it did the trick. It altered her brain sufficiently enough for her not to give a crap. Clutching her purse and keys, she marched over to the newsagent's. Once inside, she headed straight to the news section, which was out of sight of the till. Stretching on tiptoes, she reached up and grabbed the dirty magazine. Before she could chicken out, she headed straight to the till with it; she wasn't going to shoplift it, as if she was caught she'd never live down the shame of it.

Without making eye contact, she plonked it on the counter – thankfully no one else was in the shop – and opened her purse. Still looking down, she waited for the boy to tell her how much it was. He didn't. Eventually she looked up. The boy was staring straight at her, his bottom lip quivering a little, crimson-faced and frozen. He looked as if he was about to cry. Then he looked at the magazine and back at her again, still unable to speak. 'Oh, for crying out loud!' Daisy said. 'How much is the bloody thing? It's nearly 1990, you know. A girl can do what she likes!' She spun the magazine round to clock the price. 'Here!' She slapped some coins on the counter. 'Keep the change!' She picked up the magazine and waltzed out.

Back in the safety of her kitchen, she burst into hysterical laughter. A combination of the wine, the relief she felt and the look on the boy's face. Her heart was racing. She couldn't believe she'd done it. But there was still the small matter of the magazine. Curious, she sat down on the sofa to thumb through it.

Daisy had never looked through an adult magazine before. Why would she have done? And she was shocked, amused and repulsed in equal measure. She could handle looking at the women in their underwear, but it was when they took it off – some of the utterly unabashed and brazen poses they were striking, the excruciating close-ups in vivid colour. Daisy saw parts and places of a woman she had never wanted to see – and why they wanted to display their parts in this way was beyond her. It made her feel neat and tidy down there, proud of herself, in comparison. She felt like throwing the magazine away right there and then. It was so … seedy; so in your face. But she'd come this far. And, besides, some of the stories, although ridiculous, were actually quite entertaining – certainly better than the pictures. In fact, some of them even turned her on. She was aware her face and throat were flushed, her hands were shaking and her heart was pounding. It made her want to slip back into bed and touch herself.

By the time Jack got back from work, Daisy had read the magazine from cover to cover. She was cooking dinner – spaghetti bolognese – and was on her third glass of wine. Jack didn't notice her flushed face. 'Jesus! We just got absolutely butt-fucked!' he said, and headed straight for the lounge to roll a joint. This had become a daily habit.

Daisy, used to these vulgar expressions by now, merely remarked, 'Oh. When do I get mine then?'

'Hey?' he said, barely registering. And then, 'Have you seen my baccy tin …? It's OK! Got it.'

Daisy took the bolognese off the heat, wiped her hands on her apron and drained her wine glass. She wanted to get this over and done with before he started smoking. Hidden under a tea towel on the kitchen counter was the magazine. Picking it up, she headed into the lounge.

Jack was crouching forward on the sofa, leaning over the coffee table and sticking some cigarette papers together. He was getting quite deft at it. Daisy watched him for a second. He looked up at her – her face anyway – but didn't notice her hands behind her back. 'You OK?' She was looking at him in a funny way. It reminded him of something not so long ago.

'Yes, fine.'

Jack went back to constructing his spliff. Daisy walked forward and stood next to him, just out of his eye line. Without further ado, she gently tossed the magazine, face up, on the coffee table next to his tin. Some of the tobacco in it wafted out and spilt. 'Careful!' he said.

Then he noticed the magazine in all its glossy, incriminating glory. Jack froze, cigarette lighter and pebble of resin in hand, about to warm and soften some to crumble into his spliff. His face turned the same colour as the boy's in the shop. What the hell was going on? He couldn't move a muscle. It was as if something trivial – acknowledged, yes, but totally unimportant, a guilty curiosity – had been plucked from a private closet in his mind and made real, as if his very thoughts had been read and manifested themselves in front of him. He didn't know where to look – at the magazine, at Daisy or at the ground. He chose the third option.

'Stand up,' Daisy said.

He still couldn't bring himself to look at her. He was too embarrassed, his old self coming back. The black spot too, dancing with glee in front of his eyes: '*Someone's in trouble! Someone's in trouble!*' it appeared to sing. And that tone in Daisy's voice, again it seemed familiar – that day at Stanford Hall, maybe – but more commanding this time. 'What's going on? What *is* that?' He pointed, then finally turned his head to look at her.

'Don't look at me,' she said firmly. 'Look at the magazine. I think you know exactly what it is.' Jack felt like a little boy, being told off by his sister.

'Daisy, stop it now. This isn't funny.'

'Just do as I say, and stand up.'

Powerless and ashamed, he did as he was told.

She leant forward, opened up the magazine, and began to calmly leaf through it. Jack simply couldn't fathom what was going on. And like Daisy, he too had never had the dubious honour of seeing inside a dirty magazine. Not that he hadn't wanted to – that one at work had been driving him mad, the cover of this one too. But he would never have dared look inside; he was too embarrassed. But how did she know? How could she possibly know?

He was horrified by, but glued to, what he was seeing. Flesh upon flesh. A battle of guilt waged in his head against the curiosity about the unknown; he'd only ever seen Daisy, and felt as if he was cheating on her. But equally he couldn't tear his gaze away. Despite his shame, he could feel himself hardening.

'Stop me when you see something you like,' she said, continuing to leaf through the magazine. 'Which one is it? Or is it all of them? Is that her?' Daisy slowed down when she got to the model on the cover, the one in the white pants. She stopped at the centrefold and stood back up. 'Is it?' Jack couldn't answer, and didn't know where to look. 'Well, go on then,' she said, putting her hands on her hips.

'Go on what?' he said, half-traumatised.

'Don't look at me! You know what. Unzip your trousers.'

'Daisy, no! It's disgusting!'

'You didn't think that when you were looking at it in the shop, did you?'

'I wasn't!'

'Yes you were. Now do as you're told. Unzip your trousers and get it out.'

Jack felt powerless to resist, as if he was being punished. It felt as if he deserved it. Slowly, he did as she asked, ashamed at being fully aroused. He bit his lip.

'You dirty bastard,' she said. 'Well, go on then. Get it over and done with. I'm not doing it for you!'

'Daisy, no!'

'Just do it!' she shouted.

Jack took hold of himself and began to stroke.

'That's it,' she encouraged, flicking through the different pages of the same model again. She settled back on the centrefold picture, legs splayed wide, olive thighs, neatly trimmed bush, and could sense Jack's enthusiasm boiling over. She brought the magazine closer to the edge of the table, right in front of him, as if rubbing a kitten's nose in its mess. 'That's it, you dirty bastard!'

Jack's body quickly bucked and he came hard. He cried out in shame and intense pleasure, splashing the table and the image in the magazine with his mess. When he'd finished he slowed down, his body still heaving with exertion, his heart pounding, confused beyond belief. He went to stuff himself back away, full of self-loathing and on the verge of tears. 'Wait!' Daisy said, still commanding him.

She plucked a couple of tissues from a box on the table, handed them to him and told him to clean himself up. As he was doing so, she picked up the magazine and shut it. Once Jack had finished, he went to make himself decent again. 'Hold on!' she said. 'I haven't finished with you yet!'

Before Jack knew what was happening, she took hold of him, still semi-tumescent, and led him back through the lounge towards the kitchen, him in one hand, the rolled up magazine in the other. Jack shuffled after her, trying to keep up. Daisy paused when they reached the kitchen. She pushed the pedal of the bin down with one foot and dumped the magazine into it. The lid clanged shut. Then she led him over to the kitchen counter where she'd been preparing dinner. By now Jack was fully stiff again and, pushing aside some carrots she'd been chopping, Daisy yanked him forcibly onto the chopping board. He had to stand on tiptoes.

Picking up the chopping knife, to Jack's horror and exhilaration, Daisy held it in the air, hovering it over the base of him. 'Now this is what will happen if I ever catch you looking at those again, Jack Gardner … Jackeroo, or whatever your name is these days. Is that clear?' Jack didn't know how serious she was being, and he looked at her, perplexed. Had she gone mad? Was it the marijuana? She sounded serious, but thankfully there was a mischievous glint in her eye, and he nodded.

Then she put the knife down, which was a relief, and, guiding him by his shoulders, turned him to stand in front of her. Clearly still not finished with him, she pushed him down and told him to get on his knees. Jack duly obliged. He was face to face with her apron. There was one of those thunderbolt flashbacks – something about the look and smell of it, the aspect of it, that reminded him of his sister – only briefly, and then it was gone again, thank God. Then she lifted up the apron, together with her skirt. 'This is the only altar you need to worship at,' she said. 'Right here.' She took hold of his hair and buried his face in her crotch. Jack said 'Amen' in his head, and proceeded to make amends.

PART THREE

PART THREE

CHAPTER 18
Ouija Board, Ouija Board

It was Halloween, a Tuesday. Jack was walking home from work. The moon was full, pockmarked and yellow like Swiss cheese, and the brilliant stars were legion – pinhole cameras in a charcoal sky onto an unseen world. He'd always had a thing about Halloween because of stories his sister had told him. He could remember, clear as day, standing outside the back door of his house as a boy, putting out a saucer of milk for a hedgehog. Looking up at the sky he saw them – the witches – tiny and silhouetted by the moon at first, then swooping down on their brooms, large as life and cackling right above his head. He'd run back into the house, screaming. He'd always had a vivid imagination. It was like that time at Easter when he swore he'd seen Jesus in his front garden.

When Jack got home, the flat was bathed in the glow of candles and the air was thick with the sweet, pungent smell of marijuana. Stronger than ever. Skunk. It had been doing the rounds of the kitchen the last few weeks – the first time any had shown up in Cromer, that Aitch knew of anyway. And it was powerful stuff. This particular variety went by the name of Northern Lights. Daisy had given up only smoking when Jack smoked, and rolled her own while he was at work – little single-skin bombs for herself. Jack loved it. It was like when they'd first met and he'd wanted her to share his cider – to feel how he felt.

Reggae music was coming from the lounge. Bob Marley, another artist recently discovered by Daisy courtesy of an LP from the Town Hall. It suited the marijuana perfectly. Daisy was nodding her head to it, reading the lyric sheet of the album, in her own little world. 'Hi,' Jack grinned.

'Hi,' she said, looking up and smiling. He could tell she was feeling the effects of the drug just by her eyes and the way she didn't get up to greet him, as if it was too much effort, too far. He didn't mind at all. She had that languid quality about her, dreamy, her eyelids heavy, her reactions a little slow. He found it sexy.

'You OK?' he said.

'Yes, fine. Except for the phone doing that thing again. It seems to be getting worse.'

Sometimes their old phone dinged, as if it was about to ring. But then it never did. It had freaked them out at first, as if someone was trying to get through – Carol, Grandma or Haslam (still asking questions, mainly about Peasgood and the money). Daisy would put the receiver to her ear and listen, saying hello; Jack, too. But there would be no one there, no dialling tone either; all you could hear was air, whistling, like putting a shell to your ear. Then they'd have to press the buttons on the cradle a few times until the line came back.

'I've told you, it's haunted,' said Jack. 'Didn't the man in the shop say it was from the war?'

'It's all right you joking. You don't have to sit here on your own at night; it's kind of creepy when it happens.'

'What's with all the candles?'

'It's a special night. Our first Halloween together,' Daisy said. 'I've got us a nice bottle of wine in, too.' This was one of the many things Jack loved about her. Any excuse for a celebration – especially anything remotely ritualistic.

'Better go and get my bath then.'

'Hurry up then. I'll get rolling.'

Towelling his hair dry, Jack returned to the lounge after his bath. Daisy had a spliff ready and a bottle of wine and two glasses on the table.

Surprisingly, the music had disappeared. Daisy was watching TV. 'Something on?' he asked, picking up the joint and inspecting it. It was rolled tight, neat, compact. He was impressed.

'Yes, *Halloween*. Have you seen it?'

'Halloween what?' The spliff bobbed up and down in his mouth as he spoke. He lit the twisted paper end.

'*Halloween*. The horror movie.'

Jack inhaled and closed his eyes. A mild ache, a pleasant harshness, filled his lungs … and then hit his head. A rush. He blew out a stream of smoke and sat back. The world was suddenly a better place. 'You and your horror movies,' he said.

'You can't not watch *Halloween* on Halloween, especially when it's on telly. Ooh! Here we go, it's just starting. Listen to this music, it gives me the chills.' She picked up the remote and turned the volume up.

A black screen with orange writing came up. Then a repetitive piano refrain kicked in that immediately stuck in Jack's head. A flickering pumpkin appeared accompanied by some sinister, dramatic low string sounds. This came and went in time to the music, along with more of the orange writing. The whole effect was quite unsettling, and the film hadn't even started. 'I feel creeped out already,' Jack said.

'You will be. It's terrifying. Wait till you see Michael Myers.'

'Who?'

'Never mind. Just hand over that spliff and watch the film.'

They settled back on the sofa, and for the next hour and a half Jack was both captivated and traumatised. They spent a lot of the film either jumping in fright or peeking out from under the blanket. Especially during the wardrobe scene with the coat hanger. Jack had never come across such a menacing character in a film. It was relentless. Why wouldn't he die? There was something about a madman that was so unnerving. And that derelict house as well... It reminded him a little of his own house back home, which also freaked him out a little. What if part of it was still standing now? Inhabited by a Michael Myers-type character?

When the film had finished, they discussed various elements of it as Jack rolled another spliff. Elements such as 'trick or treating'. Obviously Jack had never done this. Daisy said she had a few times with friends, but hadn't dressed up. Her parents had never got involved in it, said it was 'an American thing'. Keeping with the Halloween theme, she recalled how the craze for doing a Ouija board had gone around school, and some of the spooky things that had happened.

They stayed up talking and getting stoned, the novelty of being together still new, still boundless; trying to milk every last drop out of each day, as if it was their last. Jack loved this, hearing about her upbringing, about school and her childhood. The wine was gone now, but they carried on smoking, the skunk incredibly strong. And the more stoned they got, the more honest and sentimental they became.

For the first time they discussed the loss of their baby in depth – whether it would have been a boy or a girl, and what they would have called it. With these sad thoughts there were surprise tears from both of them, Daisy setting Jack off. Jack said he hadn't given the naming thing much thought. But Daisy had: Edie for a girl and James (shortened to Jim), after her dad, for a boy. It struck Daisy that her mum and dad would have both been grandparents. Her dad a granddad. It was a funny thought. She bet he would have been a great one. Young, but a great one.

Conversation switched to their other respective losses, to Anne and to Daisy's dad. Another subject Jack had yet to talk about properly. And there were more tears as they tried to put into words how they felt. But it felt good to let everything out. Daisy summed it up when she said, 'I just wish I could speak to him, you know? That's what hurts the most. There are times when certain things happen and I just wish I could hear his voice, his laugh, get his opinion on stuff, get some advice – like with the baby thing.'

'I know. I just wished I got a chance to say goodbye,' said Jack. 'That's what eats away at me. The rest of it … how it happened, her side of the story, what he did to her…' He stopped and grimaced, having scratched the rawness within. It was like lava, always there, always bubbling away. 'I don't think I want to know. It just stirs up the hate, and the anger. But I still wished I'd got to say goodbye…' Daisy squeezed his hand, knowing exactly how he felt.

There was silence for a while; they had talked themselves dry, come to a standstill. But then Daisy said, 'You know what we should do?'

'What?'

'A Ouija board.'

'Why?'

'To try and talk to them. To say goodbye.'

'Who?'

'Dad and Anne, silly. Their spirits.' Daisy sat up, rousing herself from her stupor. She'd kind of said it without thinking, but the more she thought …

Jack stirred too, to look at Daisy, to see if she was being serious. It looked as if she was. 'No. That's weird – and creepy. I've had enough frights for one night with that film. How, anyway? You don't really believe in that stuff, do you?'

'I don't know. Kind of. It seemed to work when we were at school. You just ask questions – 'Are you there?' and that – and they send messages back by spelling things out.'

'Like I say, weird and creepy.'

'It won't be. They're good spirits – on our side – and they're recently departed. They used to use Ouija boards during the war, so loved ones could contact dead soldiers – that's how they got popular. And it's Halloween. If they're going to come through it'll be tonight! Please, Jack. I really want to. Don't you want to talk to Anne, to say goodbye? You said you did!' A manic edge had crept into her voice, a desperation, as if this was the most important thing in the world. Skunk could do that to you.

'Yes, but… I don't know. Not like this…' Jack reached for some skins to roll another spliff, as if in defence – not that he needed one. As he began to stick them together he could sense Daisy still looking at him.

'Please, Jack.'

He sighed. 'Have you even got one? I didn't see it when we were unpacking.'

Daisy sensed him weakening. 'No, but I've got a Scrabble board.'

'A Scrabble board?'

'You'll see!'

Daisy cleared the coffee table and was soon emptying the drawstring bag of plastic letters onto it. They clattered and scattered, some spilling onto the floor. 'Quick, pick them up, we don't want to lose any,' she said. Jack did so, a little wearily. It was late. It had been a long day and, more significantly, he still wasn't sure about this. Meanwhile, Daisy was turning the letters over so they were all face up. She began to arrange them in alphabetical order in a squashed circle, an oval, to fit the slim table. Jack watched her. Clearly she'd done this before. 'Damn, where's the J?' she said. 'Jack, is it on the floor?'

'No, I picked them all up.'

'Well, look again; we can't have a letter missing. Especially a J.' She looked at him to see if he understood the relevance. Not sure that he had, she began shaking the bag.

Jack sighed and ducked his head under the table. 'Nope.'

The letter wasn't in the bag either. 'Shit,' she said, her face that of a child's whose party had been spoiled. She wanted it to be perfect. 'Guess we're just gonna have to write one. Can you grab a pen and paper? There's a notepad on the side in the kitchen.'

'Really?' said Jack. 'Is one letter that important?' He could barely move. The dope had done him in, tranquillized him.

'Course it's important! How's my dad gonna spell his name without a J?'

'Oh. Well, don't get your hopes up too much. I really don't think your dad, no disrespect, is going to get in touch through a Scrabble Ouija board.' He yawned.

'You've just got to believe. It's not gonna work if you don't believe! I'll get the paper and pen. Can you keep setting this up?'

'Can you grab me some crisps, too?' he called after her. He'd got the munchies.

'You'd better take this seriously!' she called from the kitchen. 'You can't sit there munching crisps!'

Daisy returned clutching a bag of crisps in her teeth, the notepad and pen and two fat, lit candles in her hands. She placed the cream-coloured candles either side of the top of the oval of letters. The flames flickered for a moment before glowing brightly again. She dropped the crisps into Jack's lap. He was still trying, but failing, to roll another spliff, making a right mess of it. 'No more of that, please. Come on. We need to concentrate. You've got your N and M the wrong way round as well; M comes before N.'

'Does it? Oh, yes. Sorry.'

'Shit. We need to do a yes and a no as well. And a goodbye. Otherwise it's dangerous.'

'Dangerous? Why?'

'Because … never mind. Just make sure we say goodbye at the end – you have to close the board down properly, that's all.' She picked through the remaining letters, spelling a yes and a no. Then she tore out two bits of paper from the pad and wrote out a J and the word goodbye. She placed the words and letter in their relevant spots in the oval, pushing the other letters aside slightly to accommodate them. Any remaining letters she put back in the cloth bag before sticking it under the table. 'Right, sit down over there, opposite me,' she said, kneeling on her heels and pointing. She surveyed the makeshift board. 'Hold on, we haven't even got a planchette. What am I thinking?'

'A what?' said Jack, settling opposite her, cross-legged.

'A planchette: the thing you hold on to that spells out the words.'

'Well, how's it gonna work then?'

'You can use anything as long as it slides. Lids, ashtrays – we even used a deodorant can top once.' Jack looked sceptical. It all seemed a bit silly, a bit amateurish. Daisy, meanwhile, was scanning the near vicinity of the room for a suitable conductor. 'Ashtray,' she said. 'Pass me that little ashtray thing.' She had found it in the Saturday market – a little navy and brass Art Deco ashtray with a flip top lid, a lady's trinket really, not much bigger than a fifty pence piece. There was a little stand inside that you could rest your cigarette on – or in their case a spliff. The bottom of it was smooth and shiny. It was perfect. Jack closed the lid and passed it to her. She tried it out. It slid beautifully across the lacquered finish of the coffee table. It struck Daisy as funny that it was full of ash, considering what they were going to use it for. Like a miniature urn containing the remains of a beloved pet mouse whose spirit they were trying to conjure up.

And then they were ready. Daisy settled herself and closed her eyes, trying to clear her mind. She looked serious all of a sudden. Jack felt a bit foolish. He had no idea what he was supposed to do. To his surprise, Daisy began to say some kind of prayer: 'Let these candles protect this board and ourselves with The Light. Let us only communicate with good spirits and those of The Light.' *Light?* thought Jack. *What light?* Where was she getting this stuff from? Apparently done, she opened her eyes. 'Right, are you ready? Put your fingertips on the planchette.' Jack gulped, suddenly feeling serious himself. What if his dead sister did come through? What would he say to her?

He did as Daisy said and put the fingertips of his first two fingers on the ashtray. She did the same. There wasn't much room and their fingers butted up snugly. 'OK, just start moving it in a small circle with me to get used to it; this helps build energy up in the board and lets the spirits know we're here.' They both tried to go in opposite directions. Daisy tutted. 'Lightly, Jack: you don't need to crush it into the table! Here, let me lead for now.' Jack tried to relax his fingers a little. He let Daisy move the planchette in an anti-clockwise direction. Soon it began to glide smoothly, effortlessly, as if neither of them was trying at all. It was a strange feeling. He could almost feel it heating up, glowing – or was this his imagination? After a minute or so Daisy let the planchette come to rest in the middle. She closed her eyes again, and in that serious voice said, 'Dear spirits, is there anybody there who would like to talk to us?' She opened her eyes and Jack watched her eyeballs shifting around the room, as if listening, seeking out any kind of sign. Nothing happened. There was just silence in the flat. No traffic noise, no people, the music long gone. Jack tried to make eye contact with her, but she wouldn't meet his gaze. Perhaps she was embarrassed. He wanted to signal to speak, to say 'What now?' How long did they wait?

And then the ashtray began to slide.

Daisy looked at him, wide eyed. Then they both looked down. The planchette was making a beeline for 'yes'. Jack quickly withdrew his hand. 'Daisy, don't do that!' he said. 'It's not funny!'

'Jack, don't take your hand off! It wasn't me, I swear. You might have broken the connection now.'

'I don't think I want a connection.' He was rubbing his hand on his jeans; it felt clammy, tainted, a numb, tingling sensation in his fingertips.

'Come on, we were just getting somewhere. We'd connected with someone. What if it was Anne? What if she's trying to contact you, to tell you something?' It was a strange thought, that she might be trapped in some other world somewhere, trying to talk to him, just like she was trapped under that metal sheet in that tank – cue another one of those flashbacks that hurt his brain. He winced. This wasn't good for him, or his mental state.

But the thought of Anne trying to contact him and him ignoring her – the guilt that this brought – made him sit up and return to the board. Daisy looked relieved. 'Is it just me or has it got even colder in here?' she said. She pulled the blanket around her before settling herself again, her fingers back on the ashtray. Looking at Jack, she gestured for him to do the same. He did so, reluctantly.

Daisy closed her eyes again, trying to recapture the mood. 'Dear spirit, if you're still there, would you like to tell us your name?' There was another moment of inactivity. But then, sooner than before, the ashtray began to move. Jack had to fight the urge to withdraw his fingers again, as, before their eyes, it glided towards and settled on the letter J – the only paper letter on the board. Something about this struck Jack as fishy. Was she having him on? Or was she that desperate to contact her dad that she was willing to pretend? He also felt disappointed that the planchette hadn't gone to the letter A. Before he had time to dwell on this, the ashtray began to move again, that eerie gliding feeling; it kind of made his stomach spin, like that fairground ride, the waltzer. This time it swept across the oval and did indeed settle on the letter A. Daisy looked at Jack, a mixture of exhilaration and surprise on her face – her dad, James. Jack looked back sceptically, as if to say, 'really?' She shook her head, only slightly, to signal it wasn't her, desperate for him not to break the connection. Jack's mind wandered, anticipating the planchette would go to M next; he was just waiting for it. It began to move again, but not far this time; a small arc to settle on the letter C. Jack scoffed. He couldn't help himself. 'Oh, come on, Daisy. J-a-c. What, am I connecting with my own dead spirit now?'

But Daisy looked deadly serious; it was her turn to feel disappointed. 'Don't take your hand off, please. Whatever you do, don't take your hand off. It's not me, I swear. Whoever it is, the spirit's strong. Very strong. Concentrate. Just a little longer.' Jack tutted and tried to engage his mind again. 'And look at me, don't look at the board.' He did as she said, locking his eyes on hers. After a few moments the planchette began to move, almost magnet-like, a strong pull across the board. Neither of them looked down till it had stopped. An O. J-a-c-o. Jack let out a strangled yelp. He let go of the ashtray and shot backwards in horror, his entire skin crawling with goose pimples, the hairs on his forearms standing on end.

'Jacob! That's my father's name. Jacob!' he cried. And before Daisy could stop him, Jack had swept his arm across the table, scattering the letters on the floor.

'Jack, don't!

One of the candles fell to the floor with the letters, spilling wax and landing on the torn notepad. The notepad burst into flames, sending up a plume of sepia smoke. 'Aagh!' Jack cried.

'Put it out. Put it out!'

Jack stamped on the notepad, over and over, squashing out the flames. Burnt paper and ashes scattered, the acrid stench of smoke stinging the air. Jack looked at Daisy and she looked at him. Both of them terrified, both breathing heavily. Then they looked down at the letters. Some were face down, some were face up. Out of the ten or so that were face up, one of them was a B.

Daisy gasped. 'Oh, Jack. We didn't close the board. We didn't say goodbye…'

CHAPTER 19
THE FOG

That Halloween night, through the conduit of marijuana, maybe a Ouija board and maybe that film – or maybe a cocktail of all three – Jack had let the demons in. Into his head, at least. And one demon in particular. His father. The next morning neither of them could really believe it had happened. It didn't seem real. Had they just been stoned? Daisy questioned herself. Had she been unconsciously moving the planchette?

Not long afterwards, Jack started getting visions. These weren't like his flashbacks, things that had gone before; they were the present. His father sitting on the sofa and turning to look at him, speaking to him: *'You're going to hurt her and she's going to leave you. You're just like me.'* That was the first time it happened: the side of his father's head and face charred, just as they were on that sliding drawer at the morgue, the same dead eyes, that glassy stare, deep and cold as a grave. He didn't tell Daisy – telling her about the flashbacks had been bad enough, she would think he was mad. And the visions came and went, but always when he was on his own, never with Daisy around. It made him want to be always with her, even if she was just nipping to the shops; it was the only way to keep them at bay.

The weather turned colder, and so did the flat, if that was possible. But at least it was dry inside, so on days off they would sometimes barely leave at all. They'd sleep in their clothes, huddle under the blanket on the sofa with hot water bottles, smoke spliffs and watch endless films. In their own little world. They worked their way through Daisy's top twenty movies list, finishing off one drizzly afternoon with her number one, *A Streetcar Named Desire*. It was absolutely perfect to Daisy. They were stoned. The huge windows of the flat, complete now with net curtains, reminded her of Stanley and Stella's apartment in the film, the rain a lullaby of tears against the glass, enveloping them, part of the show; their own movie within a movie. That's how it seemed to her anyway. They'd even started to fight a little like the couple in the film. A few spats and quarrels were creeping in here and there, and they often ended in violence, the marijuana messing with their heads. It was always Daisy who started it. Petty things really. Jealousies spilling over from work and their social group (mainly involving Jeanie). Jack always ended up defending himself, restraining her; he'd never hit her back, all too wary of his father's prophecy coming true. But Daisy didn't seem to mind the sparring, it just made her feel more as if she was living out her life in a film. In this case her favourite film. Was that how in love with her art she was? How far she would take it? That she would pick fights on purpose? Clearly so. She liked being at the mercy of Jack's physicality, with him pinning her down, throwing her across the bed. She wanted him to be her Stanley. It turned her on. And then the makeup sex afterwards; always great, getting those coloured lights going...

Another time, again through a marijuana haze, they watched the fall of the Berlin Wall: tens of thousands of Germans swamping checkpoints, fences and gates, clambering over them, with bewildered-looking soldiers and officials powerless to stop them. For a while it looked like another Hillsborough unfolding. But it all went off without serious incident. Soon revellers were drinking champagne, letting off fireworks and sparklers, dancing and singing on top of the wall itself, partying as if New Year's Eve – the much-anticipated end of the decade – had come early. Some young men were even physically chipping away at the wall. It all seemed so very important, auspicious, momentous. Yet Jack and Daisy's detachment was complete; it was something happening in another world, not theirs.

One night that November, a fog bank rolled in off the sea, enshrouding the seaside town. Sea fog was a feature of their new home, especially since the cold weather had hit, something they were getting used to. But previously there had been nothing like this – it was the worst the town had experienced in decades. The local radio and news talked about nothing else, telling people to stay at home and not to use their cars in town unless absolutely necessary. Even the buses stopped running. It was a little unsettling to look out of the window in the morning – fascinating but sinister – to see how the buildings opposite had disappeared; the whole town in fact. It reminded Jack and Daisy of the film *The Fog* – monstrous seafarers with hooks for hands and wooden legs traversing the shore and marauding the town, sinister knocks at the door. Jack didn't want to go out and Daisy didn't fancy being left at home alone. But they had no choice. Jack had to work.

Negotiating the town was disorientating, eerily quiet save for gulls' plaintive cries; they sounded puzzled, as if searching for something. Jack couldn't see much further than a few feet in front of him. It took twice as long as normal to reach the restaurant, as he kept losing his way. Several times he nearly banged into other people, dark shapes, phantoms, appearing suddenly out of the mist, zombie-like town workers muttering apologies: like Jack, they had no choice but to be out in it. Lunchtime service was dead: they did a grand total of three covers, all regular singletons. The evening wasn't much busier, despite the fact the fog had eased enough for traffic to resume. The atmosphere was less dense, but the town was still veiled in a freezing, patchy murk that swirled and drifted about, wetting Jack's hair as he made his way home.

It was out of this lingering, clinging fog that a black car menaced. Two beams in the mist, slightly behind him. Jack wasn't aware of this as he turned the corner of the street adjoining the one in which they lived. Just as he wasn't aware that it had followed him home the previous night. Walking home with his headphones on had become habit, his thoughts centred on the spliff that Daisy would have ready for him, his personal stereo in the pocket of his new long black coat – a second-hand one similar to Tom's – with the collar turned up against the cold.

When the car pulled up quickly alongside him, the first thing Jack was aware of was a sudden movement to his right. The next thing he knew a strong arm, frighteningly strong, had him round the neck, knocking his headphones off; they dangled as he was dragged backwards, his throat in agony as it was crushed. Air left him and he choked as he tried to cry out. But a leather-gloved hand was clamped over his mouth. His nostrils spasmed as they tried to find oxygen, the panic making it worse. He saw lights in his head. Was this what it felt like to suffocate? Was he going to die here on this foggy street? Then his throat was released and he was bundled into a vehicle. A door slammed shut and the car squealed away from the kerb, the leather-gloved hand still over his mouth. He could smell it. That and tobacco and aftershave. Then another hand clamped on the back of his neck. He fought to free himself, but this hand found the pulse in his neck and applied more pressure. A voice in his ear, bad breath in his face. 'Don't struggle. If I squeeze this spot hard enough yer a goner. Just keep quiet, be a good wee boy and I'll take my hand off yer mouth. Start hollering and it stays on.' The voice was to his left, his assailant the only person beside him in the back of the car. The only person in the front was the driver: a huge fat, bald head, shaved at the back. 'Take the road past the park.'

'Easier said than done in this shite... Which one is it?'

'Ach, you've missed it. Go round again.' The men had strong Scottish accents. 'You. Get doon,' the first man said, pushing Jack down on the seat. He tried to resist, but it was no use; he considered swinging his elbow, but this was a fight he knew he couldn't win. Not with the two of them. Survival was more important than pride or being a hero. The car turned corners for what seemed like an age. Jack had no idea where he was. 'This one. Doon here.'

The car turned again, then speeded up slightly, heading in a straight line at last. 'Right, get back up.' The hand was removed from Jack's mouth and he was dragged upright, his headphones and the tail of his coat trapped under the bulk next to him. He noticed, through the window and the mist, the town's park and the pitch-and-putt golf course, the fog clearing as they headed away from the coast. Where were they going? Where the fuck were they going? It reminded him of the time he'd been captured at the station, but even that had seemed like a picnic in comparison to this. This was pure fear.

'Where are you taking me? What do you want?'

'Shut up. I'll do the talking,' the man said. 'And don't look at me. Look at Danno's head.' Instinctively Jack turned to look at the man. He didn't get far. A glove in his face and 'I said, don't look at me!' Then to the driver, 'Keep going, another half mile or so, tell we het the trees.' Trees? The wooded area on the outskirts of town. That didn't sound good. Jack thought of Daisy. She'd be waiting for him, already worried about him because of the fog. He looked at his door, down at the handle. An escape route? The man still had him round the neck, but that was it. And the car wasn't moving that fast. When they slowed down? He shifted his right hand slightly, bit by bit in the dark, trying to get it as near the handle as possible. 'It's locked,' the man said. Jack's heart sank. He considered screaming, but who would hear him?

They carried on driving for around five minutes, not passing another car. The road had become narrower, bowered by black skeletons of trees, the moon conducting a Morse code through the overhanging branches. The man leant forward. 'The next pull-in,' he said. Jack's mind was racing. What were they going to do with him? Kill him? What did they want? He anticipated the gleam of metal, the glint of the flitting moon on a gun barrel pressed to his head. Hard and cold, digging into his temple. Just like in the movies. The car slowed and bumped into a gated pull-in, not dissimilar to the one at Bunny Wood. Bunny Wood. What he'd give to be back there now. A safe and sound and familiar bosom. How had his life taken this turn?

The driver turned off the engine and all was silent, save for the creak of the men's leather jackets as they shifted in their seats, the car ticking and settling, the pellet-like drip of moisture on the roof. The driver didn't turn round. He'd still only spoken once. 'Don't look at me,' the man said again. 'Now, if I take my hand off yer neck, yer not gonna do anything selly?' Jack continued to stare straight ahead. 'Eh?' The man squeezed again, that pressure point. It made Jack want to pass out. He shook his head, never before having felt so physically vulnerable. The man slowly released his grip and sat back, placing his gloved hands on his thighs. 'Good. Thadda boy. Now. Ah guess yer wondering what we're doing out here. I know I would be if ah were yous… Well, it's quite simple, really. Or it can be. As simple as yer want tae make et. So here it is… I suggest yae listen carefully…' *Here it comes*, thought Jack, vermin crawling all over his inner organs. 'Change your story about where yer got that money from – the grand or whatever peanuts it is yer think yae earned – or things will get nasty. And, trust me, yer don't want things tae get nasty. Does he, Danno?'

'Fuck, no,' said the man from the front seat.

'This isn't nasty. This is us being friendly. Consider it a friendly warning. 'Cause if yer don't do as we're asking nicely, next time it won't be a warning. And it won't be yous either. It'll be that pretty little girlfriend of yours.' This triggered a switch in Jack. He started swinging, regardless of the danger, a gut reaction to Daisy being threatened. One punch landed and glanced off the man's head, but the next one was blocked. Violently outraged, the man dispensed an elbow blow to Jack's head that made him see stars. Then he was pinned down with a forearm to the throat and pushed into the corner of the seat, the man using all his weight. 'Easy there, wee man,' he hissed, continuing to apply pressure as Jack struggled. He'd never come up against such brute strength. Not with his father, ever.

The man in front turned round for the first time. 'Yer need some help back there?' he said.

'Now look what you've gone and done. That wasn't very sensible, was it? Now you've gone and got Danno's attention. And yae don't want that. He's not as friendly as me. No, I think I've got this, thanks!' The man was putting on an act, toying with Jack, as if it was all a game.

'Yer sure?'

Jack gave up struggling.

'Aye, I'm sure. Now, where were we? Oh yes, yer pretty … little …girlfriend.'

'Shut up!' Jack shouted. 'Shut up!'

'Boy, you really like her, don't yae. That or yer stupid. Well, good! I'm glad that yae like her!' He was shouting now; the game was over. ''Cause if yae don't change yer story then it'll be her next. But *she* won't come back. She'll disappear. Danno here likes little girls, don't you, Danno?'

'Aye.'

'And Danno's got friends that like little girls too, haven't yae, Danno? Love the new hairdo by the way…'

'You fucking bastard!' Jack cried.

'That's right. A fucking bastard. But right now this fucking bastard is the only thing that's stopping your head getting ripped off. Now listen up. Yae do as I say and yae don't go to the police. Got me? If yae do, the same thing happens. The girl disappears. We know where yae live and we know where yae both work, Crab's Claw, ennet? And I wouldn't go spilling too much to yer lady either. We hear she can be a bit feisty. A bit hot-headed. The only person yae want to be talking to is that pesky detective friend of yours. Change your story and call him off. Or else. Have I made myself clear? Have I?' Jack nodded. 'Good. Now get out of the car. Danno, unlock the door.'

Losing his headphones in the process, Jack was shoved out of the car and into the cold, black night. Humiliated, outraged and defeated. But still alive.

By the time he'd stumbled home, still terrified of the car coming after him, it was gone twelve and Daisy, unusually for her, was already in bed. Earlier she'd had a phone call from Hilary, around the same time Jack had left work, asking her to come in at lunchtime the next day; someone had called in sick. It was annoying because it was Jack's day off, but she didn't like to say no. And the money always came in handy.

At first Daisy had been worried about Jack, out there in the fog. But as time had gone on, she'd grown mad at him. There was no way they could have been busy, not with the weather. She guessed he'd gone to The Love Shack without her – and without letting her know. Then he'd expect to come home at whatever time and for her still to be up, waiting for him. Well he could think again. She decided to teach him a lesson. Sod him. If he preferred their company to hers, then fine. And woe betide him if *she'd* been there. She wished she'd asked Hilary what time he'd left – and with whom.

Jack let himself into the flat, and, without even brushing his teeth undressed and crawled straight into bed. He was shivering, wet and freezing cold. He cuddled into Daisy's back for warmth and comfort. This woke her up, and she kicked her legs at him, pulling away, 'Get off me! You're freezing cold!' Then, secretly relieved he was back safely, she fell asleep again.

Jack clung on to her again, wrapping himself around her. Savouring her warmth, her steady breathing, the fact that she was safe and unharmed. The way her back rose and fell, hot, heavy and slow, against him, her heart a muffled drum – the total opposite to him, his heart and mind still racing, his breath jerky and shallow. All the way home he'd debated whether to tell her or not. But he couldn't – not the full story anyway. He knew only too well what Daisy was like – especially when it came to injustice. Even they'd known that. How? She would kick up the biggest fuss ever. Make him go to the police. And then he'd have to tell her that they'd threatened her. She'd want to leave this place that had become home, to move back to *her* home. Where would *he* go?

He could sense this in her sometimes, especially after she'd been speaking to her mum or when they'd had a fight. Sometimes she'd threaten him with it. This was partly because a bit of a stalemate had ensued between Daisy and her mum. Weeks had quickly grown into months of Carol refusing to visit Cromer, still hoping her daughter would see sense and come home. Daisy was equally stubborn, trying to prove that she could survive on her own, that she'd made the right decision and didn't need to go running back home every five minutes. A Christmas compromise had finally been agreed: a visit back home for the festive period, an invitation extended to both Daisy and Jack.

And who was to say these men wouldn't come after them wherever they were? How had they even been found? It was Peasgood that was at the root of it. That bastard – and he was in the East Midlands. Who'd have thought he'd have gone to such lengths to protect himself?

Still traumatised and unable to sleep, Jack continued debating what he should do long into the night. All the dark thoughts, the worries, the fears ganging up on him, tormenting him. Like coal-black birds on a telephone wire. First one, eyes beady and head cocked. Then another joining it. Then another and another, twitching, screeching, mocking, gathering. Until there was a whole row of them, none of them leaving him alone. And then when he finally managed to drift off into a troubled sleep, plagued by bad dreams, it was nearly morning. He dreamt of what had happened: the car, the threats, the violence. Being cast out onto the road. The car speeding away. But Daisy was in the back seat, her terrified face staring out of the back window at him, her hands pressed against the glass.

CHAPTER 20
Peasgood

When Jack woke the curtains in the bedroom were still closed. The previous night came back to haunt him. He sat bolt upright in bed. Had it all been a dream? Or rather a nightmare? A dark, twisted vision of hell – of black cars and trees and fog and men in black coats. It was hard to separate what was real from what wasn't; the dreams were so fresh in his mind that they clung to him, a web he couldn't extricate himself from. His head was fuzzy. He felt delirious, sweaty and clammy. Hot and cold. A chill from the previous night. And where was Daisy?

He looked at her empty spot in the bed. What time was it? Eleven-thirty already. 'Daisy?' he called. There were no sounds from the kitchen or lounge. No music playing, no TV on. 'Daisy?' Jack shot out of bed, not noticing the cold mug of tea next to him. Panicking, he stumbled down the hallway, paranoid from the dreams that she'd left him or been taken away, his thoughts running amok. 'Daisy?' The kitchen and lounge were empty. He pushed open the bathroom door. She was nowhere to be seen. He'd never woken up without her before; they always went to bed together and woke up together. He wanted to cry, his worst nightmares coming true. What if she was out there on the streets at the mercy of those two men? Then he spotted a note on the kitchen counter, its corner tucked under a mug. He raced over to pick it up: 'Jack. Have been called into work today till 3. Someone's off sick. Where were you last night? We need to talk later. Daisy.x'

He breathed a sigh of relief. At least she was at work. Safe and sound. Or what if she wasn't? What if she hadn't got that far? Should he ring the restaurant? Or maybe go in? He was panicking again. *Get a grip.* They would have rung by now if she hadn't showed up. But he would meet her afterwards. At three. From now on he would always walk her to and from work: he wouldn't let her out of his sight until this was sorted. And that's what he had to do, sort it. He'd got to ring up Haslam and tell him he'd made it up, to change his story. So that Peasgood called those men off. But what did he say? Where would he have got over a thousand pounds from?

His father.

He'd say he stole it from his father.

After stumbling around for ten minutes, unable to think clearly, Jack finally located the card with Haslam's number on it. Thank God. He had to do this without Daisy around, pressuring him. With shaking hands he dialled the number. After half a dozen nail-biting rings Haslam picked up. 'Haslam.'

'Mr Haslam, it's Jack. Jack H– Gardner.'

'Jack! Course it's you. No other Jack's got my number. This is a surprise. What can I do for you? No problems I hope…'

'No. Erm, yes. It's about the money, you see. My money.'

'Go on…'

Jack took a deep breath. 'I made it up. Where I got it from. It wasn't from Peasgood at all. I lied. I'm sorry.' His voice cracked with the pressure of it all. It felt as if he actually *had* lied. He felt ashamed. He was lying now, and just wanted it all over and done with.

The detective let out a long breath. 'You lied? … Jack, why would you do that?' Haslam thought of the wasted hours: of bothering the man, visiting his factory. Only this week, against his better judgement, he'd called Peasgood again, using flattery as a way in – *'being such a busy man with such a large workforce one could understand how easily a young worker could slip through the net; maybe you left the day to day staffing mundanities to underlings, a head of personnel or payroll maybe, someone who might remember the boy in question?'*

It hadn't gone down well.

'You'd better tell me where you really got that money from, and right now, young man,' Haslam said to Jack. 'And no more lies.'

'It was my father's money. From his furniture business. He always got paid with real money; notes, I mean. I found it in a wardrobe in his bedroom, before I set fire to the house. It would have only got burnt otherwise. I needed it, so I took it.'

Haslam mulled it over. He wasn't in a position to dispute the claim. It sounded feasible – and it wasn't as if anyone had reported a robbery or having over a grand in cash stolen. It was a relief in a way: the tying up of a loose end. 'Why didn't you just tell me that in the first place? It would have saved a whole lot of hassle – and paperwork. And why the hell Peasgood? It doesn't make sense.'

'I was ashamed – and scared. I thought you'd take it off me. And once I said it I couldn't back down.'

'So you just picked him out at random? Like out of a telephone book? Out of thin air?' There was a rising note of anger to his voice, but then it changed suddenly. 'Hold on. So how did you know what he even looked like – or that he'd got a Scottish accent for that matter? I remember you saying that...'

Shit, thought Jack. *Shit, shit, shit*. He hadn't thought this through. *Think! Think!* 'Erm ... Daisy had worked there – only a couple of shifts ... he wouldn't remember her. He treated her badly. He treated her badly and she told me about it and I wanted to get my own back on him.' More lies. Jack pressed the palm of his hand against his head in anguish, then wished he hadn't; his head was hurting where he'd been elbowed.

'Seems a bit extreme.'

'I know. And I'm sorry, but I didn't know what else to say. But you've got to tell him! Tell him I've changed my mind and that I'm sorry.'

'I'm disappointed in you, Jack, I must say. You've wasted police time, lied to the police and wasted his time; he could press charges, you know.' This is what bothered the detective the most; Peasgood seemed the malicious type. Arrogant. The kid had been stupid, but he didn't really deserve that. 'You'll be hearing from me in due course. This might not be the end of it, I'm afraid. Thank you for coming clean, though. It was the right thing to do.'

'And you will tell him, won't you? You will tell Peasgood?'

'I'll deal with it, yes. Bye for now, Jack.'

Haslam hung up and stared at the phone on his desk for a while. Something about this didn't add up. He prided himself on being a good judge of character; and Jack didn't strike him as capable of being manipulative or vindictive. He'd been so adamant about where he'd got the money from, incensed almost at Peasgood's denial – for months on end. Why the sudden turnaround? And why was he so desperate for him to let Peasgood know? And then there was the timing of it. Coincidence? He would phone Peasgood again and talk to him. Maybe his guard would come down. The detective couldn't help thinking there was more to it than met the eye.

After the phone call, Jack too sat motionless, pondering. He'd done it. He'd told Haslam and changed his story. So why didn't he feel any different? Why the same anxiety? It was because Peasgood didn't know yet. He wouldn't be able to relax until he got confirmation that Peasgood knew. But would he even be able to relax then? Would he ever feel safe again, for himself or for Daisy? When you could just be snatched on the street like that and bundled into a car. But it had been dark – and foggy. They'd picked their moment. How long had they been watching him for? It could have been weeks. It gave him the creeps. Worse, that man had said he knew where they lived – and worked. How? The sooner Haslam phoned back the better. But what if it was days? He wouldn't be able to sleep a wink. He would have to phone Peasgood himself. That's what he'd do. If he hadn't heard from Haslam by five he would phone him. In the meantime he had to think what, or how much, he was going to tell Daisy. If anything.

*****

It was not long gone two-thirty. Jack was jittery and on edge and had been unable to eat a thing all day. The ghastly vision of his father had been tormenting him, making the most of Daisy's absence, *'She's going to leave you. They all do in the end.'* Jack was sick of it and sick of waiting. He wanted to reach the restaurant before Daisy finished work at three. He was just preparing to leave when the front door of the flat opened and slammed shut, making him jump out of his skin. His eyes scanned the kitchen for a knife, a weapon. 'Daisy?' he said.

No answer.

Then a head appeared at the top of the stairs, making him jump again. 'Daisy! Why didn't you answer? And how come you're home already?' His initial feeling was one of anger that she had walked home alone. But this quickly gave way to relief and gratitude that she was back safely. He had missed her and instinctively moved towards her, wanting to hug her. But Daisy put her hands up. 'Don't,' she said, her expression defiant, stony.

Jack felt hurt. He'd been through enough already. 'What?' he said. 'What's wrong?'

She put down her bag. 'Where were you last night?'

Jack didn't know what to say, still didn't know how much to tell her or where to begin. Maybe he could just say he went to Aitch's…

'Where were you?' Daisy shouted, hurt and venom in her voice. 'And who were you with? And don't you lie to me, Jack! Don't you ever lie to me, 'cause I swear to God I'll just pack my bags right now and go.'

'I…' he faltered.

''Cause I know you weren't at Aitch's last night – Tom told me. He said it was dead and Aitch wasn't even on.' *There goes that alibi then*, thought Jack, as Daisy advanced. She'd been simmering with this information all day. 'But *she* was, wasn't she? That little slut who can't keep her hands or eyes off you! So where were you, hey? Where were you till gone twelve o'clock if you weren't with Tom or Aitch?'

Jack backed away, his hands raised. He recognised that look on her face, the look that normally preceded her lashing out. 'Daisy, if you'll just calm down I'll explain everything.'

'You'd better!' She was up close now. But then her face changed. 'What happened to your head?'

Jack put his hand to the lump. It was bruised and swollen, tender to touch. There was no avoiding it; he was going to have to come clean. At least she would believe him. She got so crazy about Jeanie. So jealous and irrational. Her Achilles heel. 'I got kidnapped last night.'

'Kidnapped?' she scoffed. This was so far-fetched that it didn't help Jack's cause. Who got kidnapped in Cromer? 'By who?'

'Two men. I was walking home in the fog. They were in a car. They grabbed me and shoved me into it and drove me out of town. It was horrible. They threatened me. One of them did this.' He touched his head. 'And this.' He pulled his polo shirt collar to the side. There were two more bruises either side of his neck.

Daisy's face had gone from hurt and accusation to incredulousness. 'But why? Why would anyone want to kidnap you? It doesn't make sense. Who were they?'

'They were Scottish. Peasgood's men – or something to do with him.'

'Peasgood?'

'Yes. They told me to change my story about where I got the money from. I don't know why. Probably 'cause Peasgood's lied to the police or something.'

'That fucking bastard!' cried Daisy. 'If you're telling the truth, Jack, God… I'm so sorry.' She went to stroke his head, to push away his hair. 'Baby, I'm so sorry.'

Jack winced, a touch of indignation creeping in. 'Course I'm telling the truth. Why would I make something like this up? It was terrifying. They drove me away to some woods. There were two of them and one of them had his hand over my mouth and round my throat. I could hardly breathe. I thought they were going to kill me…'

'Jesus Christ.' She couldn't believe what she was hearing, a fury building inside her. 'Why didn't you tell me this last night? And what did the police say? You have phoned the police, haven't you?!'

'Yes. Well, Haslam anyway.'

'Haslam? What good can he do? He's miles away. You need to phone the local police.'

'They told me not to. They told me that if I did then,' he averted his gaze, 'then next time it would be worse.'

'Next time? I can't believe what I'm hearing. This is blackmail! Kidnap, assault and blackmail! The police need to know. I'll call them myself.'

'Daisy, don't!' Jack grabbed her arm. And this time there was no pleasure in it for her. This wasn't a game.

'Ow, Jack. You're hurting!'

'Leave it. I'm dealing with it. You didn't hear these people. They were very specific. They only wanted me to deal with

Haslam. It's him they want calling off. For me to change my story and for Haslam to stop investigating Peasgood. That's it.' He loosened his grip, becoming aware of how hard he was holding her. 'Sorry. Haslam said he'd call Peasgood and let him know. In fact he's probably already done it by now.'

'But why should that bastard get away with it? He's a bully and a liar and you know how I feel about bullies.'

'What does it matter? He hasn't got my money, has he? This way everyone wins. He calls off those … those thugs, and I get my money back – I hope.'

'But you'll look like a liar. Doesn't that bother you? It's like admitting you're guilty for something you haven't done – you might get in more trouble. It's the principle of the thing. Why should he get away with it? Or what if he decides to press charges for you making accusations against him. Or what if he doesn't stick to his word? Where will it end?'

'It'll end as soon as he knows I've changed my story.'

'Aaagh!' Daisy cried. 'I just can't bear the thought of him getting away with it – the sick bastard, getting men to do this to you, threatening you and scaring you half to death. You're absolutely sure they were sent by Peasgood?'

'Yes! I mean, they didn't mention his name or anything – but then I guess they wouldn't. But they were Scottish – which is too much of a coincidence – and they knew Haslam. And who else would go to those lengths to get me to change my story about the money?'

'I suppose so… But what did you tell Haslam – about where you got the money from? Actually, don't tell me. I'm gonna get changed out of these stinky clothes first. Put the kettle on – and then I want you to tell me everything, about what happened and exactly what you said to Haslam. And roll a spliff – I could use one for my nerves. Oh, Jack.' Daisy held his head and kissed him. 'At least you're safe, thank God. That's the main thing.' She hugged him, then walked off shaking her head. 'That fucking bastard,' she said again.

Jack put the kettle on. He decided to make some toast, too. It was the first time he'd felt hungry all day. As always, Daisy had calmed him down, made him feel more at ease. Just telling her about it was the lifting of a burden. Perhaps everything was going to be all right. Providing Daisy kept her cool: he'd already told her too much. He just needed to hear confirmation that Peasgood knew. Until then he wouldn't be able to properly relax.

Daisy was stunned by Jack's revelations. Stunned and angry. At the unfairness of it, and that such a thing – such violence – could visit their lives. She also, like Jack, found it impossible to fathom the lengths Peasgood had gone to to protect himself.

But then neither of them knew Peasgood. Not really. Not of his past, or what he was capable of…

*****

One of seven children raised in a Glasgow tenement, Peasgood had made his way up the hard way, unafraid of using intimidation and unscrupulous methods. And, now, a couple of years from his planned retirement, he wasn't about to have everything he'd worked for come crashing down thanks to some pipsqueak of a kid.

When the news of the fire at the house on the hill broke, Peasgood had kept a close eye on the story. He was one of the few people who had actually set foot on the land or even knew where Jack and his father lived. And when a teenage boy was taken in for questioning he'd instantly put two and two together. He'd followed the local news bulletins, the newspaper articles about Jack's reclusive father, Jack himself and the red-headed girl – fearful of any connection with him or his factory. It was a relief that the old man had gone – human bodies weren't the only thing buried on that rambling plot, and the police were snooping about, digging for things.

But there was still that blasted boy: he'd literally lead the police to him. After the dreaded call from the detective that day, and his own subsequent denial, he'd put down the phone; then, with a gnarled and shaky finger he'd dialled a number with a Glasgow area code. His old stomping ground. Just in case.

That same day, pre-empting any follow-up action, Peasgood had also called an impromptu meeting of his entire workforce. Again, just in case; he hadn't got where he was by not being ahead of the game. He'd made the matter out to be a mere trifle – a routine investigation into illegal workers being paid cash – which it was at the end of the day. Playing right into Peasgood's hands, Haslam hadn't mentioned any connection to the Bunny Hill crimes in order to protect Jack's identity, merely said it was a money matter.

Peasgood had 'requested' that in the event of any potential visit staff were to deny knowledge of anyone being paid in cash. Failure to do so would affect their Christmas bonus (which was paid off the books in cash). There might even be a little extra if they co-operated. It was a stroke of genius; Peasgood would have made a good politician.

Despite all this, it was still a bit of a shock when Haslam turned up, unannounced. Peasgood answered his questions and showed him around. Then he watched nervously as the detective spoke to a couple of random workers before leaving. Peasgood was pleased to see them solemnly shaking their heads. One of them, a long-time worker, did remember Jack – a peripheral figure who had left some weeks before – but he didn't make any connection with the house on the hill. Why would he?

It had all gone according to plan. Yet still Peasgood couldn't relax. Yes, he'd been meticulous, yes he was manipulative, but he was also hot-headed. It was his weakness. He had a dislike of authority – governments, the police. And he'd dug a bit of a hole, set something in motion, that could come back to bite him. When they are cornered, when they are pushed, men can do drastic things.

And that's why he'd taken extra precautions. Extreme precautions.

Call it security.

CHAPTER 21
December will be Magic Again…

Soon Jack was told by Haslam that Peasgood knew the accusations about the money had been dropped – but that it might not be the end of the matter. Still, this was a huge relief, but when Jack asked if he could have his money back, Haslam had become evasive, saying something about paperwork. At the same time Jack was also informed that with no new evidence forthcoming, the investigation into Anne's murder was now closed, and his father was officially considered responsible. This was also a big relief. Jack gave the go-ahead for the cremation of his sister's and mother's remains – his father's could be dumped in the bin for all he cared. Haslam had swung it so that the cremations wouldn't cost Jack a thing; and told him that he should be very grateful. He was.

Daisy fumed and sulked for days about Peasgood and the money. The injustice more than anything. Along with her father, Marlon's portrayal of Terry Malloy in *On the Waterfront* had shaped her attitude to bullies. And Peasgood had become her Johnny Friendly. She didn't understand how Jack could be so unbothered. He was more concerned with not letting her out of his sight, to the point of paranoia. She never questioned him about it, just figured he was being over-cautious after what had happened that fateful night in the fog. And who could blame him?

Hearing that the money was being held back coincided with the receipt of their first quarterly utility bills – something that in their naivety they hadn't budgeted for. They'd just been living week to week, spending their wages as and when they got them. This made it easier for Daisy to make a decision. Hilary had been badgering her about working more or less full time; they'd lost a member of staff and Christmas was just around the corner. So Daisy took her up on the offer, as a stopgap at least: she didn't see any other choice and still wasn't ready to go back to college. For some reason she felt anxious every time she thought about it. The flat, the restaurant and the gang were her own little bubble now: because of their dope-smoking she and Jack were becoming more and more insular. College could wait until the New Year.

Jack was thrilled that Daisy had decided to work at the restaurant full time. This meant he could keep more of an eye on her and wouldn't have to worry about her so much. But perhaps more than that it conveyed her commitment to the area. To them. Daisy's mum, on the other hand, was less than pleased; it was exactly what she'd been afraid of, her daughter ending up in a dead end job with no prospects. They would also have to break the news to Daisy's grandma at some point – tell her that the course didn't work out, or something...

With the Peasgood matter apparently put to bed, the threat of a further kidnapping gradually faded, along with the ghost of Peasgood himself. It had been weeks since the incident; and as December wore on, Christmas – or more specifically their first Christmas together – became the main topic of Jack and Daisy's thoughts and conversation. They talked about it late into the night. As it had been with birthdays, Jack had never experienced a proper, traditional Christmas with presents; his familiarity with it was through TV and books, watching *The Snowman* with Anne, his Raymond Briggs *Father Christmas* book or the squabbling families on *EastEnders*.

Jack had never even seen a real Christmas tree. The day had always been centred on his father, just like his birthday: keeping him happy and his stomach full. A roast dinner. Then drunk in front of the TV, watching the Queen's speech and laughing at *Morecambe and Wise*. The two children hoping the day didn't descend into violence at the merest spark. Though Anne was forbidden to spend any money on Jack, she'd always done her best, holding a little back from her meagre housekeeping in the run-up to provide him with a little stocking of an almost Dickensian nature: an old sock always stuffed with a Terry's chocolate orange, a clementine or satsuma and maybe a pack of cards that she'd use to teach him to play patience with. Or maybe some crayons. But that was it. The weight of it on the end of his bed was thrill enough.

This had made Daisy want to cry, and she took it upon herself, in her usual fastidious way, to ensure that Jack had the best Christmas ever, his first proper one with gifts galore. They were going to have an Advent calendar and their own tree and everything. She asked him what presents he'd like, so she could put them on his Christmas list, and she jokingly penned a letter to Father Christmas, saying that if he didn't believe in him he wouldn't come. It made Daisy feel like a kid again: she felt an anticipation, a buzz about Christmas she hadn't had in years. It was like that innocent summer, which seemed so long ago, when they'd sat by the oak tree in the spinney and planned Jack's wish list of activities.

Jack, as always, was swept along by Daisy's enthusiasm, but the only present he really wanted was a chocolate orange – and maybe some of the children's books he'd lost. At least this gave Daisy something to work on. They spent cold, windswept December days navigating the twinkling town, bedecked with Christmas lights that had been switched on by a *Blue Peter* presenter. Every now and again they split up, Jack having relaxed a little in that respect, to purchase each other small gifts

– work was busy and tips were especially good, as customers were so generous around Christmas time. Often they'd retreat to the Sailor (as they now called it) for a lunchtime tipple and much-needed respite from the elements. They'd grown fond of the pub: the open fire that provided such a contrast to the cold in their flat, the nets and lobster pots and tankards that hung from the ceiling, the occasional shared treat of scampi or chicken and chips in a basket. In keeping with the time of year, Daisy would order homemade mulled wine and help herself to the complimentary mince pies on the bar, urging Jack to try one. Then, rosy-cheeked, they'd settle by the fireside to tease each other about what they'd bought, Daisy clutching her warm glass and blowing on the sweetly spiced steam to cool it as Jack sipped at his cider.

Daisy had also decided to finally make Jack's follow-up compilation tape – a 'Daisy's Greatest Hits Vol. 2' – in time for Christmas. It would be perfect as a gift and she was in her element working on it; the only annoying thing was that she didn't have all of the songs she had earmarked, as some of her records were still at home. And that was another thing that needed planning: Christmas at home, which she was looking forward to. It would be nice to have a proper roast dinner with all the trimmings for once. Getting time off wasn't a problem. The restaurant was closed on Christmas Day and Boxing Day, so all the staff had a much-needed break after December's efforts. But there were no trains back until the next day, so they'd both requested the Wednesday off as well.

The main sticking point was that Carol wanted Daisy to be home on Christmas Eve. As a tradition they'd always gone to Midnight Mass at the local church; not so much for the religious side of it, more for the carols. And even though it did seem a holier-than-thou drag as the girls had got older, Daisy still enjoyed the sound of the carols being sung in the vaulted village church, it made her feel nice and squidgy inside

– childlike. But she was adamant that she wanted to be at home in Cromer on Christmas morning, with Jack, in their own flat, on their own together – enjoying the build-up of the night before as well. They both had to work Christmas Eve anyway, and they used this as an excuse.

Carol was annoyed, and in a fit of pique put the phone down on Daisy on one occasion. 'How are you going to get here if there are no trains running on Christmas Day? You know what? Don't even bother!' It took some sweet-talking from Daisy to make her understand, and even more sweet-talking to Lily to get her to come and pick them up on Christmas morning. This she finally agreed to – more to stop her mum moaning than anything. She demanded a decent present from Daisy in return; she needed a new hairdryer. Spending this extra money was something Daisy could do without. *Let's hope Grandma comes up trumps*, she thought.

December at work went by in a colourful and festive blur, mainly of Christmas parties. Everyone was in high spirits. It was infectious. There was a strong feeling of comradeship, almost of family; they all worked hard together – day and night, evenings and weekends – and then played hard together afterwards, Daisy and Jeanie being the exception.

The front of house staff were encouraged to wear festive adornments during December, Santa hats and tinsel. Not to be outdone, Aitch took to wearing an elf hat, complete with big, sticky-out ears, as he washed up. He seemed permanently drunk, or stoned, or both – possibly because Tom and some of the others kept on sneaking unfinished bottles of wine into the pot wash area and placing them by the bin. Aitch raided the plates for Christmas hats and the little toys that came from the Christmas crackers, and eventually collected a whole box of them. It was if he had his own little Santa's grotto, complete with mistletoe so he could pester the girls for a kiss. When he came across an un-pulled cracker, he crept up behind the chefs, pulled it and made them jump. Chef would bark at him to 'stop being a fucking clown'. But even he would chuckle at the sight of Aitch with half a dozen differently coloured party hats stretched over his elf hat.

It all reached fever pitch on Christmas Eve, one last mad push, the restaurant chock-a-block. Jack only had an hour off between shifts. It was a long day, but everyone knew that once it was over that was it for another year, and they had two whole days off to recover. Jeanie had gone all out and was wearing a full Mrs Santa outfit, a knee-length dress and matching hat, a belt accentuating her slim waist, the look finished with stripy tights and mistletoe in her hair. She was getting on Daisy's nerves as she waltzed about. 'Ooh, do you like my flashing fairy light earrings, boys?'

When the last turkey ballotine went out there was a huge cheer from the chefs. And once service was over, kitchen and front of house staff alike were in a desperate rush for the punters to leave so they could get the clean down out of the way as quickly as possible. The Sailor always had a lock-in on Christmas Eve night; and the kitchen staff were keen to get there before last orders, thus securing their place for the night and the confirmation that the front of house staff would be let in at the back entrance by the landlord.

Spliffs were rolled ready for the short walk to the pub. Jack gave Daisy a kiss, sorry to be leaving her behind. He said he'd see her in a bit and told her he'd get her a drink. 'Get me a pint in, boys!' Tom called as they left. 'No, get me two!' Not for the first time, he rued the day he'd chosen a job out front instead of in the kitchen.

The night was bracing, cheek-stinging, as Aitch and Jack walked to the pub together. The sea bowled an icy roar up the main thoroughfare of the town, sending the glowing reindeer and snowmen spinning; a shock to the system after the sweaty heat and madness of the kitchen. This, along with the spliffs, went straight to the boys' heads. The Sailor was absolutely heaving, the jukebox belting out Christmas classics. Again, it was a furnace compared with outside. The boys fought their way to the bar, their arrival heralded by a peppering of good-natured insults: the rest of the chefs were already there, a couple of pints in. That's how the hierarchy worked. Jack could have left earlier too, but he'd wanted to help Aitch. Even Chef was there, a rare sight indeed, but he didn't stay long.

By the time the front of house team arrived it was gone twelve, but the pub was still swinging. Jack and Aitch had managed to secure a table towards the front, as arranged. There was a rap on the window next to them. Aitch knelt on a settle to pull back a curtain and peer over the frosted lower section of the glass. Tom grinned in from the street. Aitch grinned back and signalled for them to go round the back. As the curtain closed again, all Jack could see of the girls was the top of Jeanie's Santa hat. Aitch got up. 'Just gonna get the nod from Mike to let them in. Stay here and guard the table. Same again, mate?'

Jack nodded and gave a thumbs up, glass to his mouth mid-swallow.

'Come on, you 'orrible lot, you'll get me shot,' Mike said as he let the latecomers in.

They all said, 'Thanks, Mike,' and Tom gave the landlord one of his handshakes.

'Four of yer? Is that the best yer can do? Hardly worth opening the door for,' Mike joked. 'Ooh, hello, Mrs Santa,' he said to Jeanie as she passed. He was a good sort, and he knew from experience that the Crab's Claw lot were a thirsty bunch; the hospitality trade usually were. Good spenders – especially the chefs. He wasn't too fussed how old they were, as long as they looked eighteen…

Aitch greeted the gang noisily at the bar, dishing out drunken hugs. Jack couldn't help smiling; he was so fond of them all. But it wasn't just that. The scene in front of him, as he relaxed on his bench, arms outstretched, represented just how far he'd come. To think he'd spent pretty much sixteen years of his life without talking to a soul. Never mind setting foot in a pub. Yet here he was, in a crowded room – which didn't faze him in the slightest – waiting for a group of people his age he could truly call friends.

All of them, bar Jeanie, had changed into their normal clothes. The only change to her attire was that she'd swapped her work shoes for some red Converse boots that matched her dress. Daisy looked stunning, dressed in her fur coat, a plummy shade of lipstick on, black jeans and Doc Martens. And as she waved to him, her cheeks ruddy from the cold, it made Jack glow that she was his. God, he was stoned. Aitch must have loaded that last spliff they'd had out the back before the door got locked.

An overwhelming desire to hug Daisy came over him. He wished they'd hurry up and order their drinks. But it looked as if Aitch was organising a round of shots as well. To Jack's disappointment, Daisy signalled she was going to the loo. Jack gave a 'hurry up' signal. Daisy smiled and blew him a kiss. Alison went with her, but not Jeanie; no sooner had they left, than she turned round and headed across with the first of the drinks. She was tottering slightly, spilling some of the drinks and giggling, as if she was already tipsy.

'Looks like I've got you all to myself for a few minutes. That makes a change,' she said, as she plonked the drinks a little haphazardly on the table. Jack smiled. He was used to her talking in this jokey way, but he'd noticed she never did it when Daisy was around. 'Now might be a good time for you to give me your Christmas kiss. Everyone else has.' And she stood there, swaying her hips and jingling the bell on her hat. Jack blushed, not knowing whether she was being serious or not. He laughed awkwardly and reached for his pint, taking a defensive swallow. 'Spoilsport,' Jeanie said, sitting down opposite him. As she did so, she rearranged the skirt of her dress, lifting the white woolly hem up slightly and crossing her legs. It turned out that the stripy tights weren't actually tights at all, but long stockings with their tops rolled down. And in that moment, whether it was intentional or not, Jack briefly saw a flash of her red knickers and the tops of her slim, pale thighs. One of them had a mole on the inside of it. Her pants were a tomato red; like her dress, but shiny and satiny in texture.

Jack went a similar colour himself. Instinctively, he took a large glug of his drink, but too quickly, and began to choke – just as Aitch and Tom arrived with more drinks. 'Jesus, you all right, Jack?' said Aitch. 'Go down the wrong 'ole or somethin'?'

Tom patted Jack on the back as he continued to cough, his eyes smarting. 'Steady on, fella. Jesus, what did you do to him, Jeanie?'

'Nothing. I only asked him for a Christmas kiss!' And they all burst out laughing, except Jack.

'I've just got to get the shots and then we're done,' said Aitch. 'Nice of the girls to help. Back in a sec.'

'Why do girls do that?' said Tom, sitting down.

'Do what?' Jeanie sounded distracted.

'Always go to the toilet together in pairs or groups. Lads wouldn't dream of doing that!'

Jack heard Jeanie reply but he wasn't aware of what she was saying. He felt a little strange. There was no kidding himself that he wasn't still thinking about what he'd seen. It had been shocking, yet thrilling. Like that first time he'd seen Daisy's underwear on Midsummer Eve, as if he'd seen something he shouldn't. It made his heart and head throb, his stomach a little sick. But this was new again – and confusing – to be affected this way by someone else. Or some*thing* else. Unless you counted the images in that magazine. They had given him the same sort of feeling. This had been kind of like that. A glossy, erotic image, but fleeting. He hated himself for thinking these things. Where was Daisy?

'Guess what I've got,' cried Aitch, returning with six shot glasses on a little tray. Behind him were Daisy and Alison, thank God.

'Er, it looks like tequila,' said Tom, picking up a glass that looked small in his long, tapered fingers. He put the glass to his nose. 'It smells like tequila!'

'Yes, I've got tequila, but guess…'

'Erm, sorry to interrupt you boys,' said Alison. 'But is there any chance us girls can sit down? We've been on our feet all night.'

'Of course. Sorry, ladies,' said Aitch, giving one of his trademark bows and letting them through.

The girls settled down next to their respective partners, Daisy saying, 'Budge up, Jack,' kissing him on the lips and patting him on the thigh as she sat down, Out of the corner of his eye Jack saw Jeanie tug the hem of her dress down. Or maybe he'd imagined it. *Stop thinking about it!* he told himself.

'Where was I?' said Aitch. 'Oh yes. I may have tequila, but – actually, let's do the tequila first.' He picked up a glass. 'Everybody! Happy Christmas!'

'Happy Christmas!' they all shouted in unison, picking up a glass and knocking a shot back, most of them shaking their heads, some of them slamming the table with their hands at the taste. From another table two middle-aged couples looked over and smiled at their frivolities, as if to say, 'Remember being that age?'

'Uggh! God, that's rank!' cried Jeanie. 'Give me my Bacardi any day.' She'd brought a half bottle into work with her that they'd passed around on the way down.

Daisy took a swallow of cider to get rid of the taste.

Unexpectedly, Aitch turned round, bent over and began doing some messed up version of 'The Twist', gyrating the saggy seat of his jeans in Jeanie's direction. He didn't seem to have a backside at all. 'Guess what's in my pocket? Guess what's in my pocket?' he sang over his shoulder. There was some blue paper sticking out of one of his back pockets.

'Gross. I'm not going in there!' said Jeanie.

'Oh, go on, Jeanie, it'll make his Christmas!' teased Alison.

Aitch shook his bum again.

Jeanie let out a groan, closed her eyes and began squeamishly plucking out the blue paper. It looked like tickets. 'Ooh, you'll have to dig deeper than that,' Aitch said. She reached in again, screwing up her face, and Aitch let out a high-pitched moan, twitching as if in the throes of sexual ecstasy. Everybody laughed. Daisy not so much. She got the impression Jeanie was enjoying being the centre of attention. Jeanie plucked out two remaining tickets, making six in total, and placed them on the table. She then took a dramatic gulp of her drink, as if to rid herself of the traumatic experience.

'New Year's Eve tickets!' Tom cried, turning one over.

'Aye!' said Aitch. 'Fancy dress. You all owe me two quid.'

'How come you're so flush anyway all of a sudden?' said Tom, dishing out the tickets.

'Christmas tips, baby. Plus I haven't got a girlfriend to buy presents for unlike you saps. Unless you count Jeanie here of course. How was it for *you*, darling?' He put his arm round her but she pushed him away.

Everyone eagerly inspected the tickets. Jack didn't share their enthusiasm. He immediately felt threatened by this pale blue slip of paper, a little on edge. Fancy dress. The thought of doing anything that drew attention to himself or that made a spectacle of himself was terrifying. He took a gulp of cider.

'Wow! I can't wait,' said Alison. 'I'm surprised you've got to pay, though.'

'Yes, that's not like Mike,' added Tom.

'There's a buffet and that, and a decent prize for the best costume apparently. I think he wanted to make sure it was

262

all the regulars got 'em first. First come, first served – there's only fifty or so. And what with it being the big one this year, it's gonna be rammed. All the pubs will be. They'll be turning 'em away.'

A double-tongued ripple spread through Daisy's stomach, a forked lightning flash of excitement, at the thought of the turn of the decade – the end of the '80s and the dawn of the '90s. She couldn't really remember the last time this had happened. The '80s had been her decade. The one she'd really been aware of. The music. The films. It seemed to have been the '80s forever, her whole life. She couldn't imagine it being 1990. But she was also thrilled at the prospect of dressing up. She'd always loved the idea of going to a fancy dress party; she'd never been to one. Her mind began to whirr.

The gang spent a while discussing what they could dress up as. There were some ridiculous and outlandish suggestions. Jack went a little quiet. He was still a little perturbed by what had happened earlier; about how he'd felt. He felt guilty, disappointed in himself, as if he'd betrayed Daisy somehow. The night went on. After they'd had another couple of rounds, Mike declared it really was last orders. Cue another scrum for last drinks. Someone put 'Last Christmas' by Wham! on the jukebox. And with everyone unwilling to leave, an impromptu dance floor sprang up. Jack, by now suitably inebriated enough to lose his inhibitions, let Daisy drag him up. Lost amongst the throng, they banged and fell into each other. The night culminated in pretty much the whole pub hollering out 'Fairytale of New York' – which had quickly become Daisy's favourite Christmas song. The punters' voices rose and swelled with the chorus, surprisingly tuneful: Daisy's Midnight Mass. Mike, a little drunk himself, rang out his last orders bell in time to the song, ushering in Christmas Day. Jack seemed to be the only one who didn't know the words. But it didn't matter: he was too drunk to care. And it was one of those moments both he and Daisy would never forget, a little moment of companionship and good times. Here they were, really living.

When it was time to go, Aitch's mistletoe appeared from somewhere. Hugs, kisses and yuletide greetings were exchanged. Even Jeanie and Daisy, in a rare festive truce, put aside their usual restraint and engaged in a drunken embrace. Daisy still didn't trust her, though; she wasn't so plastered that she didn't notice how her lips appeared to linger just a little too long on Jack's cheek when she finally stole her Christmas kiss from him.

CHAPTER 22

Driving Home for Christmas

'What happened?' Jack croaked. His tongue felt coated in fur, his throat like glass.

Daisy stirred next to him. It was morning. 'What? Aagh, my head.'

'What happened?'

'Oh my God. What time is it? Jack, it's Christmas morning!' She reached for the alarm clock. 'Oh, shit! It's nine already. My sister will be here in an hour. What have we done? We've ruined Christmas already!' She threw her head back on the pillow.

'What happened?' Jack said for the third time.

'Stop saying "what happened"! We need to get up.' But Daisy had no intention of doing so: it didn't seem possible. 'You passed out is what happened. Drunk.'

'Where?' He had no recollection of getting home from the pub.

'Here. On the sofa. We were meant to open a present each, remember?'

This was some relief to Jack. He was terrified he'd made a fool out of himself somewhere out there in the world. And then something embarrassing came back to him. Had he been crying last night? 'Where were you?'

'I was here. You were nearly crushing me to death.'

'Why?'

'Can't you remember at all? I was reading you *Where the Wild Things Are* and you started crying. You were lying on me, like this.' She rolled over and lay with her head on his chest. 'I got it you as a present and you said it reminded you of Anne … and you wanted me to read it to you, just like she used to. I only got as far as the first few lines and you started crying.' Jack let out a groan of embarrassment. 'It's OK,' Daisy said, picking at a button on his shirt; he was still fully clothed. 'It was sweet – at first anyway. You were like a big baby. I think it just hit a nerve with you – you know, stirred old memories and that. Look at me; it happens all the time.' Jack didn't say anything, still a little embarrassed – pondering the effects of alcohol and what it can do to you. 'But then you started muttering stuff about your father – that bastard – scary stuff about seeing him and hearing his voice. That he was here in the flat. You were drunk and you weren't making any sense. But it was quite freaky – you were scaring me actually. That reminds me: we can't smoke at Mum's, you know, so there's no point in taking any. She'd go barmy after what happened to Dad. Which is hypocritical, really, considering she used to smoke it. But I think it'll do us good anyway, to have a break from it and that – I don't think it's doing us any good.' She patted his chest for a response but got nothing back; Jack's brain was racing, trying to digest everything she was saying – the prospect of going without gear, and that he'd told her about the visions. Still a little drunk, Daisy continued to babble. 'Anyway, I shushed you and tried to calm you down. And then you passed out, lying on my chest. I couldn't bloody move you, you were like a dead weight. Oh, shit! I think we left the Christmas tree lights on!' Daisy sat up. 'We could have burnt the place down. And what about the electricity? Jack, we've got to get up. My sister'll be here soon. We haven't even opened any presents yet. Come on!' She shook him.

Jack groaned again. Being shoved was making him feel seasick – not that he'd ever been on a boat, but it was how he imagined it to be. And his brain appeared to be rattling about in his head. He didn't care if it was Christmas Day. Daisy was right; they'd ruined it already. 'I can't!' he said.

'You've got to. Mum will kill me – and Lily. I'll make you a cup of tea.' She pulled back the covers and swung her legs over the side of the bed. The cold flooded in. 'Jesus. Why does it have to be so fucking cold in here?' She too was fully clothed, Jack noticed, but she still wrapped herself in her dressing gown. He immediately pulled the covers back again. 'Jack, no!' she said, yanking them back, but he clung on, trapping them with his arm. Daisy gave up, laughing as she walked out. Clearly she hadn't had as much to drink as him.

By the time Daisy returned with the tea, Jack still hadn't ventured out of bed. She stood next to him and tutted. Tied around her neck were their two stockings, hanging like a scarf. She'd planned on playing Santa Claus during the night and putting them on the end of the bed; another thing she rued not doing. Also around her neck hung the camera. It swung dangerously on its strap as she leaned over to pass him his tea. 'Here, sit up and drink this,' she said. Then she removed the stockings from her neck and untied them. 'Happy Christmas, babe,' Daisy said, kissing Jack on the lips. It struck Jack that even in the morning her breath seemed to smell sweet, never bad like his own. As if she was made of different stuff. He managed to raise a smile.

The stocking, a scarlet and white football-type sock with tassels, was bulkily stuffed with all manner of shapes. There was a pleasing weight to it as it rested on his stomach. He began to feel along it, trying to work out what was in it. Clearly a chocolate orange box, some playing cards by the feel of it, and what felt bizarrely like a banana; it felt a little obscene as he held it through the knitted sock. He looked at Daisy, giving her a naughty smile, which she returned. 'Stop it,' she said. 'Don't get me going, we haven't got time. Here let me take a photo.'

'Really?'

'Yes! It's our first Christmas together.' Daisy positioned herself at the end of the bed. 'Now, hold the stocking – not your banana! – and look at me and smile.'

Jack did as he was told, too weary to argue. He was getting used to these random photo requests now. It was as if she had to document everything with pictures, an extension of her diary. 'Do you want me to take one of you?'

'Yes, in a minute. Let's open our stockings first. We haven't got much time.' Daisy put the camera down and came to sit next to him, and they both set about their stockings. Daisy clearly had been much more imaginative than Jack; his stocking for her consisted mainly of chocolate. He couldn't resist cracking open his chocolate orange, first smelling it through the wrapper. To him, the smell *was* Christmas. He peeled back the shiny paper to reveal the neatly clustered chocolate segments and sniffed again, inhaling deeply. It made his head swim with nostalgia and sadness. He sighed. What would he be doing now if he'd never met Daisy? Would he still be up there on that hill? Would he ever have had the courage to leave?

Daisy watched him as he plundered his stocking again, and took another photo. This was what she'd wanted to do, to create magic for him. And it was truly magical, especially those gold chocolate coins in their little orange net; they sparkled like some exotic currency in a fairy tale, payment for a mythical beast… Jack sniffed the playing cards too, opening them up and savouring their new smell. 'For Shithead,' Daisy remarked. There was one little present that was wrapped up, with a shiny gift rosette on it. 'Now this one,' she said, plucking it from his hand, 'is to be opened later. It's probably one of the most important presents, but it fitted so well into your stocking I couldn't resist putting it in.'

'I'm guessing it's a tape,' Jack said, taking it back. 'My number two tape – finally.' He gave it a dreamy sniff.

'Idiot,' Daisy smiled. 'You'll see.'

*****

By the time Lily arrived, they'd still only opened one proper present each. And she was a little late. Daisy had had to wash her hair – she would have a full shower at home. A shower. Imagine: what a luxury! The thought of stripping off and standing up in this infernal cold was painful. They'd had to pack, too. Why hadn't they done that the previous day? Even though they'd had all week, everything had been a mad rush, what with work and shopping for presents for everybody back home. Grandma was going to be there too; Daisy couldn't wait to see her, but was a bit worried about what she'd say about university.

The sudden knock on the flat door was a violent infiltration into their world from another. Though they were both expecting it, it sent them into a panic. The flat was a tip, with wrapping paper strewn about and unwashed dishes and glasses next to the sink. It wasn't the impression Daisy wanted to give of their lives. At least it was only Lily, and not Mum or Grandma. She felt a little nervous, a little shy as she descended the stairs. Her stomach dropped at the sight of her sister's shape through the ribbed glass. They'd never been close-close, but it was as if she was greeting a stranger: a reminder of how insular they'd become in the four months they'd been away. It seemed so much longer, yet had gone by in a flash.

'Aah, finally!' Lily greeted her. 'I thought I'd got the wrong flat.' *Straight in there*, thought Daisy. 'I couldn't park anywhere either, I had to go round the corner. This street's chock-a-block.'

'Happy Christmas then!' Daisy said, a little sarcastically.

'Oh, yes. Happy Christmas.' They both engaged in a stuttering, awkward embrace, two hens pecking round each other. Afterwards they found it hard to look each other in the eye. As Daisy closed the door, they made their own furtive observations. She thought Lily had lost a little weight, which was surprising – and a little galling. Lily thought Daisy had put on a little weight as she followed her upstairs. This was also surprising; she'd expected her to be wasting away, living on scraps like a starving student. She'd better not have gone and got pregnant again: Mum would go spare. 'Your hair's grown,' Lily said. 'Have you dyed it again?'

'No, it's just wet,' Daisy said over her shoulder.

They rounded the top of the stairs. Jack was standing, trapped, in the corner of the kitchen. He'd wanted to run away and hide. He'd also wanted a spliff before Lily had arrived, but Daisy had forbade him, saying her sister would smell it. Funny how the dope had replaced the cider as his way of facing things. He had the same shell-shocked look on his face, thought Lily, that he had every time she saw him; as if he still wasn't used to other human beings. Physically, he hadn't changed much, except that his hair had grown too. It looked better than it had that night they'd dropped them off. He was still wiry, with those hooded, piercing blue eyes, a good-looking lad. Just odd. 'Hi, Jack,' she said.

'Hi.' Jack blushed and shifted uncomfortably, unable to make proper eye contact. There was an awkward silence as all three of them struggled to find something to say. Jack and Daisy weren't used to visitors. The three of them standing there reminded Daisy a little of the first time Lily had met Jack – and how threatened she had been by her flirting with him. She had none of that feeling now, none of that threat. Perhaps this would change over Christmas back home. But in comparison to Daisy's new competition, her sister seemed relatively harmless.

'Do you want a cup of tea or something?' Daisy said.

'Er, no, thanks' – Lily scanned the dirty pots on the counter – 'perhaps we'd better get straight off; it's a fair drive back.'

'Thanks for coming, by the way. To pick us up. We do appreciate it.'

'No worries. Mum would have been miserable all Christmas otherwise. Right, have you got everything?'

'I think so. I just need to grab a bag from the bedroom.'

Panicked at the thought of being left on his own with Lily, Jack said, 'Me too,' and followed Daisy down the corridor.

Once they were out of sight, she turned and whispered, 'What bag? Your rucksack's in the lounge.'

'Oh, yes.'

By now they had reached their bedroom. 'You just didn't want to be left on your own with her? Did you?' And Daisy started prodding him in the ribs. 'What did you think she was going to do? You're not irresistible, you know!' She tickled him and Jack laughed, grabbing hold of her and wrestling her onto the bed. Daisy let out a scream as she fell back, giggling.

Lily heard it from the kitchen and tutted. Like a pair of kids, she thought, a little enviously; her love life was currently non-existent. She stepped into the lounge whilst she waited, to have a bit of a nosey at how her little sister was living. For the first time she properly registered that the flat smelt of stale cigarette smoke. So one or both of them were smoking. She decided not to mention it; she'd keep it as ammo, depending on how this little Christmas visit went. It was bloody freezing, too; she wrapped her coat around her. The lounge was a bit of a mess; no ashtrays, though. It seemed like a larger version of Daisy's bedroom back home: posters all over the walls, records, tapes and videos everywhere. Their own gaudy little Christmas decorations. Daisy had made coloured paper chains and strewn tinsel about the place. They even had a little tree. It was strange, but Lily had to begrudgingly admit that her little sis had pulled it off; she was managing to survive on her own. She'd flown the nest. More than could be said for her: she'd been left at home with a grieving mother. It made her feel a tad resentful, no wonder she couldn't get a boyfriend.

Lily was just about to venture over to peer out of the lovely big windows with fake snow in their corners when Daisy reappeared. She plonked a holdall down next to what looked like a large sack of presents. 'Right, I think that's it. Excuse the mess,' she said, a little embarrassed. 'We had a bit of a late one last night.'

'Well, I'm glad someone did. I had to have an early night – I had to be up at six-thirty. At least it got me out of Midnight Mass.'

'What, didn't you go with Mum?'

'Well, I couldn't, could I? Don't look at me like that! Grandma went with her.'

'She's there already?'

'Yes, she came yesterday afternoon.'

As they spoke, Jack skulked past Lily to surreptitiously grab his rucksack. Daisy was trying not to giggle again. She was in high spirits for some reason, probably still a little drunk. It was Christmas! Or maybe it was just the prospect of getting out of the flat for once. Of being somewhere else. Maybe it was the thought of seeing her mum. She'd missed her.

They set off, Daisy and Jack in the back, bags at their feet, the sack of presents in the boot. The car was Daisy's first sobering reminder of her dad. Of home. His tapes had gone from between the front seats, she noticed. Most of them anyway. She wondered why. Perhaps they were too much of a reminder for her mum – or Lily: Carol didn't drive much now. But it was scary how little pieces of evidence of someone's existence, even of a loved one, soon began to disappear. Put in boxes and packed away, somehow erasing a little part of them. Like that photo in *Back to the Future* (they'd recently watched it as part of Daisy's top twenty movies countdown) where the hand starts to disappear. What else would be missing at home?

Home. The thought of it gave Daisy's stomach another one of those nervous flutters. They'd been so wrapped up in their own little world. The thought of being back home for Christmas, the ideal of it – warmth, home-cooked food, family – had been something to look forward to. Yet the reality, now that they were physically heading back, was something different. More daunting. Already the feelings and memories, the loss, the reminders were trying to swim back in. She could sense them waiting for her, treading water. It was easier to shut them away and keep them at bay in a different area, a different home.

It was even worse for Jack. He, too, had been far too busy, caught up in work and marijuana, to think about the reality of heading back to that area. In a way he'd been blocking it out; it was something that would happen in the future. But now it had arrived, part of him was dreading it. And meeting Daisy's family properly at last wasn't even the worst of it. It was being so close to that house on the hill. And then there was going back to that police station to meet Haslam. A few days earlier they'd rung to ask if going back was OK; Daisy had insisted, in case it broke any rules. Haslam had apparently been on the verge of phoning them. He said he couldn't refuse, what with the move going so well and it being Christmas. He also said he'd got something for Jack – so his visit would 'kill two birds with one stone'. He sounded unexpectedly chirpy, especially considering their last phone call. Haslam told them to keep a low profile, not to leave the house unnecessarily. What did he think they were going to do? Take out a full page ad in the *Echo*, announcing that the two outlaws were back home for Christmas?

With all this going through their minds, there was little conversation during the journey. What there was to start with, the odd polite inquiry for form's sake, soon petered out and in any case Jack was too shy to speak. Jack and Daisy were happy to hold hands and stare out of the window as the A47 cut through the flat and frosted landscape of the fens. Lily assumed they were hungover, so she left them to it, turning the radio on. Radio One. *Uuk!* thought Daisy. At least they were playing some Christmas tunes. 'Driving Home for Christmas' by Chris Rea wasn't one of her favourites, but it seemed particularly apt. It made her feel nice. That squidgy feeling inside again. She squeezed Jack's hand and smiled at him. He smiled back pensively.

CHAPTER 23

Keeping Up with the Joneses

'Thank God for that,' said Lily, applying the handbrake. They were home. The ratcheting sound roused Daisy and Jack from their slumber; the warmth and motion of the car on top of their excesses the previous night had got the better of them. Opening her eyes, Daisy dragged herself upright. Her sister was stretching and yawning. Lily turned to peer over her shoulder, as if she knew she was being watched. She tutted at the sight of them.

The second Jack was conscious and realised where he was, he was alarmed. On edge. It occurred to him they'd missed seeing the crossroads where they could have turned right, up the main road, to his old house. Probably for the best. Inside he groaned at what he was about to go through. Spending the next two days with Daisy's family. He had a hangover and his throat was sore again; he wished he was back at the flat. In bed, Christmas or no Christmas. How much had he drunk? And what?

'Aah, look. The VW,' said Daisy. Seeing her old blue and white van sitting on the driveway made her feel warm but sad. It represented her old life, but even so she missed it. The van was looking a little sorry for itself; it needed a wash and the tyres were a bit flat. An idea came to her.

'There's Mum,' said Lily, waving and unbuckling her seatbelt.

Daisy hadn't noticed, but there she was, waving excitedly from the porch. She looked tired but flustered, her cheeks red. Older and thinner, too, with her grey hairs showing through at the roots. Daisy leant forward, smiling and waving back. 'Has Mum stopped dyeing her hair?'

'She's stopped doing a lot of things,' Lily sighed. 'But she's been better this week than since you left, what with you coming back. Getting the house ready and that. Come on, let's face the music.' She opened the car door and stepped out, letting in the cold.

Daisy turned to Jack and patted his leg. He had the look of dread on his face that she hadn't seen for a while. 'Come on,' she said. 'It'll be all right.'

'She hates me,' he said, remembering the animosity he had felt from Daisy's mum before they had left for Cromer.

'Don't be ridiculous. She doesn't hate you at all. She always asks after you on the phone. Come on, they'll wonder what we're doing.' But she practically had to drag him out of the car.

The air felt crisp and fresh, a proper winter morning, although there was no frost. It had a certain feel to it, almost tangible; a certain smell. Christmas-like. 'Hi, Mum!' She waved again.

'Hi, love!'

Jack winced as he got out of the car. His legs ached from being cramped up and seemed to have lost all their fluid. He felt completely dehydrated. 'Wave to Mum,' Daisy said through her teeth, as she shut the door. Jack looked up briefly, smiled, and raised his hand in a pathetic wave.

'We need to get the presents out,' said Daisy. She popped the boot open and Jack grabbed the Christmas sack. It looked odd, a bit childish perhaps, out here in the real world.

With Lily already inside, Carol watched them approach, her hands pressed together as if in prayer. It made Daisy feel a little awkward; and she was glad, albeit surprised, when her mum rushed forward to meet her. 'Come here, you!' she cried, holding her arms out, her face crumpling with months of pent-up emotion. She threw her arms around her daughter, hugging her fiercely, her chin nestling in the fur of Daisy's coat. As she closed her eyes, two tears finally spilled.

Jack hung back, watching from a few paces away, clutching the sack of presents and feeling uncomfortable at this display of maternal affection. He felt a pang of longing, a small stab of envy, wondering what it felt like to be on the receiving end of it, what Daisy's mother smelt like.

'Let me look at you!' Carol said, pulling away and wiping her eyes. She took a step back and held Daisy at arm's length. 'You're looking well,' she said. 'I'm surprised!'

'Fat, you mean,' said Daisy.

'Fat! There's not an ounce on you. I mean healthy. Your hair's grown,' she said, running a hand through it, 'and I love your coat. Is it real?'

'I don't know!' Daisy laughed. 'Just got it from a second-hand shop. Didn't I, Jack?' She turned, always sensitive to Jack's feelings, trying to make him feel included. Jack blushed and nodded.

'Jack!' Carol said. 'Sorry. Look at me, getting all emotional. Happy Christmas.' And, surprising both of them, she gave Jack an impromptu hug. Jack didn't know what to do – it was like the time when Anne had hugged him before he'd gone camping. He stood there rigidly, clutching the sack. Carol's perfume filled his nostrils, flowery and fruity at the same time. He thought he caught a whiff of alcohol on her breath as, to his relief, she released him.

Daisy was smiling, pleased at the gesture. 'It's so good to see you both,' said Carol, stroking Daisy's arm. 'Come on, let's get inside out of the cold. I've got the house all done up. I can't wait! Grandma's here, too.' She was like an excited child.

'Lily needs to lock the car,' said Daisy, as they stepped into the porch. 'Ooh, I love the wreath! Did you make it?'

'Of course. That's my traditional green and red one. Wait till you see the one in the lounge.'

Jack followed Daisy inside, inspecting the wreath on the way; it reminded him of Midsummer Night, only now it was mid-winter.

The warmth hit them both straight away, along with the much-missed and sumptuous smells of a roast dinner. It made them realise how hungry they were. 'Mmm, smells good,' said Daisy. 'What are we having?'

'Turkey, of course. With all the trimmings. Ooh, I need to check the potatoes for the mash. I hope they haven't boiled dry.' Carol bustled off. 'Take your shoes off; I've had the carpets cleaned,' she called over her shoulder.

Daisy and Jack were left in the hallway. 'Sorry,' said Daisy, as she put down her bag. Taking his shoes off was one of Jack's pet hates. It made him feel vulnerable, naked almost; a result of his upbringing. In their flat he wore shoes from the second he got up till hitting bed at night. It was a comfort thing.

'What shall I do with the presents?' he asked.

'Just leave them next to my bag.'

As Jack begrudgingly took his shoes off, Daisy soaked up the strange feeling of being back in her family home. Although she'd only been away for a few months, it seemed longer. She felt like a stranger. The house seemed to have evolved slightly. It reminded her of visiting her grandma's house when she was little. Everything seemed more old-fashioned, more formal – the furnishings, the decor. She felt as if she'd got to be on her best behaviour. As she placed her boots on the shoe rack, she noticed how uncluttered it was: her dad's shoes were no longer there – his walking shoes, his slippers – another one of those erasings. It made her feel a little sick; it still wasn't right that he wasn't there, that she couldn't hear his voice booming out from the kitchen, or from the bar in the lounge.

As they made their way down the hallway to the kitchen, the black spot in Jack's eye made a festive appearance, mainly at the prospect of meeting Daisy's grandma. He could still remember what Daisy had said on the day of her dad's funeral: that she wanted to hit him with her handbag. Carol was at the sink, mercilessly bashing the contents of a pan with a potato masher, the steam and effort making her face even redder. The kitchen window was clouded with condensation. She looked up. 'OK, love?' she said to Daisy.

'Yes, fine, thanks.'

'Daisy, sweetheart!' A rich, cracked voice came from the far end of the kitchen. Daisy's grandma was sitting at the kitchen table, prepping vegetables. She looked nothing like Jack had imagined – a bent-over, hooked-nosed, witch of a woman, like the grandma in *George's Marvellous Medicine*. Instead she was elegant, like her handwriting – slim with good cheekbones and wavy hair, rather than the standard old lady perm. Pretty, with make up on. 'Come here so I can have a good look at you. I haven't got my glasses on.'

'Hi, Grandma,' Daisy beamed. Jack didn't know what to do, so he loitered.

Carol looked up, mid-mash, and mouthed conspiratorially, 'Go and say hello.' Jack nodded and shuffled after Daisy. Why did people keep asking him to say hello? It was as if there was some secret etiquette at play, and he didn't know the rules.

Daisy and her grandma were hugging. 'Ooh, it's good to have you back, love. We've been worried about you. Happy Christmas.' They pulled apart. 'Now take this coat off so I can have a good look at you.'

'God, why does everyone want to examine me?' Daisy tutted. But she was glad to remove the fur coat; she was burning up and felt a little light-headed, probably from the alcohol or the heat of the kitchen. Or maybe it was the tight black roll-neck sweater she'd decided to wear. She felt like those

279

holidaymakers, used to the cold of England, who disembark from a plane in a hot foreign country in ill-chosen attire.

As she hung the coat over the back of a chair, her grandma said, 'I feel I ought to get a saucer of milk for that coat.' And she chuckled in that surprisingly deep, croaky voice.

Daisy felt a little self-conscious as she stood back up. Again, she regretted her choice of top: it seemed to be riding up and clinging to her. She pulled it down. 'Hmm, you're not wasting away, then.' Before Daisy could protest, Grandma added, 'Unlike this young man here. Isn't she feeding you properly? You could do with some meat on your bones.' And she turned to Jack for the first time. No hug or Happy Christmas for him, then. Perhaps she hadn't forgiven him for the funeral – or for whisking Daisy away. Jack smiled sheepishly, keeping his eyes peeled for a rogue handbag.

'Oh, you've got changed,' said Carol.

'Hey?' said Daisy. 'Oh.' Lily had appeared in the kitchen. She was yawning.

'Yes, it's flippin' freezing in this house.' Jack and Daisy shared an incredulous look.

'Well, the heating's been on since six. It's ever so warm in here.'

'Best spend all day in the kitchen then.'

'Cheer up, love, it's Christmas!' Carol joked.

'I'm so tired! I've been up since the crack of dawn.' Lily made her way over to the table.

'I was up before you! Who made you a cup of tea?'

'Well, that was your choice. When are we doing presents?'

'I'm not sure. Perhaps a few before dinner and a few after.'

'You need to lock the car,' Daisy said.

Lily groaned. 'Great. Can't you do it?'

'It's *so* good to be back,' Daisy said sarcastically.

They all watched Grandma for a moment. She had gone back to prepping the Brussels sprouts, her knobbly, liver-spotted hands – the only real sign of her age – clutching a small knife. 'Why do you do that, put a cross in them?' Lily asked.

'To make them cook quicker,' Carol piped up.

'To make them cook more *evenly*,' Grandma corrected.

Jack felt like wading in, telling them that Chef had said it was a mistake, as it just made the sprouts (or 'nobbies' as they were called at work) waterlogged and soggy. But he thought it would be rude to do so.

'Right, that's the mash done. Who's for some Buck's Fizz?' Carol said. 'It's gone twelve, hasn't it? Might liven you lot up a bit. Get you in the Christmas spirit.'

Buck's Fizz on Christmas Day was a tradition in the Jones household. The girls had even been allowed a weak one when they were growing up. It still amused Daisy that midday seemed to be the magic cut-off point, after which her mum deemed it OK to drink alcohol. This morning, though, the acid and alcohol combination on an empty stomach didn't seem too appealing. Perhaps it would pep her up. 'Hair of the dog' and all that. Jack was wondering what the hell Buck's Fizz was.

'Only a weak one for me,' Grandma said.

'Would you mind doing the honours, Lily? You know…' Carol trailed off. It had always been Jim's job, popping the cork. He'd loved playing the barman.

Lily, who had just sat down, huffed. 'Why have I got to do everything?'

'Perhaps Jack should do it?' suggested Daisy. 'You know, man of the house and all that.' She put her hand on his arm, thinking she was doing him a favour. He looked at her, horrified.

'Yes, I don't suppose why not. Good idea, Daisy,' said Carol.

Great, thought Jack.

He made a total mess of it. First, he nearly took one of his eyes out, the cork narrowly missing his head as it shot from the bottle before ricocheting off the ceiling strip light and plopping into Grandma's Brussels sprouts bowl. Then, as the fizzy liquid escaped in frothing rivulets, Jack tried to point the bottle into one of the slim-necked champagne flutes, already half-full with orange juice. But he poured too fast and, to his horror, the glass quickly filled and overflowed, spilling onto the table and dripping onto the floor. Daisy and Lily squealed. Carol rushed over to the sink for a cloth. Grandma merely tutted, 'What a waste of good champagne,' and plucked the cork from her bowl to smell it.

With every continued drip – as Jack tried slowly to fill the other glasses with shaking hands whilst Carol mopped up the spillage, saying 'Hmm, this is going to make the floor tacky' – his mortification grew. He could have murdered Daisy for suggesting he do it; he had no experience of anything like this and it was bound to end in disaster. Finally, they clinked their glasses together. 'Cheers.'

'Hair of the dog,' added Daisy, and looked at Jack. But he wouldn't return her gaze. She sensed that he was annoyed with her. She was a little regretful herself; she'd wanted to ingratiate Jack with her family and it had backfired spectacularly, so perhaps she should stop trying so hard…

When they were onto their second Buck's Fizz (this time poured by Carol), and the turkey had been checked and basted, they all retired to open some of their presents. The lounge was done up beautifully with traditional decorations that made the flat look positively tacky. Holly garlands of the darkest green were peppered with clusters of bright red berries. Above the fireplace there was a wreath of spruce and fir, dusted with white and decorated with pine cones, dried citrus fruits, cinnamon sticks, bells and bows. The sweet pine smell of the huge Christmas tree filled the room, tastefully adorned with white lights, copper and silver baubles and tinsel. Under it were shiny parcels, all with bows. To top it off, a fire crackled and glowed in the hearth. 'Wow!' said Daisy, echoing Jack's thoughts. 'Mum, it looks *amazing* in here! A real winter wonderland.' The fizz had gone to her head.

'Thank you,' said Carol. 'I wanted to make an effort.' She suddenly looked as if she was about to cry.

'You've done a grand, job, love,' said Grandma, shuffling her way to a comfy chair.

'Well, you've got to make an effort, haven't you? You can't just give up.' And that was it, she was off again, sniffing and wiping the corners of her eyes.

'Stop it, Mum, you'll set me off,' said Daisy, giving her a hug.

'Come on, pull yourself together, Mother,' said Lily, patting her on the shoulder. 'Jack doesn't want to see you crying every five minutes, do you, Jack?'

Jack froze. Was he meant to say something in reply? 'I'm sorry,' said Carol, producing a tissue. 'Lily's right. I'm so pleased to have you all together: I shouldn't be crying.' Jack gave his best supportive smile, but felt totally out of his depth. He nervously took another gulp of his drink. It was going down too quickly. How was everyone else making theirs last?

The family settled down to exchange presents. 'I'll just go and get ours. Have you got any cider, Mum?' said Daisy, noticing Jack's empty glass. Hers was almost empty too.

'Steady, young Daisy, you'll be squiffy before dinner,' Grandma joked.

'Yes, there's some in the fridge,' said Carol.

Daisy returned with a can of cider to share (she didn't want them to look like alcoholics) propped on a stack of presents, mainly for her family. She'd only brought in a couple for her and Jack; the rest she wanted to open upstairs later when they were on their own. She couldn't believe she hadn't visited her bedroom yet; she wondered what state it was in. Packing during that fateful week in August had been a mad rush.

Topped up with alcohol, Jack slowly began to defrost. But he still felt like an outsider, withdrawing into his shell as he watched the Joneses go about the rituals of their family Christmas. Exchanging presents in front of an open fire, laughing and kissing; festive cheer. He felt as if he was watching them all from outside. Literally. His face pressed against the window in wide-eyed wonder, like Tiny Tim in that *A Christmas Carol* movie. He felt as if he didn't belong there, didn't deserve it; not if Anne couldn't be there too. They were of a different cloth, him and Anne. Anne…

'Jack?'

'Hmm?' Daisy was nudging him.

'This is from Mum.' Daisy was giving him a look again, as if he was meant to say or do something.

'Thank you,' he said, taking the present and offering his best smile in Carol's direction.

The present felt soft and malleable in his lap as he gave it a gentle squeeze. He looked up and everyone's eyes were on him. 'Well, go on then, open it,' Daisy cajoled. Jack reluctantly surrendered his glass to the coffee table to fumble open the present, a tartan scarf that he would never wear. It looked and felt itchy. He muttered feigned thanks and grimaced. He was so rubbish at this.

'Thought it would come in handy if you go for any winter strolls on the beach. It must get quite bracing at this time of year on the Norfolk coast,' said Carol.

'Yes, it does,' said Daisy.

'It's lovely,' said Grandma, meaning the scarf. 'You'll look like Doctor Who in that.' Lily tried but failed to suppress a giggle, knowing Jack would never wear it. *Please don't ask me to try it on, please don't ask me to try it on*, thought Jack. They didn't.

Daisy unwrapped a diary that Jack had bought for her. 'Thank you,' she beamed.

'Oh, great! *I* bought you a diary!' said Lily.

'So did I!' laughed Carol. 'We know you too well.'

'Well, perhaps I can have a secret one and a secret-secret one that even Jack's not allowed to look at. Then I can privately moan when he's getting on my nerves! Only joking,' she said, nudging him. More likely she'd be slagging Jeanie off in it, she mused to herself.

Daisy had bought Jack a second-hand copy of *The Owl and the Pussycat*, which he was genuinely thrilled with – one of a handful of books from his list that she had managed to locate in the second-hand bookshop in Cromer. This, more than any other present, garnered the most attention. 'Ooh, now that's an old one,' said Carol, 'You two used to love that when you were little. So did I.'

'What is it, dear?' said Grandma, leaning forward.

'*The Owl and the Pussycat*. Edward Lear,' said Carol.

'I know who it's by,' tutted Grandma. '"The Owl and the Pussycat went to sea in a beautiful pea-green boat. They took some money and plenty of honey wrapped up in a five pound note…"' she reminisced. Carol and Daisy joined in. '"The Owl looked up to the stars above and sang to a small guitar. Oh lovely Pussy. Oh, Pussy my love, what a beautiful Pussy you are. You are, you are. What a beautiful Pussy you are!"' Daisy faltered, blushing, at the last few lines, shooting a surreptitious glance at Jack. Why had that bit never sounded rude to her before?

Clearly thinking the same thing, Lily let out another suppressed snort of laughter (the Buck's Fizz had gone to her head too). She tried to cover it up. 'Hold on, am I missing something here? Is this present meant to be ironic or something?'

'It's just nostalgic, that's all – for Jack. He lost most of his things in the … the fire,' said Daisy. She felt bad bringing this up in front of everyone. It was such a private thing for him. There was an awkward silence. Here amongst them was someone who had been part of a real-life grisly horror story – like 10 Rillington Place. Someone who had actually lived it. An oddity and curiosity, someone who could really spill some juicy secrets – but as tempting as it was, asking would just be bad form, seeking a cheap, vicarious thrill.

'Did you never go to school at all, dear?' asked Grandma, surprising everyone with her tact and sudden interest in Jack. But this was what he hated the most. Being scrutinised and quizzed on his shameful life. He reddened and reached for his drink.

'No, he didn't,' Daisy spoke for him. 'But he can still read perfectly well – proper books – and write. His sister taught him, didn't she?' She put her hand on Jack's knee. He nodded, sipping his cider. Daisy felt a guilty thrill at having a privileged insight into Jack's life: she could sense her family's eagerness to ask him things, their curiosity almost palpable as they unconsciously leant forward in their seats. 'He doesn't really like to talk about it, though,' she added.

'Seems he doesn't like to talk about much at all,' said Grandma, sitting back in her seat, disappointed. 'What time's dinner, Carol? I don't want to miss the Queen's speech.'

*****

Christmas dinner was a topsy-turvy and emotional affair. Carol was stressed because she'd always had Jim to help her before. Who was going to carve the bird? Her anxiety was contagious, and everybody pitched in, trying to help. Grandma fussed her way through making the gravy and the girls helped to dish everything up. Jack was given the job of putting the last bits on the table; a Santa and snowman salt and pepper pot set, a glass jug of cranberry sauce and some luxurious looking Christmas crackers.

Finally they were all sitting at the table, surrounded by food and wine glasses – another first for Jack. No one seemed to want the responsibility of carving the turkey, so it was left to Carol. 'If I'm going to do this, for God's sake someone pour me a glass of wine first,' she said. Lily gladly obliged. After taking a good glug of white wine, Carol brushed away the hair that was sticking to her rosy forehead. Then she picked up the carving knife and fork and held them poised above the bird. 'Here goes then. I don't even know where to start. Why didn't I pay more attention?' Feeling under pressure, she began to hack away at the turkey in the general vicinity of the breast. Fortunately she picked the right spot and breathed a sigh of relief. But it was a far cry from the effortless slicing of an unruffled Delia Smith on the telly. Carol's knife wasn't sharp enough for a start; another of Jim's jobs. 'This is where your father would say "leg or breast?" and find it hilarious,' she said, offering her first slice. 'So, Mum, leg or breast?'

'A bit of both for me, dear, I find the breast a bit dry on its own.'

'How did I know you were going to say that?' she sighed.

'You're doing a great job, Mum,' said Daisy.

And so it went on until everyone was served. 'Wait!' said Carol. 'Before we begin, a toast to … to your father… We miss you, love. So much.' And her voice wobbled. Daisy put her hand on her mum's arm.

'To Dad,' they all said, Jack under his breath, feeling foolish.

'And to Anne,' Daisy said, raising her glass again. Her family looked at her a little perplexed. But she defiantly kept her glass aloft until they cottoned on.

'Oh yes, of course. Sorry, Jack,' Carol said as the penny dropped.

'To Anne,' everyone said.

'Who's Anne?' said Grandma, leaning into Lily.

'It's Jack's sister. He lost her recently.'

'Oh, dear,' said Grandma. 'What a year!'

Jack tried his best throughout dinner to keep as low a profile as possible, quietly savouring the food. No offence to Daisy –

she tried her best – but not since Anne had left home had he tasted anything like it. Daisy kept on topping up his plate and his wine glass, so he didn't have to ask.

There was a break before pudding to retire to the lounge to watch the Queen's speech; Grandma insisted on seeing it on the big telly rather than the portable one in the kitchen. 'Ooh, she's at the Royal Albert Hall,' she said. 'That makes a change. I wonder why?' The Queen, wearing a long, flowing dress and surrounded by children, addressed the nation. In fact, children seemed to be the main theme of her speech. And the environment – something called 'the greenhouse effect'.

It was all very dull, and by the time Her Majesty started quoting Jesus Christ, Jack had given up feigning interest. A little drunk, he turned his attention to Daisy next to him on the sofa; and more specifically her breasts in that clingy black sweater. The closer he looked, the more he could see how the material was stretched and shiny around them, and how her white bra was showing through.

Her mind wandering from the TV too, and also a little drunk, Daisy turned to catch him staring blatantly at her chest. Flattered rather than offended, she nudged him with her elbow in mock disapproval. Jack looked up and grinned; he couldn't help himself. Daisy made a tutting gesture with her eyes. Then she looked around her to see if anyone was looking. They were all focused on the telly. Keeping her hands in her lap, she pretended to stretch and yawn whilst squeezing her boobs together, pushing them up and out. The look on Jack's face was priceless and she laughed. 'What are you two giggling at?' Carol said from the other sofa.

'Nothing!' said Daisy.

Later, a flaming Christmas pudding with a sprig of holly sticking out of it was brought in by Carol, along with two jugs, one of cream, one of brandy sauce. Jack looked at Daisy agog, as if to say, 'Is that thing meant to be on fire?' 'Ah, just like Dad did it,' said Lily, answering the question.

'I'm trying,' said Carol, setting her tray on the coffee table. 'It took me ages to get it to stay alight and I soaked it in brandy. It's got a twenty pence piece in it somewhere, too, just like Dad did, so watch out!'

All these odd traditions, thought Jack. They seemed kind of old-fashioned, which he liked. He'd never tried Christmas pudding before either. As with mince pies, he wasn't a fan. It was so rich and sweet. 'Don't you like it, Jack? There's sherry trifle, too,' said Carol.

'No, I'm fine, really, just stuffed, thanks.' All he wanted to do was go upstairs.

'Did someone say sherry? I'll have a glass of sherry,' said Grandma. Jack and Daisy looked at each other. How did they politely escape?

Halfway down her sherry, Grandma seemed to be taking an even keener interest in Jack. 'So, you had a sister then?' she asked out of the blue. He looked at Daisy and she prompted him to answer.

He cleared his throat. 'Erm, yes.'

'And you lost her, Daisy said.'

'Er, yes.' How much did she know, or not know, about what happened?

'Oh dear, I'm sorry to hear that. How old was she? Was she young like yourself?'

'Er, no … she was…'

'She was a fair bit older than Jack,' cut in Daisy.

'Still, terrible thing to happen, losing a sibling. I had a brother, you know.' At this point Daisy and Lily exchanged glances, knowing what was coming next – Grandma's war story of how she'd lost her brother; a tragic tale, but one often told – and it looked as if she'd found a new audience. 'You remind me of him a little bit – good cheekbones. Alfie, his name was. He was only eighteen when he was shot down…' Daisy and Lily braced themselves. 'He was a rear-gunner during the war, you know.' It was a terrible thing to find amusing, but the expression always got to them. Their mouths puckered and twisted as they tried not to laugh. For Daisy, the way Jack was listening so earnestly, so solemnly – with no inkling of the connotations – was making it worse.

Finally, Lily rescued them, saying she was going upstairs to have a lie down, using her early start as an excuse. After performing an exaggerated yawn, she left the room. Daisy breathed a sigh of relief, seeing an opportunity. 'Yes, we might head upstairs for a bit of a lie-down, too – we had a late night last night, and all the food and drink has done me in!'

'Oh, right,' said Carol. She looked a little put out. 'I thought we might play some games or maybe go for a walk, clear our heads a bit…'

'Hmm, maybe later… Come on, Jack,' Daisy said, practically dragging him out of the room. They grabbed their things from the hallway, Jack shouldering the sack of presents. 'Thank God for that,' Daisy said as they climbed the stairs. 'You should have seen your face, listening to Grandma,' she giggled.

'What? She's interesting.'

'I think she's warmed to you.'

'Well, why wouldn't she?' he joked, regaining his confidence now they were on their own.

'Come on, Santa,' she said as they reached her bedroom door. 'Let's see what else you've got in your sack.'

CHAPTER 24
Charades

Daisy's room was a strange sight. Although her mum had clearly had a tidy up, it was still a bit of a tip. To Daisy it seemed as if she'd been away for ages and that it was another girl's room. Everything looked so childish. Teenagerish. Her flowery bedcover, the acoustic guitar that she'd loved the idea of yet never learned to play properly. So clichéd. It made her cringe inside. Even some of the bands on the walls – Jesus Jones, Inspiral Carpets – bands she'd outgrown. It smelt stuffy in there, a little dusty, but it was still the warmest room in the house.

They put down their things and threw themselves backwards onto the bed. 'God, I'm stuffed!' Daisy cried, holding her stomach. 'I'm going to have to go on a diet; you'll have to roll me out of here.'

'My jaw's aching from false-smiling so much.'

'Well, stop it. You're so eager to please. A little lapdog. Are you gonna wear Mother's scarf to please her?' She tickled him in the ribs.

'Shut up!' Jack said, tickling her back. 'You want them to like me, don't you?'

'Course I do, little lapdog.'

'Right, that's it!' He sat on Daisy's legs and pinned her arms behind her head.

'Ow. You're hurting me!' she laughed.

'Good!' He ducked down to kiss her with lust in his eyes. Play-fighting for them had always been a prelude to sex, a form of foreplay.

Daisy responded but, coming back up for air, said, 'Jack, don't even think about it – we can't, not here, not with them downstairs. The bed makes too much noise.'

'On the floor then, like before.' That night they'd made love during the storm.

'No, I couldn't. Not knowing they're downstairs – what if Grandma heard?'

'Aagh!' He rolled off onto his back.

Daisy looked down at the bulge in his jeans. Then her eyes travelled back up to his face, a picture of thunder and frustration. He wouldn't look at her. It made her wonder what it was like, being a boy in a situation like this; the same as being a girl? It couldn't be. Having that thing down there with a mind of its own. They took it so hard (she smiled at the pun), so personally. She throbbed too, but it seemed easier to turn it on and off. She looked down again, turned on at the sight of it, but feeling sorry for him. Maybe a compromise was in order. Shifting in closer so that her breast was resting against him, she nuzzled into his neck. Then, to his shock, considering there was no lock on the door, she reached down to unzip his jeans...

Afterwards, they both took it in turns to use the bathroom, Jack first. When Daisy returned, Jack was rooting around in his rucksack. 'What are you looking for?'

'This.' He held up a carrier bag that had been tightly wrapped around something.

'What is it? Jack! You haven't!' The package was tin-shaped. Tobacco tin-shaped. 'Jack! I said not to bring any. It'll stink! Mum knows what dope smells like, you know. She used to smoke it.'

'That's why I wrapped it in this.' He pulled out the tin, which was also tightly bound in cling film.

'Well, don't open it up in here whatever you do! I told you not to bring any.'

'I'm sorry, I couldn't help it. It's only a couple of joints' worth. I just couldn't bear the thought of not having any for two days.' That was the difference between them, Daisy thought. Knowing she couldn't have any, it wouldn't really have crossed her mind. 'Can't we just have one out the window?' he said.

'Jesus, no! You must be mad.'

'Well, where then?'

'I don't know. Honestly, can't you go without, just for two days?' The look on his face said he couldn't.

'What about outside?'

'How? Where?'

'I don't know. What if we go for a walk?'

'We're meant to be keeping a low profile, remember. Besides, Mum'll want to come.'

Jack groaned. This was so frustrating. They'd got used to a life of no parents, being able to do what they want when they wanted. 'Well, what about if we slip out the back, into Honeysuckle Cottage?' His face lit up.

'Oh yeah, I can just see that. Mum or Grandma looking out the kitchen window and smoke pouring out of the summer house. That's if we could even slip out...' Daisy watched Jack picking at the plastic wrap around the tin, desperate to crack it open. It was almost worse than how he'd been with his cider. 'Look, it'll be properly dark soon if you can hold on a bit. That'll be our best bet. It'll be too late to go for a walk then, and the oldies *always* nod off after dinner. I bet Grandma has already. Then we'll slip out the back.' Jack didn't reply. 'OK?'

'Yes, suppose so,' he said morosely.

'Cheer up. At least you've had a little treat. Spare a thought for me…' This raised a glimmer of a smile. 'Hey, we've still got our presents to open as well. Let's do that for a bit to pass the time.'

Opening their remaining presents cheered them up, and helped take Jack's mind off the gear for a while. Daisy had managed to find him a *Mog the Forgetful Cat* book, Raymond Briggs' *Father Christmas* and *The Very Hungry Caterpillar*. Jack was thrilled that, slowly but surely, and all thanks to Daisy, he was getting his precious book collection back – they weren't his sister's, but at least he could still revel in the comfort and nostalgia of them. 'Will you read to me again later?' he said, a little embarrassed to ask.

'Yes,' she laughed. 'As long as you promise not to fall asleep this time…'

In return, Jack had bought Daisy a seven inch single of Neil Young's recently released 'Rockin' in the Free World', a photo album and a new film for her camera – which, Daisy realised to her annoyance, she'd forgotten to bring. Her last present for Jack, and the crowning glory, she saved for last – the much-awaited follow-up compilation tape. Clearly this gave her more pleasure than the giving of any other present. 'Happy Christmas, babe,' she said, handing it over and kissing him on the cheek. 'I know you know what it is.' She eagerly watched him unwrap it.

'*Daisy's Greatest Hits Vol. 2*' it said on the spine – this time in black biro. She had made a cover for it, keeping with the Christmas theme: a close up photo of frosted holly she'd taken herself. Jack stared at it for a while, thinking how lucky he was. 'Come on, look at the track listing!' she said. He opened up the case and pulled out the tape. 'Look at this as the continuing of your education,' she enthused as he studied her neat handwriting. 'A companion to your other tape. My absolute favourite songs of all time … although there were a couple that I didn't have at the flat, which was annoying.'

The track listing was as follows:

Side One
'You are the Everything' – R.E.M.
'My Time (live)' – Jane's Addiction
'Love Me to Death' – The Mission
'When You Come' – Crowded House.
'Take Me Home, Country Roads' – John Denver
'Mersey Paradise' – The Stone Roses
'Givin' the Dog a Bone' – AC/DC
'I Know it's Over' – The Smiths
'After the Goldrush' – Neil Young
'Edie (Ciao Baby)' – The Cult
'A Few Hours After This' – The Cure

Side Two
'Train in Vain' – The Clash
'Both Sides Now' – Joni Mitchell
'Whole of the Moon' – The Waterboys
'Something's Gotten Hold of my Heart' –
Nick Cave and the Bad Seeds
'Heartbreak a Stranger' – Bob Mould
'Sounds of Silence' – Simon and Garfunkel
'Anchorage' – Michelle Shocked
'How Will I Ever be Simple Again?' – Richard Thompson
'Hounds of Love' – Kate Bush
'Can't be Sure' – The Sundays
'Good Feeling' – Violent Femmes

Daisy talked Jack through the tape, saying that some of the songs reminded her of the two of them being rude together. 'You can probably guess which ones by some of the titles!' she blushed. 'Love me to Death' is just the sexiest song ever!' One band noticeable by their absence were the Velvet Underground;

they would have to earn their place on one of these tapes. 'I can't wait for you to hear it,' she said.

'Neither can I,' said Jack, knowing how much he'd enjoyed the first tape. But, truth be told, he was more concerned with when he could have his spliff.

'Shit!' said Daisy. 'I've just thought. I haven't got a tape player here anymore! We'll have to borrow Lily's. She hardly uses it anyway, except to listen to the crappy charts.' Daisy got up.

'Daisy?' Jack said. 'Can we, you know, now?' He put his thumb and forefinger to his lips in a circle.

'Really?' Daisy said. 'You still want to?' Still want to? He was dying. 'Uuh. Wait a minute then, let me just get the tape player first. Then I'll creep downstairs and see if they're asleep.'

Daisy left the room and Jack located his baccy tin. He was clutching it expectantly, like a hopeful child, when Daisy returned with the tape player. 'She wasn't in her room. I think she was in the bathroom – a good thing, really…' Daisy chucked the tape player on the bed, then looked at the tin in Jack's hand. 'Wait there,' she sighed.

A few minutes later, wearing their coats, they were tiptoeing past the open doorway to the lounge, from which snoring could be heard. It felt naughty, but fun at the same time. The kitchen was glaringly bright, but it looked as though Carol, or someone, had tackled most of the pots then given up. Daisy made a mental note to finish them off when they got back.

They slipped out of the patio door and onto the decking, lit up by the light from the kitchen window. Beyond, it was dark. So much the better. They headed for Honeysuckle Cottage, the summer house at the bottom of the long garden. The cold air was a shock after the stifling warmth of the house. A frost was beginning to form, and the shaggy grass of the lawn was slightly crispy underfoot, giving way to damp. Shame it hadn't snowed, mused Daisy; a white Christmas would have been nice.

Though they were a safe distance from the house, Daisy winced as the door of the cottage creaked as she pulled it open. There was just enough lamppost light from over the fence for them to see. 'You'll have to skin up in here, then we'll nip over the fence to smoke it,' said Daisy. 'And we can't be long.'

'Why can't we smoke in here?' said Jack, shivering slightly as he cracked open his tin. 'It's freezing out there.'

'In case they see the smoke.'

'How could they?'

'You never know. And it might leave a smell – though by the looks of it,' she said as she brushed away dust and cobwebs from the window to let in more light, 'Mum hasn't been in here for a while.'

Jack built his spliff on the inner ledge of the window so he could see. Daisy helped by holding a lighter close for him, swapping hands when it got too hot. 'Don't spill any!' she said.

'Ssh! You're making me nervous,' Jack said, his fingers already shaking a little.

Spliff rolled, they left the summer house and hopped over the fence, using one of the slanted struts for aid as they'd done many times before. Jack helped Daisy down on the other side. It was brighter there in the jitty, under the lamppost; they could see each other better, their breath streaming out in the cold air. Unable to wait any longer, Jack lit the spliff, sucking to get it going, then plucking off the fanned paper end and flicking it on the floor. Inhaling deeply, he let the sweet but harsh smoke fill his lungs. It was heaven, but rough on his already itchy throat; this took him by surprise, and a bout of coughing ensued that made his eyes stream. When this subsided, he took another drag, then offered the joint to Daisy. To his surprise, she refused. 'I'd better not. Mum's bound to smell it on my breath. She'll think I've started smoking. It's all right for you; she might disapprove, but she can't stop *you* from smoking.'

Daisy didn't really feel like it anyway, didn't feel she needed it there. She wasn't in the mood. With the afternoon's alcohol wearing off and the thrill of the presents out of the way, a sombre mood was descending, with thoughts of her dad never that far away. Jack shrugged. Normally he would be irked if she didn't partake in whatever he was having, but in this instance he understood, and as long as he got his hit that was all that mattered. As he smoked, he studied Daisy's face in the lamplight. She seemed a little preoccupied, not quite there. 'You OK?'

She scuffed the floor with her shoe. 'Yes. Just thinking about going to see Dad's grave tomorrow, that's all. I want to, you know, to have that connection with him, but the thought of it kind of makes me feel sick... You know, that feeling in your stomach.' Jack blew out smoke and put a comforting hand on her arm. He never knew what to say in these situations, and a silence descended. Soon he began to shiver and his teeth chattered. 'It's bloody freezing,' he said, stamping his feet.

'It's not that bad,' said Daisy, trying to drag herself out of her funk. 'I think you're coming down with something – you should have worn your new scarf! Come on, let's get back.'

Jack took one last drag, then pinched the glowing end of the spliff. There was about a third left. He wasn't going to waste it, and he popped the remainder back in his tin. Daisy tutted.

They slipped quietly back into the house. The kitchen was still a mess. Daisy told him to get rid of the tin whilst she hung their coats up, then they set about clearing the rest of the pots. Daisy washed whilst Jack dried. The rattle of pots disturbed Carol, and she came shuffling through to the kitchen in her slippers. 'Oh, you needn't do that, you two; I'd have finished them off.'

'It's no bother,' Daisy said. 'Honestly.'

'I can't believe I nodded off,' Carol said, yawning. 'Must have been the booze. I don't really touch the stuff these days, not since your dad...' She trailed off, as she always seemed to at the mention of his name. 'Did you have a lie-down yourselves?' Daisy and Jack thought it best not to look at each other. Without waiting for an answer, Carol continued, 'I feel a lot better for it, I must say. I can feel a second wind coming on.' She looked anything but: bags under her eyes, a little confused, her hair alarmingly grey. Smaller in stature than Daisy remembered, too. 'Shall I put a bit of a spread out?'

'God, I couldn't,' Daisy said. 'I'm still stuffed from dinner.'

'What about you, Jack? Do you fancy a bit of buffet stuff? I bet *you're* hungry, young lad like you.'

'Hm?' Jack said. He was standing, clutching a tea towel, a glazed expression on his face; the spliff had gone straight to his head.

'Do you fancy a buffet? Cold meats and cheese?'

Jack looked at Daisy, not knowing what the right answer was. He wouldn't have minded something; he felt a bit peckish. 'Maybe later,' Daisy said. 'Or why not save it for tomorrow?'

'He can speak for himself, you know,' Carol said. 'How about some pork pie, Jack? Do you want some pork pie? It's Melton Mowbray.'

'Er, yes please, if it's no trouble.'

'See?' Carol said to Daisy, toddling over to the fridge.

Daisy leant on the sink and shook her head. It was as if her mother was enjoying having a man about the place to pamper and wait on. And he was lapping it up. 'If it's no trouble,' she mimicked when Carol's back was turned, mouthing the words. And then, 'Lapdog.' Jack grinned and flicked her with the tea towel – something he'd picked up from work – glad to see her cheering up again.

'Where's that sister of yours?' Carol said, unwrapping a large pork pie. 'I hope she hasn't turned in for the night; it's still early. I fancy a game of charades actually – in your dad's honour; it would be rude not to. We always play charades at Christmas.'

Daisy groaned. 'Charades, Mum? Really?' It was as if her mum was desperate to make their first Christmas without their father a success, following his traditions almost to the letter.

'Come on, it'll be fun. I'll go and get Lily.'

Jack was on the sofa in the lounge, a plate of pork pie wedges in front of him, along with some cheese and a jar of pickled onions. The family were trying to explain the finer points of charades to him as they argued about whether to play it at all. Lily looked about as enthusiastic as Daisy. Jack was plain terrified at the prospect of standing up in front of everyone. How could he avoid it? 'Right, if we're gonna do this, I need a drink,' Daisy said. 'Mum, have we got any kahlúa?'

'If we have it'll be behind the bar. Have a look. I only got the basics in – gin and vodka and that. And sherry for Grandma…'

Daisy disappeared behind the bar in the corner of the lounge. Her dad's bar. It was his territory. She located a kahlúa bottle with a few fingers of the dark liquid left in it, enough for a couple of White Russians at least. The bottle was sticky and, like most of the bottles behind the bar, a little dusty. The kahlúa probably hadn't been touched since their summer cocktail day, the day they'd dressed up and the first time they'd had sex in the house. She paused with her hand on the bottle, picturing the memory. Her mum and dad had been away – on their fateful trip. The last time she touched this bottle he would still have been alive. Daisy sighed. 'White Russian, Jack?' she said, holding up the kahlúa. Jack nodded his head, chomping on pork pie.

'Ooh, I'll have one,' said Lily.

Great, thought Daisy. That meant there would probably only be enough for one each.

Paper and pens were handed out, and everyone began to write down books and film titles. Jack felt under pressure and struggled, his mind going blank. His film knowledge was so limited. He was a bit ashamed of his writing as well – and his spelling – and he had to concentrate, his tongue curling out of his mouth as he slowly began to write down some of his childhood books and the odd film he could remember. It didn't help that Daisy was furiously churning out one after another, folding up the scraps of paper and throwing them in the pot. Jack kept on trying to make eye contact with her to signify he didn't want to stand up in front of everyone, but she was too engrossed. She had warmed to the idea, remembering the girlish excitement she had felt when playing charades. And anything to do with films and books stimulated her; she was picking out some of her more obscure favourites (*Ciao! Manhattan*, let's see them try and do that!) but also some that she knew Jack would know.

Lily went first. After a few sips of her White Russian, she had also warmed to the idea – anything to be the centre of attention. Jack was bemused by it all at first. Syllables? What the hell was a syllable? Weren't they something you crashed together in a band? But soon he started to pick up the nuances of the game. He was still too shy to shout anything out, scared of getting the answer wrong and knowing that if he got it right it would be his turn. But when Daisy was clearly acting out *The Owl and the Pussycat*, he couldn't help himself. 'You can't shout out your own ones, silly!' Daisy said in return, recognising his handwriting. This was met with laughter from the family, denting his confidence for a while. But the more he watched the others perform so unabashedly – even Grandma was having a go – the more he wanted to face his fears and try. '*An American Werewolf in London!*' he shouted, a little too loudly.

'Yes!' Daisy said, clapping, then touching her nose and pointing to him, just like Una Stubbs and the other celebrities did on the game show version. 'Right, your turn, baby.'

Carol tutted at the familiar, rather grown-up, pet name. It was fascinating but scary to see how they were together. So young, yet so in tune and besotted with each other, but on the other hand how like a mother and child they were – the way Daisy babied him, spoke for him, rewarded and protected him at every opportunity. Hardly marriage material. What would Jim have made of it all?

Jack's heart thumped. With trepidation he picked out his charade. What if it was something he'd never heard of? Highly likely. Thankfully it was one of his own – *Jaws*. He could do this! After necking the last of his White Russian, head down and urged on by whistles and clapping, he shambled to centre stage. But standing up there with everyone looking at him wasn't so easy; and he froze, embarrassed. Sensing his pain, Daisy encouraged him. 'Is it a film?' she asked, and did the camera hand signal. Jack nodded. 'Go on then.' Feeling foolish, and looking only at Daisy, he copied her. 'A film!' everyone shouted. Then he faltered again. 'How many words?' asked Daisy. Using one finger, he signalled only at her. 'One word!' everyone shouted. Now for the hard bit. What did he do? After some deliberation, and feeling like an idiot, he turned to the side and pretended to swim, followed by the opening and shutting of his arms that resembled more of a crocodile's jaws than a shark. But it was enough. And to his relief, everyone, almost in unison, shouted out *'Jaws!'* Jack, crimson-faced and grinning, hurried back to his seat to more fanfare and the arguing over who'd said it first. He'd done it! His heart was pounding. Daisy pulled him to her and proudly gave him a kiss.

CHAPTER 25

Thanataphobia

The next morning, Jack and Daisy were woken by a knock at the bedroom door. It was Carol. 'There's a cup of tea out here for you both. It's gone nine, I'm doing bubble and squeak.'

Daisy panicked, pulling the covers up over them both. It hadn't been discussed, she and Jack sleeping in the same bed; by the time they'd hit the sack everyone had been drunk and tired. Clearly her mum had accepted it, but she didn't need her face rubbing in it with the sight of the two of them snuggled up together in their underwear. 'Thanks,' Daisy said, praying her mum wouldn't come in. She'd always used to with a cup of tea.

'I'll leave it out here,' Carol said.

'Thanks,' Daisy said again. She waited, feeling guilty. When she was sure her mum had gone, she nudged Jack.

He groaned in response: another day, another hangover. What day *was* it even? And where was he? It was too early, and his throat was like glass again. The sheets underneath him felt a little damp from where he'd sweated in the night. Why was the room so hot? It was winter, for Christ's sake. He felt Daisy get out of bed. Then he heard the door open and close. He opened his eyes just as she was putting his tea on his bedside table. Creamy thighs inches from his face, and a T-shirt just covering what he wanted to see. Instinctively, he reached out to touch, to lift up the T-shirt, but by the time he'd freed his hand from under the covers she'd already turned away. Clutching her mug, she went over to the window to open a curtain and look out. 'God, there's been a real frost.'

'Come back to bed,' Jack muttered. They hadn't got round to having sex the previous night, just collapsed into bed. It would have been the first day they hadn't had sex forever. And Christmas Day of all days: it wasn't right.

Daisy closed the curtain again and returned to bed. But instead of snuggling up, to Jack's dismay she sat up with her tea. Feeling amorous, he rolled into her, pressing himself against her and putting a hand on her thigh, sliding it under her T-shirt. 'Jack, stop it!' she tutted. 'We can't. Mum and Grandma will be downstairs. We've got to go down for breakfast.'

'Aagh!' Jack rolled away. This was getting ridiculous. Going without gear was one thing – but sex as well? He hadn't envisaged this when Daisy had told them they'd be spending Christmas away. It made him want to go home. 'When then?' he said, pouting.

'I don't know. Drink your tea.'

'Don't you want it?' He wasn't used to this; it was hurting his feelings.

'Yeah, course I do, but … it's different for me here – knowing I'm in the same house as my mum *and* Grandma, and that they could hear; the thought of it puts me off, I can't explain it. You'd probably feel the same if your mum, Anne,' she corrected, 'could hear, too.'

Jack sulked as they drank their tea and got ready to go downstairs. He didn't even want breakfast; and the mood he was in he couldn't be bothered to face Daisy's family either. He childishly conspired to turn her down next time she wanted sex, so she could see how it felt.

The kitchen was filled with the smell of breakfast frying. Carol was bustling about, determined to carry on the holiday spirit. Bubble and squeak on Boxing Day morning with the leftovers was another tradition. 'Morning, you two,' she said. 'You sleep OK?'

'Yes thanks,' Daisy said, putting the mugs in the sink. No outward signs of the sleeping arrangements bothering her mum then, she thought (they did, but what could Carol do?).

Jack grunted in reply.

'Morning, love,' said Grandma, who was sitting at the table. 'Morning, Jack.' It was like a replay of their arrival, thought Jack; and the prospect of another day here, grimacing and smiling and not being able to smoke weed or have sex, suddenly seemed suffocating. At least the apparition of his father hadn't followed them from Cromer – yet – but he'd never liked company.

They both said good morning and sat down. The table was set with knives, forks, glasses and a chilled jug of fresh orange juice.

'Poached or fried?' called Carol.

'Er, poached for me, please. Jack?' Daisy nudged him.

'Huh?'

'Egg. Poached or fried with your bubble and squeak?'

Jack shrugged. He didn't really fancy either. 'Fried with a hard yolk please,' Daisy said. She gave him a look, a prompt to say 'thank you'.

'Thank you.'

'Daisy, can you go and shout your sister again? I took her tea up the same time as yours. You kids, I don't know how you can stay in bed so long.' Jack and Daisy looked at each other. Nine o'clock was hardly a lie-in these days.

'I've been up since seven,' said Grandma pluckily.

Daisy got up to go and rouse Lily. Jack made to get up with her, terrified at the prospect of being left on his own, trying to make small talk with Grandma. But Daisy put a hand on his shoulder. Jack stared out of the window at the frost on the vast expanse of lawn, conscious of the old lady watching him. He had no idea what to say to her. Just then Sookie burst through the cat flap, announcing her arrival with a mewl, a welcome distraction. She sniffed at the cold turkey in her food bowl, turned her nose up at it and came to rub round Jack's legs instead. He bent down to fuss her enthusiastically, her nose and fur cold from outside. He rubbed her chin and she began to purr. 'Fussy thing. You like cats then, Jack?' Grandma asked.

'Er, yes.'

'Have you got one yourselves, you and Daisy?'

'No, it's a flat.'

'Of course,' said Grandma. 'What about at the old place, up there on the hill?'

'Er, no. We were never allowed one.'

'Shame,' said Grandma. 'Every house should have a pet. I'm more of a dog person myself.' Jack grimaced.

Thankfully Daisy returned. 'She's coming. In one of her morning mards as usual. Hello puss, puss,' she said, sitting down to stroke Sookie. 'Do you need a hand with anything, Mum?'

'No, nearly there now. Actually, you can get the plates out of the oven for me – watch out, though, they should be hot. Oh, and you can dunk the cafetière and get some fresh mugs; it should be ready now.'

Daisy got up. 'I'll get the plates,' said Jack, getting up with her.

Daisy tossed him a tea towel. Jack got the plates from the oven and set them on the side, then loitered with the tea towel slung over his shoulder. 'You can help me dish up if you want to make yourself useful, Jack,' said Carol, adding, 'Busman's holiday, eh?' Jack had no idea what she meant. But he *was* missing work in a strange way: the hustle and bustle, the banter. The towel over his shoulder reminded him of it.

'What shall I do?' he asked.

'A patty and two bits of streaky on each plate, please. Here's a spatula.' She passed him it. 'Ooh! Look at those burns on your arms,' she said, wincing; Jack was wearing a T-shirt and it was the first time she'd seen them.

Jack smiled sheepishly, glad that she'd noticed them. Whizz said they were like officer's stripes: the more you had, the higher up you were.

He laid out the five plates and proceeded to dish out the food. Without being asked, he transferred the eggs too, arranging everything in stacks rather than side by side, as they would at the restaurant. After finishing the dishes off with a twist of black pepper, he stood back. Carol had watched with interest. 'You enjoy cooking, Jack?' she said.

'Kind of,' he shrugged, whipping off his tea towel to carry two plates to the table.

Daisy, finishing off the coffee, gave him one of those 'goody-two shoes' smiles then, secretly proud, followed with the steaming cafetière.

The relative tranquillity was disturbed by Lily entering the kitchen. 'Daisy, have you been in my room and taken my tape player without asking?' She stood there, hands on hips, a towel wrapped round her head. Jack was shocked to see her without make up; she looked like a totally different person.

'Oh, morning,' said Carol.

'Now you're in trouble, young Daisy,' chuckled Grandma.

'Er, well. I would have asked but you were in the bathroom – as usual.'

'Well, you should have bloody waited then, shouldn't you?'

'Don't swear in front of Grandma, please, Lily,' said Carol, taking two more plates to the table.

'Sorry, but it pi – winds me up. She's only been back five minutes and she's already at it, taking things out of my room without asking…'

'It's not like you use it,' said Daisy.

'Yeah, I do. I was gonna find out who the Christmas number one is.'

'They told you that last Sunday – it's that crappy remake of the Band Aid single.'

'Daisy, language,' said Carol.

'Oh,' said Lily, disappointed. 'Anyway, it's my tape player and I want it back.'

'Well, me and Jack wanted to listen to a tape I made him as a Christmas present. We haven't had a chance yet. Mum, tell her.'

'Don't drag Mum into this. Your breakfast's getting cold. Daisy, you shouldn't have taken it, and Lily, if you're not using it then it would be a nice gesture – season of goodwill and all that... Now, please, can we just eat our food in peace? Coffee, Mum?'

For a while there was silence, save for the clinking and scrape of cutlery. Jack couldn't help keep stealing glances at Lily. She'd obviously just come out of the shower, hence the towel round her head. But seeing her without makeup on was freaking him out. It wasn't the first time this had happened with girls. Daisy wore little makeup, unless she was dressing up to go out, and looked the same to him with or without it. She, too, was a little surprised at seeing her sister 'au naturel' – especially in front of a man. Little did she know that Lily had given up flirting with and trying to impress Jack; he seemed immune or oblivious to her advances. Must be simple in the head, she'd concluded.

Carol broke the silence by clearing her throat. 'I thought it would be a good idea to visit the cemetery today whilst we're all together.'

Daisy stopped eating and stared into space. That was exactly what she'd been planning on doing – but with Jack, not some bloody family outing. She'd wanted some alone time with her dad, to talk to him. Jack could have had a smoke as well – she knew he'd be gasping by then. 'That's if you feel up to it?' Carol added, trying to read her youngest daughter's silence. 'Then I thought we could have a little Boxing Day walk and a drink in front of the fire at the GB. You know, make an occasion of it, rather than something sombre...' Still no response. 'Lily?' Carol tried.

Lily shrugged noncommittally. 'Suppose,' she said.

'We're meant to be lying low, remember,' said Daisy gloomily, her plans hijacked. 'No one's meant to know we're back.'

'Says who?' said Carol.

'Haslam.'

'I wouldn't flatter yourself,' said Lily. 'Your fifteen seconds of fame are over – no one's interested in you anymore.' Daisy glared at her sister.

'Well, there's always the Red Lion if you're worried. No one knows you in there, I bet.' Jack and Daisy looked at each other, remembering how Daisy had had her bum pinched by a sleazy regular there, and Jack had been barred for punching his lights out. 'It's changed hands, you know. It's a lot smarter now.'

'Since when?' said Daisy.

'Ooh, the beginning of December, I think. They wanted to make the most of the Christmas trade.'

'Interesting,' said Daisy.

'What is?'

'Nothing.'

'You're being very cryptic, young lady. It was just a thought anyway, the pub after... I've bought a poinsettia. Not that it'll last long in this frost ... but at least it's alive. I don't want to put cut flowers down...'

Daisy noted how her mum seemed to avoid saying 'grave'. 'I don't know,' she sighed.

'What?' said Carol, raising her voice and surprising everyone. 'What don't you know?'

'Can I be excused?' said Daisy, getting up with her plate.

Carol stared after her. 'It's not just you that's lost him, you know. We're all feeling it!' An awkward silence descended. Grandma looked upset, and picked up a napkin before dabbing at her mouth. Lily, head down, prodded her bubble and squeak with a fork. Jack didn't know what to do. Should he get up and follow Daisy?

Some moments later, after an awkward exit, they were both back upstairs. 'You OK?' said Jack; he could tell she wasn't.

'Yes.'

'What was that all about?'

'Oh, she's putting on a brave face, you can tell – trying to do all the usual stuff, Dad's stuff, but she's trying too hard. I wish she'd just stop; underneath she's clearly a mess. And now I feel guilty. I just wanted it to be me and you...' Daisy was interrupted by a knock at the door.

'Can I have a word, please?' It was Carol.

Daisy gave Jack an exasperated look. 'Yeah, coming,' she said, torn between being pissed off at her mum and the guilt. She opened the door. Jack heard Carol speaking quietly. He caught the word 'private'. Daisy tutted, looked at Jack again, then walked out onto the landing, closing the door behind her. Jack heard muffled voices, but had no idea what was being said. When Daisy returned, shutting the door behind her, her eyes were teary. She made a beeline for the bed, throwing herself down and lying on her side, facing away from Jack. He went to her and curled into her back, putting an arm round her. 'It's OK,' she said through her sniffles. 'We've made up. But we're all going together...'

*****

Almost as much out of habit now as caution, and to her family's bemusement, Daisy said they'd meet the rest of them on Church Lane; she and Jack were going the back way, over the fence, to the cemetery. The frost had set in overnight, and the over-long grass was now cemented in place, unruffled by the chill breeze. The garden, Carol's usual pride and joy, looked a little neglected in the unforgiving light of day. The flowers had been left to grow straggly, their summer growth still attached like soggy, wet straw, rather than being pulled out or cut back for the winter; it was the same with the clematis over Honeysuckle Cottage. Daisy brought this up when they reached the lane. 'Not been doing much gardening lately, Mum?'

'No, it hasn't been the weather for it – it can sulk till the New Year now.' This wasn't like her. She seemed to have lost interest in things – she wasn't even drinking, or so she said.

It was strange for Jack, being back on these narrow lanes – there was the church that he'd sat outside during Daisy's dad's funeral. And there was the cemetery – waiting, ancient and restful, behind its rusty black gates; the only movement a swirling confetti of dead leaves in one corner, tawny, russet and gold, whipped up by the breeze. Visiting the grave, Jack had the feeling of being an outsider again, an intruder at a private family moment. But he didn't feel as if he could wander off either, it would be disrespectful. The last time he'd been there he'd discovered that the woman he'd thought was his mother, Carla, wasn't his mother at all. He'd stumbled across her grave. There was part of him that wanted to look at it again, to pay his respects in his own way.

Carol was the only one who said much. She called her dead husband 'love' and patted his gravestone as she knelt down with the poinsettia. She was used to this because she visited the grave regularly, but for Daisy it was a shock. It brought everything back – the reality, the finality. In the end it overwhelmed her, and she sobbed silently with Jack's arm around her. That's the thing with grief: it's like a well that never runs dry. And the amount you draw from it, how often and how deeply, isn't up to you; *it* decides.

Sensing Daisy wanted some time alone, Carol said, 'We'll wait at the gates. Then we'll go and have that drink. It's a bit fresh here. But have five minutes – or as long as you like. Talk to him. It's OK. I do it all the time. Come on.' She gestured to Lily and Grandma. 'You coming, Jack?'

'Er, I'll wait with Daisy if that's OK.'

Carol put her hand on Daisy's shoulder. Then she and Lily walked slowly away, shepherding Grandma back down the slippery path.

'I'll go and have a wander,' said Jack.

'You don't have to. It's OK.' Daisy wiped her nose with her sleeve.

'No, I'll leave you to it.' He kissed her and made for Carla's gravestone, remembering exactly where it was. It looked older than he remembered, more weather-worn than Daisy's dad's. There were no flowers on it either; that there was no one left to do this made him feel sad – for her and for himself. It made him think of his sister. Anne was Carla's daughter. This was her mother, which made Carla his family in a way. Didn't it? Perhaps *he* should have brought some flowers, and he decided to in future. Who would look after it if he didn't? As he stood there he heard Daisy speaking to her dad – just as she had last time – and a powerful sense of déjà vu washed over him. How many times would they come and do this? Until they died themselves? Death again; that unseen trapdoor waiting at the end of a conveyor belt that nobody can stop. From a very early age he'd been all too aware of it, and here in the cemetery Death's constantly ticking clock got louder, deafening, panic-inducing. He shuddered to snap himself out of it.

Respects paid and ghosts visited, Jack and Daisy made their way out of the cemetery. They closed the gates behind them, as if trying to shut their feelings away. The others were waiting for them in the lane. 'You OK, love?' said Carol. Daisy nodded. 'So, the Red Lion then? I think we could all use a drink.'

Jack knew he certainly could – especially if he couldn't have a spliff. But Daisy said, 'I think we'll give it a miss, thanks, I don't really feel like it – but you go.'

'Ah, that's a shame,' said Carol. 'We don't have to go. It was just a thought...'

'I'd like to go,' cut in Lily loudly, sick of her opinion not counting – everything had been all about Daisy since she'd got back. 'Saves being stuck in the boring house all day.'

Carol looked at Daisy, unsure. 'Honestly, you go,' said Daisy. 'We'll have a little wander or something.'

'Well, if you're sure...'

The group split up, Jack and Daisy heading back in the direction of the house. Jack, a little put out at missing out on a proper pint of cider, trudged after Daisy who, now they were out of sight of the others, was walking quickly. 'How come you didn't want to go to the pub?' he called after her.

'Do you want a spliff or not?' she said over her shoulder.

Jack's face lit up.

After a hastily rolled spliff, which they'd smoked in an out-of-the way spot outdoors, the two of them were back in Daisy's room. The spliff had done wonders for Jack and, to his surprise, Daisy had partaken too – she needed a release and figured she'd got enough time to brush her teeth and scrub her fingers to get rid of the smell. They were both feeling contemplative, woozy, a little melancholic maybe, but certainly more relaxed as they listened to Daisy's new tape and drank cider. The music worked its magic on Daisy, and she thawed, becoming more animated, more like her usual self.

When the others returned, there was the traditional Boxing Day buffet and more drinks. Carol had put on a fine spread and Jack and Daisy were both starving, having not eaten since breakfast – and barely anything then. Later there were more games and drinks, and Daisy and Jack relaxed into the evening, enjoying the warmth of the house and being waited on hand and foot – especially Daisy, it made a change from doing the cooking all the time. 'Mum, am I still insured on the van?' she asked, out of the blue, moving her Monopoly piece to the 'Just Visiting' square. Jack was loving it – he'd never played Monopoly before and it was as if the money was real to him; he wanted a board for home.

'Christ, now you've got me,' said Carol, picking up the dice, flummoxed after a few G and Ts. 'I haven't even thought about it – it's just been sitting out there on the drive since you left. I *suppose* you are… I certainly can't remember cancelling it – and I can't remember any renewal papers coming through… Why? You're not thinking of driving the old thing again are you?'

'Yes, I was actually. I'm thinking of taking it back to Cromer.'

'Really? I'm not sure if that's a good idea. Is it still roadworthy? I'm not even sure if it's got an MOT or not… And what about Haslam? Didn't he say…'

'Oh, screw Haslam,'

'Daisy. Grandma.'

'Sorry, Grandma. But, as Lily so eloquently put it, nobody's interested in *me* anymore. I'm sick of us not being able to drive anywhere out of Cromer – it gets a bit boring.'

This was news to Jack, and he looked up at her. Was she bored living at the flat with him? When he was so happy and looking forward to getting back – just the two of them again. The mention of Haslam was sobering, too. The meeting Jack had with him the next day was looming; he'd been pushing it to the back of his mind. What did Haslam want from him? It would have been nice just to get straight off in the morning.

'Well, good luck getting it started – I bet the battery's flat, the tyres too – and if it's not MOTd you're not taking it anywhere!' said Carol.

CHAPTER 26
Surprises

'Mum, do you know where the jump leads are?' Daisy asked, bursting into the kitchen the next morning. After scraping the frost off the van, and topping it up with oil, she'd found out the battery was dead. At least she hoped it was the battery.

Carol looked up from the kitchen drawer she was rifling through. 'God, they could be anywhere. Try the boot of the Montego – or the garage. Aah, there you are!' The MOT certificate she'd been searching for. She consulted the expiry date, confirming the VW was still in date. Was that a good thing, though? Daisy driving the van all the way back? Carol knew her daughter; if she'd got her mind set on something that was it. 'You're in luck!' she said. But Daisy had already gone. Carol smiled sadly; she'd enjoyed having Daisy back again; she brought some much-needed energy and life to the place; and she'd missed this – being needed and solving family problems, however trivial.

Daisy extracted the tangled jump leads from the boot of the car. Funny how she hadn't noticed them when they'd arrived – but, then again, she hadn't been looking for them. 'Hold these and untangle them whilst I move the car closer,' she said, handing them to Jack. Jack did as he was told, while Daisy, head out of the window, inched the Montego right up to the side of the van. Having left the van's lights on several times, she knew how to jump start it from watching her dad – just about. Its side door was already open and the front seat was slid forward, revealing the battery that was located in a hole in the floor. Daisy jumped out and turned the car's engine off. Then she grabbed the leads off Jack. 'Right, red is positive, black is negative,' she said. 'So, red or black first?' She looked at the cables, as if they were going to answer her.

'What? Don't you know?' said Jack alarmed. Car engines and electric cables seemed like a dangerous combination to him.

'Red. It's red. I think…' How could she be so casual about it? 'Good battery or dead battery first,' she said, looking from one vehicle to another.

Jack let out a groan. 'Daisy, do you think this is a good idea? You might blow up your mum's car – or electrocute yourself.'

'Don't be silly,' she said. 'Good battery first…' Leaning under the Montego's bonnet, she squeezed the red cable's jaws open and attached them to the car's battery. Jack stood back, wincing, terrified of Daisy getting an electric shock. But nothing happened. He watched as she attached the other end of the red cable to the van's battery. 'So far, so good,' she said, standing back up; she'd gone through a stage of wanting to be a mechanic, like Charlene on *Neighbours*. After Daisy had attached a black end to the Montego again without any incident, Jack dared to move a little closer, intrigued. Finally, she put the other end of the black one in place. 'OK, let's give her some power,' she said. Hopping back into the Montego, she made sure the car was in neutral, then started the engine before getting out. 'Right, this is the exciting bit – I hope! We'll give it a few minutes … fingers crossed.' Jack followed Daisy round to the driver's side of the van.

She waited a few minutes, impatiently drumming her fingers on the steering wheel and rocking backwards and forwards. She fiddled with some of the knobs on the tape player, wanting to turn it on, but not daring to. Maybe there was a forgotten tape in there, she thought, pressing the eject button. There wasn't. 'How long do you have to wait?' asked Jack, beginning to grow impatient himself.

'A bit longer, you can't rush it – the battery's totally dead.' After five minutes, she was ready to try. Carol had come to the front door to watch. 'OK, here goes,' Daisy said. She closed her eyes, as if it would help, and turned the key. The van's engine whimpered a few times, but didn't catch. Jack was disappointed – it would have been better than getting the train. 'That's good!' said Daisy. 'There's life in it. It was totally dead before. It just needs a bit longer, that's all.' After another five minutes of excruciating waiting, she tried again. The engine whirred, coughed and then, amazingly, with an exhalation of smoke from the exhaust, jumped into life. Daisy revved the accelerator pedal and squealed, 'Woohooo! Good old VW!' She patted the steering wheel in delight. Jack grinned, awestruck, as he so often was, at this independent, worldly-wise girl and her many hidden talents. Carol laughed from the porch, despite her reservations, caught up in the moment. Daisy continued to rev the engine, as she'd seen her dad do, filling the drive with pungent petrol smoke in the process. Even Grandma appeared to see what all the fuss was about.

Satisfied the battery was OK, Daisy hopped down and planted a kiss on Jack's lips. 'Clever girl, aren't I?' she said, wanting some acknowledgement. Jack grinned again. She certainly was, and he planned on giving her plenty – back at the flat later, it couldn't come soon enough. But first there was the little matter of that meeting with Haslam…

After a tearful and protracted goodbye – Carol hated letting Daisy go again – they were on their way. By Jack's choice, they took a route that avoided his old house, pumping up the van's tyres and buying petrol on the way. Although he was curious about the state the house was in, he wasn't ready to see it. It was a pity, he wouldn't have minded driving past Bunny Wood; now that he *did* miss. Daisy was a little miffed as she was burning with curiosity herself, and it seemed stupid whilst they were in the area not to take a look. When would they get the chance again? But she had to bite her tongue and respect Jack's feelings; the place obviously held deep-rooted trauma for him, as well it might, as he'd seen his entire family – if you could call them that – perish there; and his childhood home, the only one he'd ever had, go up in smoke.

Talking of smoke, Jack couldn't wait to get a spliff rolled and sparked up. This didn't help his state of mind, and by the time they pulled into the police station car park at West Bridgford he was a mess. Just seeing the place was enough – the place that he was brought to after being captured, and where he was put into that hellish cell. The questions, the not knowing if he was ever going to see Daisy again. 'Best get it over and done with,' he sighed, unbuckling his seat belt. To his surprise, Daisy left the engine running.

Unlike Jack, she was a little better at hiding her feelings. She put her hand on his knee. 'Do you mind if I don't come in with you?' Then, seeing the look on his face, she added, 'I mean, I will if you want. If you really want me too … it's just…' She trailed off. Jack searched her face, seeing the rare vulnerability there, the worry lines and frown. Oh. The penny dropped. The baby. What had happened in that corridor. The blood. What she'd lost. What they'd both lost. Funny how he didn't really think about it much. Clearly she did. This was *her* house of horrors.

'It's fine,' he said. 'I can do this. Jack Gardner can do this.' Daisy smiled, leant across and kissed him, then they hugged.

'Thank you. Good luck,' she said. 'Whatever he's got in store for you, I'm sure it's nothing to worry about. Didn't you say he sounded chirpy on the phone?'

Haslam was still chirpy when he greeted Jack at the front desk. 'Jack!' he said, shaking his hand. 'So good to see you! You're looking well. All that sea air doing you good, eh? No one followed you in, I hope.' He pretended to look over Jack's shoulder and out of the window. Jack didn't feel well – on top of his nerves, he still felt ill. But to someone who hadn't seen him for a while, he would look a little healthier, his hair growing back, a bit of colour about him. 'Come on then, let's get this over and done with – I don't really need to be here today to be honest. Joan, can I have two cups of tea brought in please? You drink tea don't you, Jack? I can't remember?'

'No, yes. I'm fine, though,' he said.

'Yer sure? One tea, thanks, Joan. The usual. Right, follow me, young man – you know the way!' Why was he so jovial? thought Jack. Smug almost. 'A belated Happy Christmas by the way. Did you have a good one?' Haslam said over his shoulder.

'Yes, fine thanks.'

'Back in the old neighbourhood, eh?'

'Er, yes.' Jack was distracted; the smell of the police station was setting off triggers in his mind. The black spot appeared. Powerful flashbacks rocked him as he negotiated the corridors, the light bulbs exploding in his head making him feel dizzy – being shackled, the sickening sound of a heavy door clanging shut and being bolted.

'Here we are,' said Haslam, stopping at his office. Jack followed him in, relieved. This room held no bad memories for him. 'Sit yourself down.' Haslam gestured to a chair at his desk. Jack did as he was told. The detective sat back and put his fingers together. 'How's that girlfriend of yours – young Daisy?' he asked. 'I'm surprised she's not with you…'

'Oh, she's in the van – the car. She's fine.'

'Feeling a bit shy, was she?' he joked. 'Anyway, I'm glad you're still making a go of things … you young uns today don't seem to last five minutes. Especially shacked up together.

It's not easy. I should know! Thirty-two years I've been with my wife…' He trailed off, staring into space. Then his face changed, becoming more serious. 'Listen to me prattling on… Let's get down to business. I'll think we'll get the serious stuff out of the way first.' He leant forward to fish in his trouser pocket. After some jangling he pulled out a bunch of keys. Then, as Jack watched, he reached down to unlock and open a drawer in his desk. Shooting Jack another serious look, he pulled out a white cardboard box and placed it on the table between them. It was like a large, more robust, shoebox – or a heavy duty paperwork box – the kind the shelves lining the room were filled with. Jack had no idea what could be in it. 'Now, I know this might be a little upsetting for you…' Haslam was interrupted by a knock on the door. 'Come in!'

'Sorry. Hope I'm not disturbing anything. Here's your tea. I've brought you some mince pies too. There were some left over.'

'Thank you, Joan. Mince pie, Jack?' The lady scuttled out of the room.

Even if he liked them, he wouldn't have been able to eat a thing. He just wanted to know what was in the box. He couldn't take his eyes off it. 'No, thank you.'

'I know what you mean… Mince pies never seem to taste the same after the big day's gone. I'm waffling again… I guess you're wondering what's in the box. Well, how do I put this…' This bit was always hard: you never knew how people were going to react, especially in this case when the boy wasn't expecting it. Haslam placed his startlingly white hairy hand on the top of the box and splayed his fingers, one of them with a gold wedding band on it. 'In here is what we discussed on the phone. It's been done…'

'Done?' said Jack.

'Your family. Your mother and sister. These are their ashes…'

Jack felt his skin crawl and he recoiled in his chair, as if trying to put distance between himself and the box. All the repressed feelings about Anne crowded in and seemed to rush to the fore, as if they wanted to pour out of his mouth in a hot stream. He had kept them at bay. It was easier with distance, with not seeing; he didn't even have a grown-up photo of her. But here she was. His sister, a living, breathing human being with blood coursing through her veins, reduced to some dust in a box. 'I think I'm going to be sick,' he said. The colour had drained from his face.

'Oh shit! Use this!' Haslam grabbed a wastepaper basket and shoved it across the desk. Jack grabbed it and bent forward to retch. His stomach went into spasms, but nothing came out. He heaved again, dry-retching until his face was mottled and he saw lights in front of his eyes. But still nothing came out. He was dimly aware of Haslam saying something and leaving the room.

When he returned, Jack was sitting back in his chair. His eyes were watery and he looked a state. His stomach was still clenching and unclenching like a fist, but the worst had passed. 'Here, try and drink some water,' Haslam said. He passed Jack a glass and put a loo roll on the desk. Jack took the water from him, but couldn't bear the thought of it hitting his stomach and triggering him off again.

Haslam sighed and ran his fingers through his thinning hair. He felt guilty. He shouldn't have sprung it on the boy, but had never imagined he would react like that; he thought he'd be relieved for the chapter to be closed. 'I'm sorry,' he said, putting his hand on Jack's shoulder. 'I should have given you a bit of warning. The thing is, that wasn't why I asked you here today – I didn't know myself until this morning. The box appeared at the front desk on Christmas Eve apparently and no one told me; we've had a skeleton crew on, see. But I thought it would be a double surprise...' *Double surprise?*

thought Jack. 'Anyway, do you want to look or shall we move on? They're neatly labelled in separate canisters…' Jack shook his head violently. 'OK, we'll move on, not a problem. I've got something that might make you feel better.' Haslam patted Jack's shoulder again and returned to his side of the desk. Jack put the wastepaper bin back on the floor, and Haslam respectfully placed the box on the floor as well, so it wasn't between them. 'Right, on to more cheerful things… You'll be pleased to know that our mutual acquaintance, Mr. Peasgood, is very shortly going to be in serious trouble. He already is, but he probably doesn't know it yet…'

'What?' said Jack. 'What did you say?'

'This morning, or whenever the post is back to normal and when his factory reopens, whichever comes first, our Mr Peasgood is going to receive … let's call it a belated Christmas missive, giving him seven days to produce his last ten years' figures for inspection and all his personnel records and wage slips.' Jack couldn't believe what he was hearing: this was worse than having your dead sister's ashes sprung on you.

'B-but, why?'

'Why? 'Cause the man's a crook and his game is up. We've got good reason to believe he got his entire workforce to lie for him – and that's only the beginning. I was investigating him anyway, mainly in my own time – I had a hunch. There was something about the man I didn't trust. It opened up a right can of worms, I can tell you. Anyway, check this out.' Haslam leant forward on his desk excitedly, propped on his elbows, 'A disgruntled worker came to me off his own back! Pissed off – excuse my language – about being unlawfully sacked in the run-up to Christmas. He'd barely been there a month, but once the Christmas orders were out of the way Peasgood got rid of him – you and Daisy weren't the only people who he mistreated. Hold on, did Daisy even work there? 'Cause I know…'

'I never worked there!' Jack cut in, horrified at what he was hearing. 'I told you where I got the money from!'

'Jack, it's OK. This guy Roberts, Alan Roberts — you wouldn't know him, it was way after you left — says he overheard on numerous occasions other workers talking about an extra Christmas bonus they were expecting for keeping quiet about an illegal worker some months back. Now don't tell me that wasn't you. We certainly haven't been there asking about anyone else!'

Jack sat stony-faced. He was running out of answers. His worse fears were being realised.

'Is there anything else you're not telling me?' Haslam continued. 'Did Peasgood threaten you? Did he contact you somehow? Put pressure on you to change your story? We now know he's got some very, how shall I put it, dubious acquaintances — especially across the border — and that's another story in itself. But if he did, it would be the icing on the cake. We might be able to get him put away. You've got to tell me…'

Jack could feel Haslam studying him, looking for a breakthrough. Meanwhile his brain was whirling. So was his stomach again. He heard the vile, menacing Scottish voice in his head: 'Change your story and call him off. Or else… We know where yae live and we know where yae both work…' 'I need to go,' he said. 'I need to see Daisy.' He made to get up, scraping his chair back.

'Wait,' said Haslam, getting up himself. 'I'm not finished yet. Look, sit down a minute. I know Peasgood has put the fear of God in you somehow, I can see that, so I'm going to go easy on you. For now. Give you some time. But this isn't why I got you here today either; this has all been off the record, by the way — to be continued at a later date. Let's see how Peasgood reacts to that demand first…'

'When will he get it?' said Jack, closing his eyes and covering his face with his hands.

'Any time. Maybe today. Maybe tomorrow. Like I say, I'm not sure when the post is back to normal, or when the factory reopens, or even who opens his post. Anyway, sit down a minute. I've got something else for you.'

Jack reluctantly sat back down and Haslam reached into his desk again. He came back up with an envelope and put it on the table between them. 'What is it?' asked Jack.

'What is it? Let's call it an advance.'

'An advance?'

'On your confiscated money. Which I was hoping to be able to give you back by now – or at least some of it – but the powers that be won't allow it, not whilst the investigation is ongoing. It's got a certain someone's fingerprints all over it for a start – and they're not Santa Claus's!' Haslam had that smug look on his face again, as if he'd got his man. 'We already had them on file. Can you believe that? Like I said, Mr Peasgood has a chequered past. This isn't the first time he's had a brush with the law. We know you worked there, Jack, whether you want to admit it or not. He knew your father, didn't he? That's how you got the job there...' Jack was beyond denying it now. What was the point? Yet still the admission wouldn't come.

Haslam studied him for a moment. He had a soft spot for the boy; he'd done nothing but tell the truth, or at least tried to, until Peasgood had put the frighteners on him. The detective tapped the envelope, then pushed it towards Jack. 'There's two hundred quid in there – money out of my own pocket, I hasten to add – but I want it back as soon as you get yours – the missus'll kill...'

'I don't want it,' Jack said.

'Don't want it?' Haslam's face changed; he looked offended. 'You *will* take the money and you'll be grateful for it – or I'll shove it somewhere the sun don't shine! There's two hundred quid in there – now take it and get out of here before I change my mind! And take your family with you. What's left of 'em,

God rest their souls…' He gestured to the box on the floor. 'Their death certificates are in there with them and there's a form I need you to sign, but you can post that back to me.'

Jack didn't know how serious Haslam was being, but figured he'd already used up the detective's patience. He bent down to pick up the box – no time for squeamishness now – grabbed the envelope and went to leave. It felt as if a death certificate had been slapped on *him*. He shuffled to the door. What was he going to tell Daisy? Where did he start?

'Cheer up,' Haslam called, his voice mellowing again. 'Buy your little lady something! I'll be in touch. Keep you informed. Have a good New Year.' Jack gave the detective one last look, then went to close the door. 'Oh! One last thing. I nearly forgot!' Jack groaned inwardly and paused, his hand on the door; he just wanted to be with Daisy, to know she was all right. 'Do you know a Verity Storm?' Jack looked perplexed. What was a verity storm? He shook his head and shrugged, not knowing how to answer. 'A family member?' Jack shook his head again. 'What about a Carla Storm?' Jack gave a start of recognition and Haslam registered it. 'You do know a Carla Storm.'

'I know a Carla Hemsley…' Wait a minute: he did remember seeing that name somewhere. Where was it? Yellowing old-fashioned paper… Carla's birth certificate that he'd found in the box from the attic. 'It was his wife … my father's,' he said. 'Anne's mother.' The woman he'd thought was *his* mother. 'She was born Carla Storm.'

'That would add up, then. Do you know if she had a sister? A Verity Storm?'

'No idea,' said Jack. 'Why?'

'We've had her solicitor on the phone, saying she's laying claim to your old place on the hill and all that land.'

CHAPTER 27
Jinkies!

Daisy had mixed feelings about going back to Norfolk. Leaving her mum behind in such a state had been hard. It had felt like abandoning her all over again. The same with her dad's grave. It was nice to be near it, to be able to visit it whenever she wished. It was comforting in a way and made her feel close to him, more in touch with him. On a more selfish note, being back home had also felt like a kind of holiday. A break. The warmth of the house. The luxury of a hot shower. Being cooked for. Not having to work – at the restaurant or at home. At least they'd both got the rest of the day off, she supposed. It was good to have the van back as well. The thought of the freezing cold flat, however, wasn't so appealing.

She had no idea how Jack was feeling. He'd been acting strangely ever since he'd come out of the police station. On edge, but quiet. Worse than before he'd gone in. Hardly surprising considering what he'd come out of there with. That box. It had obviously affected him. She'd suggested scattering the ashes somewhere local, whilst they were still in the area. Maybe in the spinney near the crab apple tree. Jack had snapped at her and got all defensive, which wasn't like him. Then he'd proceeded to skin up. Again. It was starting to make her feel how she'd felt about him and his cider. His dependence on it and her inability to stop it. That feeling of being second best.

Daisy looked across at him, glancing in the rear-view mirror again. You could hear the jars of ashes clinking and rolling about in the back. She put Jack's new tape on to drown them out. The thought of the ashes coming back to the flat bothered her. It was a little macabre, a little weird, knowing they would be in the same place as them. It would be the same for her, she supposed, if the shoe was on the other foot and they were her dad's. But at least he'd died a natural death, as opposed to... She shuddered. 'Do you mind closing the window when you've finished that one. It's freezing!' She spoke as kindly as possible. Jack took one last drag, blew the smoke out and closed the window. 'Thanks. Hey, what do you want to do for the rest of the day? Or, more to the point, what do you want to blow all that cash on, Richie Rich?' She patted his leg, still amazed at the detective's kind gesture.

Jack shrugged in response. 'Don't know,' he said. Daisy couldn't understand why he wasn't more excited about the money. Or that bastard Peasgood getting his much-deserved comeuppance. OK, it wasn't the full amount. Far from it. But it was a start, an unexpected surprise. It would give them some financial breathing space; they could spoil themselves a little. They were both working and, as Aitch had pointed out, Christmas tips at the restaurant had been amazing. Grandma had come good as usual too, bless her. They were flush for once. This in itself should be something to celebrate. And they'd got the big New Year to look forward to. That reminded her. They needed to get costumes. They'd left it late.

'What's wrong?' she said, turning the music down a little. 'I thought you'd be excited that we're on our way home. That's all you've been moaning about for the last few days! We can get those coloured lights going again ... just you and me...' She looked at Jack cheekily, thinking this would raise a smile. It didn't. She turned back to the road. 'It's the ashes, isn't it?' she said. 'Is that what you're thinking about?'

The ashes were the least of Jack's worries. They could wait. He still hadn't told Daisy the full extent of Peasgood's threats, the ones against her. He'd chosen not to. Again. How could he when he'd already kept it from her? She'd go ballistic, probably wouldn't even want to go back to the flat. He wouldn't be able to let her out of his sight. Not for a second. Day or night. Not till all this was over, and hopefully Peasgood went to jail. Perhaps he should have told Haslam right there and then. About the kidnapping. Perhaps it would speed things up. But he'd been so horrified at what the detective had done, the direct opposite of Peasgood's wishes, and the consequences that came with this. Would revealing the truth about the kidnapping be a red rag to a bull and make Peasgood even angrier? More likely to act, to send men out again? Jack became aware Daisy was waiting for an answer... 'Suppose,' he lied.

'What about the sea?'

'What about it?'

'You know. For Anne's ashes. Didn't you say she loved the seaside? That was where you thought she'd gone. Then that way at least she'd have made it in the end. I guess...'

'I'm not chucking my sister in the sea!' Jack said, aggressively.

'Sorry,' Daisy said. 'It was just a suggestion.'

*****

After finding a parking space on their street, the pair of them lugged their belongings, presents, box of ashes and all, up to the flat. Stepping out of the warmth of the van was a shock. It was bitter by the coast. But even that didn't prepare them for the cold of the flat. 'Oh-my-fucking-god! It's freezing in here!' said Daisy, dumping her bag on the kitchen floor. 'Oh great! No wonder. We left the bloody window open!' She had opened one of the top windows in the lounge before her sister had arrived. In the rush of leaving she'd forgotten to close it. *We?* thought Jack, as Daisy went over to close it, standing on tiptoe. 'I don't fucking believe it. It's bad enough as it is in here,' she said, hugging herself and shivering, still wearing her coat. 'Look at this!' she said, picking up a leftover glass of water off the side. It's actually got ice in it!' She shook the glass. 'That does it. We can't carry on like this – I can't *live* like this. We need to get a heater or something. One of those little fan heaters. Mum uses one in the cottage – or used to anyway. I should have brought it back with me.'

'What about the electricity?' said Jack. 'I remember my father saying they were expensive to run. He used to have a gas one in his workshop.'

'A gas one? We're not lugging one of those and a bloody great canister through town and up the stairs! Besides, we've got some money now – we don't need to have it on much. Just to sit next to in the lounge for a bit. Or to warm the bedroom up before we go to bed.'

So it was decided. After unpacking they headed into town in search of a heater and some fancy dress outfits. Their departure was delayed by a slightly heated debate about where Jack should store the ashes. He wanted to stick them under his side of the bed, but Daisy refused, saying it was creepy. She didn't want to have to stare at the box in the lounge either, especially when she was on her own in the house. That Ouija board incident had scared the crap out of her. Jack was offended, saying it was his family. And he – more so than Daisy – was only too aware of his father's malevolent spirit. What if *he* got wind of the fact that Anne was with them in Cromer? The thought of this made Jack want to keep a close eye on the ashes. It was as if he'd gone from being repulsed by them to being possessive. In the end they went in the spare room, along with the vacuum cleaner and Daisy's excess clothes.

Town was surprisingly busy: people off work between Christmas and New Year, older children, teenagers, eager to spend their Christmas money. Jack lurched from shop to shop, surreptitiously keeping his eyes peeled for a sinister black car. They stopped at Boots to get him some Lemsip, paracetamol and Lockets. His cold seemed to be getting worse; he was shivery and burning up and his throat was still sore. They had no luck with a heater: the only shop that would have sold one was closed until the New Year. It had a sign on the door saying so. 'A HAPPY NEW YEAR TO ALL OUR CUSTOMERS!' it cheerfully read. 'Yes, here's to another week of freezing our bloody arses off! Thank you very much!' Daisy said, stomping off. Next she dragged Jack, under duress, to the fancy dress shop. She had walked past it many times and it had always fascinated her. Stepping inside wasn't a disappointment, and it instantly cheered her up. The interior smelt and felt old. Despite a fair few empty racks, there was still a pleasing number of costumes left. Gladiator outfits, mummy outfits, chef outfits (no good to them!). She imagined all the parties they'd been used for over the years, and by whom. Running her eyes round the shop, Daisy was reminded of the *Mr Benn* cartoon that she'd watched growing up. The theme music ran through her head and she felt dizzy with nostalgia; that stealthy assassin who liked to creep up on you and knock you for six. She imagined the narrator's kindly voice: 'and, as if by magic, the shopkeeper appeared...' And there she was: an oldish lady with half-moon glasses emerging from behind a curtain. 'Hello,' she said, a local twang in her voice.

'Hi,' Daisy said.

'After anything specific, dear?'

'Erm. Not really. Just something for New Year's Eve.'

'Hmm ... you and the rest of the town. There's not a huge amount left, I'm afraid. All your classics have gone, your superheroes, your *Star Wars*... Still, you should be able to find something if you're not too fussy. Was it for both of you or just yourself?'

'Both of us,' Daisy said, turning to Jack. He was staring out of the window, looking up and down the street.

'OK. Size could be an issue. Especially for you. You're quite petite.' Daisy blushed, pleased. In her head she was a big, fat, post-Christmas blob. 'How do you fancy being a nurse for the night?' the lady said, stepping from behind the counter where there was a little rat-sized dog curled up in front of a gas heater. 'I could see you as a nurse.' She walked over to a rack and pulled out a costume. 'It's about your size,' she said, holding it up. It was the skimpiest nurse's outfit Daisy had ever seen – more like a child's dressing up costume. She could imagine it clinging to her and riding up all night. She wouldn't be able to sit down.

'I don't think so,' Daisy said diplomatically.

'OK. Erm … what about Wilma Flintstone?' The lady pulled out a white dress and orange beehive wig combo. 'Fred's gone, I'm afraid, otherwise you could have gone as a couple.' The dress was flimsy. Like a thin white cotton bed sheet, it was hacked into zigzags at the hemline. She'd catch her death in it; and she could make something similar for nothing at home.

'No thanks,' Daisy said.

'I think you're after something more conservative…' The lady put the costume back. 'I know, what about *Hi-de-Hi?*' A yellow tunic, short black wig and white shorts were pulled out, echoing Ruth Maddock from the TV show. *God, no*, thought Daisy. This wasn't as easy as she'd envisaged. She shook her head again, shyly. 'I'll leave you to it, dear,' said the lady, sighing a little impatiently. She went back to the warmth of her gas heater.

'Can't we just go home?' Jack said, speaking for the first time. 'This is pointless.'

'No. I haven't looked properly yet,' Daisy said, frustrated at his lack of interest. She perused the racks as Jack hung back. The old lady watched from over the top of her glasses.

Nothing seemed to pique Daisy's interest. All the female ones were so slutty. A St Trinian's outfit with another skimpy hemline. A rubber getup, more like bondage gear, which even had its own whip. Was it supposed to be Catwoman? She wanted to stand out, but not in that way. She could always dress up as Madonna again, she supposed, but it was a bit of a let-down. Then the bell of the front door dinged, making Jack spin round. Daisy wondered why he was so on edge. Another young couple, about their age, entered. Jack slunk further into a corner, embarrassed. Daisy continued to search, unperturbed, sighing occasionally. Growing more impatient, Jack began to hop from one foot to the other. Daisy had all but given up when a familiar outfit caught her eye. A bright orange roll-neck jumper and scarlet skirt. Hung round the jumper's neck on a string was a pair of glasses. Velma from *Scooby Doo!* Now that was something she could work with. Kooky and nerdy, but something she could sex up a bit. A sexy Velma! She didn't need the wig as her hair was already a short-cropped bob. And those awful orange football socks could go. She'd got some knee-high brown boots that would work with the outfit. Yes! That was it. She held it up to Jack. He shook his head, as if to say 'really?' not seeing or unwilling to see the potential.

'I've got a Shaggy left to go with that one!' said the old lady.

*****

Daisy insisted that they were going to have a Chinese takeaway for supper; if she was going to be cold, at least she was going to have something nice to eat. Besides, she'd got used to not cooking, and it wasn't as if they couldn't afford it. Jack, in turn, insisted that they should get it delivered. It was dark out. Daisy grumbled at the extra charge, then, unable to help herself (she'd had a couple of glasses of wine), questioned Jack about his skittishness and over-cautiousness. Surely they should be able to relax now that Peasgood was being dealt with by the police?

Jack, a little drunk himself, hopped up on a combination of wine, marijuana and cold remedies, gave an impassioned, spur-of-the-moment speech about how it was his job to protect her. It just came to him, but it was true. He'd let Anne slip through his fingers, something he would never forgive himself for, and he wasn't about to have the same happen again. After having experienced first-hand what Peasgood was capable of, who knew what else he might try? What if he decided to retaliate? Until he was dealt with they had to be cautious and vigilant, and take no chances. Both of them. They had to stick together at all times.

This did the job, and Daisy understood and loved him all the more for it. He was right. When there was a knock at the door, Jack was the one who got up to answer it and collect their Chinese. He was feeling brave after his speech and because of the drink in him; he had also already stashed a rolling pin in the gas meter cupboard by the front door.

Getting everything off his chest (or most of it anyway) was a relief. He felt he'd done his duty. They had their Chinese and continued to drink. And the more Jack drank, the better he felt. This was what he had missed for the last couple of days. Just the two of them. Snuggled under the blanket together with their hot water bottles, smoking, drinking, listening to his new tape. The phone did that odd dinging thing at one point, startling them. At first Daisy thought it was her mum, checking they'd got back safely – which reminded her she was meant to call. This she did, stealing the blanket, whilst Jack skinned up a stingy spliff (his supply was running dangerously low), and signalling her to hurry up because he was getting cold.

By the end of the evening they were both wasted. Especially Jack. Adrift on a raft of medication on a narcotic sea, he'd been able to temporarily banish his fears. They could wait till tomorrow. He felt invincible. Nothing could touch him while they were locked in that flat. Neither Peasgood nor his cronies.

Before bed Daisy gave Jack a drunken preview of her New Year's Eve outfit – only she could make Velma look sexy – then they finally got the coloured lights going. She insisted on keeping the outfit on throughout, complete with the glasses. Jack didn't mind; he was too far gone, it was like making love to a stranger. Afterwards, as he drifted off, still high as a kite, he couldn't work out if she'd actually said 'Jinkies!' as she came or if he'd imagined it…

CHAPTER 28

The Cromer Carrot

The following morning Jack had the mother of all come downs, both mentally and physically. The Peasgood situation hit him first. The enormity of it. The reality. It wasn't just a dream you could wake up from. And it seemed all the substances he'd put in his body the previous night had been filtered of the good stuff – the euphoria, the dreamy light-headedness, the invincibility – and left him with a bitter residue. Like a paracetamol lodged in his throat. His head throbbed. His brain felt frazzled, his body fried. He really shouldn't be going to work; he was too ill. But he wouldn't have considered staying at home. He didn't want to let anyone down or risk his job, especially after being off for three days. Not only that, he needed to see if Aitch had got some gear. What Jack had left wouldn't last the day; not that he wanted a spliff straight away, his throat wouldn't take it. But it was the fear of running out.

Daisy wasn't working at lunchtime, so she asked if they could nip to the shops in the afternoon as she wanted to get a few more accessories for her New Year's Eve outfit. It was the last thing Jack needed; all he wanted to do in between shifts was curl up in bed. Already in a foul mood he snapped at her, asking if it was really necessary. Hungover herself and feeling a bit suffocated, Daisy bit back, 'I can always go on my own, you know!' Jack grudgingly agreed.

Tidying up the mess of the freezing flat on her own, Daisy had her own little come down. It surprised her. She felt slightly deflated by being back, and didn't know why. She put it down to her three-day hangover and post-Christmas blues. It was like all the decorations. They seemed pointless now, a little pathetic. Same with the tree. She could quite easily have taken them down right there and then. Jack being so ill didn't help. Didn't Mum always say that about Dad? That men were a nightmare when it came to being ill. That they turned into big babies?

As she walked round town later, the same jaded feelings returned. Feelings of displacement. Going back home had messed with her head, no doubt about it. Cromer was great in the summer: the beach, the pier, the carnival. Even the fair had been fun up to a point. But on a cold, nondescript winter's day it held no charm at all. The place seemed quite dreary and drab. Daisy tried to cheer herself up with thoughts of New Year's Eve.

Jack had an even worse day in the kitchen. Still tortured by indecision over what to do – whether to come clean with the full story to Haslam and Daisy – he was unable to concentrate properly; and was barked at by Chef on several occasions for messing things up. But he was held back by that warning, the threat that carried so much weight. By keeping quiet, at least he was sticking to his side of the bargain and not breaking any rules. Surely Peasgood would see that? That it was Haslam and this disgruntled worker and not him? It was a thin thread of hope to hold on to. Jack had also picked up on Daisy's mood, a slight melancholia about her that worried him. He clearly remembered the throwaway comment she'd made at her mum's house about being bored in Cromer. He didn't want to do anything that would spook her or give her an excuse for them to leave.

And so it went on for those strange few days between Christmas and New Year that nobody knows what to do with.

Daisy feeling a little suffocated. Jack being at Death's door. Going from the heat of the kitchen to the cold outside didn't help; coupled with the drugs he was on, he felt as if he could faint sometimes when he was walking home. He really should have gone to the doctor's, but they'd never got round to signing up. Foolish really. And dangerous. Being so ill, he'd cut right down on his dope smoking; it was physically impossible to hold the smoke down without going into a coughing fit. Aitch had only got what he called some 'personal' anyway. 'It always goes dry over Christmas,' he explained, but he was expecting a delivery of solid before New Year's Eve. Something called soapbar. He'd given Jack a couple of spliffs' worth of his own stash to tide him over.

New Year's Eve arrived without incident. Jack was starting to wonder if Peasgood had got the letter. Perhaps the factory was closed until New Year, like some of the shops in Cromer. Or maybe he'd been locked up already. Not being familiar with the slow-turning cogs of the law, Jack expected things to happen overnight. He'd never got round to phoning Haslam, still unsure if it was the right thing to do. Poking the hornet's nest, so to speak. Maybe it had all been hollow threats and scare tactics after all.

As on Christmas Eve, Jack had to work the day and night shifts. Daisy just the night. That evening, along with the rest of the gang, they took their costumes in to work in bags and hung them up in the changing rooms. They'd all made a pact to keep their chosen outfits a surprise, to be revealed on the night. There was much ribbing about what everybody might have chosen. Jeanie had booked the evening off in advance, in order to get ready. 'I'm not going out stinking of food!' she'd said. This suited Daisy; she wouldn't have to watch the skinny wretch get dressed. It was nice not having her around during service as well; it meant she got Alison to herself. They'd grown close, and had swapped phone numbers since Daisy got back. This seemed like a big step. Alison had asked if she could borrow Daisy's fur coat for the night, but even with some new blonde streaks in her hair nobody guessed who she was going as.

Finally service was over, and once dessert was served Hilary let all the young ones go. She and Dan were there till the death anyway – the joys of the catering trade, serving people on New Year's Eve whilst everyone else had a good time – so it made no odds to them. Daisy finished at about the same time as Jack for once, which was nice. The night ahead was a big deal, and everyone was in high spirits – except Jack; he felt like an idiot changing into his Shaggy costume, a knitted green sweater and brown flares. He refused to wear the wig that came with it. Aitch kept knocking on the wall between the changing rooms and making lewd comments. And then on the girls' door, too, telling them to hurry up.

'Are you ready, boys? Here we come,' said Alison, as they finally emerged. 'Tadah!' All eyes were drawn to Daisy first, who was wearing a pair of conker-coloured boots to go with her outfit. She'd tacked the scarlet skirt up a bit, so she had plenty of leg on show, and the thin sweater clung to her chest. Her hair was fluffed forward in a bob with a little bow in it off to the side, and she'd drawn freckles on her cheeks with a makeup pen. To finish it off, she was wearing Velma's trademark glasses. They suited her in a sexy, sophisticated way.

Aitch wolf-whistled.

'Zoinks!' said Tom, lowering the impenetrable dark sunglasses he was wearing.

Daisy blushed.

'Ahem! Boyfriend,' said Alison, drawing attention to herself and theatrically taking an imaginary drag on a cigarette holder held in her red-gloved hand.

'Cruella de Vil!' cried Aitch.

'The very same,' said Alison, pleased he'd got it.

338

'You look incredible, babe,' said Tom, giving her a kiss. 'A bit old perhaps...' She removed one of her gloves and gave him a playful slap with it.

It was hard to say who Tom was trying to be. He looked pretty much the same – long coat, drainpipes, pointy boots, all black – save for the addition of a dusty wide-brimmed black hat and sunglasses.

'No offence, Tom, but who are you?' said Daisy.

'See, I told you no one would get it,' said Alison.

'Andrew Eldritch! The Sisters of Mercy singer!'

'Ah, yes. Of course,' said Daisy.

'And you are, Aitch?' said Alison, giggling at his outfit. A long, curly ginger wig and kilt combo. Knobbly knees on show.

'I'm a Scotsman!' he announced in a surprisingly good Scottish accent, which was a little too close to home. Jack and Daisy shared a look.

'What Scotsman?' said Alison.

'Just *a* Scotsman.'

'Why?' said Alison.

'My family's Scottish. My dad's side anyway. This is his kilt.'

'Well, I never knew that,' said Alison.

'At least I've got somewhere to stash me gear for the night,' he said, picking up his sporran and shaking it. 'I've even got some ready-rolleds. That reminds me, Jackeroo, I've got a little something for you later.' Then he adopted the Scottish accent again. 'And if you wee lassies play your cards right yer jus' might get tae see the Crown Jewels!' He flapped the kilt about, and Daisy blushed again.

'Please tell me he's got something on under there, Tom,' said Alison.

'I'm saying nothing,' said Tom.

Aitch then walked about ten yards down the corridor, suddenly bent over and lifted his kilt up. 'Nooo!' the girls cried together, turning away in horror. But not before a pair of pasty legs and tartan boxer shorts had been revealed.

'Haha! Got you!' said Aitch, straightening up, his face red. 'Don't tell Jeanie, though! I'm gonna wind her up all night.' Everyone shook their heads. If he was like this sober, what was he going to be like later?

'Talking of Jeanie, we'd better get off,' said Alison. 'She'll be waiting.'

They walked to the pub together, Shaggy, Velma, Cruella de Vil, Andrew Eldritch and a Scotsman, sharing a spliff on the way. 'Jesus Christ!' cried Aitch, his kilt flapping about in the wind. 'It's cold as a wetche's tet! I'm glad I'm wearing me kecks. Me balls a-be shrivelled up like walnuts! Now I know how you lassies feel!'

'Too much information as usual, Aitch,' said Alison, laughing.

Jack, who'd remained pretty quiet so far, was thinking that the accent could get a little grating if Aitch kept it up all night. He was starting to relax a little, though. He'd been stuffing himself full of paracetamol and Lemsip during service to try and keep the fever at bay. But his stupid jumper was scratching his skin and he wasn't looking forward to entering the pub stone cold sober. 'You OK?' said Daisy, linking her arm through his.

'Yes,' he sighed. 'Just want to get a drink down me, that's all.'

'Same here,' she said. Then she whispered, 'How do I look? Do you like the glasses?'

'You look amazing.'

'Good,' she said. 'Maybe I can be your secretary later and take down your particulars...'

This cheered Jack up and he grinned.

His smile disappeared as they turned the corner to the pub. Daisy had a flutter of butterflies, too. There were hordes of people, all dressed up, heading towards the Sailor, or standing outside smoking. The place looked rammed. 'Hope you've all got yer tickets,' said Alison, opening her matching red handbag.

'Mine's in me sporran!' said Aitch.

'Yep, in my bag,' said Daisy – along with some makeup, Jack's baccy tin and his medication; not really in keeping with Velma.

As they neared, seeing all the people dressed up reminded Daisy of Halloween night in those American films, where everyone got into the spirit. It gave her a buzz of excitement. There were superheroes, Vikings, a Rubik's cube, a Michael Jackson. And was that a Staypuft marshmallow man going in? That or a Michelin tyre man. It was all very surreal, but kind of cool. They handed their tickets to the man on the door, a regular who was being paid in pints. 'All right, Tony,' Aitch said. 'You the bouncer for the night or something?'

'Something like that,' he said, stamping the back of Aitch's hand with ink. 'In case you come out again. Like the skirt, by the way.'

'Ha. Cheers, pal.' Aitch walked in, nearly bumping into a fluffy green Orville on his way out, giant nappy and all.

'Sorry, mate, can't see a thing in this,' the Orville said.

Tom stood aside to let him pass. 'All very formal,' he said to Tony, offering his ticket and then his hand.

'Well, you know. There's some idiots in this town…'

It was getting on for quarter to eleven and the pub was packed. Loud music was playing. The gang fought their way to the bar, which was about three deep, everyone in costume. Queuing up, Aitch spotted Jeanie. He'd done well, considering she was wearing a black wig. 'Oh my God! Jeanie!' he shouted. She was standing at the bar, flirting with a John McEnroe character, complete with a wooden racket, and a tall youth dressed as Indiana Jones, both of them a fair bit older than her. Letting out a squeal and a wave, she said something to the lads, then tottered over with a drink. She hugged and kissed everyone, clearly already drunk. 'Ooh, hi, Shaggy,' she said, hugging Jack a little too enthusiastically for Daisy's liking. Daisy rolled her eyes, then took her turn in giving and receiving a false hug. Jeanie reeked of perfume. 'So, what do you think everybody?' She stood back and did a twirl, still clutching her drink. *Great*, thought Daisy. *Bloody Wonder Woman*. The outfit left nothing to the imagination, especially the shorts. Jack didn't know where to look.

'Sorry, Daisy,' said Aitch, 'but that pips you! Please, don't ever take that outfit off, Jeanie – unless you're going to bed with me!'

'I had to improvise with a pair of hot pants,' she said, ignoring him. 'The costume ones were way too big. Do you like my nails? They took me ages.' She splayed out the fingers of one hand. The nails were decorated in the stars and stripes of the American flag. Boy, she really wanted to win that prize, thought Daisy.

'Wow! They're so cool,' said Alison.

'Thanks. You guys look amazing, too!' she said. 'God, I'm so excited! Can you believe it?' She let out another squeal.

'How many you had already?' Tom laughed.

'Too many. But not enough. Men keep buying me drinks… Must be the outfit. Perhaps I *shouldn't* ever take it off!' *What a dreadful idea*, thought Daisy.

Everybody ordered two drinks to start off with to save queuing again. Then they all proceeded to get drunk, stoned or both. Mike must have known everyone was smoking marijuana out the back, but he seemed to turn a blind eye to it.

The big moment arrived before they knew it. They only seemed to have been there five minutes. Daisy would have preferred a bit more warning and a build-up, to really savour the night. But there was Mike, dressed as a Mexican bandit, ringing his bell as hard as he could. The music was turned off and suddenly everyone was shushing and calling for silence, save for a few hecklers. 'Shaddup everybody!' Mike called out. He was fiddling with the stereo behind the bar, and a horrendous blast of static blared from the pub speakers as he tuned in to the radio. Finally he got the right station and looked at his watch, panicking. The countdown was under way. 'Ten, nine' – everyone joined in, holding glasses aloft – 'eight, seven' – it got louder – 'SIX, FIVE, FOUR, *THREE, TWO, ONE!*' The chimes of Big Ben were drowned out by a deafening roar of cheers and '*HAPPY NEW YEAR!*' It seemed a significant moment, the end of an era and the dawn of a new decade. 'Happy New Year!' they all cried, hugging and kissing each other. All around them, everyone was doing the same. Strangers were wishing anyone near them a Happy New Year, hugging and shaking hands, Jack included. It was all quite bizarre to him. He'd never experienced a New Year celebration of any sort before. Some people had broken off into groups and were holding hands in circles with their arms crossed to perform an impromptu 'Auld Lang Syne'.

'Auld Lang Syne!' cried Aitch. 'We've got to do it! I'm Scottish!' They tried but no one really knew any of the words, and it soon petered out. Mike rang his bell again anyway and called for quiet. 'Right, you 'orrible lot. The buffet is now being served' – this was met with more cheers and heckles – 'and meanwhile I'm gonna be going round and checking out your costumes to see who's worthy of the big prize. It'll be announced in approximately fifteen minutes. Enjoy!'

Aitch made straight for the buffet. The rest of them couldn't be bothered and carried on drinking. From time to time Daisy kept whispering 'Jinkies' in Jack's ear in a sultry voice. It was driving him mad. The trio of narcotics had done for him again, fooling his body he was OK, making him lightheaded and banishing his worries.

Soon, the fancy dress prize was announced. For pure inventiveness, unsurprisingly, Staypuft marshmallow man won. Jeannie, however, got the runners-up prize for her Wonder Woman outfit. There were wolf whistles and rude things shouted out by drunken men as she tottered up to collect her prize, a bottle of champagne. The gang ribbed her when she returned, saying it was because Mike fancied her and calling him a dirty old man. Aitch suggested they should go back to The Love Shack for a 'proper smoke'. He wanted to build something called a 'Cromer Carrot' (his own version of the Camberwell Carrot made famous in *Withnail and I*). Jack and Daisy weren't that fussed as it was in the opposite direction for them – and they had other things on their minds. Tom suggested they should all go back to the flat for a change. And once this was mooted there was no stopping them, everyone begging for this to happen. Especially Aitch. 'Ah, come on, it'll be amazing!' he cried. 'We always go back to mine!'

Despite being drunk, Daisy wasn't sure. Handing over their phone number was one thing… She looked at Jack. He looked back at her. Although clearly plastered, he wasn't sure either. There were those ashes knocking about for a start. As if reading his mind, Tom said, 'Jesus, what are you two hiding in there, dead bodies?'

'Flat! Flat! Flat!' Aitch started chanting, and the others joined in.

Jack couldn't help but break into a grin. And to Daisy's surprise, he said, 'Suppose so.'

'Yes!' cried Aitch. Everyone cheered.

'Jackeroo! Jackeroo!' they chanted, piling onto him. Daisy rolled her eyes. At least they could listen to her music, she supposed.

'We can crack open my champagne!' said Jeanie. Daisy hadn't really expected her to come and wasn't best pleased about it, but what could she do?

They walked out of the pub and into the night of a new decade. The '90s, the topic of conversation all the way back to the flat. As they were on the quieter streets of the town, it really hit home. Even saying it felt strange. 1990.

It seemed another massive step to Daisy as she pulled the key from her bag; not just letting people into their house, but into their lives. The gang were so excited you would have thought they were being let into Buckingham Palace. Being so eager to get inside, they pressed forward and literally fell through the door and onto the porch floor together. Everyone was in stitches, especially when Aitch said from somewhere, 'Och, no, I think I've split my sporran!' By this stage everyone was howling, and Jeanie announced she was going to wet herself if she didn't get upstairs quickly. Daisy couldn't help but get caught up in it all. They were such a bunch of idiots.

She felt surprisingly house proud, showing everyone the kitchen and lounge. Something she'd never experienced before. At least it was nice and tidy. It was so strange having people in the flat. But she was worried about it being so cold; they were used to it themselves. Jeanie immediately asked where the bathroom was, and disappeared. 'If you need a hand getting those hot pants off, just let me know!' called Aitch.

'You wish!' she called through the bathroom door.

Then there was an awkward moment when everyone could hear Jeanie peeing. The boys looked at each other and sniggered; much to Daisy's dismay, even Jack. She hoped he wasn't picturing her doing it. God, now she was herself. It was disgusting, the tramp. 'I'll put some music on, shall I?' she said. 'Come on, Jack, take everyone into the lounge.' She took his hand, drawing him away.

'I'm gonna crack this champers open. You got any glasses, Jack?' said Aitch.

'I'll get them,' Daisy tutted. 'Jack, go and put some music on.' She pushed him into the lounge. Tom and Alison followed him.

'I love all your posters, Daisy!' Alison called.

'Jesus, look at all these albums!' said Tom. 'I thought *I* had a lot.' Daisy was pleased. She was also pleased when she heard the sweet opening harmonica strains of 'My Time' by Jane's Addiction from her new tape emanating from the stereo.

'That's only about half of them,' she called. 'The rest of them are at home.'

'Where is home exactly?' said Alison. 'You never said.'

'Oh, a couple of hours or so from here. You wouldn't know it…'

Soon they were all gathered in the lounge, clutching various random receptacles full of champagne. 'Here's to the '90s!' said Aitch. 'Happy New Year!'

They all drank and toasted.

'And here's to us!' said Alison, 'The Cromer Six!'

'The Cromer Six!' they all said, and drank again.

'Right, to *really* celebrate New Year, I'm gonna build you the biggest spliff you've ever seen in your life,' said Aitch.

'I don't know whether I can take it,' said Alison. 'I'm already done in.'

'Me, too,' said Daisy. The champagne had hit her head. 'I'm just gonna nip and get changed.' She didn't think she'd be able to sit comfortably in her skirt.

When she got to the lounge door she waited, hoping Jack would look over. He didn't. He was too busy listening to Aitch describing how you needed twelve skins to construct a Cromer Carrot. She cleared her throat loudly, but he still didn't hear over the music. No one did. There was nothing else for it. 'Jinkies!' she said, as if she was calling a pet dog or cat. Jack immediately looked over. So did everyone else. Inebriated as she was, Daisy wasn't embarrassed.

'Back in a minute,' said Jack.

'Oh, aye?' said Aitch. 'Where are you two sneaking off to?'

'Got a mystery to solve or something?' said Tom. Alison laughed. Jeanie didn't; just curled her legs up on the sofa and watched Jack go.

Alone in the bedroom, Daisy pushed herself against Jack, her tongue searching his mouth. 'God, I've been wanting to do that all night,' she said in between kisses.

'Me, too,' he said.

'How do we get rid of them?' She took his hand and put it on her hip underneath her skirt.

'We can't. They've just got here. It would be rude.'

'I want to be rude,' she said, moving his hand between her legs. He couldn't believe how brazen she was being.

'Oh, God, Daisy, don't.' It was so warm there. He could feel her through her knickers. So warm and familiar. He could feel himself hardening. 'Daisy, we can't. Not with them in there.' He tried to push her away.

'Jack, I'm so horny. I don't care. I think it's this outfit...'

'Daisy, stop it. Seriously. It'll be too late in a minute.'

'Good.'

'You'll catch my cold.'

'I think I already have.' Jack wrested himself free, an obscene bulge in his trousers.

'Look! How am I supposed to go back in there now?'

'Don't,' she said, slowly hitching up her skirt, 'stay in here with me.'

'No. They'll be wondering what we're doing. They will be now. Daisy, stop it. Don't do that.' She was still lifting up her skirt. 'I'm not looking, I'm going.'

But he did look. And underneath were a pair of cotton pants he'd never seen before. They kind of matched her jumper, a burnt orange colour the same as the butternut squash he'd been prepping that day at work. 'Do you like them?' she said, swivelling her hips back and forth.

'Yes, but I've got to go!' And he turned away, snapping himself out of the spell.

'Boo!' she said, knowing he meant it, and dropped her skirt. 'Spoilsport!'

'Ha. Now you know how it feels,' he said, finally getting his revenge.

'I guess I'll just have to please myself then,' she said in a lustful voice he knew only too well.

'You wouldn't?' he said, shocked, his hand on the door.

'Wouldn't I?' she said.

Jack made straight for the bathroom until he'd calmed down, which probably looked even worse. All eyes were on him when he tried to slip inconspicuously back into the lounge. Jeanie, curled up under the blanket on the sofa, leered at him drunkenly. Jack sat down quickly next to her. 'Everything all right, Jackeroo?' said Tom, a smirk on his face.

'Yes, fine.'

When Daisy returned wearing some jogging bottoms and a sweater, she wouldn't look at Jack. He tried to read her face but it was inscrutable. Everyone else still had their coats on, Daisy noticed. Probably too polite to say how cold it was. 'Aah, where's Velma gone?' said Aitch, through a mouthful of sausage roll he'd brought back from the buffet in his sporran.

'Velma's gone to bed,' said Daisy, yawning. 'Which is where I'll be going soon.' It wasn't till she settled herself, sitting cross-legged opposite Jack on the other side of the coffee table, that she finally met his gaze. She looked straight into his eyes, causing a pulse to go through him, then raised her eyebrows and cocked her head just the slightest bit. As if to say, 'You'll never know.' And, boy, was he desperate to know.

The giant spliff was something to behold. A monster that looked almost comical in Aitch's hand. None of them really needed it, especially the girls, but as Aitch had said, it was the ritual of it, the significance. It blew their heads off, and after a few puffs Daisy said she was going to bed. She was spinning out. Alison asked Tom if they could go home too. 'Yes, in a minute, babe.' He was still enjoying his 'boy's time' with Jack and Aitch, and the novelty of being at the flat.

'Jack, you coming?' Daisy said.

'Yes, in a minute, babe,' he said, mimicking Tom. Tom gave him one of his handshakes.

'Well, don't be long. Are you guys all right letting yourselves out? Or crash if you want. But if you go, make sure you take

Wonder Woman there with you.' Jeanie looked as if she'd passed out under the blanket.

'I'm not planning on crashing anywhere,' said Aitch. 'It's the '90s, man. I'm gonna see how long I can stay awake into this new decade.'

'Don't be long, Jack,' Daisy said. More serious now. Already at the corner. She didn't like it that Jeanie had got comfortable so quickly.

'I won't.'

'Jinkies,' she said woozily.

'What is that? Some kind of code with you two?' said Aitch.

Jack smiled a dreamy smile.

*****

The next thing he was aware of was burning up. Horrendously. It was dark and he was delirious and he didn't know where he was. He hadn't taken any paracetamol for hours and now he was paying for it. Why was he still wearing that goddamn itchy hot sweater in bed? It was damp and sticking to him. He sat up to take it off and felt Daisy lying on him. She murmured and helped him remove it. Then they both lay back down. Her with her head and hand on his bare chest.

CHAPTER 29
Femme Fatale

And that was how Daisy found them the next morning. The first thing she registered was the emptiness of the lounge. Where had everybody gone? She expected them all to be crashed out. Then she noticed the black wig on the floor. That's when she got the first inkling that something was wrong. Then she saw two feet sticking out at the end of the sofa, the closest end to her. That's when her world began to crash down around her. One foot was unmistakably Jack's; she recognised the sock. The other was bare and small and slender.

Her stomach sank like an anchor cast overboard.

She moved into the room, silently and in slow motion, unable to comprehend what she was seeing. As if watching herself from above. Was she still asleep? Was this a bad dream? She wanted it to go away. To un-see it. But there was Jack, still fast asleep, on his back with no top on. And there *she* was. Jeanie. Her head tucked into his chest, her blonde hair tied up in a bun. Her hand with its manicured nails, painted with the American flag, placed protectively on his shoulder. As if laying claim to a new state. The blanket was down just far enough to reveal her neck and slim, bare shoulders, the morning sun highlighting the impossibly fine and pale hairs across the top of her back.

Daisy immediately assumed the worst. She was naked under there. They had all gone home and she had slept with him. If she pulled the blanket back, she would see, from the side, one of her perfect tits squashed against him. Against *her* lover. Skin on skin. Her leg draped across him. It made her feel sick to the stomach, and a strange noise escaped her throat. A barely audible whimper. But part of her wanted to do it, to pull back the blanket and torture herself. Another part of her couldn't bear to.

A myriad of emotions flashed through her mind in a second, a dozen actions. Anger. Disbelief. Hatred. Betrayal. How could the rest of them have let this happen? She wanted to shake him and yank her up to claw at the bitch's face. But there was hurt, disappointment and, strangely, resignation. That something had happened she had feared would happen all along. Ever since she'd clapped eyes on the girl, with her honey-blonde hair, dimples and Timotei advert smile. These last few months Daisy had watched her work up close. How she used everything at her disposal. Not just with Jack, but with all the men. Daisy had known girls like that at school. And girls like that were exercising their right to take what they wanted. Last night she'd seen her chance and taken it. Jack had merely succumbed. Not that that was an excuse. But why wouldn't he? She was prettier. Her legs were longer, slimmer. Her waist thinner. Her tits jutted out more – like a bloody Barbie doll's. 'Oh, Jack,' she said, but the words caught in her throat and came out as a sob. A sob that no one heard. For she knew that she could never forgive him. And that was the saddest part. She could never let him near her again, inside her again. Not now. It was disgusting. Dirty. Sullied. She wanted her mum. More than anything else in the world she wanted her mum. And her dad. It was like a weight crashing down, everything she'd been feeling for the last few days. Suddenly she felt very far from home.

Slowly and silently, just as she'd entered, she backed out of the room.

Jack was woken by the sound of a vehicle starting up on the street below. His frazzled brain tried to piece together what had happened. His neck was cricked from lying on the sofa. The sofa? Why wasn't he in bed? He gingerly opened his eyes. The light was wrong, the ceiling was wrong; he was definitely in the lounge. Why were they sleeping in the lounge? He looked down and pain shot through his neck again. That was when he saw the blonde hair and the painted fingernails on his shoulder. What the fuck? Before he could react he heard the vehicle again, revving too hard and quickly pulling away. The engine sound was familiar. The VW. *'Daisy!'* he cried, shooting upright. He pushed Jeanie off him and rushed to the window, still wearing his brown flares. Sweeping aside a net curtain, he pressed his face to the glass, trying to see down the street. Through the condensation, he saw the rear of the van disappearing in a cloud of smoke, leaving behind an empty parking space. *'Daisy!'* he shouted again, pressing his hands to the glass.

He rushed out of the lounge, unable to look at Jeanie. Where was everyone else? He tore down the stairs and out onto the street. Rounding the corner, he pounded the pavement to the T-junction, desperately hoping to see which direction she'd gone in. It was futile. The van was nowhere to be seen. Dressed only in socks and trousers, he called out in anguish and ran his hands through his hair. A car rounded the corner with its windows down. 'New Year's Day' by U2 was coming from the stereo. 'Happy New Year!' the driver called out the window. 'Dig the flares, man!'

Jack stormed back to the flat. Now the adrenaline had worn off, his feet hurt, he was freezing cold, shivering and felt like death. He ran up the stairs, into the lounge and glared at Jeanie. 'Get out!' he shouted. 'Just. Get out!' She flinched at the venom in his voice, as if she'd been slapped; Jack had always been so placid, such a softie.

Just then the bathroom door opened and Jack turned, surprised. It was Aitch, totally confused, his ginger wig askew. He'd made a makeshift bed in the bath out of coats and towels. 'What's going on?' he said. Then he saw Jeanie getting up off the sofa. She was still wearing her outfit from last night, the sparkly boob tube top and shorts. She had panda-eyed mascara and looked bewildered, dazed and sorry for herself. 'Oh shit,' Aitch said.

Jack turned back to her. She cut a pathetic sight, collecting up her things, her wig and her rope and her boots. He wanted to shout and bawl at her: 'Have you any idea what you've done?' She looked up and saw him glaring at her, as if he wanted to kill her. 'I'm sorry, Jack,' she said. 'But nothing happened. We didn't do anything – I was just cold, that's all.' She looked as if she was about to cry.

'Jeanie, I'd just leave it if I was you,' said Aitch. 'Come on, let's go.' He checked his sporran for his skinning up paraphernalia whilst Jeanie put on her boots. It was awkward waiting; no one knew what to say. Finally, Jeanie walked quickly past Jack. Her bare arm accidentally brushed against him and he recoiled. Aitch gave Jack a sympathetic shrug from the kitchen. 'Hope you sort it, buddy. See you at work. She'll be back…' Jack watched them descend the stairs.

'Nothing happened, I swear,' he heard Jeanie say again in a muffled voice. Then he thought he heard her sob. Aitch put his arm round her waist. The door slammed shut.

Outside, they crossed over the road and headed in the direction of town. A car was reversing into the space vacated by Daisy's van. As they walked past it a man leant across and wound down his window. ''Scuse me, pal, yous just come from Daisy's?'

Aitch thought he was having a laugh with the Scottish accent, seeing as he was still dressed in his kilt. But though the man's tone was light and conversational he didn't appear to be joking. Aitch wasn't in the mood for banter anyway. 'Yes, mate. Why?' he said.

'She in?' the man said.

'Er, no. She's not.' They went to walk off, but the man carried on.

'Gone off to work, has she? Bit early…' He looked at his watch.

'No, she er … she shot off about five minutes ago… Bit of a fallout, long story.' Jeanie looked shamefaced. 'Who's asking anyway?' said Aitch, realising he was probably saying too much. Who was this guy?

'Oh, I'm a friend of the family's. We're down this way for New Year… So, she's not with her laddie then?'

'Jack? No, he's inside.'

'You've no idea where she's gone or when she'll be back?'

'No, sorry, pal.'

'Maybe to her parents,' said Jeanie, trying to help. She wrapped her jacket around her, shivering now.

'OK. Cheers, guys. Happy New Year.'

'Yes,' said Aitch.

The man wound the window back up and watched them walk away. Once they were out of sight he smacked the steering wheel twice, hard. 'Fuck's sake!' He had a hangover and didn't want to be there – even though he was being paid handsomely. He glanced at his watch again, then got out of the car. After looking up and down the deserted street and up at the flats, he crossed over the road and walked towards the phone box.

Back in the flat, Jack was left on his own with the reality of the situation. What had happened? *What had just happened?* None of it seemed real. He couldn't even ask Daisy about it. Had she really gone? *Where* had she gone? What had she seen? Surely she'd seen they had clothes on? He tried to picture it, how he'd woken up. She must have only just left. Then he saw that hand again, those painted fingernails on his bare shoulder.

He winced. None of this looked good, whichever way you looked at it. What would he have thought if he'd found her with Tom like that? Under a blanket together with no one else about? He would have gone mental. It would have destroyed him, sickened him. Even the thought of it made him feel ill. But he'd thought it was Daisy last night. He'd been that far gone, that delirious; he honestly had. But *she* didn't know that. *What had he fucking done?* He wished he could take it back and rewind time. He should have just gone to bed with Daisy last night. His beautiful Daisy. Why hadn't he? She'd wanted him to. Pleaded with him to. And why hadn't Tom and Alison taken *her* home? Daisy had asked them to, he remembered that now – as if she knew something was going to happen. And he'd gone and proved her right. 'STUPID. FUCKING. IDIOT!' he shouted, banging his fist on the table. Then he broke down and cried, collapsing onto the table with his head in his hands, overcome with despair.

He stayed like that for a few minutes, his head devoid of anything but his own misery. But when his brain started functioning again, he knew he had to pull himself together; that this wasn't helping. He needed to think of a plan: how to find her, how to get hold of her. As he became aware of his surroundings again, he felt as if someone was watching him. And he looked across at the lounge, through the crooks of his elbows with blurred, teary eyes. There was his father sitting on the arm of the sofa, that familiar, mocking look of disdain on his face. Burnt and disfigured, just as he always was. But it was still a shock and made Jack shrink back in fear. Especially when he spoke: '*See, I told you she would leave you… They always do in the end…*'

'You're not real!' Jack shouted, picking up a salt cellar and hurling it at the apparition. His father ducked and the salt cellar smashed into the wall at the far end of the lounge, narrowly missing a window. When Jack looked back again his father had gone.

Good.

Think, Jack, think… Where could she have gone? Surely not all the way back home? What about Alison's? She'd grown close to her. Did she even know where she lived? He remembered they'd swapped numbers recently – Daisy had asked him if she should. He grabbed the little phone book by the phone. There were only a few numbers in it. Alison's was one of them. Typical Daisy. She loved to write things down. Her handwriting ripped through him. Made her absence seem worse. He picked up the phone, then froze. He'd barely made half a dozen phone calls in his life, and pretty much all of them were to Daisy. The thought of it made his head swim. What if Alison's parents answered? What if no one was up yet? What time was it anyway?

Taking a deep, shaky breath, he slowly began to dial the number. When he'd finished the phone rang and his heart began to pound. He nearly chickened out and hung up. But he had to do this; Daisy could be there. He could tell her the truth. Make her see sense. Plead with her and make it all right. The phone clicked in his ear. 'Hello,' a voice said, startling him. It sounded young, like a little girl.

This threw Jack for a second. 'Hello… is Daisy there. Shit!' The girl giggled. 'I mean Alison. Is Alison there, please – this *is* Alison's number?'

'Yeah, she's my sister. Hold on, I'll just get her. I think she's still in bed – as usual…' The phone was set down heavily, a rustle and a clunk loud in Jack's ear. *Still in bed*, he thought, his stomach sinking; that would mean Daisy wasn't there. He felt stung by disappointment and considered hanging up. What was the point in talking to Alison now? But he had to make sure. After waiting for what seemed like an age, the phone was clumsily picked up. 'Hello,' said Alison in a croaky bed-voice, sounding put out.

'Alison, it's Jack.'

'Jack.' She sounded surprised and a little awkward. 'It's barely nine o'clock. Everything OK?'

'I'm sorry. Is Daisy with you?'

'No, why? Why would she be?' Now that it came to it, Jack felt ashamed that they'd fallen out, and how it had happened. It was a private matter. He faltered. He was about to open his mouth to speak when Alison said, 'Hold on. Jack, hold on a minute, there's someone at the door. Fuck's sake…' His heart leapt. Daisy! The phone was put down again and he strained to hear what was going on. There were voices, a commotion, but he couldn't make anything out. He thought he heard a female voice, but it sounded like crying. Eventually the phone was picked back up. 'Jack. Sorry, Aitch and Jeanie have just turned up – she's upset. I'm guessing this is connected?'

Jack was bitterly disappointed. Again. He felt lost and alone. Embarrassed that he was going to cry. 'I've got to go,' he said.

'Jack, wait!' Alison said. 'I'll call you back. I'll speak to the others to see what's happened, then I'll call you back. Or Tom will, OK? If Daisy's missing and upset, we need to find her…'

'OK. Thank you.' It was a small ray of hope, to know he'd got people helping him. On his side. But for how long would she be once she found out more?

'Bye for now,' Alison said.

Jack hung up the phone.

He paced the lounge. Out of habit, he craved a spliff. But for once, seeing his baccy tin on the coffee table didn't do anything for him. It was the last thing he needed: he had to keep a clear head. It was the gear that had caused all this, he told himself. He should have gone to bed. That thing Aitch had rolled at the end of the night had blown them away. He could have done anything and not known about it. Thank God he hadn't.

Jack paced and fretted some more. Where would Daisy be if not at Alison's? The more time passed, the more a worry that she was heading back to her mum's began to nag at him. Where else would she be? Sitting in the van somewhere? At the restaurant? She wasn't even working today. He would have to ring her mum: he didn't have any choice. And that would be much worse than admitting to Alison they'd fallen out. But he would have to wait. She wouldn't be there yet. What time had she left? He'd lost track. It must have been around 8.45. How long did it take? Two hours or so? He couldn't wait that long. He'd go insane.

Then something occurred to him. He dashed to the bedroom. Only her side of the bed cover was pulled back. Another wave of guilt and misery. But that wasn't why he was there. Her clothes. Had she taken any with her? He pulled open the bedside drawer with her underwear in it; it looked undisturbed. He yanked open the wardrobe. Nothing seemed to have gone. He rushed to the bathroom and her toothbrush was still there. Her fur coat was hanging up in the corridor, too. Going over to it, he buried his face in the collar. To his surprise and disappointment it smelt strongly of Alison, that scent she wore – Sandal something – Daisy said she liked it. But at least it meant she was coming back, didn't it?

The next two hours were the longest of Jack's life. He should have been going into work, or at least phoning in sick, but he couldn't even contemplate it. It wasn't important. Nothing mattered but Daisy. After grabbing the alarm clock, he tried to go to sleep on the sofa under the blanket. He set the alarm for eleven and put it right next to him; and the phone was right next to the sofa as well. It was so loud there was no way he wouldn't hear it. When it rang unexpectedly, he jumped, then reached out and snatched it. 'Daisy?' he said breathlessly.

'No, sorry, it's Alison. You still haven't heard from her then?' Jack didn't say anything. All these false hopes were destroying him. 'Jack, you still there?'

'Yes.' He held the receiver against his cheek for a moment.

'Good. Right, I've spoken to Jeanie. She's told me everything. Not that there's anything to tell. She's really upset. But the main thing is nothing happened. She said so and I believe her. And I believe in you too. I know we haven't known each other for long, but you're not that kind of guy. And I know Daisy's cleared off somewhere – probably thought the worst when she found you two. I know I would have done if it was Tom – I'd have gone spare! But as soon as you explain to her, she'll come round. She's got to. I'll speak to her as well if you want. The way I see it – and the way she's *got* to see it – is that you passed out, drunk and stoned and God knows what else, and Jeanie cuddled up to you 'cause she was cold. I know it's not ideal, but that's it! End of story.' She made it sound so simple and straightforward. If only. 'The main thing is, we've got to find her. It's a bit worrying if she was in a state. Especially if she's still drunk or hungover. I take it you've tried her parents?'

'No, not yet.'

'Not yet? Why not?'

'She wouldn't be there yet. It's miles away.'

'So? Ring them anyway. Tell them what's happened, and ask if she can ring you as soon as she turns up. Even if it's just to let you know she's safe.'

This made sense. A voice of reason. He'd never heard Alison sound so grown up, so caring.

'It's just her mum, but yes I will.'

'Do it now. And let me know as soon as she turns up. *If* she turns up – I'm not at work today, and I won't be able to relax till she does. There are some weirdos out there…' This sent a chill through Jack. In all the commotion and panic and feelings of abandonment he'd forgotten about Peasgood and his cronies. How could he have done? Alison was right. He needed to call Daisy's mum straightaway. He thanked her and hung up.

After locating the number under 'home' in the phone book, and pushing aside his fear of doing so, he picked up the phone again and dialled.

Daisy's mum answered, sounding cheery.

Jack didn't know what to call her. 'Mrs Jones, it's Jack.'

'Jack! This is an unexpected surprise. Happy New Year! Is Daisy too hungover to call herself?'

'Er, no. That's why I'm calling actually. She's not with you, is she?' Why did he say that? She wouldn't be there yet.

'No. Why would she be?' A slight note of concern had crept into her voice.

He avoided the question, too ashamed to say it. 'Well, if she turns up, will you tell her to call me – please?'

'Yes. But why? Why would she be coming back here? You two had a falling out or something?'

'Sort of – but it was a misunderstanding.'

Carol sighed. 'I always worried this might happen. Storm in a teacup, though, no doubt.'

Jack had no idea what she was talking about. 'Please, just tell her to call me if she turns up.'

'Don't worry, I will. How long's she been gone for?'

'I don't know: about an hour, hour and a half.'

'An hour and a half? Well, she wouldn't be here yet. But that's a long time to be gone. I hope she's not driving around still drunk from last night in that old van! It must have been something quite serious for you to think she'd drive all the way back here. Care to enlighten me?' Jack didn't answer; didn't know what to say. 'Ookay… Well, I'll let you know if she turns up. And if she hasn't in half an hour or so – the roads'll be quiet today – I'll be calling you back anyway. And then you'd better tell me what's going on, 'cause then I *will* be worried!'

An agonising three-quarters of an hour later the phone rang again. This time it had to be Daisy. Or what if it was Chef, ringing up to bollock him? Jack had no choice but to answer it. 'Hello,' he said, mentally praying.

'Jack, it's Carol.'

He felt like crying. 'Is she there? Is Daisy there?'

'Yes, she's here.' Immense relief washed over him; at least she was safe. But it was short-lived. 'That's the only reason I'm calling, to let you know she's safe. Daisy doesn't want to speak to you right now and I don't blame her. She'll call you if and when she's ready to, so don't bother calling again today. She turned up in one hell of a state … and you, well, after all she's been through for you, you ought to be ashamed of yourself.' And with that she hung up the phone.

'No!' Jack cried. 'No!' He needed to speak to Daisy. He kept pressing the buttons on the top of the phone, as if this would magically make her voice appear. He couldn't believe how cold her mum had sounded; and despite her warning, he found the number again and called straight back.

Carol picked up immediately. Before Jack could utter a word she said, 'I said not to call, so don't make a pest of yourself. She doesn't want to speak to you right now. Please don't call again.'

'But…' The phone line went dead. When, in desperation, he called the number again, it just rang out for two minutes, maybe more. Eventually he gave up and slammed the receiver down. Then he broke down in tears, sobbing uncontrollably in frustration and at the rejection. He felt a panic, a sickness and a dread that Daisy was so far away and didn't want to speak to him. But what if she did want to? What if her mum was just being a bitch? She'd never liked him. He had to go to her. To make sure. He couldn't just sit at home all day, or even worse all night, waiting for her to call. He wouldn't be able to do anything else, wouldn't be able to function until it was sorted.

Jack got up and ran to the bedroom. From under his bed he grabbed his old battered tin, the one that had come from up on the hill. The one with his photographs and the map of the American states in it. But more importantly, with his money from Haslam in it. Train money. He had to catch a train to see Daisy, to plead with her and make her see sense. The tin went into his rucksack along with some underwear; he didn't know how long he'd be gone for. Then he thought of the ashes. They would go with him, too; he didn't like the thought of leaving them behind. And as he stuffed the canisters into his rucksack it felt like old times; his mind felt like old times. Childlike. A little unhinged. He was going on a journey.

His journey didn't last long. When he got to the railway station it was deserted. No guards. No staff. No potential travellers on the platform. Stuck on the board that held the timetable was a printed notice. 'PLEASE NOTE: DUE TO ENGINEERING WORKS THERE WILL BE A REDUCED TIMETABLE ON NEW YEAR'S DAY. FOR TRAINS THAT ARE STILL RUNNING, PLEASE SEE BELOW. APOLOGIES FOR ANY INCONVENIENCE CAUSED'. There were only three trains all day – none of them going anywhere near Loughborough, or even Peterborough for that matter. They all ran between Sheringham and Norwich (Daisy had mentioned this place, but Jack hadn't a clue where it was or how far). And the earliest didn't arrive for a couple of hours. No wonder there was no one about. It was New Year's Day. He was stuck. He wouldn't get there till tonight, even if he was lucky. And what if her mum still wouldn't let him see her? He'd be cast out in the dark. Alone. She'd have to let him in, surely.

Jack racked his brains. Walking? Hitchhiking? What direction did he even go in? He hadn't got a clue. It was miles to a proper main road anyway. And how many cars were going to be about today? There must be another way. Plane? Don't be silly. Taxi? What about a taxi? How far did taxis go? Surely they couldn't refuse if he was paying. And he had money. Lots of it. He ran back to the flat.

In the porch was a Yellow Pages that they'd never looked at. Remembering Daisy finding the factory number in it that day long ago, he picked it up and frantically thumbed through it, randomly at first, not realising it was alphabetical. Once he was back upstairs with the directory he eventually found the taxis section, and picked up the phone. The first five he called were either not interested, busy or too far away to come and collect him. He quickly realised he needed someone nearer. He found a few with the same area code as Cromer. One of them, when Jack said 'East Midlands', said, 'Sorry, mate, I don't do airport runs.' Airport runs? Another laughed and hung up. Just when he was starting to lose hope, a local guy from Sheringham sighed and said, 'Yes, I can do it. Ain't got nothing better to do. But I warn you, it's gonna cost you an arm and a leg.'

'Sorry?' said Jack.

'It's gonna cost yer! It's New Year's Day, mate!' The man sounded angry that Jack had called him.

'How much?'

'Dunno. I'll have to work out the mileage and call yer back. It's double for a start. What's yer number?'

'It doesn't matter, really. How much?' said Jack. He was wasting time.

'Eighty quid – and that's just one way!' the man said aggressively, expecting Jack to baulk, to say he wasn't interested.

Jack swallowed. Eighty quid. What did he care? It was money he wouldn't have had; he would have given him the lot. 'That's fine. How long?'

'Oh.' The man sounded surprised. 'Be there in twenty minutes. I'll need the money up front. Cash.'

And so, for the first time in his life, Jack found himself in the back of a taxi. He looked up at the big windows of their flat as the car pulled away, wondering when he'd see them again. If ever. His father appeared at one of the windows and watched him go; and inside the flat the phone rang. Again.

Soon he was on the very same roads that Daisy had been travelling on herself only a few hours before. The taxi driver had softened once he'd met Jack and been given his money. He'd been expecting one of those rich kids from the posh school, probably missing Mummy and Daddy and wanting to go home on the spur of the moment. Money no object. Not this nervous wreck, clutching on to his rucksack for dear life, looking as if his world had ended. He'd tried to make conversation at first, but had soon given up. This suited him. Jack kept nodding off in the back, the trauma and worry on top of the previous night exhausting him. The canisters of ashes in his rucksack kept clinking together, just as his cider bottles used to. Lulling him to sleep. He had that feeling of going on a journey again, of regression, of returning to a former state. The old Jack. Jack Hemsley. Not the new Jack Gardner.

CHAPTER 30
Lout

Daisy was lucky to make it back home safely. She was in such a state, and to add to her trauma the needle on the petrol gauge was at rock bottom for the final twenty minutes or so of her journey. She hadn't passed a single open petrol station the whole way back; something she hadn't thought about before setting off.

It still didn't seem real. The whole thing. She was confused. All she knew for sure was that she wanted to get home to her mum. It was the betrayal that stung the most. Burned like poison. The fact that he'd chosen someone else, regardless of the consequences, shared that thing that was most precious, that was theirs and no one else's. She couldn't stop her brain from picturing them together. How she'd found them and what they might have been doing. She tortured herself with it, conjuring up the most lurid, destructive images and poses. Their bodies entwined. Her legs wrapped round him and those nails scratching down his back. Or her on top of him, riding him. Had she been better at it than her? Lord knows she'd had enough practice. Had she given Jack more pleasure than she ever had? Had he compared their bodies as he touched her? Her tits, her flat stomach? Her arse? At around that point she had to pull over and throw up.

As the journey wore agonisingly on, the anger gave way to despair and self-doubt. Had she overreacted? Jumped to conclusions? She tried to recreate the scene; the sofa, the lounge. Had there been clothes or underwear lying about? Bizarrely, out of habit, part of her was still worried for Jack. The fact that she was out of touch and so far away from him. She knew he would be going out of his mind, and it killed her. It occurred to her that the last thing she would have said to him was 'Jinkies'.

After pulling up on the drive at home, she practically fell through the door and threw herself at her mum. Carol hated to see her daughter in such a state, and was furious at Jack for causing it. But a small part of her enjoyed the feeling of being needed, of being the source of comfort. She made Daisy a hot chocolate, just as she had when she was a little girl, and listened as she told her what had happened. Lily hung around in the background, eavesdropping. Eventually Daisy retired to her bedroom and, like Jack, fell asleep, exhausted, blocking it all out.

She was still in bed when Jack turned up. The doorbell rang, and Carol, who was in the kitchen, was immediately alarmed. She couldn't imagine Jack would actually show up there. And so soon seemed an impossibility. But who else would be calling on New Year's Day? Still, she took a step back in surprise when she opened the front door to see him standing outside the porch with his rucksack. It was like seeing a ghost. 'I don't believe it,' she said, putting her hand to her chest. She didn't need the hassle, and wished her husband was there to deal with it. 'What are you doing here, Jack? How did you get here so soon?' She looked past him for a car. There wasn't one. It was as if he'd appeared out of thin air.

'I got a taxi. Mrs Jones, I need to see Daisy. Please can I come in?' He put his hand on the glass.

'No, you can't. She's asleep. I told you on the phone – she'll speak to you when she's good and ready. You've had a wasted trip. Now don't cause a scene.'

'Please, Mrs Jones, I just need to talk to her for five minutes. To explain.'

He turned the handle of the porch door and opened it to step in.

Carol was outraged. 'Oh no you don't! You can't come in here!'

'Daisy!' Jack shouted, his eyes searching the hallway. 'I didn't do anything, you've got to believe me! Daisy!'

'Get out!' Carol tried to close the door on him. 'I'll call the police!'

At the word 'police' Jack instantly backed off and let her close the door. That was the last thing he needed. Carol turned the key. 'Go on, clear off!' she said through the glass. Lily appeared sheepishly behind her. 'Lily!' Jack said. 'Please tell Daisy nothing happened. I swear!'

'I'm not getting involved in this.' Lily held up her hands. 'She's upset, and now you're upsetting my mum. You need to go. Come on, Mum. Sorry, Jack…' She closed the inner door.

Woken by the commotion, and hearing Jack's voice, Daisy had instinctively begun to make her way downstairs, drawn to it. When the stairs creaked, Carol and Lily turned round. 'Don't even think about it!' Carol said. 'You're not going out there!'

'But, Mum…'

'No! That boy's caused enough trouble as it is. Stay upstairs until he's gone. We're dealing with this.' Carol and Lily stood defiantly in front of the shut door.

'But where's he gonna go? You can't just turn him out on the streets! It'll be dark soon.'

'That's *his* problem. He should have thought about that before coming all the way over here. Stupid boy. He's not stepping foot in this house again and that's final!' Daisy turned and stormed back to her room, distraught. 'After all we've done for him as well,' Carol continued, moving to the bottom of the stairs. 'Trust me, you'll thank me for this one day! To think you were going to have a baby with him!'

This hit a nerve. 'Stop talking!' Daisy yelled, and slammed her bedroom door shut.

Outside, Jack was fighting back tears, stunned at how cold Carol and Lily had been. He looked up at Daisy's bedroom window. Then he looked at the porch door and back up at the window. He moved across the drive to stand underneath it. 'Daisy!' he shouted. 'Daisy, I didn't do anything, you've got to believe me! Daisy, I love you!'

Daisy crept to the front of her room and listened, out of sight behind a curtain. She so wanted to look, so wanted to see. But she knew that if she did – if she saw him – it would break her. And him. Listening to his strangled cry was bad enough; it was one of the worst things she'd ever had to go through. 'Daaaiissy!' She sobbed into her hands. Where would he go? How had he even got here? With one of the gang? 'Daaaiissyy!' If she wanted her life to imitate art, it had come back to bite her. It was like listening to Stanley howling 'Stella!' in the courtyard after they'd fallen out in *Streetcar*. Stella had succumbed and gone to him. But Stanley hadn't been unfaithful. Yet.

Incensed, Carol rushed to the lounge window. What would the neighbours think? Feeling safer than at the porch, she opened the window a crack. 'Pack that in! I'm warning you. You keep that up and I'm calling the police!'

'Daaisyy!'

'Right, that's it. I'm calling the police. I mean it!'

Just then, hearing the commotion, a neighbour appeared, a man. 'You there, what are you doing? It's New Year's Day. You're disturbing the peace.' Jack turned. He felt cornered. Threatened. Helpless. Seeing Carol, the man said, 'Do you need a hand? Do you know this boy?'

'Unfortunately, yes. And if he knows what's good for him, he's going. Right now.'

She glared at Jack. The man looked at Jack, arms folded. Jack looked up at Daisy's bedroom one last time. He wanted to shout again, but knew it was futile.

With a strange, defeated cry – that of a wounded animal – he turned and ran. The man braced himself, ready for an attack, a fight. But Jack darted past him. 'And don't come back, you lout!' he called.

Unable to hold back any longer, Daisy appeared at the window. She expected to see a car with one of the gang in it, on the drive or on the road, but all she saw was their neighbour staring after Jack as he sprinted away, his rucksack bobbing on his back. She let out a cry and put her hands on the glass, just as Jack had downstairs. Then she dropped onto the bed, sobbing hysterically and hating the world – her mother, Jeanie, herself. Never had she felt such pain, such anguish. Not since her dad had died anyway; and, oh, how she wanted him.

There was the sound of footsteps. Carol knocked on the bedroom door and walked straight in. 'It's for the best, love, you'll…'

'Go away!' Daisy shouted. 'I hate you! I don't want to see you!'

'Don't say that! You don't mean that. I'm your mother and I'm just trying to protect you. Somebody's got to!'

'You don't understand. Nobody understands,' Daisy wailed.

'We do. I do. We've all been young once…'

'That's your answer for everything, isn't it? We've all been young once! It's not the same!'

Carol tried to sit on the bed, but Daisy flinched and rolled away. Her face in the duvet, she said, 'Please, just go away… I want to be left alone.'

Carol got up and tearfully walked out of the room.

Some time later, it could have been minutes or hours, Daisy became aware of the phone ringing. She'd been drifting on a magic carpet of despair in a numb no-man's land. The sound brought her back round, and despite the hurt and confusion she felt, her heart leapt. It could be Jack. Despite everything she still wanted to speak to him. More than ever now. To hear him say it. The truth. To get it over and done with – even if it killed her. She got up off the bed and made her way to the door.

Carol, whose first thought was also that it was Jack, snatched up the phone, ready to let fly. She was surprised to hear a girl's voice on the other end. A girl asking to speak to Daisy. 'It's not the best time at the minute, I'm afraid,' Carol said frostily. 'She's asleep. Who's calling?'

'Who is it, Mum? Mum, who is it?' Daisy said from the landing.

Carol listened, then looked up, a guilty look on her face. 'Just a second,' she said, putting her hand over the mouthpiece. 'Alison. Is that *her?*'

Alison? thought Daisy. *How did she get this number?* Hearing her name was a painful reminder – of what had happened and how Daisy in a way blamed them all. And 'her'? Oh, *her.* 'No. It's a friend. I'll take it upstairs.' Daisy picked up the phone in her mum's bedroom. 'Hello,' she said, nervously.

'Daisy, thank God! It's Alison.'

'Mum, you can put the phone down!' After a slight delay the downstairs phone clicked. 'Sorry.'

'It's OK. Daisy, I'm so glad I got hold of you – and that you're safe.' Alison sounded urgent and breathless, but Daisy cut her off again.

'How did you get this number?' she said.

'Oh, erm ... from work. Bit naughty, I know. It was in the staff personnel book – you put it down as your emergency contact number and I took a chance. I didn't know what else to do. None of us did. I've been trying the flat all day. And been round. So has Tom. Where's Jack? Aitch said he didn't turn up at work. Is he with you?'

'No, yes, sort of...' She felt guilty and didn't know what to say.

'So he *is* with you? Has he explained? About what happened?'

'What is there to explain?' Daisy felt that numbness again, that deadness and despair.

'Well, nothing happened for a start. You do know that, don't you? Absolutely *nothing* happened…' She waited for a response, but got none. Daisy's heart was speeding up, in her mouth; she wanted to hear, but didn't want to. Didn't dare to hope. 'I've spoken to Jeanie.' Daisy winced at the name. 'She's been round at mine all day. She's distraught. I've never seen her like that.' Daisy rolled her eyes. 'She said Jack passed out – he was nodding off when we left – and then she was freezing cold, so she cuddled into him. She knows she shouldn't have and she's really sorry. She said Jack was delirious and burning up so he took his jumper off – but that was it! They had their clothes on and everything. He even said your name a few times. He thought he was with you!' By now Daisy's heart was pounding. She was overcome with emotion. With relief and happiness, but sadness too, that she'd jumped to conclusions and hadn't listened to him. Still unable to speak, she began to cry. 'And I believe her, Daisy,' Alison continued. 'And she's really sorry. I've never heard her like that. Ever. She really opened up to me – she was still drunk – saying how her dad left when she was young, and she knows she's a nightmare around men – craves attention and all that. And she may come across as confident, but she's not. Not really. She looks up to you, you know, your style and how you're totally yourself. Sometimes she feels left out of the group, what with me and Tom and you and Jack together. She gets a bit jealous, a bit envious – I shouldn't say this, but sometimes I do too – the way you and Jack are together, the way he looks at you. I wish Tom looked at me like that! Hey, don't cry. You're setting me off now!' she laughed. But it was no good. Alison had opened the floodgates and Daisy wept uncontrollably. 'Oh, babes. It's all gonna be OK, I promise. This is nothing. Not worth breaking up over…' After a pause, she said, 'Daisy, there's something else, too, something I wanted to ask you...'

'Huh?' Daisy was barely listening.

'Your name in the personnel book...' She faltered again. 'I hope you don't think I'm being nosey, but ... are you *that* Daisy Jones, the one in the news a while back?'

It took some moments for Daisy to be able to speak, to compose herself. She looked out of the bedroom window, where a whit of winter daylight remained, and said, 'Alison, I've got to go.'

CHAPTER 31

Back to the Old House

Taking the back way out of the village, Jack ran and ran. Faster and faster. As if he could outrun the pain. The rejection. Leave it all behind. An age-old indignation snapped at his heels, urging him on. That feeling of not being heard. Of being ignored. Of injustice. Just how his father made him feel growing up, and more recently the police. But he never expected it from Daisy. Not ever. It was like being stabbed by an angel.

It wasn't until he'd vaulted the kissing gate, hurtled down the overgrown path and hit the main road that he realised where he was going. Home. His old home. The one on the hill. When Daisy's world had crumbled around her earlier that day she'd instinctively craved the comfort and sanctuary of family; her mum, her childhood home. In Jack's case that house, or what remained of it, was all he had left. A thread of something familiar to hold on to. A connection to his poor, dead sister and mother. It wasn't a conscious decision. It was something hard-wired inside. Gravitational.

Lungs bursting and legs on fire, Jack reached the bottom of the pot-holed lane that led up to the property, the bungalow where he'd spent the first sixteen years of his life. Practically a prisoner. Even now the lane stopped him dead in his tracks.

As if a force field were at play. When he was a child he'd been forbidden from using it, lest he be seen. He bent over, hands on knees, gasping for air. Dizziness hit him and he stumbled, nearly falling forwards. Steadying himself, he tore off the rucksack that had been chafing his shoulders and armpits. As he caught his breath he turned to look up the lane. He hadn't been there since the fateful night of the fire and it immediately reminded him of Anne. The first of many new flashbacks hit him. A powerful surge. Of him crouching in the verge at the entrance of the property as a boy, watching her leave to catch the bus to school and later the shops. Sometimes on her bike. And how much he'd hated it. Her leaving him at the mercy of his so-called father. Sometimes he'd cried, which made her cry too. She'd been practically a child herself. And then how he'd steal across the lane and wait and watch for her to come back from his vantage point.

And now he *was* bringing her back. Cradling his rucksack and still breathing hard, he began to make his way unsteadily up the lane; he hadn't run like that in months and his legs seemed to have lost all their strength. Because of the tall hedges the property wasn't visible. It never had been. And this lulled him into the false sense that it was still intact. Exactly how he remembered it. It was a shock when he reached the opening of the driveway. The first thing he saw was the police tape blocking the entrance, the same stuff that had been temporarily placed at the bottom of the lane. He wasn't expecting this and it sobered him further. The tape was tattered, flapping in the breeze and sagging in the middle, as if people had been climbing over it.

Beyond this in the distance, facing him, and again a shock, was a huge space where his father's workshop had stood. He thought he could make out some of the machines, in the open air now but still hulking, dark and solid against the backdrop of the hedge and the poplars. He expected his father's rusty old van to still be on the drive. But that had also gone. Where? Who had taken it? Cautiously, he negotiated the criss-crossed tape, barely able to lift his legs over it. Then, not knowing what to expect, he made his way up the drive.

A scene of devastation hit him.

The wooden lean-to at the end of the property, like the workshop, no longer existed. And the bungalow itself was a scorched shell. A higgledy-piggledy mess. An unfinished Lego house of jagged edges. Some outer walls remained. Some were curved inwards. Others had collapsed entirely so that you could see right through to the garden on the other side and that the floors inside had disappeared. The roof had gone, and so had any remaining window frames.

Jack's lips involuntarily trembled as a feeling of desolation rocked him; he had nowhere in the world to go. Sobs rose in his throat. He had caused this. If it weren't for him this building would still be intact; he could slip inside right now and curl up in his old bed with a roof over his head. He felt the sickening ache of loss, of wanting it all back as it was before.

Drawn onwards nevertheless, he made a beeline for what had been the back door, the only door they ever used, now just a gap into the space that used to be the kitchen. Being made of stone and furthest from the source of the fire, the kitchen floor was the only one that still seemed to be fully intact. But still Jack trod gingerly, expecting everything to give way beneath him as he stepped inside. As he surveyed the scene, more flashbacks hit him, bombarded him. Like an already wounded soldier being peppered with a fresh spray of bullets. They made him stagger and hold on to a wall for support. The stale bite of smoke still hung in the air, stirred up by the cold and damp. Everything was coated in black.

In the middle of the kitchen were the remains of the old pine table at which he and his sister had spent so much time. Now just charred wood and metal casters strewn across the floor, one of them still attached to a leg. Echoes of ghosts rebounded off the walls. His father's voice and recriminations, 'You're lazy!' and then his sister's, 'Mind out the way, Jack.' Her apparition nudged past him with their father's breakfast tray. His eyes followed her fondly into the parlour where he used to sit on the rug by the stove. And where she taught him to read and write. The rocking chair had gone, the dresser too, but the stove remained in its hearth. The rest of the floor had collapsed entirely, leaving a pit of scorched joists and wires, as if the house's guts or intestines had spilled out. But worse, much worse than all of this, to his shock there was spray-painted graffiti on the walls, and the foundations were littered with debris. Cans, bottles, cigarette packets. People had been up here. The house had become a grisly attraction; and kids dared each other to stay up there all night.

Jack turned away in disgust. His eyes returned to the kitchen and the gap where the door to the cellar used to be. The stone steps were still intact. He edged forwards to look down them, and more flashbacks hit him. Of how he used to jump down them in one go. How when he landed at the bottom he would grin and look up, knowing Anne would be watching him worriedly from the top; she would tut and shake her head before walking away. It had made him feel warm inside, knowing that she cared. It was dark in the stairwell at the bottom. And though he was curious to see what state the freezers and the cider-making kit were in, he refrained from venturing down, afraid of the other ghosts that lay in wait for him in the dark.

An overwhelming feeling of depression poleaxed Jack and he sat down heavily on the top step, placing his rucksack next to him. Despite his troubled upbringing he'd always had a cheerful disposition, a childlike wonder at the world, its seemingly infinite secret treasures, its smells. Nature. Bunny Wood. A sunny day. The man in the moon. A sunset. Cider, butterflies, crickets. His story books. His dreams of America. Seeing the house had temporarily occupied his mind, crowded out the dark thoughts, but now they returned. The thoughts of Daisy and her rejection. There was no magic in the world anymore. Nothing to hope for or look forward to. Never before had he considered killing himself, of ending his life, but such was his despair that he did then.

Tears rolled down Jack's cheeks, and he hugged his knees and rocked. Just as he used to. He craved some comfort. Anyone or anything. He had no cider or marijuana – didn't even want any. Then he remembered the ashes in his rucksack. His family's ashes. His sister and mother. He picked up the rucksack and hugged it to him to feel less alone. Through the canvas he could feel the canisters, and knowing their ashes were inside stirred something in him. A fierce loyalty and a flicker of fight. This was still their home. Still their land. And no one was going to take it from them. Not this Storm woman that Haslam had mentioned, not anybody. In his scrambled mind he pictured rebuilding it. Repairing it. There were hundreds of bricks still in the yard – providing they hadn't been taken. Without his father, he would be king of the castle. He would stand guard and protect his boundaries from interlopers, trespassers, this woman and her solicitors. Let them come. They'd better bring an army. Sparks danced in his mad eyes as he pictured it. He took the thought and nurtured it, retreated with it to the closet in his mind and locked the door behind it. He began to rock again. To rock and hum, still cradling his rucksack, sitting on the cellar steps amongst the ruins of his home.

*****

Daisy put down the phone and quietly crept out of her mum's room. She went back to her room, where she knew she had a box of old shoes. Locating a pair of trainers that pinched her feet, she fumbled them on in a panic. *Oh, Jack, what have I done?*

she thought, wiping the tears from her eyes. *I am so, so sorry, baby*. This nearly set her off again, but there was no time to dawdle. She thought she'd lost him once and she couldn't bear the thought of it happening again.

Stepping out onto the landing, she paused to listen. The telly could be heard from the lounge. She had to get out of the house without her mum knowing; she wouldn't let her leave, and Daisy didn't have time to explain about Alison's phone call. Creeping down the stairs, she avoided the steps she knew that creaked – and skipped the last two entirely. Her keys were still on the table in the hall. She carefully picked them up and clutched them tightly to stop them from jangling. The lounge door was open, but her mum always sat on the sofa opposite the telly, out of sight. It would have to be out the back and round the side of the house. The front doors were too noisy; her mum would be sure to hear and would be up like a shot.

Daisy tiptoed past the lounge door, holding her breath, and prayed Lily wasn't in the kitchen. She wasn't. There was only Sookie, sitting on the windowsill, staring out into the garden. She miaowed in greeting and hopped down, hankering for food. Daisy shushed her and gave her a quick pet, but didn't have time to feed her. She unlocked the patio doors and slipped out. Closing the doors behind her she ran round to the driveway. The van was still unlocked and she jumped inside.

This was it, she thought, putting the key in the ignition. It made her feel guilty, but she would explain when she got back. Got back with Jack. Because she *was* bringing him back. If her mum didn't like it they'd just clear off back to Norfolk. Shit! Petrol! There was barely any left in the van and nowhere open. They wouldn't be going back to Norfolk tonight. And what if she ran out? She briefly considered slipping back inside and grabbing the Montego's keys. But it was too risky. The van had got to make it to Bunny Hill. If not she'd get out and walk. She said a prayer and turned the key. The van started, and she quickly reversed out of the drive and onto the close. Out of the corner of her eye she noticed light spill from the lounge window onto the drive as a curtain twitched open. Without looking back, Daisy pulled away.

There was only one place she thought Jack might be – well, three if you counted Bunny Wood and the spinney – but she was banking on the house. Despite Jack's reluctance to go up there recently, she guessed it would be a source of solace in his hour of need; and more guilt ripped through her at how she'd not given him the benefit of the doubt, at how she'd jumped to conclusions. She cursed her jealous streak. But despite her need for haste, she didn't dare accelerate too hard, trying to preserve the petrol that was left.

Turning left at the crossroads, she joined the main road. She was just passing the brook when she looked in the rear-view mirror for the first time. A car had joined the main road and was heading in the same direction as she was. *Shit*, she thought. *Please don't let that be Mum.* The car didn't have its lights on, even though it was nearly dark. Despite Daisy's slow speed the car wasn't gaining on her. It couldn't have been her mum, thank God. Or Lily; she drove like an idiot.

By the time Daisy had reached the council houses on the left, the car wasn't any closer, and still hadn't put its lights on. She was now at the bottom of the steep Bunny Hill. The lane to Jack's house was about a hundred yards further on, halfway up the hill on the right-hand side. *Nearly there, nearly there*, she thought, changing into a lower gear and pressing harder on the accelerator. And that was when the van began to chug and struggle; that sudden loss of power that makes your stomach sink. She pressed her foot down again, but it was worse. The van quickly lost all speed and began to judder. Having run out of petrol before, she knew the feeling only too well. 'No, no! Not now!' she cried as the van began to grind to a halt. Daisy had no choice but to pull over, onto the grass verge.

She quickly put the handbrake on, but it strained to hold the van, which groaned and rocked back slightly at first. Of all the places to run out of petrol, halfway up a hill. It wasn't important, though. Jack was. The van could be dealt with later, tomorrow, whenever. Remembering her dad's advice, she put her hazard lights on.

After checking the rear-view mirror again, she opened the door; she was in a dangerous spot and expected the car soon to be passing her. But it didn't. It had stopped just past the council houses a way back. That was when she first thought there was something a little odd about it. It still didn't have its lights on, as if the driver didn't want to be noticed; and wouldn't any normal motorist have come to see what the problem was? In the parsimonious light it was hard to make out what type of car it was or what colour. It just looked dark. Or black. A shiver of fear ran through her. Peasgood's men. Like Jack, with everything else that had been going on she had forgotten all about them. It made her want to stay in the van, but what would that achieve? She had to get to Jack. With one last look, she slammed the door and dashed across the main road.

Behind her, the car had put its lights on for the first time. As she watched, it pulled away from the side of the road and began to head towards her. It sent another chill through her. There was something about it that reminded her of a crocodile, lying in wait under murky water, then surfacing, opening its yellow eyes and moving in for the kill. Still looking behind her, she broke into a run. The car was gaining on her fast. Too fast to be a Good Samaritan coming to help her out. The lane was coming up on her right. Ten yards, five yards. She reached it, and without looking back again began to sprint.

She heard the car behind her brake hard on the main road, then skid on the gravel as it turned up the lane. *Shit, oh shit*, she thought as she ran. What if Jack wasn't there? What then? It made her feel trapped and vulnerable and isolated. Her legs were agony and she got a stitch as she approached the driveway to Jack's house. The car was not far behind her, the angry revving of its engine, its lights reaching beyond her, casting her desperate silhouette on the lane. Without slowing down, she pretended she was carrying on up the lane, but then at the last minute swerved, hurdled the police tape, and darted up the driveway. It did the trick. As she looked behind her, she saw the black car hurtle past, a large, bald-headed man at the wheel, staring straight at her.

The car skidded to a halt somewhere up the lane; then there was the crunch of its gears. 'Jack!' she screamed. 'Jack, where are you?' She frantically looked about her, up the garden, and then into the remains of the property, barely visible in the gloom. She heard the whinny of the car reversing on the lane. 'Jack! Where are you? Please be here!' She ran to the back door. At that same moment a dark figure appeared in the doorway. She banged right into it and screamed.

'Daisy?' Jack cried, grabbing hold of her, his rucksack dangling from his arm.

'Jack, thank God. Run!'

'What? Why?'

A car door slammed.

'Just do as I say and run!'

He did.

And they ran.

Many thanks to PC 2397 Jon Stevens of
Nottinghamshire Police for his invaluable
advice on all police matters.
Eternally grateful.